# MATTHEW HATTERSLEY

# A WORLD OF SUN AND VIOLENCE

Vinci Books

vinci-books.com

Published by Vinci Books Ltd in 2025

1

Copyright © 2023 Matthew Hattersley

The author has asserted their moral right to be identified as the author of this work in accordance with the Copyright, Designs and Patents Act 1988. This work is a work of fiction. Names, characters, places and incidents are the product of the author's imagination or are used fictitiously. Any resemblance to actual persons, living or dead, places and incidents is entirely coincidental.

All rights reserved. No part of this publication may be copied, reproduced, distributed, stored in any retrieval system, or transmitted in any form or by any means, including photocopying, recording, or other electronic or mechanical methods, nor used as a source for any form of machine learning including AI datasets, without the prior written permission of the publisher.

The publisher and the author have made every effort to obtain permissions for any third party material used in this book and to comply with copyright law. Any queries in this respect should be brought to the attention of the publisher and any omissions will be corrected in future editions.

A CIP catalogue record for this book is available from the British Library.
Paperback ISBN: 9781036700843

The EU GPSR authorised representative is Logos Europe, 9 rue Nicolas Poussion, 17000 La Rochelle, France
contact@logoseurope.eu

## By Matthew Hattersley

The John Beckett Series

*Darkness On The Edge Of Town*
*When The Kingdom Comes*
*A World of Sun and Violence*
*A Bullet For The Past*
*A Line in the Sand*

## Chapter One

The sun had long since set over El Tigrito, the Anzoátegui state located in the east of Venezuela, yet the oppressive warmth of the July heatwave lingered, clinging to the skin like a second layer. In the southern outskirts of the city, in the Zona Industrial San José de Guanipa, the atmosphere crackled with anticipation. Distant barks from stray dogs intermingled with the blare of police sirens and the sharp staccato of gunfire. El Tigrito might not have been as dangerous as Caracas, some five hundred kilometres northwest, but it was no stranger to violence. Trouble hung heavy in the air, like a silent, unseen energy prickling the skin and raising the hairs on the back of one's neck. This was not merely a place where threats lurked in the shadows. It was where danger was the rule, not the exception.

At the heart of the Zona Industrial stood a multistorey car park, a looming concrete relic of urban brutalism. Built in the early eighties, it was now showing signs of neglect. Weeds sprouted through the cracks in the asphalt, and every available surface was adorned with the splattered colours of gang signs and graffiti. Now no longer used as a car park, the imposing structure lay all but forgotten by the city – yet not by those who thrived in the darkness.

Once a month this venue transformed into the epicentre for all that was corrupt and sinister in El Tigrito. It was a place where deals were made and lives were traded, where the currency was not just money but power, loyalty, and often betrayal. There were no vehicles onsite, however, this evening. Those attending the venue knew to park some distance away and walk the rest. That was one of the rules – no cars. There were few other rules. People came on foot, some left on stretchers or carried out by their cronies. Others left in body bags.

At the main entrance two men stood guard, their bulky frames and stern expressions acting as silent warnings, informing those who approached to treat them with respect. The assault rifles slung over their shoulders only emphasised the point. These men were the gatekeepers of this underworld, collecting tickets and removing those they suspected as being troublemakers, their vigilant eyes scanning each arrival in turn. The local cops wouldn't dare venture here, but these men were not just warding off law enforcement; they were on the lookout for those carrying weapons or grudges for rival gangs, and those who sought to conduct business without the proper authorisation.

In this charged atmosphere a man and woman approached the entrance, their arrival eliciting an immediate reaction from the two guards who snapped to attention, their hands darting to their heads in sharp salutes.

"Lieutenant Peroza! Welcome to El Campo de Batalla," greeted one guard. "We are graced with your presence this evening."

No one knew if Victor Peroza was a genuine lieutenant

– or where he might have earned such a distinction if he were one – yet he was granted the title by all who knew and feared him, which were often the same people. To know Victor Peroza was to be afraid of him. He was unpredictable, cruel, with a vicious streak that often bubbled up out of nowhere. Tonight, however, he dismissed the guard's formal introductions with a smile and a wave of his hand. Although he loved being saluted and would have had both their heads if they hadn't done so, he liked to play it down, especially when entertaining a lady.

Tall and good-looking, Peroza exuded an air of natural authority mixed with street-smart swagger. His skin was weathered, telling of years spent under the harsh sun, but he was still ruggedly handsome, with deep-set eyes that were sharp and calculating. His thick glossy hair, now peppered with grey, was combed back from his face in a slight quiff, giving him the look of an ageing matinee idol.

A dark, well-fitted suit clung to his frame, the sleeves rolled up to reveal forearms covered with scars and faded tattoos, most of them done in prison using a razor blade and a mixture of ash, shampoo and Styrofoam. Underneath the suit he wore a crisp white shirt open to below his sternum, and on his feet were a brand new pair of Giorgio Armani loafers – emerald green with a gold stirrup bar. Only the best for Lieutenant Victor Peroza.

"I see your man is fighting tonight, Lieutenant," the second guard said, grinning as if he were speaking with the president himself. "Good luck."

Peroza glanced at his woman friend, a sharp grin splitting his tanned face, exposing two rows of perfect white teeth.

"Luck? We do not need luck. He will win. He always

wins." He placed his arm around the woman. "Come, darling. Let us find our seats. Thank you again, gentlemen."

He took four COP 50,000 notes from out of his jacket and slid them into the nearest guard's top pocket like he'd done it hundreds of times before. Being a proud Colombian, he always carried pesos rather than Venezuelan bolívares. "For you both," he said. "Buy yourselves something nice."

Peroza didn't pay for things here, but he still liked to play the big shot. He liked the status. He liked the power. He liked the way these two huge men nodded and scraped their boots, thanking him politely as they waved the two of them through. Grinning to himself, Peroza placed his hand on his companion's lower back and guided her through the gate. He didn't know the girl's name, but he didn't care to know it either. Just like his Gucci suit and his Armani loafers, she was an accoutrement of wealth and success. A high-end escort who cost more than these poor bastards would make all evening, she wore a form-fitting red dress, tastefully accessorised with a gold chain and earrings. Her blonde hair fell over her shoulders and her make-up was impeccable, enhancing her features without overshadowing her natural beauty. Just as he'd requested – sexy but classy.

Together, Peroza and the woman made an intriguing pair as they moved through the venue towards the back of the room and up a flight of steps to a special mezzanine level. From up here their seats, velvet-cushioned and reserved for VIPs only, overlooked the floor of the main car park, now transformed into a raucous arena. Below them, in the centre of this makeshift colosseum, a ring had been erected, a simple square delineated by ropes strung between metal posts. The ring's floor was a patchwork of mats, worn and already stained with the blood of many men. Around it spectators gathered, a motley assembly of the city's underworld – gang members, high rollers from the shadowy fringes of society, thrill seekers drawn to the forbidden nature of the event. The air was thick with the smell of sweat, cheap alcohol, and the metallic tang of blood.

"We have got here just in time," Peroza rasped in his date's ear.

The woman feigned a smile. "I can't wait."

Peroza sat back and made himself comfortable, scanning the sea of faces below. Over to his left, a man appeared at the top of the steps and, on seeing the lieutenant, hurried over. This was Jesus Salinas, the main promoter here at El Campo de Batalla. Peroza disliked Salinas immensely. He was a smarmy character, his entire demeanour oozing a greasy and insincere charm.

"Lieutenant Peroza, what an honour it is to have you join us tonight," he began, his smile a little too wide, his eyes a little too eager. "The main event is about to start. I trust your man is fighting fit?"

"You bet he is," Peroza growled. "He will put on a good show for you. As always."

"The whole place is buzzing about it," Salinas continued, leaning in closer as if sharing a secret. "He is fast becoming a celebrity around here. As are you, Lieutenant."

Peroza's lips curved into a half-smile, his gaze shifting to the woman beside him and gauging her reaction. "Hussam Bracho," he explained. "My fighter. He's a beast in the ring. He's a beast out of it too." At this he exploded into laughter, the comment eliciting the same from Salinas.

The woman asked what he meant, but a moment later the lights dipped. The noise from the crowd rose to a deafening crescendo before dropping away as the ring announcer's amplified voice boomed over the speakers hanging from the ceiling. "Ladies and gentlemen, the moment you've all been waiting for! Tonight's main event is about to start…"

"There he is," Peroza said, watching the woman's face as he pointed to Bracho clambering over the ropes into the ring.

"That's your man?" she asked, narrowing her eyes at the sight in front of her. "What…? What's wrong with him?! Why is he like that…?"

Peroza didn't answer. He just chuckled to himself as the announcer continued.

"Your fighters for the final event this evening. Ramon Osario, and Hussam Bracho, otherwise known as El Demonio Roto!"

The crowd roared, the noise almost deafening as the spotlights shifted to the ring. Peroza and his companion watched intently as Bracho lunged toward his opponent, an immense figure of unrelenting aggression. He dominated the fight in seconds, his moves as brutal as his physique, each punch and swipe delivered with a ferocity that left no doubt about his reputation.

"Seriously, why does he look like that?" the woman whispered.

"It's a long story," Peroza replied, sitting back. "For now, let's watch."

As the fight went on, his attention was split between the ring and the reaction of the woman beside him. Her initial look of curiosity had quickly morphed into one of horror and grim fascination as Bracho pounded Osario to within an inch of his life. Peroza didn't blame her for looking shocked. Bracho's almost seven-foot frame and grotesque appearance were startling enough, but the ferocity of his attacks and their brutality only added to the macabre spectacle.

## A World of Sun and Violence

Hussam Bracho was a man forged by the slums of Caracas. Chucked out of an orphanage to fend for himself, his life had been sculpted by violence and survival. It was said he possessed the mental capacity of a ten-year-old, but Peroza thought of him less like a remedial adult and more like an animal. He was an attack dog, a beast who knew nothing but the language of brute force.

"My god. He is so powerful."

The woman's eyes widened as she watched on, unable to look away yet clearly repulsed by what she was witnessing. She was seeing up close the raw, unmasked face of the world Peroza inhabited. A world where ruthlessness and violence were not just accepted but celebrated.

The climax of the fight arrived abruptly, as Bracho halted Osario with a heavy punch to the guts before knocking him out with a swift and devastating blow that sent blood and teeth flying into the crowd. As his opponent fell, Bracho stepped back, roaring into the heavens and drawing a collective gasp from the crowd followed by deafening applause. Peroza felt his date shudder beside him.

"Would you like to meet him?" he asked her.

The woman turned. "Oh... I don't know."

"Come with me." Peroza waved at the crowds as he got to his feet, then saluted the beast in the ring who was staring up at his master, eager for validation. "If you think he's ugly from here, you should see him up close."

Peroza laughed at his own joke. He was feeling good tonight. After bets and prize money came in, he was set to make over fifteen thousand US dollars. Not bad for a few minutes' work. Most of the money would be sent back to Colombia to finance the cause, but as usual he planned on skimming a couple of thousand off the top for his own pocket. The woman would need paying and he'd earned a little reward for all his hard work. It was important to allow oneself some downtime on occasion.

As the crowds continued to chant, he led the woman over to the stairwell, waving as he went. Sometimes you made money, sometimes you made art, and sometimes you made both. Tonight had been one of those nights. And it was only going to get better once he got this bitch home and showed her what else he was good for.

But as he guided his companion down to the lower level, his mind drifted to more pressing issues. In just three days, General Murcia was scheduled to visit him, to check on how operations were going this side of the border. Peroza knew the meeting, while routine on the surface, carried with it a weight of unspoken expectations. He and Jalen Murcia had been like brothers once. They had come up through the ranks together, fought side by side with shared dreams of a transformed Colombia free from the chains of corruption and foreign influence. Murcia was not just a comrade, he was a visionary, a man whose charisma and resolve had given real weight and importance to their cause. But of late, Peroza had sensed a change in him, subtle yet undeniable.

Where once Murcia spoke of liberation and justice, now his conversations veered towards consolidation of power and wealth. The ideals that had once been their guiding star seemed to dim in the light of newfound opportunities for personal gain. It was as if the man Peroza had once known was slowly being replaced by a stranger, one whose ambitions no longer aligned with the cause they had both bled for. This new Murcia was someone who viewed their recent discovery not as a means to further their mission, but as a step towards his own career. And this shift wasn't just disappointing, it was dangerous. Peroza knew all too well the corrosive effect of power and greed. He had seen it erode the strongest of bonds, turn allies into adversaries, and transform revolutions into mere power plays. The Murcia he'd known – the fiery revolutionary, the unyielding fighter – was being overshadowed by a man who seemed increasingly consumed by a thirst for wealth and influence.

Peroza couldn't help but wonder if their shared vision was gone, and in the back of his mind the seeds of a new rebellion were beginning to be sown. But for now he shook the thoughts away. Tonight his focus was solely on having a good time.

He let his hand travel down his date's back, feeling a flush of warmth as it came to rest on her sizeable buttocks. He squeezed tight, showing her and the world who owned what. Tonight he was a king and no impending visit from General Murcia was going to change that. He would introduce the woman to his prize fighter, collect his money, and then take her home for some fun. It was his night, after all. He deserved the best.

## Chapter Two

The hot sun beat down on Guayana City, its rays reflecting off the vibrant market stalls and bustling crowds as Vanessa Adler made her way across the main square. Having not been able to sleep the previous night, she now felt jittery and uneasy. Sweat glistened on her brow and made her thin canvas shirt stick to her back as she moved with purpose between the busy stalls. Despite this, however, she remained alert, scoping out her surroundings, focusing in on the detail – the eager faces of the vendors, the hushed conversations between traders, the subtle undercurrent of tension in the air.

The market was a colourful array of fresh produce, vibrant textiles and local crafts. Yet beneath the surface was a palpable agitation. The smiles of the sellers were strained, their eyes darting nervously at any sign of trouble. It was a community living under the shadow of fear, their normalcy disrupted by the growing unrest in the region.

While Adler weaved through the crowd, she ran through the next few minutes in her mind – what she would say, how she would act – steeling herself for the encounter whilst at the same time slipping seamlessly into her role as Julia Gray. To anyone who asked, and that included passport and border control, Gray was a journalist for the New York Times, working on a story about local culture and the impact of the political climate on daily life. In reality, as a CIA paramilitary operations officer, she'd been embedded in the country for the last six weeks, her mission part of a broader strategy to gather intelligence on the rapidly evolving political and military landscape in the region.

Her primary target was Jalen Murcia, leader of the Colombian Liberation Army – or the ELC, as they called themselves. Murcia was a figure who had risen to prominence through a combination of guile and brutal efficiency and had been flagged on the CIA watch list numerous times over the last few years. The ELC, a breakaway faction from the more established ELN, had gained true notoriety under his leadership and the situation was becoming a concern. Murcia's methods were unorthodox, his vision ambitious, and his reach extended far beyond the jungles and mountains of Venezuela and Colombia.

Adler dipped her head as she made her way through the marketplace, the straw Panama hat she wore serving the dual purpose of shielding her from the sun whilst adding an extra layer of anonymity in her attempts to blend into her surroundings; not so easy with her fair skin and strawberry-blonde hair. Against the vibrant, sun-drenched backdrop of Venezuela, her appearance gave her the unmistakable air of a westerner. Yet her cover story was tight and she wasn't expecting any problems today.

Even so, Adler was well-prepared to defend herself if necessary. Of average height, her physique was toned and athletic for her thirty-one years, shaped by her past as a high school swimmer and track and field athlete. Before joining the agency she'd harboured dreams of being an Olympian, yet it seemed fate, or maybe genetics, had other plans. But her background in sports came in useful. It had not only sculpted Adler's physique but also her endurance and agility, qualities that served her well in the demanding role of a deep-cover officer.

As she walked, her thoughts were focused on the upcoming meeting with Castillo and what information he had for her. She hoped it was something useful, something concrete. She'd been in the country six weeks already and was starting to get antsy. The longer she stayed here, the more dangerous it became for her and the slimmer her chances of success. Castillo, a local police officer turned asset, wasn't high-ranking but had lived in the region his entire life and knew a lot about everything. The CIA also knew a lot about everything, but you couldn't beat local insights to help with the finer details.

Castillo had agreed to provide Adler – or rather, Julia Gray – with vital information on Murcia's upcoming visit to the area. This was for her 'article', with Castillo to remain an unnamed source, ensuring no repercussions for him. By this point, Adler had met him on three separate occasions and his intel was good. She trusted him. He would be compensated well for any information, of course, but Adler suspected the gruff local cop would have shared what he knew regardless if it meant exposing the evil underbelly at play in his once fine country. He was a good man, tired of the violence and corruption in Venezuela.

In front of her was the café where they were to meet, El Flamingo. It was a nondescript establishment, with a faded red and white facade that blended seamlessly with the surrounding buildings. Adler stepped inside, the cool interior a welcome respite from the overbearing heat. An elderly woman looked up from the counter, her dark eyes twinkling despite the lines on her face, evidence of a hard-lived life. Adler greeted her with a smile as she approached.

"I can get you something?" the woman asked, speaking English with a heavy accent.

"Thank you," Adler said. "Two coffees with tamarind milk and two plates of fried sweetbreads." She'd already eaten a hearty breakfast back at her hotel, but the order was what she'd been told to ask for. The old woman squinted at her for a moment, leaving Adler to wonder if she'd got it all wrong. But then she nodded, gesturing for her to follow.

The woman led her through to the back of the café and down a narrow corridor. The air was thick with the smell of strong coffee, old cigarettes and a faint musty dampness that seemed to seep out of the walls. They reached a door at the end of the corridor, and the woman knocked softly before opening it.

The back room was small and poorly lit, the only light coming from a single flickering bulb hanging from the ceiling. The walls were bare save for a few peeling posters, and the floor was covered in linoleum cracked and stained with age. A small, rickety table stood in the centre of the room, surrounded by a few mismatched chairs.

Edgar Castillo was sitting at the table, his bulky frame making the chair beneath him creak as he turned to greet her. "Julia. How are you?"

He was a stout man somewhere in his fifties, with thinning hair and a round face that could have made him look incredibly jolly if he ever smiled. Maybe in better times he had done. His clothes, although clean, were worn and stretched tight over his overweight frame. As their eyes met, she noticed his were as tired and wary as her own.

"Good to see you, Edgar," she said, taking a seat opposite him, facing the door. "This is all a bit cloak and dagger, isn't it?"

Castillo blew out a long breath. "It is what it is. I have to be careful. We both do, Julia."

Castillo had seen the dramatic changes in his country firsthand. Since the nineties, the ELN had been establishing positions in Venezuela, building alliances with Venezuelan officials, particularly during Hugo Chávez's presidency, and using the country as a base to help fund their rebellion back home in Colombia. Murcia, once a mere rebel soldier, had transformed into a major player in this complex web, establishing links with Cuba and Hezbollah for arms and heroin trafficking, escalating his influence and notoriety. His ambitions posed a threat to global security, and his ruthlessness was legendary. Murcia had wiped out entire factions of FARC militants and was now raising funds in Venezuela to support insurgencies in Colombia and, according to recent intelligence, a possible military coup. He fancied himself as the next president of Colombia, and to many global observers this seemed increasingly feasible.

The United States' concern over Murcia's plans was significant. So locating him while he was vulnerable – visiting Venezuela without his full security detail – had become a critical mission. It was the reason Adler was now sitting in this stuffy backroom trying to play it cool.

"What do you have for me?" she asked. "I heard General Murcia was due to visit his operations over here soon." Adler already knew about Murcia's visit from agency intel but wanted the word on the street.

Castillo sucked in air through his teeth. "One of the men at the station has a brother-in-law who works in… private security, if you know what I mean. He does work off and on for Lieutenant Victor Peroza. You know of him, yes?"

Adler nodded. Everyone in these parts knew of Victor Peroza.

"Well, this security guy told the brother-in-law there's been increased activity recently as Peroza prepares for General Murcia's arrival."

"Activity where?"

"At Peroza's main compound. In the jungle outside of El Tigrito."

Adler leaned forward, trying not to appear too eager. "Right. And did this security guy mention the location?"

The ELC were shrewd operators. They moved around a lot to avoid detection and often set up camp in the jungle, hidden from drones and satellites by heavy leaf canopies. The CIA had four possible sites listed for Peroza's Venezuelan headquarters but currently no confirmed locale.

"Anything would help," she added.

"No. I'm afraid not."

Adler noticed Castillo was sweating profusely, more than could be attributed to the heat and the room's lack of ventilation. She watched him, her pulse rising a little. Did he know who she was – who she really was? There was no reason for her to think that except for her instincts. But something wasn't right. She didn't like the way he kept glancing at his watch.

"Is everything okay, Edgar?" she asked. "As we've already agreed, you'll be paid well for any information you can provide, and you have my word I won't mention you by name."

"Yes, yes, I know all this."

Adler tensed, glancing around her. The door to the room was closed and she heard no sounds beyond it except for the flow of water in the pipes and the occasional clink of crockery from the café.

"When is General Murcia expected in Venezuela?" she asked.

Castillo's eyes widened. "Two days from now. But"—he glanced at his watch again—"I think there's something else. Something bigger. Beyond their usual operations."

"What is it?"

"I am not sure. And that's all I know. You should go. Right now." His eyes, previously weary, now widened with alarm.

"Edgar," Adler whispered, rocking forward onto the balls of her feet. "What did you do?"

Castillo's lips moved silently, forming the word 'sorry'. But before Adler could react, the door flew open and three men burst into the room.

Adler's instincts, honed by years of training and field experience, kicked in at once. She grasped the edge of the rickety table and heaved it upwards, sending it hurtling towards the intruders. The table was a flimsy barrier at best, but bought her precious seconds as she lunged towards the nearest assailant. A swift kick to the man's knee buckled him, which she followed with an elbow to the nose, sending him reeling backwards. The men clearly weren't expecting her to fight back and now the others froze, their enthusiastic grunts ceasing as they glanced at each other and then back at Adler.

They were young men, maybe even in their late teens. They wore old US army fatigues with no specific insignia, but she guessed they were Peroza's men. Probably recruited from the local townships around Caracas and El Tigrito. Poor kids with no other opportunities available to them.

But even if they were just teenagers they were bigger

than she was, with keen eyes and determined expressions. As they closed in on her she stepped back, eyes scanning the room for a weapon or a way out. There was neither. Adler danced from foot to foot while the two men advanced, her fists raised in readiness as one blocked her path to the door and the other moved around the side of her. She threw a punch but he evaded it, and as she tried to correct herself the other barged towards her, throwing his arms around her waist and slamming her into the wall. The room shook. She saw Castillo getting to his feet, saw the look of pain and regret on his face, saw the second man rushing at her, pulling something from his pocket.

"Get the hell off me," she wheezed. "I'm an American citizen. A journalist. I'm protected by international humanitarian law. You're making a big mistake." Even as she said this she knew that in ninety percent of cases where a journalist was killed for doing their job, those responsible went unpunished. Peroza undoubtedly knew it too; the percentage was probably a lot higher in Venezuela.

Despite her skill and agility, the two men together proved too strong for her. She tried to fight back, even landing another solid blow, before they spun her around and pushed her face against the wall. She struggled some more. Then a coarse bag was thrust over her head, plunging the world into darkness.

"Shit. Get off."

The disorientation was instant, her senses thrown into chaos. Blind and struggling, Adler became desperate. She swung wildly, trying to fend off the unseen men, but her fists found nothing but air. A muffled commotion behind her made her freeze. She heard Castillo's voice, him begging for mercy in Spanish. She heard the sound of a struggle, then a brief scuffle followed by a heavy thud. It seemed Castillo had been silenced, likely knocked unconscious.

Before she could process this, a crushing blow to the back of her head sent a sharp jolt of pain through her skull. Her legs buckled. The sounds of the room began to fade. It felt as if she were sinking into deep water, the world above growing distant and muffled.

This was bad.

This was really bad.

She heard the men talking, felt zip ties being strapped around her wrists. Another sharp blow to the head sent her crashing to the floor, and the fading sounds in the room became a distant echo. Her mind spun with a thousand troubling thoughts, none of which she could grasp hold of. Then her mind clouded over, and there were no more thoughts at all.

## Chapter Three

Beckett was already regretting his decision. In front of him an older American couple were holding up the line, speaking with the local tour guide in loud voices. The young man was doing his best to field their scattergun questions, but was clearly out of his depth in terms of both language and customer service skills.

"We just want to be absolutely certain it's safe," the American guy was saying. "You hear rumours about these places. There aren't any of those militant guerrillas out there, are there?"

The young man behind the wooden shack blinked and smiled. "No problem. Is all fine."

"Okay, if you're sure. But my wife can't walk far, so we don't want to be trekking through the jungle for miles. You know what I mean?"

The local man remained positive, not taking the older man on. "Is all good, sir. You want to go? Both?"

Beckett turned around, purposely removing the couple from his field of vision. He stretched his arms wide, feeling the burn across his chest and shoulders. It was a hot day but he was well rested, if not a little stiff after spending the previous night in a small hotel half a kilometre from Maiquetía Airport.

He'd travelled to Venezuela from Portugal on his Michael Day alias and had initially considered spending a few days in Caracas. But even as he'd stepped off the plane he'd sensed the air prickling with anarchic energy and had decided to get on his way as soon as possible. Beckett had been to Venezuela once before but under vastly different circumstances. That time he'd been part of a covert mission involving Sigma Unit and Delta Force that had seen him fly in under the cover of darkness, extract two British nationals and an American, and leave before sunrise. This time he was here for a different reason. Pleasure, rather than business.

Ever since his abrupt and objectionable departure from the secret service, Beckett had set his sights on a new mission – to travel, to experience the wonders of the modern world up close, and as a tourist rather than a soldier. Angel Falls, located deep in the jungles of the Canaima National Park, was his first port of call.

Reaching the front of the line he spoke in Spanish, telling the tour guide what he wanted and sliding over a stack of bolívares as payment. The man stared at him for a moment, perhaps trying to assess where he was from, what his story was. Beckett's cap was pulled low over his brow, shadowing his features, a precaution against any rogue CCTV cameras that might have caught his likeness at the airport. His hair, which previously he had let grow for a while, was now cropped short – a return to the familiar, to a sense of self that he felt most comfortable with. The tour guide took his money and handed him a handwritten ticket that could have been for anything. Beckett pocketed it and glanced around.

"When's the next flight?" he asked.

"In one hour," the man said. "If you wait over there, someone will collect you." He pointed to a row of plastic seats where the American couple were sitting, reading a guidebook. Standing next to them were two men in their early twenties who looked European.

"I don't suppose I could wait for the next one?" Beckett asked, lowering his voice.

"Only one plane a day. Next flight is tomorrow afternoon."

Beckett nodded. He'd assumed as much, but it was worth a try. A loner by nature, he preferred his own company and the quiet of his thoughts to the bustle of a group. Yet he knew the falls were hidden deep in the jungle and he would have to travel some distance to reach the Canaima camp, the starting point for expeditions to the base of the falls. Navigating the dense wilderness and unpredictable rivers would require the expertise of a Pemon guide. And that meant joining a tour party.

"Thanks anyway," he told the man behind the counter. "I'll take my chances with this one."

He was travelling light, having placed all his possessions – a bag, his passport, his father's watch – in a locker at the airport, so he dropped his hands in his pockets and wandered over to wait with the rest of the party. The Americans looked up as he approached, the woman smiling so sweetly at him that he felt a twinge of guilt for thinking badly of them.

"You going to Angel Falls too?" the guy asked. Up close he looked to be in his late sixties. He was overweight but Beckett felt it kind of suited him. He was wearing a red and yellow aloha shirt, cargo shorts, and a pair of mirrored aviator shades that were pushed up by his cheeks as he smiled.

"Yes, I am," Beckett replied.

"Oh, you're British!" the woman exclaimed. "How delightful." She was about the same age as her husband, with dark, greying hair. She wore a pair of red-framed sunglasses and a creased summer dress. "I'm Kathleen Dixon, by the way. And this is my husband, Bruce."

"Bruce Dixon, pleased to meet ya." The man stood and held out his hand for Beckett to shake.

"Michael Day. Good to meet you both."

"These boys here are coming too," Bruce said, indicating the two men standing a few feet away. They were both tanned, with wavy blond hair and could have been brothers but Beckett didn't think so. They each had a backpack slung over their shoulders and were wearing shorts and t-shirts. Bruce leaned in and whispered, "Germans."

"Ah." Beckett looked over and nodded politely. "*Du bist aus Deutschland?*"

"That's right. But English is fine," one of them said. "My name is Finn Martin and this is my friend, Niklas Lange."

"You're backpacking?" Beckett asked.

"Yes. We have just arrived here from Peru after visiting Machu Picchu. It was amazing."

"I bet. Well, it's good to meet you all."

"Likewise," Bruce said. "From what I can gather from this guidebook, it's going to be pretty cramped on the flight over to the first camp and even more so in the riverboats. I'd say we're going to know each other a whole lot better by the end of this."

Beckett turned away, adjusting his cap to shield his eyes.

## A World of Sun and Violence

The prospect of spending a few days up close and personal with a group of strangers made him grimace internally. His past life had been about solitude, blending seamlessly into the background, avoiding small talk and the usual social pleasantries. But that was the old version of him, the soldier, the deep-cover operative. Today he was nothing but a simple man looking for peace in the beautiful surroundings of one of the most impressive waterfalls in the world. All would be well, he told himself.

Besides, in his old line of work, expecting the unexpected was part of the job. Adaptability was key, and what was this if not just another adaptation, albeit a much less dangerous one than he was used to?

Hell, what was the worst that could happen?

## Chapter Four

Bruce Dixon had been correct. For a man of Beckett's build – broad-shouldered and tall – the six-seater Cessna 206's interior offered a challenge. The seats were narrow and the legroom negligible.

Far below them, the lush greenery of the Canaima National Park stretched to every horizon, the dense jungle cover punctuated only by the occasional lake and clearing. Through his small, oval window Beckett could see the Orinoco River over to the north, snaking through the landscape, its waters reflecting the afternoon sun in a dazzling display of light. It was an amazing view and a welcome reminder to him of the raw, untamed beauty that lay just a few hours away from the hustle and bustle of civilisation. Yet, an hour into the flight the novelty of the journey was already wearing thin.

As well as the cramped interior, it was an old, rattly plane, seemingly held together by rivets and sheer willpower. It buzzed through the air like an angry mosquito, whilst inside, the air was filled with excited chatter and the occasional squeal from Kathleen as the plane rocked through pockets of turbulence. The Germans had pulled out guidebooks and were excitedly poring over them, reading passages out loud for the group.

"'The highest uninterrupted waterfall in the world'," Lange read. "Imagine that."

Kathy sighed. "I can't wait to see it with my own eyes."

"What does that mean – uninterrupted?" Bruce asked.

"It means it falls straight from the top to the bottom," Lange replied. "No rock pools on the way down or anything like that. Crazy, huh? More than three thousand feet."

Lange and Martin were sitting up front, with the Dixons in the middle, and Beckett in the rear of the plane. Everyone onboard seemed pleasant enough, but despite the friendly atmosphere Beckett remained quiet. Polite nods and half-smiles were his currency of interaction, offering no more than necessary. He wasn't here to make acquaintances. He was here seeking solitude and the quiet majesty of nature. Once they arrived at their destination he planned on trekking off by himself to experience the wonder of the falls up close, away from the chit-chat and the selfies.

In front of him, Kathleen began pointing out the window and giggling excitedly as the plane began its descent. A few minutes later the pilot's voice rose over the hum of the engines, announcing their approach. "Ten minutes!"

Beckett returned his attention to the view, catching sight of the waterfalls in the distance, their mist rising to greet them like friendly smoke signals. As the plane got lower, the landscape opened up before them to reveal the expanse of the Canaima Lagoon.

The pilot brought the plane down on a narrow landing strip near the lagoon. Beckett braced himself, pressing his hand onto the roof of the plane, but it was a decent landing considering the size of the engine and the uneven terrain. They'd been told to carry light, so once the few bags had been gathered together, the group disembarked, Beckett allowing the others to go first before jumping down onto the grassy runway. As he glanced around, the dense tropical heat enveloped him like a wet, heavy blanket.

They were quickly ushered to a boat waiting to transport them across the lagoon to Campamento Bernal, where they would stay for the night. There, they met their Pemon guide who introduced himself as Anku, which he went on to explain meant 'eagle' in his language.

Anku was a small, wiry man in his mid-thirties with kind eyes and thick black hair. Dressed in an old Manchester United jersey and a pair of ripped jeans, he was a far cry from the image Beckett had in his head when he'd first heard the words 'Pemon guide', but that was on him. Normally, Beckett never made assumptions about anyone or anything until he had enough information to go on. That he was doing so now, suggested civilian life was finally seeping into his bones. He wasn't sure if that was a good thing.

As soon as they'd all made their introductions, Bruce lifted his phone and tilted it into landscape mode. "Anku? Mind if I get a photo of you with Kathleen here?"

Anku's smile didn't waver but he raised his hand. "I prefer to remain in your memories, not your cameras."

Bruce's face fell, but he lowered his phone and smiled. "Of course. Yes. My apologies."

Beckett remained at the back of the group as Anku stepped up onto a tree stump to address them all. "We have a long day ahead of us tomorrow. Tonight we will rest at camp and I will prepare dinner for us all. You will eat well. You will need your strength. Please follow me."

The camp was a simple setup of tents arranged around a central fire pit. Beckett was relieved to discover that except for the Dixons, who chose to share, everyone else had their own tent. He had no bag to unpack, but took off the grey linen shirt he'd been wearing and hung it over the top of his tent to air. It was now dusk, the blue hour, and the air felt good against his bare skin. It was a pleasant evening, soundtracked by the creak of crickets, the chirp of exotic birds and the rustle of critters in the undergrowth, and Beckett allowed himself to relax, finally. Despite his initial reservations about group travel, he was glad he'd made the journey. The Dixons, in particular, were growing on him. Their infectious enthusiasm, and the attentive way Bruce made sure to include his more demure wife in conversations, was endearing.

As night fell and Anku began to cook, the aroma of searing meat and wild herbs filled the air. Beckett took a seat on a fallen log, far enough from the rest of the group to have some space, yet close enough to not seem aloof. The only light came from the fire, casting flickering shadows and a warm orange glow on everyone's faces. Leaning back, Beckett closed his eyes, listening to the comforting crackle and pop of burning sap mixed with the distant roar of waterfalls.

Once dinner was ready, Anku served up the robust stew he'd prepared. It tasted as good as it smelled, and as Beckett ate he allowed his thoughts to drift back over the past eighteen months. Not so long ago he'd been a key operative for Sigma Unit, deeply embedded under the guise of London crime boss Rufus Delaney's right-hand man. A lot had happened since then. It felt like another lifetime.

Before departing Portugal, Beckett had put some feelers out, using an encrypted forum to communicate with his former handler, Jacob Beaumont. According to Beaumont, both the heads of Sigma Unit and MI6 seemed content to forget John Beckett had ever existed. That didn't mean he'd be welcome back in the UK, but it indicated that the British SIS weren't actively pursuing him.

However, the situation with Xander Templeton, the CIA section chief based in London, was another matter entirely. Templeton had been collaborating with Sigma Unit and MI6 when Beckett disappeared, and was reportedly still irate. He hadn't said anything specific regarding Beckett to anyone, but Beaumont advised caution, aligning with Beckett's own instincts. Staying under the radar as Michael Day seemed the best course of action for now. Besides, returning to London wasn't in his plans anyway. He had a whole world to explore.

Finishing his stew, his thoughts shifted to his niece, Amber, currently living in Spain with his friend Miguel Santos and family. What happened last year had been hard for her too, but the last time he spoke to her she seemed to be thriving. Perhaps in a year or two he'd go back for her, but for now he took solace in the fact she was happy and she was safe.

A loud 'oohing' noise from the Dixons brought his attention back to the moment, and he looked up to see Anku standing in front of the fire, the light from the flames reflected in his dark eyes. He was telling stories, as guides often do, entertaining the delighted thrill seekers with tales of the region.

"Many travellers think of Canaima as just this land," Anku was saying. "But for the Pemon, Canaima is more than just the name of a place. It is the spirit of the evil that stalks us, the danger that lurks in the beauty of the Gran Sabana."

Beckett shifted on the log so he was facing the fire. Anku noticed he was now paying attention and grinned mischievously at him.

"Canaima is the snake hidden among the leaves, the branch that whips back to strike your face. The Pemon do not believe in a death that comes without reason. Canaima is our explanation for the unexplained, the ender of lives." He leaned closer to the fire, letting the flames cast eerie shadows on his face. "Canaima can be the jaguar that watches from the darkness of the trees, or the spirit that slips through our homes in the dead of night. Every accident, every injury, it is his doing."

The Dixons exchanged glances, Kathleen giggling nervously. The Germans, Martin and Lange, huddled closer to the fire as Anku continued his ghost stories, but Beckett had heard enough. To him the tales were fanciful, the kind of myths and legends people created to explain the unknown. He didn't believe in spirits or monsters; he believed in the tangible, in things that could be seen and touched and fought if needed.

He got to his feet, causing Anku to pause. "Is everything okay, my friend?"

"Oh yes," Beckett replied with a smile. "But I'm rather tired, so I think I'm going to turn in for the evening. Thank you all for a pleasant day and I'll see you in the morning."

The others bid him goodnight, and after a polite wave he strolled back to his tent, still half-listening to Anku's tales and half-smiling to himself as he did.

"What's his story?" he heard one of the Germans ask, a tad too loudly.

"Oh, I think he's just a little shy," Kathleen replied. "I'm sure he'll come out of his shell once we get to know each other better."

Beckett's smile spread.

*Good old Kathleen.*

He removed his shirt from the top of the tent and shook it out before unzipping the tent's front flap. Once inside, he stripped down to his underwear and settled into the sleeping bag provided. It was surprisingly comfortable in the tent, but Beckett had trained himself over the years to sleep anywhere. Lying on his back, he began the familiar routine that had become his ritual for sleep – a breathing exercise, followed by the methodical relaxation of each muscle group in turn. One by one he released the tension from his body, from the broad muscles of his back down to the soles of his feet.

He was drifting off to sleep when he thought he heard a gunshot off in the distance. Sitting upright he listened for more, but there was nothing. It had sounded like gunfire, but if so it would have been far away, and he was probably imagining it anyway. That happened on occasion; especially when he was tired.

He lay back and closed his eyes. All around him the night was alive with the sounds of the jungle, a symphony of insects and the scuffles of nocturnal creatures. But within the confines of his tent and his own mind, there was now a quiet solitude. He smiled to himself, thinking about Anku's demonic jaguars and vengeful spirits as he drifted off to sleep. Beckett enjoyed the tradition of such stories, but in his world there were no such things as supernatural beings – only flesh and blood, only man-made dangers. And against those he had always known how to defend himself.

## Chapter Five

Beckett woke early the next morning, his internal clock nudging him conscious at what he guessed was around 5 a.m. He always woke at the same time. It was a habit from his military days that he had felt no reason to break now he was a civilian.

Dressing quietly, he unzipped his tent and stepped out. The last embers of the campfire were still glowing in the pit as he approached, stretching his limbs whilst being careful not to wake the others. Dawn was a short while off and a calm hush hung over the camp. Seeking to clear his head and prepare for the day, he took a walk over to the lagoon, which looked so inviting in the early morning light.

Reaching the lagoon's edge he didn't stop, but walked straight into the still water and immersed himself entirely. He stayed under for a count of twenty, cocooned in the lagoon's cool embrace before surfacing and letting the water cascade off him. It was exhilarating, the best morning wash he'd ever had, and a stark contrast to the heat already prickling at his skin.

He lay back and floated on top of the water, his thoughts drifting again to his former life as an SIS officer. It was happening more and more lately; he didn't know why. He supposed it was the routine he missed, the structure. Being a covert operative was a life of risk and uncertainty, but also one of purpose. He knew there was a part of him that still ached for that life – for the clarity of the mission, the identity being a soldier had given him – but he also recognised the need to forge a new path, to find a new sense of self away from that world.

Before him the jungle was a silhouette against the morning sun now making itself known over the treetops. The air was filled with the promise of the new day, the smells of earth, water and leaves mingling together in a scent that was uniquely the jungle. He dipped his head under the water for a few more seconds, then got out and made his way back to camp. Despite the early hour, he was almost dry by the time he got back. Anku had already roused the others and they were sitting around the dead firepit, rubbing at their eyes and muttering to each other. Aside from Beckett and their guide, they had all changed into fresh clothes. Something light and practical for the day ahead.

"Good morning," Beckett greeted them. "Beautiful day for it."

"Yeah, sure is, Mike," Bruce replied, groggily. "Can't wait to get going."

"You've been up and at 'em early!" Kathleen said, a glint in her eyes as she looked Beckett up and down. "Have you been for a walk?"

"I've been for a swim," he said, grinning. "Down in the lagoon."

"Well, what do you know? Did you hear that, Bruce? I bet it was cold."

"It was lovely." He smiled at Kathleen. This was Beckett coming out of his shell. Trying to, at least. Because why shouldn't he if they were all here together?

He glanced over at Anku who was busying himself with two pans of water balanced on the mangled burner covers of an old butane-powered camping stove.

"Do you need some help?" Beckett asked him.

Anku shook his head. "I am good, sir. You sit down. I'll bring it over."

Breakfast consisted of coffee and cornbread. It was simple fare, but consumed by the group with the enthusiasm of those preparing for a big adventure. Beckett wolfed his down in about a minute. The cornbread was stodgy and a little sweet and the coffee was strong and bitter, just as he liked it.

They set off not long after, the group divided among three flimsy old kayaks that seemed to Beckett to be far too fragile against the powerful currents of the river. The Dixons were in one boat, Martin and Lange in another, with Beckett and Anku in the third. Before they set off, Beckett enquired whether Kathleen should ride with Anku – or even himself – but she and Bruce were both adamant they go in the same boat, so that was the way it was.

Bruce had also informed them all, after reading his guidebook, that it was a gruelling four-hour boat ride on a pair of rivers, the Rio Carrao and Rio Churún, before they reached their next destination, then another ninety-minute hike to get to the lookout for Angel Falls. It was going to be another long day, but Beckett was ready for it. However, with his considerable frame, he felt every jolt and sway of the river as he struggled to find a comfortable position on the hard wooden bench.

The kayaks were narrow and the sides low, leaving the travellers exposed to the choppy river. There were lots of squeals and yells as they passed through areas of white water and the group were splashed by the foam. Hours passed whilst they navigated the serpentine waters, and the air grew thick and heavy with heat. The sun was now high above them, its rays spearing through the leaf canopy in shafts of golden light.

Despite the uncomfortable kayak, Beckett found he was actually enjoying himself. Yes, he was stuck with a group – who all seemed much chattier now they'd got over their early morning start – but they weren't bad people, and he was also in the middle of nowhere, away from the bustle and flow of civilisation. The call of birds, the rustle of leaves and the distant roar of waterfalls were a fitting soundtrack to the journey, and the air was filled with the pungent aroma of tropical fruit and foliage. As the boats hit a swift current he sat back and closed his eyes, feeling the heat on his face and the vast expanse of nature all around him. It was still and yet powerful. Quiet and yet full of danger.

The same could be said about himself.

Their route took them through the very heart of the jungle, and as the river opened out, Anku pointed out a group of Guiana spider monkeys up in the trees, which elicited a flurry of activity from Bruce and the Germans as they pulled out their phones to capture the moment. Beckett had never understood the appeal of camera phones. It seemed to him that you often missed what was right in front of you by focusing on that tiny screen. But there was much about the modern world he didn't get.

It was late afternoon when Anku called out to them all. "There is a bank around the next bend. We shall stop there for an hour to rest and eat. Everyone, please start making your way over to the side."

Beckett and Anku navigated their kayak to the riverbank first. After securing their craft to a tree, they both waded into the water to help guide the others to shore.

"Thank you so much," Kathleen told Beckett, as he helped her out of the boat and onto dry land. "What an adventure, huh?"

"Indeed," Beckett replied. "I've always wanted to see Angel Falls."

"Oh, you're English! Of… course."

It was an odd thing to say, and he was about to respond when Bruce hurried over and took his wife away. "You know the man's English, sweetheart," he whispered, placing his arm around her. "Come on, let's get you sat down and have some food." He looked back at Beckett and smiled. Beckett returned the gesture, before helping Anku tie up the kayaks.

The rest area was a sandy patch under a thick canopy of leaves, providing them with a welcome respite from the sun's intensity. They stretched out as Anku assembled a meal of cured sausage, cornbread and mamey apples from the small hamper he'd brought with him, all washed down with bottles of fresh water. The food was simple but satisfying, providing them with the energy they would need for their trek.

As they ate, Beckett chose to sit apart from the others, listening to the distant call of parrots, trying to pick out any foreign sounds. After hearing the possibility of a gunshot last night, a part of him had been alert for similar noises, but he heard nothing. Now, lying here in the sand with the sun blazing overhead, he closed his eyes and relaxed his muscles. This was exactly what he needed, the change in pace he was looking for.

But then, just as he began to surrender to the calm, he heard the sharp crack of splintering wood. And everything changed again.

## Chapter Six

Beckett rose from the sandy riverbank, his instincts on high alert and a silent alarm chiming in his head. There was a dissonance in the sounds of the jungle, a note out of tune with the natural order of things. He scanned the treeline, scrutinising the interplay of light and shadow for signs of danger.

Over to his right, the others were oblivious to his tension. They were chatting and laughing with one another, showing each other the photos they'd taken so far on the trip. It had been a long day already and even Anku was joining in with them, glad of the downtime. But Beckett's heart was thumping in his chest and his abdominal muscles were gripped in readiness.

His body knew. His body always knew.

Keeping his movements deliberate but casual so as not to alarm the group, Beckett made his way to the nearest kayak. Over the chatter he heard a distinct rustling sound coming from the trees. It could easily be a critter looking for food, or a bird flapping its wings. But if it wasn't…

He froze, adrenaline and caution coursing through his veins like a streak of white lightning. His gaze never left the treeline as he reached down and his fingers found the rough texture of one of the oar handles. Gripping hold of it, he lifted it out of the kayak and felt its weight. It was some sort of pine and less dense than he'd have liked, but it would suffice as a makeshift weapon in the right hands. And it was all he had.

He hoped he was just being overly vigilant – his keen ear and military training overtaking reason – but as he gripped the oar in both hands, evaluating its balance, the underbrush rustled and then three figures emerged from between the trees. They were young men; no more than boys, really – rebel guerrillas if the mismatched military attire was anything to go by, costumed for a role they didn't fully understand. But their expressions, eager and determined, told a different story. Kathleen screamed.

"What the…?" Bruce yelled, scrambling to his feet.

Anku was on his feet instantly, followed by the Germans. Now there were six of them facing the three intruders, which would have improved the odds except for the fact that the three young men were all carrying assault rifles.

"Nobody move," commanded the leader, his weapon sweeping across the group. He was broad-shouldered, with greasy jet-black hair and a perma-sneer. "You are Americans?"

Bruce glared at the rifle. "W-we are. Myself and my wife Kathleen here."

Anku stepped forward, his hands raised in the universal gesture of peace. "I am a Pemon guide," he said, his voice steady. "I work for a tourist company in Puerto Ordaz. We are travelling to Angel Falls. We are no threat to you."

Beckett remained still, his sharp focus on the gunmen as

they jerked their attention around the group, communicating back to each other with their eyes. They were nervous, that much was clear, and the tense way they were gripping their rifles betrayed a lack of experience. Beckett sighed. Kids with guns. They were probably part of some rebel outfit based here in the jungle. But he also knew amateurs like these – hopped up on a cause and with a loaded rifle in their hands – could be just as dangerous and more unpredictable than trained mercs.

"We carry nothing of value," Anku told them, his voice steady. "But you are welcome to search us. We want no trouble."

The others began to murmur among themselves, fumbling with their belongings under the assumption this was some kind of robbery. Bruce removed his phone from his pocket; Kathleen touched her hand to the gold crucifix hanging around her neck. But Beckett already knew this was no robbery. He gripped the oar tight as Anku stepped towards his backpack.

*Don't be stupid, Anku…*

But with a rifle aimed at his chest, Beckett was powerless to do anything. He watched on as Anku reached down and pulled something from the side pocket of his bag. He saw the flash of a blade and felt the atmosphere shift as the guide lunged towards the nearest gunman. But Anku wasn't fast enough. With a grunt, the young rebel squeezed off a flurry of shots that jerked Anku back as the bullets tore through his chest and neck. He cried out, his body contorting for a moment before it hit the ground.

Kathleen screamed. Lange did too.

Beckett's jaw tightened as a familiar rush of adrenaline flooded his system, his body instinctively readying for action. He glanced over at Bruce and Kathleen, who were frozen in shock, staring at Anku's lifeless body. The Germans hadn't moved either, but without weapons, and stood too far away from the gunmen, they were of no help.

Beckett remained still, assessing his odds. He was outgunned and outmanoeuvred, but the young rebels had let their guard down after the attack. If he timed it right he could take out the nearest one with the oar, then using him as a human shield he could grab the kid's rifle and deal with the others. It would be over in less than two seconds. He shifted his weight, ready to move. But his plan was halted as the lead rebel pointed his rifle at Kathleen's head.

"Oh golly no," Bruce stammered. "Please. No!"

"Drop it," another of the rebels barked, aiming his gun at Beckett. "Now."

Beckett held the young man's gaze. He was a lanky kid with a scar running up his jawline, and Beckett would have knocked his head off in any other circumstance, but with the others present he couldn't risk it. Instead he let the oar slip from his fingers and it landed with a muted thud on the sandy riverbank. Bruce gave out a whimper, but Beckett ignored him, not taking his eyes off the three armed men.

These jungles, Beckett knew, were home to rebel militias. Often they were Colombian nationals, exploiting the Venezuelan unrest to fund insurrections back home. He'd heard such activities had died down since Maduro took over as president. But maybe not.

"You come with us," the one with the scar ordered, motioning with his rifle for the group to start walking. Beckett's mind was racing for ways he might turn the situation around, but as the gunman shoved his rifle into his side, he had no choice but to comply. "Move, tough guy," he hissed. "Or I'll kill you right here!"

## Chapter Seven

Adler had no idea where she was. In fact, for a few seconds on waking she had no idea *who* she was. As her consciousness clawed its way back through the layers of syrupy memories, a dull pain in her sinuses was the only thing anchoring her to reality. She swayed with the motion of the room she was in, feeling more disoriented than ever. She was yet to open her eyes and something in the back of her mind told her not to. Her hand instinctively went to her head and she felt a sticky wetness.

*Blood.*

*Oh shit.*

Her eyes snapped open as a deluge of images flashed through her mind – the meeting with Castillo, the men in army fatigues, the bag over her head, then the blow to the head that had sent her into oblivion.

She looked around her, blinking into the gloom. She was in the back of what appeared to be an old military flatbed truck, and she was propped up against the driver's cabin wall. Her hands and feet weren't bound and there was no gag around her mouth. That was something, at least. In front of her a young man sat on the wheel arch with an assault rifle on his lap pointed straight at her, though his expression was one of boredom rather than threat.

As her awareness spread further, she realised two other men were sitting huddled on the other side of her. The first was a stranger, in his thirties with short mousey hair and a worried expression. The second was Edgar Castillo.

"I'm so sorry," he murmured, his voice barely above a whisper. "They threatened my son… my grandson… I had no choice." His round face was pale and creased. He looked both terrified and angry.

Adler nodded, but it was more out of understanding than forgiveness. "It's not your fault," she told him. "You did what you had to."

The truck rumbled on, the engine's growl undercutting the hushed conversation. The heat beneath the truck's canvas cover was stifling, the air thick with the stench of diesel and sweat. Now fully awake, Adler began analysing her situation but she needed more to go on, a sense of where they were heading, and what awaited them there.

The mousey-haired man leaned back to get a better look at her. "Are you hurt?" he asked, nodding at her forehead. He sounded British, his voice high and nasal.

"I'll live," she told him.

*For now*, the voice in her head said, unhelpfully.

"Do you know why they took you?" he asked.

Adler glanced over at the guard. His posture remained one of indifference, but it wasn't wise to discuss personal information, even if her alias was watertight.

"I was taken from my hotel room," the man volunteered. "It was awful. I had no idea what the hell was going on. They gagged me and bundled me into a car. I thought I was going to die."

*Yeah, well there's still time for that.*

"My name's Andrew Price," he continued, lowering his voice, the tendons in his scrawny neck straining as he raised his head to peer at the guard. "I'm a British news journalist. I'm here writing a piece for the Daily Record."

"No way, man. She's a journalist, too," Castillo whispered. "That's how we met. She's Julia Gray and I'm Edgar Castillo. I'm a cop, and she's been interviewing me about the area, the politics… the kidnappings."

Adler glared at her asset but he didn't catch it. "We shouldn't talk about this," she said.

"Yeah, but what if it's relevant?" Castillo replied. "Before, you were asking me about Peroza and the ELN. The people who approached me about you didn't tell me who they were working for, but I'd bet my house it was the ELN. If so, we should be fine. The ELN take hostages for ransom a lot, it's part of their MO."

"Not always."

But Castillo wasn't listening. "The way I heard it, they made two billion US dollars through ransom payments alone these last twenty years. Two billion! They call it their 'economic retention' policy or some shit like that. If this is the ELN then it's going to be just a waiting game. Their hostage-taking is about money, not politics, and my government usually pays up behind closed doors. As long as we keep our heads down and do what they say, we'll live. They get their money, they let us go."

Adler stared at him. "You sound very sure about that."

"He has got a point," Price said. "These groups have to

support themselves and one of the ways they do that is with ransoms. I know the West claims they don't negotiate with terrorists, but that's more of a public stance, isn't it? To deter others?"

"I don't know if it's that straightforward," Adler replied.

"But it makes sense, what he's saying," Price went on, wagging a finger at Castillo. "It is about money for these people, and if our governments don't pay up, there are plenty of other options – family, personal wealth, public appeals. In fact, I know many companies operating in Central and South America who even have ransom insurance for such situations. I think The Record has a policy."

"What are you even doing in Venezuela?" Adler asked him, eager to change the subject.

"I'm working on a piece for our weekend supplement. Investigating the ties between the Venezuelan government and a man called Jalen Murcia. Have you heard of him?"

Had she heard of Jalen Murcia? He was only the reason she'd ended up in this godforsaken mess. Adler leaned back, her head resting against the cold metal of the truck, and fought the urge to close her eyes, or let out a heavy sigh.

"You must have heard of General Murcia," Price continued. "I mean, he's everywhere in the news right now. A one-time rebel, now trying to play proper politician."

Adler maintained a calm façade as she replied. "Yes, I've heard of him. He's still a dangerous man, by all accounts."

"Absolutely. I mean, these guys are no saints. You mentioned Victor Peroza – or Lieutenant Peroza, as he likes to call himself. He runs this whole region with an iron fist and the word is he pumps all his ill-gotten gains into Murcia's bid for power." He tutted camply. "Typical Third World despots."

Adler tensed, her gaze shifting to the guard, who

seemed to be growing more attentive to their conversation. "We should keep our voices down," she whispered, giving Price a hard stare. But he seemed oblivious to the danger of their situation.

"But it's fascinating, isn't it?" he went on. "Some say there are links between the Venezuelan government and these Colombian rebels. It's what I was digging into before… well, before this."

"I know about the links," Adler said, hoping that would be an end to it. "But let's not assume anything about who these people are, okay?"

"Hey." Castillo whistled, making the guard look over. "*Eres E-L-N? E-L-C?*"

The gunman smirked but didn't respond. He did raise his rifle a touch, however, his finger resting on the trigger.

"So who is it you work for, Ms Gray?" Price asked.

"She's New York Times," Castillo announced before she had a chance to reply. "She was ready to pay me big bucks for what I knew."

Adler chewed on her lip, resisting the urge to karate chop Castillo in the throat.

"Oh?" Price said. "Have you worked there long?"

"A couple of years."

"So you'll know Robert Marple?"

Damn Castillo and his big mouth. This was what she'd been worried about. "I'm more of a freelancer," she replied. "I know who Robert is, obviously, but I've not spoken to him all that much. When I see him in the corridor I say hello."

"At The Times?"

"That's right."

Price nodded but seemed confused suddenly.

*Shit.*

Had she made an error? As always, she'd done extensive research whilst building her alias, and the name rang a bell…

Yes. Robert Marple; long-time business correspondent. That was him. He definitely worked at The New York Times.

"But like I say," she continued, eyeing the guard, "it's not wise to give out personal information. Not unless it's absolutely necessary."

"Yes. You're right." Price seemed to finally grasp the gravity of their situation, nodding in understanding. But that didn't stop him muttering under his breath. "What about bloody press impunity, that's what I want to know?"

Adler closed her eyes, trying to steady her racing heartbeat and busy mind. Either Price was too arrogant or too stupid to realise the danger he was in. Or perhaps he believed, like Castillo, that they'd have a relatively easy ride of it – that they'd be used as financial pawns in the rebels' power play, then released once the ransom was paid.

She wished she felt the same.

It could happen that way. Kidnap for ransom cases were a serious issue around the world, to the point that insurance companies offered special KFR policies. But Price's other point was where it got messy.

Whilst the official stance of the US government was not to negotiate with terrorists and kidnappers, the truth was it did happen from time to time, albeit it was more a matter of national pride than finances. Adler knew the US would rather spend ten million dollars on military operations to rescue one hostage before they paid a ten-thousand-dollar ransom. But she also knew that, in her case, a rescue was unlikely. Acknowledging her presence in Venezuela, and her true role, would risk too much exposure.

So whilst Price and Castillo might comfort themselves with stories of prompt ransom payments and speedy releases, Adler suspected the reality of the situation was a lot grimmer and more uncertain.

And should these people discover her true identity, the shit was really going to hit the fan.

## Chapter Eight

The sticky heat enveloped Beckett and the others as their captors marched them in silence through the jungle. The sounds of the river had faded now, replaced by the buzz of insects, scampering critters, and the distant call of exotic birds. Time, too, had lost all meaning. The sun, hidden by the trees, provided no clue to the passing hours, but their sweat-drenched clothes and growing exhaustion told Beckett they'd been walking for some time.

Everyone in the group looked shell-shocked, their faces sagging with the weight of misery and dread. The rebels had ransacked their bags, pocketing their phones and any other valuables, so they had nothing left, not even a bottle of water. No one spoke except for Kathleen, who kept muttering to herself. "Poor Anuk... Poor, poor Anuk!"

The fact that their guide's name had been Anku wasn't lost on Beckett, but he supposed the sentiment was there.

The three rebels had positioned themselves strategically around the group, with one leading the way and the other two bringing up the rear. Initially Beckett had been walking near the front behind the first rebel, but had dropped back, letting Lange and Martin take the lead with the Dixons in the middle. This way he could keep an eye on everyone, whilst also listening out for clues in the conversation between the two men at the back. So far he'd got nothing. They spoke little, their words limited to barked commands for them to 'keep going' or to bum cigarettes off one another.

But that didn't mean Beckett was simply ambling along passively. Beckett never did anything passively. As they walked, his mind was working overtime, assessing their position on the map in his head, recalling everything he knew about the region, as well as considering the identity of their captors. Were they guerrillas as he'd first suspected, or something else altogether – drug dealers or human traffickers perhaps, using the dense jungle as a cover for their operations? The political situation in Venezuela had grown increasingly complex of late, and Beckett had been out of the loop for almost a year. But whatever the situation was, it didn't look good.

With each step they took deeper into the tropical wilderness, Beckett weighed his options, his eyes tracking their captors' habits, their communication, looking for an opening, a mistake he could exploit. But his priority was the safety of the group. There were too many variables, too many unknowns for him to make a move yet. He surmised the gunmen were not seasoned soldiers, which should give Beckett an advantage, except their youth and inexperience only added to their volatility. The smallest spark and they could go off like a bunch of defective Catherine Wheels.

As the hours ticked by, the sticky heat of the day gave way to the cooler air of dusk and then early evening. The light filtering through the canopy took on a soft glow as the sun set over the horizon. In any other circumstance, the beauty of their environment would have been overwhelming. But its majesty was lost on the group, overshadowed by the three young men with guns and faces twisted in grim determination.

A little further and they came upon a wide clearing in the undergrowth. Kathleen glanced around, her usual cheery face creased in a deep frown. She rubbed at her neck. "I don't know if I can walk much farther," she mumbled. "Bruce, can you ask them if we can stop?"

Beckett had noticed the Dixons' pace beginning to falter a while back, their age and the relentless march taking its toll.

Bruce stared at his wife for a moment, then at the nearest gunman. "I mean... sure I will... Umm..."

"They need to rest," Beckett said, turning to address the two men behind him. "And it's getting late. I don't know where you're taking us... but if it's much further, we should make camp for the night."

It was a statement designed to gain information, or at least agreement, but he received nothing but a sneer from the young men.

"Please!" Kathleen begged, throwing her arms in the air. "I'm exhausted."

"Yeah, come on," Martin joined in, as he and Lange stopped and turned around. "We've been walking for hours. We're all tired. We need food, water, rest. I need to take a piss."

The three gunmen exchanged glances and muttered in Spanish to each other. Beckett looked from one to the other. They seemed annoyed but unsure of what to do. Finally the front one, the taller of the three with the scar on his jaw, stepped forward.

"Okay, we make camp for the night. But no one does anything stupid. You understand?"

"Thank you!" Kathleen gasped, more to the heavens than the rebels.

The decision to camp for the night brought with it a mixture of relief but also heightened tension within the group. As Scar got the Germans to build a fire, Beckett settled down against a tree to observe. Lange and Martin were both young men, fit with athletic builds. They could potentially be allies if he decided to take action against their captors, but he was unsure how they'd fare under pressure. Also, he didn't like the way Martin kept glancing at Scar's gun as he marched back and forth gathering wood. Beckett sensed the German was planning something; but he also knew any action driven by fear or desperation was only going to go one way.

As darkness shrouded the camp, the group settled down for sleep. But the night brought with it a new set of jungle sounds that were both intriguing and unnerving, reminding them all exactly where they were.

"Don't worry," Beckett reassured the Dixons, who had flinched at the sound of a distant growl. "No animals will dare come near the fire. And these people are carrying assault rifles."

And didn't he know it?

He had hoped the rebels might have set their weapons down, or at least relaxed their guard. But the three men had formed a triangular perimeter around the camp, a tactical arrangement that indicated a level of sophistication Beckett hadn't initially given them credit for. Or perhaps it was just a fluke. Either way, it meant his options were limited.

Lying back down on the forest floor he closed his eyes, feigning sleep whilst remaining keenly aware of every movement and shift in their captors' positions. Just a single slip or a lapse in judgement. That was all it would take.

As the night wore on, the rebels' alertness started to fade. Their postures relaxed, their hold on their rifles loosened, and their eyes grew heavy. Perhaps to help stay awake, they began to talk amongst themselves. They were speaking Spanish in a strong dialect, but Beckett understood most of what they were saying.

"Lieutenant Peroza will be pleased," one of them said, his hushed tone unable to contain his enthusiasm. "This is our chance to prove ourselves as soldiers. And get a big bonus also."

"That's if we don't have to shoot any more of them," said another, the bravado in his voice not quite pulling off the statement. Yet it elicited hearty laughter from his cronies.

Beckett's eyes remained closed; he listened intently as he pieced together their chatter. As he'd first thought, they sounded to be amateurs – young Venezuelan men with no prospects, most likely recruited from a local town by Colombian rebels and now finding purpose in a cause they barely understood. At one point, one of them mentioned the *Gran Jefe* – the big boss, the chief – who was on his way to Venezuela to oversee operations. Beckett's mind raced, sifting through his knowledge of the region's tangled political landscape but not coming up with anything concrete.

Who was this person? And what was the endgame here?

Another half hour ticked by. Beckett sensed it was now past midnight. If he was to be any use tomorrow, he would need actual rest. He was just starting to relax his muscles when his senses, sharply tuned as always, picked up a change in the atmosphere.

He opened his eyelids a crack, peering around the camp

while remaining still. Two of the gunmen had settled down for rest, leaving just one on guard. On the opposite side of the clearing, Beckett noticed Martin was also awake and his eyes, wide and frenzied, flicked to the young man on watch who was leaning against a tree, peering into the undergrowth, his rifle loosely gripped in one hand. Martin had a chance, but it was a big risk. Beside him, his companion, Lange, was whispering urgently in German, trying to dissuade him, but it was clear desperation had taken hold. Beckett pulled in a slow breath as Martin, his face gripped with determination, commando-crawled closer to the oblivious gunman.

*Come on.*

*You can do it.*

The German's movements were slow and cautious as he reached out, his fingers inches from the barrel of the rifle. The kid was still looking the other way. If Martin tugged down and away hard enough, he could wrestle the weapon away and use it to take out the youngster whilst he was still coming to terms with what happened. Then all it would take would be to adjust his position and shoot the two rebels across the clearing before they had a chance to wake and grab their guns. It could all be over in a second or two. Beckett could have pulled it off, but it had to happen fast and there would be plenty of luck needed.

Beckett tensed as Martin's hand inched closer to the rifle. He was going for it, but he was on his own if things went south. Beckett was too far away and he couldn't intervene without endangering the Dixons and Lange.

In a burst of energy the scene erupted into chaos. Martin's hand clamped on the rifle, yanking it towards him, but his movements were hesitant, fuelled more by fear than strategy. The gunman's reaction was one of surprise and alarm, but he managed to maintain his grip on the rifle.

*Shit.*

That wasn't supposed to happen.

The young rebel stumbled back, yelling out as his finger reflexively squeezed the trigger. A pulse of gunshots shattered the silence of the night and Martin dropped to the ground, a zip line of bullet wounds already darkening the front of his shirt.

The remaining rebels were awake in an instant and on their feet, rifles drawn, as Lange's screams for his friend filled the air. The Dixons sat up and looked about them with bleary eyes while the rebels tried to regain control of the situation, shouting at them all to 'get down', to 'stay down'.

Only Beckett remained still, a sense of inevitability washing over him. The opportunity he had been waiting for had gone. The young rebels' initial shock had now morphed into a display of force as they reasserted control over their captives.

"Oh Lord!" Bruce cried out, holding his wife close as he stared at Martin's lifeless body. "What did you do? What did you do?!"

"Shut it, old man," Scar snarled, raising his rifle as if about to slam it into Bruce's face. "You don't get to ask questions."

"He's fine," Beckett said, keeping his voice low and calm. "He didn't mean anything. He's just shaken. We all are."

Lange looked over at him, his face white. "He… They…"

"I know." Beckett maintained steady eye contact. "I'm sorry about your friend, but we all need to hold it together. We need to do as these people say." He glanced over at Scar, reinforcing his words with a nod. "We understand. There won't be any more trouble. No one else has to die."

Scar held Beckett's gaze for a long time. Beckett didn't look away. He wanted the young man to feel he could trust him.

"Anyone else moves tonight, they die," Scar muttered. "Got it?"

"Understood," Beckett replied. "We're sorry."

A sense of hopelessness now descended over the group. Lange curled up into a foetal position, quietly sobbing to himself. The Dixons huddled together, Bruce whispering reassuring platitudes into Kathleen's ear. Beckett lay back onto the soft moss of the jungle floor, all too aware that the window of opportunity had now slammed shut. The rebels were on high alert, their keen eyes darting around the camp with newfound vigilance, rifles at the ready.

Closing his eyes, Beckett was overtaken by a rare and uncomfortable sense of vulnerability. The uncertainty was the hardest part. If he knew where they were heading, and what these men planned to do with them once they got there, he could assess and plan. But for now it was a waiting game. All he could do was try to get some rest and see what tomorrow would bring. After what had happened today, it couldn't get much worse.

## Chapter Nine

It was hard to fall asleep with an assault rifle aimed at your head, but Beckett and the others must have managed it at some stage because they were now being prodded awake by those same rifles. The cold muzzle poking into Beckett's chest was a harsh reminder of their predicament.

"Hey! Wake up! Time to move."

Beckett sat upright and glanced about him. It was early morning, the sun barely visible through the dense canopy above but the air already filled with the sounds of the jungle. A few feet away, the Dixons were awake, their faces puffy and expressions distraught. Bruce was gently explaining the previous night's events to his wife, speaking to her as one might to a child. Beckett didn't catch Kathleen's response, but the fear and grief in her voice were unmistakable. Lange was also awake, sitting in silence and staring at the spot where Martin had been lying just a few hours earlier. Thankfully for the group, the rebels had dragged Martin's body into the trees, though there remained a dark, dried streak of blood on the ground.

Beckett got to his feet, prompting one of the men to shove his rifle at him with a grunt.

"Hey, it's okay," Beckett told him, raising his hands. "I'm just feeling a little stiff. I need to stretch."

The man glared at him for a moment then gave him a curt nod. "Fine. Go."

Beckett straightened, placing his hands on his lower back and leaning forward to stretch his spine. Having put his body through so much over the years – and with him not getting any younger – he made a point of stretching every morning. Today, however, the routine also served as a good cover story, and he used the time to observe the rebels, assessing their demeanour and alertness.

The three young men seemed more confident in the daylight; the amateurish edge they'd displayed yesterday replaced with a newfound assertiveness. The man who had shot Martin was acting particularly brash, strutting around like he was some big-shot military hero. Beckett knew all too well that killing a man was a transformative experience, and usually it went one of two ways. Either you went to bits and prayed to God you never had to do it again, or you became a god in your own eyes. One moment you're a fresh-faced kid without a care in the world and the next you're a warrior, brutal and cold, hardened to the ways of the world.

As he finished stretching, Beckett noticed Kathleen and Bruce watching him. He gave them his most reassuring smile. It felt false and did little to change their anxious expressions. A smile could only do so much.

"How are you holding up?" he asked them.

Bruce gave a half-hearted shrug. "Not great. Do you think we might get some food? Some water at least?"

Beckett turned his attention to the rebels. Scar and one

of the others were huddled together in a deep discussion whilst the third kept watch, his rifle at the ready.

"Hey!" Beckett called out, getting their attention. "We're all hungry and thirsty. If you expect us to walk far today, then we need something to keep us going."

The rebels stared at him a moment before returning to their huddle, their conversation now louder and more harried as they discussed whether to provide them with supplies.

"You've brought us all this way," Beckett interjected, keeping his voice calm but authoritative. "If you're planning to use us as hostages, we're no good to you dead. We need water at the very least, especially if there's a long walk ahead."

After more back-and-forth, Scar marched over to one of the backpacks they'd been carrying and returned with a small canteen of water and four foil-wrapped cereal bars. He handed the bars out to each of them and gave the water to Kathleen. Beckett nodded to him in thanks. It was a small concession but a telling one.

Once they'd all drunk from the canteen and eaten the cereal bars, the group set off. It was the same formation as before – one gunman leading, two at the rear, with Lange at the front, the Dixons in the middle, and Beckett following on behind. The only difference now was that Martin was no longer with them, a fact that was not lost on any of them.

It wasn't long before the path grew challenging. The undergrowth was dense and unyielding and the air thick with humidity. Beckett kept a close eye on the Dixons, assisting them through the more demanding parts of the journey. Their resilience, despite their obvious fear and exhaustion, was admirable. Up ahead Lange walked in shocked silence, and it was hard to tell what he was thinking. Maybe he was thanking his lucky stars it wasn't him currently rotting in the bushes, or maybe he was thinking about avenging his friend's death somehow. Beckett hoped it was the former, for all their sakes. He was now all but certain the men were rebels and that they'd captured them for financial gain, but that didn't mean their youthful exuberance and keen trigger fingers wouldn't get the better of them if provoked.

Behind him the young men chatted in Spanish, their conversation a mix of cocksure posturing and naive claims. They spoke of how pleased the lieutenant would be with their catch.

"We could be bringing back five if it wasn't for you," one of them hissed.

"Go to hell," the other snapped. "What was I supposed to do? He came for me. I did the right thing."

"You panicked. You were scared."

"I was not. I meant to shoot him."

"Sure you did. That's why you went white."

"Screw you. We have four, at least. That's still good. We'll get a decent bonus."

Beckett kept his head down, pretending not to listen but keeping an ear out the whole time. They were confirming to him exactly what he'd assumed. These young men were new to this world of armed conflict and kidnapping, their actions driven more by the promise of reward than any ideological commitment. Yet there were people above them – a lieutenant –driving the situation. Once they got to wherever they were going he'd know more, but Beckett had to assume this lieutenant person was the real deal.

As the bickering continued behind him, Beckett

wondered about making a move. A feigned stumble, a quick snatch of a rifle during the ensuing confusion – it would be quick and easy. Yet with the Dixons and Lange in such a vulnerable position in front of him, it was also too risky. Despite the opportunity, Beckett wasn't going to put the others in danger if he could help it. It was frustrating but he remained alert, biding his time.

After another two hours of trekking through the dense jungle, the group suddenly emerged into a large, open clearing, the fresh air and sunlight a shock to the system after spending so long in the claustrophobic undergrowth. The area appeared to have been deliberately cleared, the edges of the expansive space defined by a border of trees on either side. A makeshift runway extended across the clearing in front of them, and beyond this stood an imposing building that could have been a prison, with its high walls and barbed wire running around the perimeter. The setup seemed far more advanced than the makeshift guerrilla camp Beckett had anticipated. The presence of the runway, in particular, indicated a significant level of operational capability. It was clear that whoever controlled this camp had both resources and connections.

"Keep moving!" one of the rebels snarled, nudging him with the butt of his rifle.

Beckett followed the others as they were led across the grass towards the rebel base. Up close, he saw the outer walls were made of thick concrete.

"This looks like something out of the movies," Bruce whispered. "I don't like it one bit."

"Oh, shut up!" Lange sneered. "You know, you two are starting to get on my nerves."

"Hey…!" Beckett was about to step in – to tell Lange

that wasn't helpful – but before he had a chance, Scar turned around and shoved his finger in the German's face.

"No talking!" he spat, glancing at each of them in turn as his lips spread into a malicious grin. "We are here now. You are about to meet the great Lieutenant Peroza. And let me tell you – you'd better act respectfully. Because he is not as friendly as we are."

## Chapter Ten

Beckett glanced at Lange as the other rebels snickered at Scar's remark. The German's face was set in a hard, determined expression, the muscles in his jaw rippling with restrained anger. Thankfully he stayed silent. That was something, at least. Beckett had been worried that after Martin's death, Lange might lose the plot. But for now he seemed to be holding himself together. The laughter from the rebels faded as they approached the building.

The main gate was an eight-foot wooden construction, crudely held together by rusty iron rivets and tar. Scar banged on the wood with his fist and the group waited in tense silence until it creaked open to reveal two young men in military fatigues. Like their comrades, they were armed with Galil Córdova rifles, but that made sense. Galils were Colombian-made and used by both the Colombian Armed Forces and National Police, easy to traffic across the border.

"Four. You have done well," one of the gatekeepers commented.

"We know," Scar replied. "Is the lieutenant here?"

The guard nodded. "He's busy preparing for the visit, but he'll be pleased to see what you've brought." He stepped aside to let them in.

The original three captors moved behind the group, prodding them forward with their rifle muzzles. Kathleen let out a small cry, and Lange muttered something sharply in German. Beckett gave them both a pointed look, silently urging them to keep their composure. Now wasn't the time for any outbursts. They needed to stay calm and alert.

But the group's arrival hadn't gone unnoticed. As they were ushered forward, other men dressed in the same generic military attire paused in their tasks, smiling encouragingly at Scar and his men and regarding the group with a mixture of curiosity and contempt. The gate closed behind them and the Dixons glanced back, their eyes wide and their mouths hanging open. Kathleen, already shaken by the ordeal, clung to her husband's arm. Beckett moved closer and patted Bruce on the shoulder. He needed them both to hold it together.

As they were escorted across the compound, Beckett took in every detail – the gate's construction, the layout, the number of guards, what weapons they were carrying. The facility appeared to have indeed once been a prison, although Beckett couldn't recall hearing of any prison out here in the Venezuelan jungle. There was a possibility it had been out of use for many years. It certainly looked that way.

The high walls surrounding them were crumbling in places, and where there once might have been cells or administrative offices, there was now just a large, open expanse. Either by bombs, age or design, this central area had been gutted, leaving only two solid concrete structures at either end of the compound and a smattering of smaller units. Between these two-storey buildings stretched a vast training ground, worn and dusty. Around the edge of the space, three huge canvas tents and two awnings had been erected, reminiscent of the makeshift barracks Beckett had called home in his SAS days in the Middle East.

Another wooden gate was situated at the compound's opposite end, as well as three more brick-and-mortar outbuildings that looked to be storage facilities. There was also a long, low tent that Beckett assumed to be the latrine; and in front of the wall on the far side, a wooden hut with a black velvet curtain pulled across its entrance. The hut's purpose was unclear, but Beckett wondered if it was a prayer room or perhaps even a confessional booth.

As they were herded across the prison grounds, Beckett took in the faces of the rebels milling about them. Most of them were young, like their captors, but their expressions were twisted into grim sneers all the same. The air was filled with the smell of cooking and diesel fuel, and an undercurrent of damp earthiness lingered beneath. Due to the thick, high walls, it was cooler inside the compound and the external sounds were muted somewhat, but as they were brought to a halt in front of the closest of the two main buildings, Beckett heard a strange noise in the distance. It sounded like chains or perhaps machinery, rhythmic and metallic – an incongruous sound in the middle of the jungle, and he could see nothing close by that would make such a noise. He felt as if he recognised the sound, but he couldn't quite place it.

Beckett was considering this when a figure appeared from the main building. The man was tall and well-built, and unlike the mismatched fatigues of the foot soldiers, his uniform was immaculate. He carried himself with the confidence of a man who had known power for a long time. He had good bone structure and almost Hollywood good looks, but his eyes lacked any compassion or warmth as they swept over the new arrivals.

"I am Lieutenant Victor Peroza," he announced, his voice deep and resonant. "And you are now political prisoners of the Colombian Liberation Party."

So not the ELN – the National Liberation Party of Colombia – as Beckett had first thought. He'd heard of the Colombian Liberation Party but didn't consider them as major players. That said, things could change quickly and he hadn't been keeping up lately.

In a brief moment of levity, he thought of Monty Python's *Life of Brian* and the People's Front of Judea versus the Judean People's Front. Maybe he'd bring it up with Bruce and Kathleen later, make light of the situation to try to cheer them up. Or maybe not. Maybe there was no making light of any of this.

"What do you want with us?" Lange asked. "We are here on holiday. We are not part of any war!"

Peroza glared at him. "You should watch your mouth. This is no holiday for you any longer." He paused as if for effect, then grinned. "But no one will be harmed if you do as we say."

"Your men shot my friend!" Lange cried. "He's dead!"

At this Peroza frowned, turning to the three men who had abducted them. He spoke to them in Spanish, asking if what Lange was saying was true, and if so, who the killer was. Beckett glanced around as the men shuffled their feet and mumbled under their breaths before the one who'd shot Martin stepped forward.

"It was me, Lieutenant. He tried to grab my weapon. I had to do it."

Peroza exhaled through his nose, sounding a little like a horse. "Idiot," he snarled, still speaking in his native tongue.

"This is not good. General Murcia arrives tomorrow morning. Do you want to explain to him how you have killed a hostage? Not only is that a lot of money wasted, but it makes us look like brutes, savages – terrorists. This is not what he wants."

The man didn't blink but his Adam's apple bristled as he tried to swallow. "No, Lieutenant Peroza."

"Hmm. Take him away," Peroza instructed his other men. "If he can't be trusted to carry out orders, he can entertain us as a fighter."

The young man's face dropped. "No! Please, Lieutenant! Not that! Not him…!"

But Peroza was done. "Get him out of my sight."

The man continued to scream and yell as two more guards arrived to take the place of Scar and the other man, who dragged their friend away. Like their captors, these men were young but full of bravado – this despite one of them looking as if he hadn't started shaving yet.

"Take our new guests to the custodial tents," Peroza told them, then smiled and turned back to the hostages, slipping back into English. "You will be held here whilst we make arrangements for payment in exchange for your release," he informed them. "This is a secure unit, once a prison, and is well guarded day and night. You should sit tight, stay quiet, and nothing bad will happen. But anger me in any way, do anything stupid, and you will regret it. I am not a monster, but I can become one if you anger me. Understood?"

The group nodded in unison, even Beckett. There was no point rocking the boat at this stage. He had to take Peroza on his word until he knew more. For now it was enough to observe, getting a lay of the land until he could make a better judgement of the situation.

"We already have guests onsite who arrived before you,"

## A World of Sun and Violence

Peroza continued, turning to address one of his henchmen. "For now, put the woman in with the American journalist but keep the men together."

The guards stepped forward and the group was quickly split up. The men were lined up on one side, Kathleen on the other. Already terrified, she burst into tears.

"Bruce! What's going on? Help me!"

Bruce, too, began to protest, his own fears trumped by his need to protect his wife. "Please, she needs me. She's not well. I have to stay with her—" He stepped forward, reaching out for his wife's hand, but was met with a sharp slap from one of Peroza's men.

"Get back!"

Bruce, in shock, glanced at Peroza, his hand going to his cheek. "Please, I have to be with her." He stepped towards the lieutenant, but his path was halted by one of the guards who raised his rifle at Bruce.

"Hey, there's no need for that," Beckett said, positioning himself between the older man and the rebels. "These people are just worried and upset. They're no threat to you." He turned to Peroza. The lieutenant was clearly playing a bigger game here than his amateurish lackeys suggested and he hoped to appeal to his sense of international law. But as he moved, Peroza drew a pistol from the holster on his hip and aimed it between Beckett's eyes.

"So, you're English, huh?" he asked, a smirk playing across his lips. "You think you can speak for the world, police us all, just like always?"

For a moment it felt as if the entire compound was holding its breath. Beckett certainly was. Peroza shoved the gun forward, grinding the muzzle into Beckett's forehead. He noted it was a Magnum Research Big Frame Revolver, probably carried as a status symbol because, like the man said, it was the most powerful handgun in the world. At this range, it would blow the back of Beckett's skull clean out. If Peroza was using 700-grain hollow points, the blast would take his entire head off.

At least he wouldn't feel it.

"I didn't mean to speak out of turn," Beckett replied, keeping his voice steady despite the adrenaline surging through his system. "These people are scared and weary. We all are. We don't want any trouble. We just want to go home."

Peroza pressed the gun harder for a moment, then suddenly let out a harsh laugh that echoed around the prison walls. He holstered his pistol and signalled to his guards. "Take them," he ordered.

Beckett observed the lieutenant for as long as possible as they were led away.

*Sit tight, stay quiet, and nothing bad will happen…*

That's what he'd said, but Beckett had seen something in Peroza's eyes just now. The man was unhinged, impulsive. He didn't like that.

"Mike," Bruce whispered as he shuffled closer. "What's going to happen to us?"

Beckett gave him a sideways glance. "Don't worry, we'll be okay," he assured him. "We need to stay strong. We'll make it through this. I promise."

Yet the grim reality was they were trapped in Peroza's compound, pawns in a game run by men with a lust for power and egos bigger than their guns. Beckett had been in worse situations over the years, but he'd been in better ones too. Whilst Peroza's methodology appeared to be a classic kidnap for ransom, still prevalent in this part of the world, there was no assurance they wouldn't all be executed should complications arise or the payment not materialise quickly enough.

Beckett might have been out of the loop for the last year, but he was well aware of the broader geopolitical landscape. With the ongoing conflicts in Ukraine and the Middle East, the US and UK were preoccupied with larger issues than a handful of hostages held by Colombian rebels.

And the last thing he wanted was to commit himself to film in some appeal message. That was a scenario he was determined to avoid at all costs. The possibility of the UK government agreeing to a ransom was slim, but even that came with its own set of complications for someone like Beckett. If he were released only to be handed over to the authorities back home – or even worse, to the Americans – then Peroza might as well have shot him in the head just now. If MI6 or the CIA got hold of him, the very best he could hope for was to be locked up in some secret detention facility for the rest of his life, his identity reduced to a number on a piece of paper, a hidden expense.

No. Wasn't going to happen.

He needed a third option, but right now he was out of ideas. All he could do was watch, listen, and try to keep the others calm.

*We'll make it through this. I promise.*

He also had to start believing that.

## Chapter Eleven

General Jalen Murcia peered out the window of his private plane, observing the sprawling jungle below. As the aircraft began its descent towards the crude runway, the fading light of dusk cast a golden haze over the treetops stretching into the distance like a vast green ocean. But despite the impressive view and the comfort of his private jet, Murcia found himself tense and irritable. The prison compound here in Venezuela – built by the COPEI party to house political prisoners and enemies of the state away from the world's gaze – had been a valuable discovery and a necessary evil at the start of his campaign, but the more time passed, the more his visits became a source of discomfort. The prison represented the brutal, unsavoury side of his quest for power, a side he was increasingly eager to distance himself from. Indeed, whilst orchestrating his journey here, he had sent a lookalike to a meeting over in Barranquilla, a tactic to throw off the press and his political enemies.

As the plane touched down on the uneven runway, the familiar sense of unease settled in Murcia's stomach. He anticipated that, given the recent developments, these check-in visits would soon be unnecessary. Yet for the moment it was crucial to monitor his subordinates, especially his old friend, Victor Peroza, whose growing ambition and independence he found troubling.

Back in Colombia, Murcia's political advisors were pressing him to wrap up operations here at the prison and concentrate on the newly discovered site. Peroza, they warned, was becoming unpredictable; a loose cannon, they said, and Murcia was well aware of the rumours circulating of what went on here in the Venezuelan compound. Originally intended as a secure and covert location where they would hold hostages whilst negotiating a price for their release, there were now whispers of illegal gambling operations and fight clubs on the site. More disturbing were the reports of Peroza's men raiding villages under the pretence of recruitment, forcibly taking women to use as sex slaves, a tactic that bred fear and resentment among the locals. Murcia also suspected his old friend of embezzling funds meant for their cause, siphoning off resources for personal gain, which further undermined the party's financial stability.

The young rebels Peroza had recruited were another issue. They were mostly dumb kids from nearby villages, young and inexperienced, as well as being far too eager to get their hands on a rifle and play GI Joe. Murcia now envisioned the ELC as a legitimate political party, not a renegade guerrilla faction. Being seen as a lawless group akin to Al-Qaeda was contrary to his larger, more sophisticated objectives. The ELC needed to maintain a semblance of order and legitimacy; something that seemed increasingly compromised under Peroza's unchecked leadership.

Stepping out of the plane, Murcia was struck by the

absence of a welcome party. This oversight was disrespectful and another rock in the box against Peroza and his operations here. Accompanied by his security detail, he marched over to the main building. The air was thick with the smells of the jungle, a heady mix of decaying fruit and moist earthiness that did little to improve his mood.

Upon reaching the prison's main entrance, his men knocked loudly on the gate. A siren sounded, and the gate creaked open to reveal two young guards. Thankfully for them, they appeared to know who he was and saluted with enthusiasm as he filed past, dismissing their exuberant stance with a wave of his hand. Formalities were the last thing on his mind; he was here strictly for business.

Murcia cast a critical eye over the situation as he made his way across the prison grounds towards Peroza's quarters. A group of young men who'd been sitting under one of the awnings playing cards jumped to their feet and saluted as he approached. That was something at least, but their keen, youthful faces, untainted by experience, did little to reassure him. These were not the battle-trained men Peroza had promised him; they were boys playing at war, their discipline questionable, their loyalty untested. As he got closer, Peroza emerged from the main building, tucking in his shirt as he walked down the steps. He looked angry and frustrated, caught off-guard. But that was what Murcia had been hoping for, having informed Peroza his visit wouldn't be until tomorrow morning. He noted the look of unease on his old friend's face with sombre satisfaction.

*Patético idiota!*

Good. Peroza's discomfort was precisely what Murcia had intended. It was a reminder of who was in charge. This visit was not just an inspection, it was also a demonstration of his power and control.

"General!" Peroza exclaimed. "This is a surprise. Your assistant informed us you'd be here tomorrow."

"Is that so?" Murcia replied, feigning surprise. "A misunderstanding, then. I'll have a word with him later. I assume everything here is in order?"

"Of course."

The two men faced each other, their postures rigid, a tangible tension hanging in the air between them. Peroza was the taller of the two, the most striking, but Murcia held his ground, his status more than making up for his stature.

Not that he was a weak man, by any means. Despite being in his mid-fifties, he maintained a robust physique, his posture straight and commanding, exuding an aura of seasoned confidence. Like a lot of men who'd seen action over the years, he had a rugged, worn complexion and sharp, dark eyes that sometimes gave the impression they'd seen too much. His hair, peppered with grey, was neatly trimmed into the haircut of a politician, complementing his strong jawline.

The men continued to hold each other's gaze, and for a moment it seemed as if the standoff might escalate. But then, almost reluctantly, they embraced. It was a gesture that spoke more of past camaraderie than present affection.

"Still filling your ranks with boys rather than men, I see," Murcia commented as they stepped away, his eyes scanning the compound. "You know my feelings about that."

Peroza's response was a tight smile. "They work hard. They are loyal. They know what will happen to them if they step out of line."

Murcia cleared his throat, his gaze fixed on his old ally. *And what about you?* he thought. *What happens when you step out of line?*

"How are you, Jalen?" Peroza asked him. "I hear things are going well for us across the border. Our goal is in sight. I trust you won't forget about us and all we have done for you once you gain power."

Murcia let out a chuckle. "But of course, my friend. And, yes, everything is progressing as planned. But we are not there yet and we must remain vigilant and stay focused." He opened his eyes wide. "Which is why I'm here. I trust you're keeping everything under control?"

Peroza nodded, a flash of pride in his eyes. "Oh yes. We have a new shipment."

"Oh?" Murcia raised an eyebrow. "Arms? Heroin?"

"People."

Murcia's expression hardened. "More hostages? I thought we agreed to move away from this, that it is no longer aligned with our objectives. We no longer need the money."

"But it's easy money, good money!" Peroza barked, his voice echoing off the high walls of the compound. "Among them are two journalists – an Englishman and an American woman. Journalists always fetch a high price and prompt payment. Don't worry, brother. I know what I'm doing."

Murcia held Peroza's gaze. His old friend did know what he was doing, that was precisely what he was afraid of. But he held back from further questioning, allowing Peroza to lead him through the compound. He was to be accommodated in the building on the other side of the grounds, where he always stayed whilst onsite.

"Is your pet still around?" Murcia asked, as they passed the large wooden hut on the far side of the exercise yard. "Your attack dog, I mean."

Peroza snorted. "You mean Bracho? Yes, he's still here."

Murcia shook his head in dismay. He'd never cared for

that beast of a man, considering him more a gimmick than an asset, a joke that had worn thin a long time ago. Keeping such a character was indicative of Peroza's flawed approach to how he ran things here, more befitting a ragtag rebel unit than a group preparing for a military coup. In Murcia's eyes, Bracho was an oddity, a freak. He should have been put down a long time ago.

He told Peroza as much. "I want you to get rid of him. He's a liability and a pointless expense."

Peroza shrugged, unconcerned. "He serves his purpose," he said, as though that settled the matter. "How long do you plan to stay?"

"A few days."

"Oh?"

"You were hoping for less?"

Peroza hit him with that tight smile. "I wasn't sure, that's all."

"I want to get a feel for how operations are progressing here," Murcia explained. "And, of course, I want to visit the new site and check on the work."

Peroza bristled at this, his annoyance clear. "This is my base, Jalen. I understand this discovery has changed things, but you gave me control of this region."

"Yes, but you don't seem to appreciate just what we have at our fingertips, Victor. What we have now changes *everything*! You have to start thinking bigger. We are on the brink of legitimacy, yet you're still fixated on petty kidnappings and playing with your silly toys."

Peroza stopped. "I am still a part of this cause," he snarled. "I love my country. I love what we are doing for it. But we still have a way to go. The money from these hostages is vital for us. Let's not run before we can walk, brother."

Murcia eyed Peroza warily but remained silent as they set off again. He was weary and needed time to reflect. Except he couldn't ignore the fact that Peroza was growing restless. Perhaps even volatile. Peroza had been a useful ally once, an essential flame in Murcia's rise to power. But now the real kingmakers behind the general saw his old friend as a threat, a wild card who could jeopardise everything he had worked for.

"I'll leave you to freshen up," Peroza said, gesturing towards Murcia's accommodation as they arrived at its entrance.

The site, once the prison kitchen and mess hall, had been done out as a living space, with a large lounge and office area on the ground level, and a luxurious apartment on the upper level. It boasted a king-size bed, a bathroom with whirlpool bath, and a well-stocked drinks cabinet. Because one didn't have to live in squalor to be a rebel. Far from it. And once the ELC's coup d'état was successful, Murcia planned on having only the best – of everything.

"I'll have my chef create a feast for us this evening," Peroza added. "Once you have rested, come and find me."

"Thank you," Murcia said. "We'll talk more later."

But as they parted ways, Murcia's mind was spinning with thoughts and plans. If Peroza had indeed become too much of a risk, then decisive action would be necessary, and soon, to extinguish Peroza's flame before it burned everything to the ground. The two men might have been like brothers once, but Murcia knew more than anyone – in the ruthless pursuit of power, there was no room for sentimentality.

## Chapter Twelve

Vanessa Adler was alone, seated on a hard wooden bench that might have once belonged in a church. The humidity clung to her skin, making even the air in the large tent dense and suffocating. When she'd first been brought here, she'd paced up and down in anger and frustration, yelling to anyone who could hear that she needed to speak with someone, but had got nothing back. At one point, she'd poked her head through the canvas flaps of the entrance, only to be met with fierce snarls from the two guards standing outside.

Now she sat. There was nothing else to do.

The tent was sparsely furnished; just three more benches like the one she was sitting on and two battered tables. In one corner there was an old tin basin and a bar of soap, and beside this, a pallet of bottled mineral water. Despite her efforts to stay calm and focused, the uncertainty of her situation, compounded by the heat and lack of food, was taking its toll, making her feel sick.

Suddenly the tent flap was thrown open and a new

guard entered, dragging an older woman with him. "Here," he ordered, pushing the woman towards Adler. "You sit here. You stay quiet."

The woman appeared to be in her early sixties, with a sturdy build that suggested a life of comfort before her current predicament. Her clothes were practical but dishevelled, the stains and wrinkles indicating she had been wearing them for some time. Her face, framed by uncombed grey hair, was taut with stress and worry, yet there was an underlying resilience in her demeanour. Adler guessed she was American before she even spoke.

"Oh my gosh!" the woman exclaimed in a distinct Midwestern accent, possibly from Minnesota. "I have no idea what's happening! Can you help me?"

Adler watched the guard for a moment, but once the woman had settled on the bench, he sneered dismissively at them and left the tent. The older woman, obviously distraught, began to sob.

"Hey, hey, come on now." Adler shifted around and placed a hand on her shoulder. "I know things look pretty bad, but there is a way through this. You're an American, right?"

The woman sniffed and nodded. "Kathleen Maria Dixon from Ramsey County, Minnesota. Maplewood, if you know it."

Adler inclined her head, trying to establish eye contact. "Nice to meet you, Kathleen. I'm… Julia Gray. I'm also an American. From South Dakota." This aspect of her story was partly true. Vanessa Adler was born in South Dakota. Although, she left out the fact it was actually at Ellsworth Air Force Base, Box Elder. But if she told anyone here that, along with her real name, they might start putting two and two together and that would be bad.

"My sister-in-law lives in South Dakota," Kathleen replied in a small voice. "It's beautiful up there." Then the tears started again. "Oh Lord, I'm so scared. I don't know what to do. I need my Brucey. I need my husband."

Adler leaned back. "Is your husband with you? In the prison, I mean?"

"Uh-huh." Kathleen nodded. "We were in a tour group heading for the... you know... the big old waterfall. Then these men with guns came out of nowhere. They killed our guide."

"I'm sorry you had to go through that." Adler extended her arm across Kathleen's shoulders, pre-empting more sobs. "It must have been awful. How many of you were there? And how did you get here?"

Kathleen's expression clouded. Clearly she was struggling with the overwhelming exhaustion and fear. "I... I can't remember. They separated us," she stammered. "Bruce tried to... to protect me. They hit him." Her voice broke and more tears flowed as she buried her face in Adler's shoulder. Before Adler could respond, the tent flap opened and a man stepped inside.

"Good evening, ladies," he said, drawing out the word 'ladies' with evident relish. *Lay-deez.* "I am Fernando Lugo, Lieutenant Peroza's deputy here at the base."

Lugo was a large man in both height and width, with a swollen belly and thick, unkempt hair that was plastered across his forehead with sweat. It was hard to pinpoint his age – he could be anywhere between thirty and fifty – but he certainly looked older than the young men who had snatched Adler. His cheeks were mottled with acne scars and his dark eyes, set too close together, darted around the tent before landing on Adler. He leered at her.

"You are both Americans, yes?"

"That's right," Adler responded, maintaining her composure.

"And you – you are a journalist?"

Adler nodded as Lugo stepped in front of her. His worn uniform stretched awkwardly over his bulky frame as he moved, undermining his attempt at authority.

"What do you plan to do with us?" Adler asked. "This woman shouldn't be here. She is scared. She wants to see her husband."

Lugo's grin didn't waver as he kept his gaze locked on Adler. "She will see him. In good time. Once you are all processed."

"Oh, thank God," Kathleen whispered. "I don't feel so good."

Adler held her hand. It would provide little comfort but was the best she could offer at this moment. She kept her eyes on Lugo. "And then… you'll be seeking ransom?"

Lugo stuck out his bottom lip. "Maybe," he said. "Or maybe you'll all be executed. It's not my decision. But a journalist… that's a great prize. We always get a lot of money for journalists, especially Americans. But…" He looked away, his expression morphing into a mask of mock sadness. "I don't think it would be the worst thing to happen if a journalist disappeared. That way you can't write your slander about us and our cause."

"What is your cause?" Adler asked, refusing to be intimidated by his posturing. "Are you part of the ELN?"

"We are the ELC!" he spat. "Stronger, fitter, better. We are the true revolutionaries. The party that will finally take back our great country."

"You think kidnapping civilians is going to have people take you seriously?" Adler asked, her fatigue and frustration breaking through her usual composure. "That's the behaviour of terrorists, not freedom fighters."

"Enough!" Lugo closed in on her, invading her space. She felt his rancid breath on her cheek as he grabbed her face. "You know you're a very good-looking woman," he sneered, dropping his other hand onto her thigh and sliding it up her leg. "Things could go a lot easier for you here."

"Hey!" Adler reacted swiftly, gripping Lugo's hand to halt his advance. Her instinct was to jump to her feet and twist his arm around his back until she heard his joint pop, but she stopped herself as she caught sight of the young soldier by the tent's entrance, his finger twitching near the trigger of his rifle. It wasn't the time for drastic actions. She shoved Lugo away, holding back her anger as he let out a cackling laugh devoid of any joy.

"You are a strong woman. I like that." He straightened and folded his arms, attempting to reassert his dominance in the room. "Once we secure ransoms, you will go free. *Hopefully*. But it would be a tragedy if any accidents happened before then..."

"Please can I see my husband?" Kathleen wailed, clearly not reading the room. "I need him. He's called Bruce. Bruce Dixon. He's got a bald head and he's wearing a red and white shirt. Or was it blue...?" She trailed off. Adler squeezed her hand tighter. "We were taken at the same time but then split up, I know that. Is he okay? Does he know where I am?"

Lugo gritted his teeth and made a low growling noise as if he'd suddenly rather be anywhere else but here talking with them. He wagged his finger at Kathleen as if about to say something, but then thought better of it. Rising to his full height, he addressed them both. "You will stay here for now. Two of my best men will be on guard at all times with instructions to shoot if you try anything stupid. So don't."

"What if we need to use the bathroom?" Adler asked, glancing around the tent. "I don't see any facilities."

"If you need to take a piss, tell one of the guards," Lugo replied. "They will escort you to the latrines. That is all!" And on that last instruction, he strode out of the tent.

*Thank God.*

But with Lugo's words about ransoms echoing in her head, Adler's sense of vulnerability deepened and the reality of her situation began to sink in. Her position as a CIA operative on a Black Ops mission meant she couldn't rely on government support. Diplomatic relations between Venezuela and the United States had deteriorated badly after Chávez's stance as an OPEC price hawk raised the price of oil. But since Maduro came to power, there had been successful moves to re-establish ties between the two countries. Meaning the US would undoubtedly prioritise deniability over an exposed agent. It was a harsh reality to deal with, but even someone with her background could be abandoned in this volatile situation.

Her thoughts were broken as Kathleen's sobs grew louder. "I need my Brucey," she whimpered.

"Don't worry. You'll see him soon," Adler told her. "I know it."

"You think?"

"Yes. I promise." She hugged the older woman close, waiting until she'd calmed a little before shuffling around to face her. "Kathleen, do you remember who else was in your group?" she asked.

The older woman's brow furrowed as she tried to recall. "Two foreign boys. But one of them... they..." She screwed up her face as if the words were too horrible to say. Adler waited. "And an Englishman. He was real nice. It felt like he was looking out for us all. But now it's just me."

"I'm here, Kathleen." Adler's tone was resolute. "I'm going to get us out of here."

Kathleen stopped sobbing momentarily to stare at her. "How?"

Adler didn't have an answer to that question right now but she knew she had to find one. Lugo might have been a slimy creep, but she felt like she had a good read on the guy. His threats weren't empty, and the danger they were in was all too real. She had to stay alert and ready for any chance to turn the tables. The CIA may leave her high and dry, but if her identity was discovered they wouldn't even need to make that decision. If the rebels found out who she was – and, more importantly, who her father was – nothing and no one could save her.

## Chapter Thirteen

On the opposite side of the compound, Beckett and the remaining hostages were marched along under the watchful eyes of more armed guards. For the last minute or two, Beckett had been deliberately dragging his heels. It was a way of testing his boundaries but it also allowed him time to scope out the prison layout some more. There was plenty to look at, but his opportunities for action seemed limited. As he stopped to assess the closest of the two large concrete buildings that stood on either side of the prison, he felt the sharp dig of a rifle butt in the small of his back.

"Keep moving."

Beckett did as he was told and the guards herded them towards the nearest green canvas tent. Two more men with assault rifles stood guard out front. They looked to be about the same age as all the others on the base. Maybe even younger, Beckett thought as they got closer, clocking their bright eyes and patchy facial hair. Their escorts exchanged glances and nods with those outside the tent, who then stepped aside to allow the group inside.

Beckett entered the tent first, blinking into the gloom as the stuffy heat hit him in the face. There were two men already in the tent, seated together on a rickety old church pew. They looked up with wide, expectant eyes and one of them got to his feet as Beckett and the others were bustled inside. A quick assessment told him they were also hostages. Both men looked exhausted and scared, but that was where their similarities ended. The standing man was small and slim, with neatly parted mousey hair. Despite his dusty clothes, he maintained an air of composure and precision, albeit with a weariness in his eyes. In contrast, his cellmate had the look of a man who'd seen better days; his appearance rugged and unkempt, his dark, thinning hair stuck out at all angles, and the clothes he wore were loose-fitting and creased.

"You stay here for now," one of the guards said. "There is water in the corner. You can wash. Do not piss or shit here. We will walk you to the latrine if you need to go."

Beckett glanced at Bruce. The old man's lips were shuddering as if reciting a list – or a prayer, more likely – but no words could be heard.

"Keep it together," Beckett said, nudging into him. "We're going to be fine."

But as the guards backed off, Bruce broke away from the group and followed them to the exit. "I should be with my wife," he pleaded, grabbing the guard's sleeve. "Please. She needs me. She is not well."

The guard shrugged him off with a gruff sneer. Beckett was beside the older man in a second. "Come on, Bruce. This isn't helping." He held up his hand to the guards. "It's okay. He's okay."

He guided Bruce back over to the benches as the guards shuffled out.

"*Mutterfickers!*" Lange snarled once they were gone.

"I know," Beckett said. "But let's try to stay calm. It won't help anyone if we get worked up."

"Easy for you to say. They killed my friend," Lange spat.

Beckett was about to reply when the small, mousey-haired man stepped forward. "What happened? When was this?" He was English and sounded to have been well-educated.

Lange scowled at him. "Last night. We camped out after they took us hostage. He tried to escape. They shot him. Those bastards."

"Where did you come from?" the man asked.

"We were part of a tour group," Beckett cut in, sensing Lange was too upset to properly engage. "They ambushed us at a rest stop and killed our guide. We're just civilians. You?"

"My name is Andrew Price," the man replied. "I'm a foreign correspondent for the Daily Record in London. I was taken from my hotel room two days ago. I think they were worried I was writing some kind of exposé on their operations."

"I see. So you know about these people?"

Price sniffed and glanced at the other man. "That's right. The Colombian Liberation Party. Although at one time it was 'Army', not 'Party'. Now they purport to be a legitimate political organisation. But they can call themselves whatever they want, when they're kidnapping innocent people there's only one word for them in my book. Terrorists."

The other man got up from the bench. "Maybe so, but with General Murcia in charge, I have strong suspicions they could achieve their goals."

"Which are?" Beckett asked. "A coup d'etat?"

"I'd say so. I'm Edgar Castillo, by the way. I'm a cop from Guayana City."

"Why'd they take you?" Lange asked.

Castillo clicked his teeth. "I was stupid. I've been around a long time and I keep my ear to the ground. I know everything that's going on with the Colombians in my country. I thought I could sell this knowledge, make some money. I was meeting with an American journalist. But they found out, made me a rat. I thought after that they'd let me go free, but… here I am. Like I say, I was stupid."

"This journalist…?" Beckett said. "He's here too?"

"*She*," Castillo corrected. "Yeah, they took us both at the same time. I don't know where she is."

"She'll probably be held with Kathleen," Beckett said, turning to Bruce. "That means your wife won't be alone."

"It's not that." Bruce sighed heavily, slumping on the nearest bench. "Kathy was recently diagnosed with Alzheimer's. It's early days so she still remembers things. That makes it worse in a way; she knows she's ill. But she's getting more and more forgetful." He paused, his eyes moist. "We used our life savings for this trip, to see the world together before it's too late. I wanted to take plenty of photos so I can show her later… you know, when she might not remember."

The tent fell silent. Price looked down and shuffled his foot in the sand.

"We never took a lot of photos, not like the kids today," Bruce added. "We didn't have children, didn't go on many holidays. Always saving… but what for, eh?"

It was a heartbreaking story, but one that Beckett had already come to terms with after spending time with the Dixons. He'd been in two minds whether Kathleen's behaviour was due to a recent stroke or dementia. If it was

Alzheimer's, that was a real kicker. Such a diagnosis was devastating in any circumstance, but especially so in their current situation.

While Bruce and the others carried on talking, Beckett slipped away, his tactical mind already racing through possible scenarios as he examined his surroundings. The canvas walls of the tent were thick and reinforced, not the usual flimsy material of such structures. They were also triple-stitched to the heavy ground sheet, clearly designed to prevent any tampering or escape attempts. He ran his fingers along the fabric, searching for overlooked flaws or weaknesses, any small oversight in the construction that could be exploited, but he found none.

In the centre of their temporary prison cell were four wooden church pews and a bowing trestle table. He knelt and examined each item closely. There were no loose nails, no sharp edges – nothing that could be repurposed into a tool or a weapon. His attention shifted to the structure of the tent itself. The poles were solid and anchored firmly into place with rusty metal clasps. They ensured the tent's stability but offered no hope of using them for leverage or escape. Their captors had been thorough, leaving nothing to chance.

Castillo was speaking as Beckett returned to the group. "The leader – the acceptable face of the ELC – is a man called Jalen Murcia," he told them. "He calls himself a politician now, but he was once a nasty gun-running, drug-dealing piece of shit who was rumoured to have killed his entire crew when he suspected one of them turned snitch. He can wear a suit and a nice smile all he wants, but you ask me, he's still a street thug at heart, born from a world of sun and violence."

Beckett sat. *Born from a world of sun and violence.* He knew what that was like. Although, coming from England, maybe without the sun.

"And what's your story, friend?" Castillo asked, turning to Beckett.

He raised his head. "Nothing much to tell."

"Oh yeah? The strong silent type, huh?"

"My name's Michael Day. I was over here seeing the sights. Hoping to, at least."

"You're English," Price said. No flies on him. "Whereabouts are you from?"

"Cheltenham," Beckett responded. It wasn't a lie. But almost everything else he would subsequently tell them about his life would be.

As the minutes ticked by, the five strangers each told the group a little about themselves. Beckett was wary of getting involved, but he understood the human need for connection, especially in these circumstances. When it was his turn to speak, he told the same story he'd been telling for the last eighteen months – that he had been a financial advisor in London, but after his father died and left him a large inheritance, he'd decided to leave his job and travel the world while he was still relatively young. The story was well-rehearsed and plausible. Plus, after a career spent working in deep cover, inhabiting many different personas, lying was second nature to him.

By the time they'd finished it was dark outside. Beckett had hoped the cooler air might relax the group a little, but if anything they seemed more tense.

"We have to get out of here!" Lange hissed, his voice low and urgent. "There are five of us. We can do this. We have to!"

"I agree," Price said. "I know how these things can play out. These people are savages. Most of them are young kids, probably bored locals, excited to fight for a cause and have a bit of purpose in their lives for once. We only have to look at Afghanistan and 1930s Germany to know how that goes. No offence."

"None taken. You're right." The skin around Lange's eyes was tight with emotion. "They say not to worry, that they'll release us soon enough. I don't believe a word of it."

Beckett sat back as the others leaned in. Price had been quick to use the 'T' word, but the rebels' MO was likely to be kidnap for ransom as they'd stated, not a political statement. He also knew it could go either way regarding government involvement. Whilst he knew the old line that western governments don't negotiate with kidnappers wasn't entirely true, he doubted their release would be a top priority given the current global climate. But the longer they were held here, the more of a drain on resources they'd become, and the more chance someone would do something that got them all killed. Then there was his other problem. The last thing Beckett wanted was for MI6 or the CIA to know his whereabouts.

"Do you think we can overpower the men outside?" Price whispered, glancing at Beckett as he spoke. "There are only two of them. If we can grab their guns we have a chance."

Beckett remained still, having already contemplated and dismissed that idea. He'd had a good look at the guards earlier, and despite their youth, their vigilant posture and alert expressions told him they were more than ready to act at a moment's notice. Even if they did manage to overpower the two of them, then what? The walls were too high to scale and there were likely more armed guards patrolling the grounds.

"Come on!" Price snapped. "We can't just sit here and

rot. It's our duty to try to escape." He spoke eloquently but looked to Beckett like a man out of his depth. It was concerning.

"We need to keep calm," Beckett said. "All of us. Letting your emotions get the better of you, that's what will get you killed."

"I just want to go home," Bruce muttered.

"I understand. But we need to be patient." Beckett knew he was speaking to himself as much as the others.

Bruce nodded sadly. "I need to see Kathy."

"You'll see her soon," Beckett told him.

He glanced around the group: Castillo, the old cop who seemed to be holding up despite everything; Price, the arrogant journalist struggling to cope; Bruce, a man lost without his poor wife; and then Lange, still understandably angry at what had happened to his friend. They were different people from different walks of life, thrown together by fate in the direst of circumstances. But at this moment they were united by a common goal. Survival.

Beckett sat back. He just hoped they could hold it together long enough that an opportunity to escape would show itself. Because one thing was certain. Beckett could not stay here. He could not be turned over to his country.

## Chapter Fourteen

The first light of dawn brought little comfort to Beckett and his fellow captives as two new guards entered the tent and shook them awake. Beckett had slept surprisingly well despite the circumstances and the hard, unforgiving ground, but felt the stiffness in his muscles as he got to his feet. He glanced at the other men as they rubbed their faces and brushed themselves down. The morning air coming in through the open tent flaps did little to ease the dark mood hanging over the group.

The guards gestured for them to follow. They were led into the main space of the compound, and over to the shade of a large awning comprising another thick piece of military-grade canvas stretched over six posts. A trestle table stood on the dusty ground beneath the cover, surrounded by ten white plastic chairs speckled with mould and grime.

"What the fuck is going on?" Lange whispered, leaning into Beckett as the guards hustled them under the awning. "Are we having breakfast here – like we're in some shitty holiday camp?"

Beckett didn't reply. He was too busy taking in the prison, more visible now in the bright sunshine. The high walls of the compound stood impenetrable on all sides, a physical and psychological barrier to any thoughts of escape. Beckett assessed them all the same, searching the perimeter for weak points or lapses in security. Over on the far side of the prison, in the area that once would have been the exercise yard, he noticed Scar and one of the other young men who had brought them here, running laps barefoot on the rough terrain. They looked worn out, their faces grim with fatigue as if they had been running up and down since daybreak. Another armed guard watched on, perhaps instructed to impose punishment if the runners slowed their pace. The constant running was possibly a form of castigation, Beckett surmised. He'd seen Peroza's expression when he'd learnt there were originally five in their party. But if so, the men had got off lightly, which maybe hinted at a certain level of leniency in the camp.

*Or maybe not.*

As Beckett scoped out the setup inside the prison walls, he noticed a wooden structure over in one corner. It was hard to make out from this angle but it looked like an old sawhorse stood on its side, and there was no question that the man strapped to it was dead. His neck had been broken, his head hanging loosely to one side. Beckett narrowed his eyes at the grisly scene. It was the young man who'd shot Martin.

*What was that about leniency?*
*Definitely not.*

"You see that shit?" Castillo said, standing beside him; he clicked his teeth. "Maybe I was wrong about this. These rebels are bad news, man. We're fucked."

"No. We're not," Beckett told him. "And keep your

voice down. We don't need people getting more upset than they already are."

Castillo snickered bitterly. "You seem very confident that everything is going to work out okay for us. You know something that I don't?"

Beckett rolled his shoulders back. He didn't know anything. Only that it never helped to wallow. He turned away from Castillo to see two guards approaching from the main building carrying a tray of food. Behind them, another armed guard was escorting two women out of one of the tents.

"Kathy!" Bruce cried, holding his arms out as his wife got closer. "How are you, my sweetheart?"

"Oh Bruce. It was awful. I hardly slept." She went to him and they hugged, Bruce screwing his eyes up tight and burying his face in his wife's neck.

"Don't worry, I've got you."

It was a moment of humanity, quickly brought to an end as an armed guard positioned himself at one end of the covered seating area. His rifle was aimed down, but his stance indicated he was ready to act at a moment's notice. Beckett observed this briefly before his attention shifted to the second woman, likely the American journalist Castillo had mentioned. She was medium height with an athletic build, and he might have thought her attractive if he was thinking that way, but now definitely wasn't the time.

The guards set the food trays on the table, revealing a selection of fruit – oranges, apples, berries, guavas – along with a pile of thick cornbread and a large bowl of stewed black beans. It smelled good and everyone ate greedily, having not had any food since yesterday lunchtime.

Beckett grabbed himself a piece of cornbread and chewed it as he manoeuvred over to where the American journalist was standing. Her long strawberry-blonde hair was tied back in a ponytail and she looked remarkably fresh-faced considering what they'd all gone through. She saw him approaching and turned, regarding him with bright blue eyes.

"You're the Englishman, right?" she said.

"Word travels fast in these places. And you're the journalist. Sorry, I don't know your name."

"Julia Gray. I'd say it's nice to meet you, but under these conditions…"

"Yes. I get it. I'm Michael, by the way, or Mike. Either is good."

She managed a strained smile as she looked up at him. "Kathleen said you've been looking out for everyone."

"I do what I can."

"What are you, military?"

"No," Beckett answered without hesitation. "But my father was. I work in an office. Or I used to. I've been travelling for the last year. I was here visiting Angel Falls when they captured us."

She frowned. "Travelling? What is it, a delayed gap year?"

"Something like that."

"Well, Kathleen speaks very highly of you. It sounds as if you did a good job keeping everyone calm."

"It's the best way to be in situations like this. Composed, you have more chance of noticing things that might be useful and adapting to the fast-changing circumstances."

Her frown deepened. "You sure you're not military?"

"No. Are you?"

She smiled. "I'm a journalist. With The New York Times."

"That's right." He didn't like the way she was scrutinising him, as if she knew there was more to his story. He told her it was good to meet her and returned to the table to pick at what was left of the food.

Price sidled up to him and lowered his voice. "I don't trust that one," he said, looking away but jerking his head towards Gray.

Beckett glanced over then averted his eyes immediately. She was still looking at him. "Why do you say that?"

"She said she works for the New York Times, but I mentioned an acquaintance of mine, Robert Marple, and she said she nods to him in the corridor. Present tense. As if it still went on. But the thing is, Marple retired eighteen months ago. He lives in Florida now. She didn't mention that. She didn't know."

Beckett met Price's wide-eyed gaze. "Are you sure you're not reading too much into it? When did she say these things?"

"In the back of the truck, when we were being transported here."

"Right. And you were thinking clearly at the time?"

"No, but… I think it's odd. There's something not right about her."

Beckett didn't respond further. He was feeling uneasy about his countryman's paranoia; the man was too worked up about a lot of things. He finished his cornbread and grabbed an apple off the tray, crunching it as he went back to observing his surroundings. In the distance he heard the same clinking noise he'd heard yesterday, but what it was still eluded him.

His attention drifted to the secluded hut on the far side of the compound, away from the tents and the other buildings. It was the size of a large garage, made of wood with a piece of thick, fraying velvet covering the entrance. Last night he'd thought it could be a prayer room but now he wondered if it was used by the rebels as a space for solitary confinement. His curiosity piqued, he sidled over to the young man watching them, holding eye contact and raising his hands as he approached.

"Can I ask you a question?"

The man glared at him, a flicker of panic and confusion on his face. "What?"

Beckett pointed over to the hut. "What do you keep in there?"

The man shuddered as he looked over at the ramshackle wooden building. When he looked back at Beckett his expression was serious, almost fearful. "You don't want to know," he said. "Believe me."

But Beckett did want to know. He was about to enquire further when the obnoxious buzz of an air horn reverberated around the prison grounds. The young man stood to attention as three men emerged from the nearest building and made their way over.

Beckett rejoined the group, and Price shuffled over to him. "Hold onto your hat," he whispered. "These are the leaders. Now we'll find out what's really going on here."

## Chapter Fifteen

The captives huddled together under the large awning as the men approached. Beckett's eyes were on Peroza, the man who had tried screwing a magnum into his forehead the day before. The lieutenant and his companions halted a few metres from the captives, and it was Peroza himself who stepped forward to address them.

"You are now prisoners of the Ejército Liberación de Colombia," he announced, his voice echoing across the open space. "We are the liberators of the Colombian people, operating here in Venezuela to fund our revolution and free our country from the leftist devils. We are a legitimate group. We are strong. We are many."

"What are you going to do with us?" Price asked, his voice wavering.

Peroza glared at him, clearly annoyed at the interruption. "You will not be harmed as long as you do as we say."

The captives exchanged anxious murmurs but Beckett remained silent; he was observing the man over Peroza's shoulder. He hadn't been present the previous night and

## A World of Sun and Violence

Beckett noted the way he was standing and listening as Peroza spoke. He seemed to be overseeing the proceedings, his demeanour slightly awkward, as if he was not all that comfortable with Peroza's bluster. He was the true leader here, Beckett thought. Possibly even this General Murcia guy Castillo had mentioned.

What was it the old cop had said – the 'acceptable face' of the rebellion?

Beckett knew from experience how that usually went. These despotic politicians acted just acceptable enough to the world's media, to the public at large, while continuing to be torturous and brutal behind closed doors.

Peroza continued, his gaze sweeping across the captives. "We will soon demand ransoms," he declared. "If your governments refuse to negotiate, we'll turn to your families. If they can't pay up… well, you need to hope someone will."

"I think I have insurance to cover it," Price interjected. "Or at least my employer has. When can I contact them? How long will we be here?"

Peroza's expression hardened. "Each of you will undergo a vetting process. We need to know who you are, where you are from, what you do… then we will decide our next move."

His words triggered another flurry of anxious questions from the prisoners. Who would go first? What did they want to know about them? Would who they were influence how long they'd be held captive?

Beckett remained composed, processing every detail of the announcement, weighing it against what he already knew to be true. Years of experience had honed his skills in patience, observation, and situational analysis. He studied Peroza's mannerisms, the other man's subdued presence, the evident power dynamics at play – it was all information.

The mention of a vetting process confirmed to Beckett they were a valuable commodity to these people. While this might have offered some solace to the others, for Beckett it wasn't so simple. This meant their fate was dependent on diplomatic and financial negotiations, and decisions made far from the compound's walls by those engaged in unwinnable wars who were gripped in the throes of a crippling economic crisis. It was hardly an ideal scenario.

"Deputy Lugo here will start processing you right away." Peroza rested his hand on the third man's shoulder. "Answer his questions truthfully and with detail. We will know if you are lying, and it will not go well for you if you do. Do you all understand?"

A ripple of stoic agreement rippled around the group.

The man called Lugo stepped forward, his chest puffed out. He had the sort of face Beckett wanted to punch and not stop until the smug grin had been wiped off it, especially as his gaze lingered on Gray. "Don't worry," he said, with a lascivious grin. "I shall be gentle with you. As long as you cooperate, all will be well."

Beckett watched as Peroza turned to the mystery man, but couldn't hear their hushed conversation. The relationship between the two men could be crucial: Peroza, with his bravado and apparent authority; and the mystery man, who was more reserved but potentially a more powerful figure.

"You and you," Lugo said, pointing at Beckett and Gray. "Come with me. The rest of you – sit tight, relax. Someone will come for you soon."

Beckett glanced at Gray. "Aren't we the lucky ones?"

"Let's get this over with," she replied.

Lugo led them alongside the main building where two

box tents had been set up. Beckett was directed into one, while Lugo marched Gray over to the second one. But of course he did. Beckett had noticed the way he'd been looking at her. He caught her eye as she was led away but she didn't seem fazed.

The tent's roof cover was high enough that Beckett didn't have to hunker down when he stepped inside. A young man wearing a military cap and a sneer was sitting at a table, facing the entrance. In front of him was a clipboard and a pad of yellow paper. "Sit down," he said, pointing his shiny silver pen towards the plastic chair opposite him.

Beckett did as he was instructed. The tent was cramped and stifling, the oppressive heat accentuated by a musty odour that clung to the canvas walls. The distant buzz of chatter and occasional shouts filtered in from outside.

The man across the table didn't introduce himself; he didn't even look up from his notes as he began to read. His questions were routine, as Beckett had expected: full name, age, occupation, employer, country of birth, any medical issues. He answered them all under the guise of Michael Day, thirty-seven, former financial advisor, now nomadic backpacker.

"Backpacker?" the man repeated. "What is this?"

"I'm travelling the world," Beckett replied. "I have no job, no family, no one waiting back home for me. I'm essentially a nobody." The statement was far from subtle, but he needed these people to see him as insignificant. "The other hostages here are more important than me. Send them home first."

It was clear to Beckett these interviews were a type of triage, aimed at determining which hostages had the easiest access to ransom funds, either through insurance, employees or rich family members. For now, Beckett wasn't even considering potential government intervention.

Most likely the rebels would stagger the release of the hostages, holding back for maximum financial gain, playing a game of chicken with their lives. But that meant at some stage the rebels might need to do something to move the process along, and the longer Beckett was here the more his safety hung in the balance. Still, he'd rather chance his arm with a bunch of rowdy rebels than be handed over to the likes of Xander Templeton. Beckett suspected the CIA's London-based section chief was still furious after what had happened last year. Men like him held a grudge for a long time and would relish the chance to capture the former SIS agent John Beckett.

And then what? A lifetime spent in a dark room at an undisclosed location in the middle of the Atlantic? No, thank you. Here in the Venezuelan jungle, at least he had a chance to escape.

Beckett leaned back, observing the man scribbling down his responses. "What about you?" he asked him. "How long have you been committed to this cause?"

The man's expression dropped. "I am the one asking the questions."

"But you must feel strongly about what you're doing to justify kidnapping innocent people and holding them hostage," Beckett continued, speaking Spanish now, aiming for connection. "Is this what you signed up for?"

"That's enough for now," the man said, turning the clipboard over.

Beckett nodded. This guy was no revolutionary. Maybe there were some hidden away, but the majority of the soldiers he'd encountered seemed more like hired guns, and predominantly young men as Price had mentioned. Price had viewed this as a bad thing, but to Beckett it was a sliver of light in the darkness. Because mercenaries could be turned; inexperienced teenagers could be defeated.

The man called out in Spanish. "We are done!"

A moment later, Beckett sensed movement behind him and a rush of fresh air entered the tent. He gave his interviewer a nod of thanks before a hand grabbed his bicep and hauled him to his feet. "Come," the armed guard said, leading him out of the tent.

As the man escorted him back to the shaded seating area, Beckett heard more clearly the sound of clinking metal echoing in the distance. He still couldn't shake the feeling that it sounded familiar. Like a dockyard perhaps. Yet they were nowhere near water.

As he rejoined the main group, Julia Gray was returning from her interrogation also. "Did that creep give you any trouble?" he asked, as she grabbed a bottle of water off the table.

"Nothing I can't handle." She twisted off the bottle cap. "How did yours go?"

Beckett shrugged. "I answered everything honestly. I don't think I'll be sent home first. I'm no big draw to anyone."

Gray didn't respond. They settled down in the plastic chairs as the group made small talk, trying desperately to act normal and upbeat, whilst the rest of the interviews took place. Price and Castillo were next, followed by the Dixons and finally Lange. After the vetting process concluded and Lange was back with the group, Peroza appeared once more, this time flanked by two armed guards.

"For your comfort and wellbeing, you will be housed together from now on," he told them, eliciting gasps of relief from Kathleen and Bruce. "If you need to use the latrines, tell one of the guards. If you are sick, tell one of the guards. Other than that, you will stay quiet and cause us no trouble. If you do this, you will be returned home in due course. But believe me when I say that anyone trying to escape, or anyone who disrupts our operations in any way will face severe consequences. My soldiers will be patrolling the grounds at all times and they are instructed to shoot on sight." He turned to his men. "Take them away."

"Do you think we'll be home soon?" Kathleen asked, as the group was led across the prison grounds to the nearest of the two holding tents.

"I wouldn't bet on it," Lange grumbled under his breath. "We can't trust these people. Remember that."

Beckett was about to say something, but his attention was diverted by a young soldier carrying a tray containing two whole roast chickens to the mysterious hut on the outskirts of the compound.

"What the hell is in there?" he muttered to himself, slowing to watch.

"I've been wondering the same thing," Gray added. "They all seem terrified by it."

As they watched, the soldier placed the tray of food outside the entrance to the hut before hurrying away. A moment later a monstrous hand reached out from the shadowy interior. The thick fingers were bent and gnarly, and on the back of the hand and forearm were what looked like lumps of gristle and bone stretched at the skin. The sheer size was alarming enough, far larger than any human hand Beckett had ever seen.

"Who the hell is that?" Price asked, spinning around to address the nearest guard.

The young guard screwed up his face. "He belongs to Lieutenant Peroza. But... he... is bad."

"They say he is not human," another guard added, his tone a mixture of fascination and fear. "He cannot feel pain, or be killed."

"Oh, come off it," Price scoffed, though his pale face and wide eyes told another story. "That's not true."

The young guards exchanged worried glances.

"Some people call him El Demonio Roto, the broken demon," the first man said. "But us Venezuelans have another name for him."

"Oh? And what's that?" Price asked.

The soldier swallowed hard, his eyes darting nervously to the hut. "The Canaima," he whispered. "The Spirit of Death."

## Chapter Sixteen

The man called Bracho sat huddled alone in the back corner of his private hut, his eyes wide with delight at the sight of the two chickens on the tray in front of him. The chef had sprinkled them with that powder he liked that made his tongue tingle and they smelled good.

Bracho loved chicken. Along with steak and hamburgers, eating a roast chicken was one of the few things that made him truly happy. Although, he liked most of the food he was given here. Except for eggs, which was strange, because someone told him they came from chickens and were a sort of baby chicken. Yet they made sick come out of his stomach, and whilst he was numb to that experience, he hated the smell.

These chickens were big and juicy and hot from the oven. He grabbed the first one, the large bird tiny in his huge hands, and began tearing into it with a childlike enthusiasm. The act of ripping apart the carcass, feeling the bones crack and give way, was usually deeply satisfying to him. But sometimes, like today, the act of breaking the chicken bones, a task so easy and natural to him, made him reflect on his own body.

He glanced down at his arms and legs, his gaze travelling over his rugged, uneven torso. His body was thick with muscle and little body fat, and in some areas, splintered, unset bones protruded beneath his skin. Across his arms, chest and back, his skin was mottled with cigarette burns and bulbous purple scars.

Some people called him Chico Dragón – *dragon-boy* – but he thought that was silly, as he'd seen dragons on the television Victor had provided and he looked nothing like one. Most of the people, like Victor, called him Bracho, which was a part of his real name, but when he was fighting in the big events Victor took him to, he was known as El Demonio Roto.

From somewhere in the recess of his memory he remembered his first name was Hussam. That was what the nuns had called him at the orphanage where he spent his early years. It was at the orphanage where he had first learnt the harsh lessons of life. He still remembered the beatings and the bullying. The nuns had reacted first with shock, then with a mixture of concern and fear. But no one really knew how to help him; the other kids in the orphanage called him names like 'freak' and 'devil child', and the more he hurt others and injured himself, the less the nuns could cope. When he was twelve years old, he was cast out onto the mean streets of Caracas.

Homeless and without the intelligence or knowledge to properly care for himself, he'd endured countless injuries, breaking bones in fights or in accidents. It was while he was living on the streets, drunk on wine, that he got knocked down by a trolley bus that had subsequently crushed his right hand. He'd walked around for months with shattered bones but no one took him to a doctor, no one seemed to care enough to intervene. The bones, left untreated, healed badly, further deforming his already imposing figure. Now, a bony spike jutted from his neck, making it difficult to sleep in some positions, and his hand had healed into a mangled, club-like appendage. In the ruthless world of underground fight clubs, his deformed, callused body and ability to keep fighting despite severe injuries had made him a legend. Each protruding bone, each callus, told a story of survival, of vicious fights fought and won. Yet despite his formidable appearance, there was a simplicity to Bracho, a childlike innocence that had never been allowed to mature.

Surviving on the streets had been a brutal rite of passage. But at fifteen, his size and apparent insensitivity to pain caught the attention of a man named Diaz, who recognised his potential and set him up as a fighter in the many illegal clubs around the city. It wasn't long before Bracho gained notoriety on the fight circuit, even at his young age. Diaz was pleased with him but treated him badly. He'd promised him good food, money, his own house, but nothing ever came his way. Bracho often saw Diaz drinking and laughing with other men, but whenever he tried to join in he was sent away. Other fighters told him he should get rid of Diaz, that he was being exploited by him, but Bracho didn't understand what they meant.

But then Victor found him. Victor Peroza, the man who brought him to this compound and made him into the prize fighter he was today. To Bracho, Victor was more than just a boss; he was the closest thing to family he'd ever known. Victor was nice to him, he gave him food, and let him watch television. In return, Bracho fought in Victor's name and followed his commands without question.

Now, as he stuffed pieces of chicken into his mouth with

his good hand, he was happy with his life. Living here, having his meals brought to him, being able to watch television whenever he wanted, it was the best he'd ever had it. He still remembered what life had been like before Victor found him.

Finishing off the second chicken, he let out a large belch, snickering to himself at the noise and enjoying the regurgitated taste of his meal.

"Good... chicken."

A while later the guard returned to collect the empty plates, giving Bracho a wide berth as he always did despite him attempting a smile. Bracho knew everyone in the compound was scared of him, but he didn't mind; he was used to being feared, used to being alone. To the world he was a monster, a freak of nature, but under Victor's watch he felt more human than he'd ever done. Victor was a nice man. He'd die for Victor, and he'd kill for him, too.

He had done. Many times.

## Chapter Seventeen

The stifling late afternoon heat made the air inside the tent almost unbearable. Adler sat alone, her back against the canvas wall, observing the dynamics in the room in quiet reflection. Since being brought here a few hours earlier, the group had splintered off into smaller clusters. Coping levels were low and weariness levels high.

Across the room the Dixons were huddled together on one of the old church pews. They were speaking too softly for her to hear the content of their conversation, but she could tell from their mannerisms – the way Bruce was gently stroking his wife's hand – that they were desperately trying to reassure one other. It was understandable. She hoped to God one of them was rich and significant, or they had links to someone who was; that way they might stand a chance of being ransomed off sooner rather than later, but she doubted that was the case. It wasn't fair. They shouldn't be here. This wasn't their fight.

Near to the Dixons, on a separate pew, Lange and Price were speaking in similar hushed tones, but rather than comforting each other they seemed to be plotting, their voices low and intense. Castillo, who she hadn't spoken to much since they'd arrived at the prison, was sitting alone. As was the Englishman, Day.

She turned her attention his way, moving only her eyes lest he catch her looking. Despite his rugged and weathered appearance, his eyes were sharp and intelligent – they seemed to be always watching, always alert.

She considered approaching him, but was distracted as Price gasped loudly before being shushed by Lange. Trained in real-time observation and analysis, Adler sensed the rising tension. She rose and made like she was stretching her legs, casually sauntering over to sit on the end of the bench, hoping to catch a snippet of their conversation.

"We can't just sit here and do nothing," Lange was saying, his deep voice tinged with desperation. "We have to make a move, find a way out."

Price seemed less convinced. "But it's too dangerous," he hissed. "You heard what Peroza said. There are guards on patrol."

"I won't let what happened to my friend happen to me," Lange replied. "These others are stupid if they trust these bastards and think their governments are going to pay the ransom money. It doesn't happen! So what then? They kill us. I'm not sitting on my ass waiting for that to happen. We need to take action."

Adler chewed on her lip as she listened. Lange was emotional, not thinking straight. A hasty escape plan, driven by panic, could endanger everyone. She glanced at Day, noticing he too was listening. He caught Adler's eye and walked over to stand behind Price.

"You need to stop this kind of talk," he said, his voice calm but firm. "Lange, I know you're upset about Martin, but if you try anything rash you could get yourself killed. As well as other people."

Adler sat back. Day had pretty much voiced what she was thinking.

"We can't just wait around for them to decide our fate!" Price scoffed, in that haughty way of his that was starting to grate on her.

"I'm not suggesting we passively await their decision," Day replied. "But we need more information before we act, a better understanding of the compound, of their routines and their procedures. Now is not the time."

Price and Lange exchanged glances. "What the fuck do you know?" Lange muttered.

"I know enough. Please, for everyone's sake, cool it. We've been here less than twenty-four hours. Let's see what happens over the next day or so, then we'll talk again."

"Whatever."

Day puffed out his cheeks. Leaving it there, he wandered back to where he'd been standing previously. He raised his eyebrows in solidarity with Adler as she approached and did the same.

"We've got some hot-headed folks here," she said. "Those two are winding each other up, but it was good what you said to them."

"Do you think it made a difference?"

She watched Lange. "I'm not sure. He's angry as hell and not thinking straight."

"Exactly. In the worst possible state of mind to make any decisions. We need to keep an eye on him."

Adler stepped back to take in the Englishman. He was tall with a muscular frame, his physique suggesting a life of strength and resilience rather than protein shakes and gym sessions. It certainly wasn't the body of a financial advisor who'd worked in an office for almost two decades. His posture was relaxed yet alert, his movements measured and purposeful. But it was his demeanour that was particularly telling; he had the watchful, calculating look of someone used to assessing situations, constantly on guard. She couldn't shake the feeling that there was more to Day than he was letting on.

"How are you holding up?" she asked him.

"Ah, you know,' he replied. "As well as can be expected under the circumstances. What about you?"

"Yeah. Same. I just hope these people are true to their word." She paused, shifting her tone to one more casual. "This must be quite a departure from your usual travels."

Day remained non-committal. "You could say that. Not the kind of adventure I was looking for."

"I get it. I once found myself in a bit of a sticky situation in Russia of all places. I lost my bag containing my passport and all my money… It was quite the ordeal."

Day raised an eyebrow. "Sounds rough. How do you get out of that one?"

"A bit of luck and a lot of negotiation – with the police, border control, my embassy. I've always been good at talking my way out of problems."

It was a classic technique to gain information from someone – sharing a piece of her past in the hopes of coaxing out a similar revelation. But Day wasn't playing ball. He just smiled.

She sighed. "Damn. What a life, huh? I thought last year was tough. You see, I was supposed to be married by now." She held her hand up to show there was no ring and shrugged. There was also no fiancé in reality, but he didn't need to know that. She continued her story. "He was a journalist too. For a rival newspaper. We were set to leave on a month-long trip to Asia, but then I discovered he was using my sources to get information for his own stories. The relationship didn't last long after that."

Day's expression softened. "That's rough. Betrayal like that can affect a person for a long time."

"I know, right? I guess it's why I tend to keep people at arm's length."

"Oh, I understand that all too well."

He was still holding back but it was a start. Adler leaned closer, smiling up at him. "It's tricky. Especially in situations like these. You never know who you can really trust."

Day nodded, his gaze lingering on her for a moment as if trying to get a read on her. "Well, you can trust me," he said.

"You sure you aren't military?" she asked, dispensing with subtleties and observing him as she asked, searching for any micro expressions that might tell her more than words ever could. "It's just… you've got a way about you that suggests you're… well, more than just an office worker or backpacker."

Day's response was a casual shrug, his face giving nothing away. Adler, however, was not easily swayed. His guarded nature, the way he avoided direct answers, it only fuelled her suspicions. In her line of work, instincts were often as important as facts, and her instincts told her Michael Day was not who he said he was

She was considering delving further when a heated exchange between Lange and Price drew her attention. Looking over, she saw they were now sitting on either side of the Dixons, no doubt scaring the poor older couple half to death with their ideas. Even the lethargic, self-serving Castillo had wandered over to listen. Adler didn't like this one bit. The notion of escape, risky as it was, appeared to be gaining momentum.

Without a word said, she and Day approached the group. "You need to stop this," Day said, pointing a finger at Lange. "I mean it. These people will be sent home soon enough. They don't need you dragging them into a suicide mission."

Kathleen and Bruce, visibly shaken by Day's mention of a 'suicide mission', looked up at him with wide, fearful eyes. Adler stood her ground beside him, her arms crossed as she observed the individuals in front of her. They were all terrified, just dealing with it in very different ways.

"Mike?" Bruce's voice quivered as he addressed him. "What do we do? We're scared as hell and we don't know what to think." He lowered his voice as if trying to protect his wife from what he was about to say. "We've all seen the news... We know what sometimes happens to hostages..." He didn't do the clichéd gesture, the finger slicing across the neck, but the way he clicked his mouth as he jerked his head back suggested the same thing

"Exactly," Lange hissed. "They've already killed the guide and my best friend. You want me to believe they'll just send us home with no bother. You are deluded."

"He's right. We can't just hang around waiting to die," Price spat, his words stirring up fearful mutterings within the group. "We have to do... something."

Adler and Day exchanged a look, both understanding the precariousness of the situation.

"So what are you going to do?" she asked Price, looking him up and down. "You fancy yourself as an action man? Are you going to overthrow the guards and shoot your way out of here?"

Price raised his head. "There are other ways. We might be able to negotiate our way to safety."

"How?"

"I don't know! But every second that ticks by I'm growing more and more terrified. I can't just sit here. I need to do something!"

Adler pulled in a long breath, working on calming her system. Suddenly the tent flap opened and two guards entered carrying assault rifles. Kathleen let out a small yelp as all eyes turned to the newcomers.

"You!" one of them barked, pointing to Price. Then his finger shifted to Adler. "You too. Come with us!"

*Shit!*

Adler locked eyes with Day, who gave her a brief reassuring nod. She tried to return it but she couldn't move. Her head was spinning with troubling thoughts and ominous possibilities. As the guard grabbed her arm and led her away, she glanced back at the group.

"Stay calm," Day called after her. "It'll be okay."

This time Adler nodded. She even forced a smile. But it was for herself as much as him. She wished she shared his optimism. To her this looked bad.

This looked very bad indeed.

## Chapter Eighteen

Adler remained quiet, trying to organise her thoughts as she and Price were marched across the prison grounds by the two guards. In contrast, Price's previous state of anxious indignation had now morphed into blind panic. It was all Adler could do not to reach over and shake him as he babbled to their captors in a desperate attempt to negotiate his way out of danger. It was as if all reason and logic had dropped away in favour of anger, bargaining and denial – all the stages of grief coming out at once. Except for acceptance. That would come later perhaps.

Or perhaps not.

"Look, I can pay you," Price stammered. "I'm well off, and I have wealthy connections. We don't need to wait for an insurance company or my government to pull their fingers out, I'll pay the ransom myself. Whatever it is. I can transfer the money today. Please, just let me go."

Adler looked away; she couldn't bear to listen to the man. And it did no good anyway, his words were met with cold indifference from the two guards. Either they didn't understand him or they didn't care.

"Let me help you," Price continued. "You don't need to do this. I am a journalist. Think about it. I can be a worthy ally. I'll write sympathetically about your cause."

*Jesus.*

The poor bastard was crying now, but his desperate pleas had no effect whatsoever. All that pathetic whining and treacherous promises for nothing.

They arrived at an area behind the nearest of the main buildings, which contained a low, single-storey structure Adler hadn't noticed previously. Unlike the rest of the prison, it looked to have been built recently, the raw breezeblocks and uneven mortar seemingly the result of a rushed, amateur build. One half of the building was split into two units with solid doors but no windows, perhaps used as offices; whilst the front of the other half comprised a large roll-up blind, similar to those found on commercial garages. The blind was currently hoisted open, but from their angle of approach Adler couldn't see inside. This secluded space, nestled behind the main building and enclosed by the high walls, felt distinctly isolated from the rest of the compound.

*But was that the point?*

Trying to ignore the bristle of nervous energy running down her spine, Adler stood her ground as one of the guards grabbed her arm and bustled her towards the second unit.

"Hey, watch what you're doing," she snapped. "I can walk there on my own."

To her right, Price was pleading with the other guard as he was led to the first door. "Please, I don't want to die. I can be useful to you. There are other people here who…

who can…" He cast a frightened glance at Adler. "Help me. I don't want to die!"

Well, that made two of them, but Adler endeavoured to maintain a sense of rationality as the guard opened the door and pushed her into the room beyond. Following her in, the guard slammed the door shut and flicked a light switch. The room was a sparse ten-by-ten-foot square, with no windows, and furnished only with a small table and single chair in the centre of the room. Facing the chair was a digital video camera on top of a metal tripod.

For a moment Adler thought she was going to throw up. Her mind raced with the possibilities of what this setup could mean. She had seen too much footage filmed in rooms similar to this one and they never ended well for the person facing the camera. Yet, she reminded herself, these people weren't ISIS. Their motives were financial, first and foremost. Nobody was going to die. Not today at least. But the uncertainty of what was to come was still unsettling.

"Sit," the guard barked, shoving her towards the chair.

"All right! I'm perfectly capable of walking!" she snapped back.

She was losing her cool. She had to keep it together. Pulling in deep breaths, she moved around the table and sat on the chair, casting her gaze around the room to try to focus her attention. A crumpled banner lay in one corner, the initials 'ELC' visible among its folds, along with a motto she couldn't make out. Turning, she noticed two nails in the wall behind her with remnants of the same material as the banner hanging from them. She turned back.

*Why remove their insignia?*

*And why leave the banner screwed up in the corner of the room?*

It didn't make any sense. But it also didn't make her feel any better about the situation.

Sitting alone, facing the camera's unblinking eye, she felt more vulnerable than she had in a long time. The guard was standing in front of the door, holding his rifle at waist height, not aimed at her. If she jumped up and flipped the table she could grab his weapon in the confusion. She paused. She was confident she could pull it off, but what then? Any noise and the guard next door would hear, maybe others...

*No.*

For now it was too risky. But if it came to do or die, there was still a chance. She found some solace in that.

Remaining focused on the camera, she mentally prepared herself for whatever was to come. She knew the importance of staying calm, of not showing fear.

The door opened and Lugo walked in carrying a cardboard folder. He was the last person she wanted to see. He closed the door and grinned at her with all the flare of a cheesy game show host.

"Ms Julia Gray. Our journalist from the USA. How are you today?"

"Oh, I'm doing great," she replied. "Can't you tell from my cheery manner?"

Lugo laughed. "You're funny. I like this." Adler looked away and sighed, unable to contain her distaste as he leaned over the table, close enough she could smell his foul breath. "You are also a very pretty woman, like a homecoming queen, yes? Did you go to prom?"

"I was busy that night."

"Oh no. What a shame. Maybe you and I can have our own prom here."

"I'll pass." She met and held his gaze. "Why am I here, Lugo? What are you going to do?"

His grin didn't falter. "I'm not going to do anything. You're going to do all the work, Ms Gray."

Out of sight from the two men, Adler grabbed the table legs. Was this it? Did she go down fighting? But then Lugo stepped back and opened the cardboard file under his arm. He took out a piece of paper and slid it across the table in front of her.

"I need you to read this," he said. "Nice and loud. Straight down the camera."

## Chapter Nineteen

Adler sat rigid in the chair as Lugo stabbed his stubby finger at the paper in front of her. "Read! Word for word."

She scanned the page. It was a script, freshly typed on a piece of white paper. She read the first few lines.

*My name is [insert name here]*
*I am X years old.*
*I am a citizen of [insert name of country]*

As Lugo dealt with the camera settings, Adler closed her eyes, focusing on maintaining her composure despite her mind racing with the implications of recording this video.

The script was straightforward enough – a scripted plea to those back home – but Adler knew any video message showing her face was potentially a double-edged sword for her. On the one hand, her people would know she'd been captured and could arrange an extraction mission for her and the other hostages. Yet, she was here on a deep-cover mission that would have to be denied by all parties if it came to light. Her journalist cover was solid enough to dupe her captors; but when her ransom video reached the media, they'd know she wasn't a journalist and questions would be asked regarding her identity, complicating matters for her and her superiors. And if the rebels got wind of the situation, it would spell real trouble.

Real trouble, as in they'd likely execute her.

Even if the rebels didn't find out, it still put the CIA in a tricky position. If they were found to be operating in Venezuela, diplomatic relations would turn sour and no one wanted that. Least of all the US government.

If she were anyone else, she imagined it would be an even decision for the agency between an extraction mission and a media blackout whilst they washed their hands of her. But she wasn't anyone else. She was Vanessa Adler.

Another double-edged sword for her to carry.

"Okay, we're ready. When I say go – you start reading." She opened her eyes to see Lugo standing next to the tripod, his finger poised on the control panel on top of the camera. "Stick to the script. Nothing clever, no coded messages. Just read."

Adler nodded, her eyes fixed on the camera. "Understood."

"Good. Now... action!" He pressed the button and pointed his finger at her as the camera light blinked red, indicating she should begin.

Adler took a deep breath. "My name is Julia Gray. I am thirty-one years old. I am a citizen of the United States of America..." She sat straight-backed in the chair, keeping her expression cold and neutral. Her voice was clipped and devoid of emotion, an ironic contrast to the turmoil brewing inside her. She told whoever would be watching that she was a journalist for the New York Times, that she had been kidnapped from Guayana City two days previously, and that she was being treated well but hoped her government would act quickly to ensure her release. It was a good performance, one with high stakes. But as she spoke, something was bugging her and she couldn't quite put her finger on what it was.

As the recording concluded, Lugo flicked off the camera. "All done now," he said, walking over and taking her by the wrist. His grip was clammy as he pulled her to her feet and she could feel his eyes lingering on her body. For a fleeting moment she imagined grabbing his hand and twisting it violently, using the momentum to throw him to the ground. It would be a swift, brutal takedown, then a satisfying crack as her knee connected with his jaw. But she restrained herself, aware that any physical altercation would only worsen their situation.

"You did well," he said, leading her to the door. "You should be an actress, huh?"

She didn't reply. Because she'd just realised what had been bugging her. She'd been concentrating so much on reading off the script it hadn't hit her initially, but there had been no mention of any organisation in the message she'd made. Not the ELN, not the ELC. No one. In the part where she spoke of where she was and who had taken her, it was almost deliberately ambiguous.

*I am being held hostage by a group of rebel guerrillas situated deep in the Venezuelan jungle. They are treating me well. They have not harmed me. They will not harm me as long as you comply with their demands promptly and in detail.*

No mention of who the rebels were, or even what they stood for. Even when kidnappers' primary focus was financial gain, they often used these videos to justify their actions or to project their message to a wider audience. But not here. It seemed odd, and Adler imagined it would complicate matters even more at the agency.

## A World of Sun and Violence

The armed guard opened the door and the three of them left the unit. "Wait here for the others," Lugo told the guard, before turning his attention to Adler with another slimy grin. "Thank you for your cooperation, Ms Gray. I hope I see more of you while you are staying here with us."

Even with the late afternoon heat, the way he said this made Adler's skin crawl. But before she could reply, Lugo walked back inside the unit, letting the door close behind him.

Adler stood facing the guard, considering her next move, assessing whether she could overpower him. The main gate was less than fifty metres away and there was no one else around. The gate would be locked but the wooden frontage was gnarly in parts, with large metal bolts protruding from the metal bars top and bottom. It would be tricky and she'd leave herself vulnerable if anyone was alerted, but she could climb it.

She gritted her teeth, ready to spring into action, the adrenaline coursing through her veins.

Should she...?

She glanced at the guard once more. He was watching her, his face tight with focus. He looked scared. That worked for her.

"Oh my God!" The door to the other unit opened and Price stumbled out, cursing and shaken, alongside the second guard.

*Damn it.*

She'd hesitated too long. With two armed guards present now, it was too much of a risk.

*Next time.*

Relaxing her muscles, she regarded Price. His face was more ashen than usual and he looked as if he might pass out at any moment. "Are you okay?" she asked him. "Did they hurt you?"

He shook his head. "No... but... I don't know... It suddenly all feels very real. And very bleak. I had to record a video message."

"Same here," Adler replied, hoping her sharp tone would convey to him that now was not the time for detailed explanations.

"What if they don't get the ransom in time?"

Adler offered him a tight-lipped smile. It was the best she could do as the guards moved around the back of them and shoved them forward. It would be fine, she told herself. She just had to stay alert for other options.

As they were herded back to the holding tent, they passed the open unit at the end of the block. Glancing inside, Adler immediately wished she hadn't. The room was dimly lit, with a tripod in the centre of the room facing a single chair. The back wall, originally painted white was covered in blood stains, like a macabre modern art painting in crimson and brown. As far as Adler could tell, there was no fresh blood, but the amount of spillage and extensive spatter marks made it clear there had been many violent encounters there. The presence of the tripod added a darker, more heart-stopping dimension to the scene. There was no getting around it. This was a kill room. Most likely the place where these bastards executed those whose governments didn't play ball.

Price's already frayed nerves seemed to unravel at the sight of all that blood. "No! I knew it!" he gasped. "I bloody knew it!"

He kept muttering the same thing as they continued their journey across the compound. He was in a state of shock, but she couldn't blame him. She suspected he'd tell the others what he'd seen when they got back. He'd have to. He was too broken by the sight of the kill room to keep quiet. People would be distraught, the Dixons and Lange especially. Panic would surely then ensue, bringing with it more chaos and putting them all at greater risk.

She considered talking to Price before they reached the tent. Try to reason with him to remain silent about their discovery. But she knew it was pointless. Price was a dam about to burst, and no words would patch the cracks.

Besides, she couldn't shake the image of the bloodied wall from her own mind and needed to talk to Day at least. She hoped the room was a hang-up from a different time, that with the advent of legitimacy the ELC had ceased such practices. But she knew blood spatter, and she knew some of the stains in that room were only a few months old. She wouldn't tell the Dixons and Lange that, of course. She'd play it down for them, reassure them as best she could. But whichever way she looked at it, that room confirmed everyone's worst fears.

## Chapter Twenty

Peroza settled in his office, the black leather chair creaking beneath him as he arranged the two laptops on the desk in front of him. The room, which doubled as his video editing suite, was stark. The only other furniture was a single wooden chair pushed to one side of the desk and an old rug in front of the door he'd purchased from a street vendor in Caracas ten years earlier. He'd brought it with him when he first moved here to the prison, with the idea it would make his office look expensive and more in keeping with an elite soldier. But looking at it today with its faded pattern and worn patches, it was no longer fit for purpose.

To his right, two shelves lined the wall, stacked with piles of tapes and recording equipment. There were VHS and VHS-C tapes, 8mm, Hi-8, Mini DV tapes, CDs and DVDs; along with plastic boxes overflowing with flash cards and USB sticks, all meticulously labelled and dated. His life's work.

There was a knock on the door. Peroza leaned back in his chair and ordered whoever it was to enter, grinning as the door opened to reveal Lugo carrying two digital video cameras.

"All done?" Peroza asked.

Lugo nodded. "Yes, sir. We started with the journalists as we arranged. I have just watched the recordings. The woman kept her cool. The man, not so much." He chuckled, the phlegm in his throat rattling as he did. "Cowardly bastard."

"Good work," Peroza told him. "Let's get these uploaded quickly. Before Murcia... Ah, never mind."

Lugo raised one eyebrow, his upbeat demeanour fading. "Trouble, Lieutenant?"

"Hmm." Peroza waved his hand dismissively. "Between you and me, a lot is changing. I sense Murcia is focused only on our recent discovery. He's eager for us to move away from our established operations, but I don't believe we're in a position to do that. We have to be careful right now. He may be getting recognition in the media back home, but our mission is far from over."

"Is the general still here?" Lugo asked.

"Yes. I was hoping his visit would be a short one, but he wants to oversee work on the new site. He also says he wants to observe our procedures and day-to-day operations." He lowered his chin, observing his deputy closely. He knew he could trust him, but he had to be careful what he said. "Don't worry, my friend. I am still the commandant of this base. Your loyalty is to me."

"Of course, Lieutenant. Always." Lugo clicked his heels, standing to attention.

"Good. You did well today. We shall stagger the release of the ransom videos as usual. But the two journalists are a good start. They always bring the highest attention. Let me see them."

He watched as Lugo placed the two cameras on the desk and set about extracting the memory cards from inside. With his bulbous, callused fingers, it was no easy task, and at one stage Peroza felt like grabbing the equipment and dismissing him. But he held his tongue and eventually Lugo handed over both cards.

"Okay. Leave me," he told his deputy. "I have work to do."

As Lugo backed away, Peroza got up and walked over to the shelves, taking down two card readers and inserting one into each of the laptops. He felt the same glimmer of satisfaction he always felt as he watched the status bars on the screen showing the fresh footage being extracted onto the laptops' hard drives. In his own twisted way, Peroza liked this part of the process. He fancied himself as a movie director of sorts, playing a pivotal role in the grim theatre of war. He often contemplated that after the revolution he might pursue his passion further. Why not? He would be part of the new elite by then. A star in his own right. Why couldn't he be the next Michael Mann? The next Michael Bay, even?

Once the ransom films were uploaded, he watched them one after the other, then spent some time topping and tailing the edits to ensure they looked professional. It didn't take long; he knew what he was doing by now. He enjoyed making these ransom videos, seeing the anguish and fear on the captives' faces as they peered down the unforgiving lens – but he preferred editing the beheading videos even more. They felt more like real art to him. He'd even created a compilation movie of his favourite ones and wondered whether he should release it for sale on the dark web. He could make a fortune in the right circles. But of course if Murcia found out he'd be furious.

The fact the general was distancing himself from their past and now reinventing himself as the moderate leader of an authentic political movement gnawed at Peroza. He hated that these might be some of the last hostage videos he'd ever make. But Murcia had all but told him as much – stating that now they had the other site it was no longer a requirement, nor did it fit with their new mission. He'd forced Peroza to alter the script and remove any mention of the ELC, and to take down the banners that had provided the backdrop to their previous recordings. Peroza had refused at first but Murcia had been insistent, leading to Peroza storming out of their meeting and ripping the banners down in a fit of rage. He understood why Murcia wanted it this way, but it felt like a betrayal. He was turning his back on everything they'd fought so hard for. It was now all about public perception for Murcia. He'd gone soft.

Content with the final cut of the footage, Peroza transferred the files onto a pen drive before yanking the drive free and striding from the room. He found Lugo in the office next to his, lounging with his boots up on the desk. He sat up promptly as Peroza entered.

"Take this to El Tigrito and upload the files," Peroza said, handing him the pen drive. "Don't use the same place as last time."

This was the usual procedure with these recordings. Lugo would travel to a different city each time, and find a backstreet internet café where he would upload the videos onto a secure site before forwarding the link to the relevant parties. They used VPNs and TOR browsers for all their communications regardless, but this way they added an extra layer of security and protected the location of their base. Which was now more important than ever.

"You got it!" Lugo said, slipping the drive into his jacket

pocket and getting to his feet. "I'll take one of the jeeps and leave immediately."

He gave a sharp salute and left the room. Peroza waited a moment and followed him outside, heading for the building on the far side of the compound where Murcia had taken up residence.

As he walked, a deep feeling of righteous indignation overcame him, which he tried but failed to suppress. He knew anger was a liability in negotiations, a sign of weakness, and he was determined not to display any vulnerability. But his resentment towards Murcia, once his brother-in-arms, was too strong.

Arriving at the building, he pounded his fist on the door. A moment later one of Murcia's security detail eased open the door and peered out.

"Is he here?" Peroza asked, stepping forward but finding his path blocked by the man. "I need to speak to the general."

He glared at the guard, his fists balled in frustration. How dare he stop him from walking freely in his own base? They remained in this tense impasse for a few seconds longer before the guard relented and stepped aside.

"Jalen?" Peroza called out, storming into the main space and casting his gaze around the lavish setup. Everything in this building was here by order of Murcia and contrasted greatly with the rest of the compound. The front room – *La Sala de Guerra*, as Murcia had once referred to it – exuded an almost western opulence. Peroza had once enjoyed sitting here with his old comrade, discussing their plans and dreams for their great country, but now the lavish décor and furniture felt too much like a calculated display of comfort and power. Plush leather couches were arranged strategically around a low coffee table, and along the walls, large mahogany bookcases groaned with books that had never been read but added a scholarly air to the room.

"Murcia? Where are you?"

He walked through into the next room to find the general sitting behind a huge leather-topped desk with his eyes closed. He opened them slowly as Peroza approached.

"Victor. All is well I hope."

Peroza cleared his throat, trying to maintain his composure. "Were you sleeping?"

"I was meditating. I was thinking. I was planning." He smiled serenely but it looked rehearsed, fake, perhaps even the work of a PR person or media training expert. It made Peroza sick. "Is there something you need?" Murcia asked.

"I was wondering how long you planned to stay here."

The general frowned as he leaned back. "Are you wanting rid of me, brother?"

"Not at all. But I need to know what to tell the men. Your presence here is unsettling them."

"There's no good reason why it should."

Peroza attempted his own fake smile.

*The fact they're receiving mixed messages is a good reason.*

*The fact that rumours are going around the camp that what we're doing is no longer in line with ELC policy is a good reason.*

Peroza knew the young men he'd recruited idolised him and viewed him as a sort of folk hero, a true revolutionary, but he couldn't live up to this status and he couldn't do what was needed if his hands were tied by protocol and procedure. Standing in front of Murcia now – who wore that stupid beatific expression on his face – Peroza's mind churned once more with thoughts of betrayal. Because two could play that game.

"I shall be staying a few more days," Murcia continued.

"Enough time that I can oversee things at the new site and satisfy myself everything is going to plan."

"Very good."

And it was good. Or at least it could be. With Murcia here at the prison, accompanied by only a modest security detail, Peroza wondered suddenly if the time was right for him to leverage the situation and seize control. The thought was certainly tempting, a seed of ambition planted in his mind. Lugo and his men would have his back, and with Murcia growing increasingly distant from the group's original ideals, he had an opportunity to position himself as the true leader of their movement.

"Is there anything else?" Murcia asked. "Because I was in the middle of something when you strode in."

"No. That's all." He bowed, slapping his hands on each thigh. "I will leave you to your... plans."

*And I will continue with mine*, he thought, as he left the building and stepped out into the afternoon sun. The idea of usurping Murcia, of taking control of the ELC, grew more appealing. He knew it would be a gamble, but Victor Peroza had never been one to shy away from risk, especially when power was at stake. It would be risky, he'd need to consider all his options, but the notion was now forming in his mind, taking shape, growing legs. He could do this. But he had to make a decision, and fast.

## Chapter Twenty-One

In the humidity of the holding tent, tension was mounting. Beckett watched from the sidelines as Price paced in front of the group, his brow furrowed, his mouth puckered into a sharp pout.

"They're going to execute us!" he hissed, his tone bristling with panic. "We saw the room where they do it. There was dried blood all up the walls, on the floor and ceiling too. We have to do something or we're dead."

"He's right," Lange whispered, also on his feet. "This settles it. We have to get out of here. By any means possible."

Beckett remained where he was. He hadn't spoken since Price and Gray had returned a few minutes earlier in a flurry of nervous energy, but he didn't like how this was going. Price and Lange were winding each other up and all it would take was for Castillo and the Dixons to join in and there'd be unbridled chaos. People did stupid things when they were agitated and in a group mentality. They took risks. They egged each other on. They got themselves killed.

He had to admit, the discovery of a kill room was not on his list of things to hope for whilst being held captive, but he understood the importance of keeping a level head.

"The fact you've made a ransom video should be a clear sign they're not planning to execute anyone soon," he told Price in a low voice, mindful of the guards outside.

"Forgive me if I don't feel very reassured," Price spat.

"What was in the script they made you read?" Beckett asked him. "What did they make you say?"

Price spluttered. "Just basic details. We gave our name, our nationality… who we worked for… We said we were being held captive by a guerrilla group."

"Did they have a special message they made you read out? Like a political statement?"

"No. Nothing like that."

"Okay, great." He glanced at Gray. "If they're not asking us to declare our faith in their cause, it's a good sign. ISIS get hostages to proclaim their support for the caliphate – it's an extra kick in the teeth to the West and they get off on it. But if these people aren't doing that, it's more evidence that what everyone is telling you is true – we're a source of income for them. Nothing more. Meaning they want us alive." He held Price's gaze, hoping this would ease his panic.

"Mike's right," Gray added. "I know it looks bad. But from everything we've seen and know about this group, they're motivated by money. If your employers have an insurance policy to cover the ransom, then they'll pay up and you'll be released."

Price rounded on her, his eyes wild. "And if they don't? That's my last chance. The British government doesn't negotiate with terrorists!" He stormed over to the other side of the tent, muttering to himself.

## A World of Sun and Violence

Beckett watched him for a moment. Did western governments negotiate with terrorists and pay ransoms?

Officially – no.

Unofficially – all the time.

Yes, there was the line everyone knew, which safeguarded against any old tinpot terrorist group trying their hand at extortion. But the reality was often more nuanced. If it was possible, money did change hands to secure the release of captured British nationals. Beckett had seen it happen firsthand. On one occasion, in Lebanon, he'd led the central negotiation and extraction team.

He didn't say any of this to Price. Maybe he would say it later, but at this very moment the man was too worked up to hear anything. Looking past Price, he saw Gray was now sitting with the Dixons. From what he could hear of their conversation, she appeared to be explaining to them – in a roundabout kind of way – that the US were happy to negotiate behind closed doors if it meant saving their citizens.

She was a strong woman. She spoke a lot of sense.

Lange and Price, however, were beyond consolation. Lange was now pacing the tent, trying to psyche up the group as if he were leading them into battle.

"We are nothing to these people," he said. "They look at us and see piles of money or bodies to dispose of when the deal doesn't happen. I will not be a passive victim. I will not sit here and do nothing. We have to act. We have to escape. There are seven of us and we have all commented that these soldiers are mainly young men. They have guns, yes. But we can overpower them. We can do this!"

Beckett held Gray's worried gaze as he moved closer to Lange. "This is foolish," he said, his voice quiet but firm. "We can't all run for it when things go wrong. You'll get people killed."

"Nothing will go wrong if we time it right," Lange snapped.

"And that time might be now," Price added, walking over and placing his hand on Lange's shoulder. "When Julia and I were escorted back here, I didn't see any soldiers on patrol. It's quiet out there. But it's early afternoon, hot as anything; I'm wondering if perhaps they take siestas in shifts at this time."

"I doubt it," Gray said.

Price threw her a nasty look. "Did you see any patrols?"

Gray frowned. "Come to think of it, no."

"Exactly. As far as we know, there's no one around except for the two men who brought us here and the two on guard outside this tent."

"That's still four soldiers with four assault rifles against seven people with no assault rifles," Castillo piped up, from where he was lying on one of the benches. "I don't like those odds, *amigo*."

"Me neither," Beckett said. It was clear to him that Price and Lange were spiralling, feeding off each other's desperation.

But Lange's resolve didn't falter. "So we just wait for our turn in front of the camera then?" he hissed. "Have our heads cut off by savages, miles from home? Come on, guys, we have to try."

To any of the people in the tent, Beckett – as Michael Day – remained stoically calm. Yet under his shirt his abominable muscles were clenched with apprehension. He could sense the situation escalating quickly and it wasn't going to end well. He had to think fast, come up with a plan that didn't involve a reckless attack on armed guards.

He moved closer to Gray, lowering his voice so the others wouldn't hear. "We need to talk them out of this," he leaned in to say. He was still wary of the American woman, but she seemed to have her head screwed on and understood the gravity of their situation. "They have no real plan. This is driven by fear and rage."

Gray didn't take her eyes off Lange but nodded in agreement. Together they approached the two men.

"Listen," Beckett urged, maintaining a reassuring but authoritative tone. "A frontal assault on four – or even two – armed guards is suicide. We need to be strategic, wait for a proper opening."

Price was already shaking his head. "We don't have time! That room…!"

Gray stepped in front of him, her voice steady. "Andrew, we need to stay alive to have a chance. Acting impulsively will end any hope of that. Right now we're safe. But if we try to escape and fail, that could change drastically."

"What if we succeed?" Lange argued. "We can do this!"

Beckett could sense Price was wavering, uncertainty creeping in. He pressed on. "Think about it. These people have invested time and resources in us. We're more valuable to them alive than dead. That's our leverage."

Bruce interjected, his voice frail. "But my Kathy… she's not well. We can't just sit here and do nothing."

"Doing *some*thing doesn't mean rushing into a fight we can't win," Beckett told him. "It means being smart, waiting for a genuine opportunity."

"Fuck you!" Lange snarled, shoving past him and walking to the far side of the tent. "This *is* a genuine opportunity. It's the first one we've had since we got here. They've relaxed their security. Who knows if that will happen again. Now is the time."

Beckett cast his attention around the tent. Everyone looked like tightly coiled springs ready to snap. He took in the Dixons' terrified expressions, the panic in Price's eyes, Lange's frantic desire to act. The young German was nearing breaking point, but short of physically restraining him, there seemed little else Beckett could do.

He sat down, gesturing for Gray to join him on the bench.

"This is bad," he told her, as she sat next to him and they observed Price and Lange plotting across from them.

"Do you think we've a chance?" she asked. "To escape, I mean?"

Beckett rubbed at the stubble on his chin. "Maybe, for one or two of us. But there's no way the entire group is going to make it to safety. What happens to those left behind, Castillo and the Dixons? Regardless of the kill room, we're being treated reasonably well right now. But that could all change if they stage a breakout."

They watched in silence as Lange and Price continued to whisper conspiringly. Lange was the most animate, waving his hands around and pointing to the tent flaps, like an overzealous sports coach explaining tactical manoeuvres. Beckett raised his head and subtly shifted his weight forward onto his feet. The situation was on a knife edge. He knew Lange was too far gone to be reasoned with. He was going to attempt something.

All their lives were now hanging in the balance.

## Chapter Twenty-Two

Adler gripped the edge of the bench on either side of her, her fingernails digging into the wood. She felt helpless and angry in equal measures. She'd seen the kill room too and understood its grim implications. Yet, as Day had pointed out, there was no immediate reason to believe they were in danger of being executed. However, if they antagonised their captors, and proved themselves to be pests and a threat to their methodology, it could mean a one-way trip to that bloodstained room sooner rather than later.

Lange was now backing away from Price, moving to the side of the tent nearest to the entrance flaps. Once there, he flattened himself against the canvas and gestured at Price. "Go on," he hissed. "I'm ready."

Adler and Day shared a look of disbelief and frustration as Price positioned himself at the tent's entrance.

*They were going for it, the stupid bastards.*

She felt Day tense beside her as if he was about to jump up and tackle Price to the ground. But before he could act, Price launched into his performance.

"Hello! Guard?" he called out, his voice trembling with a level of distress that seemed only slightly contrived. "I need help. I'm not doing too good. I feel very sick!"

Adler seethed at Price's stupidity. This was not the plan. Almost instinctively, and in unison, she and Day rose and headed towards the tent entrance, her going for the nearest side and Day circling around to where Lange was waiting. They needed a clear line of sight, and if the situation spiralled out of control, they needed to act.

She prayed Day would reach Lange in time to stop whatever he was planning. But as the tall Englishman was traversing the edge of the tent, two armed guards stepped inside.

Adler and Day froze in place as the guards waved their rifles around the interior.

"Help me!" Price whined, bending double and moaning. "I'm sick!" He was overplaying the discomfort, but it seemed to work on the guards. They lowered their weapons.

"What is wrong?" one of them asked, stepping forward.

In that moment of distraction Lange made his move. With a sudden burst of energy he lunged at the nearest guard, shoulder first, sending him tumbling into his buddy and knocking him to the ground. Kathleen screamed. Adler stepped forward and kicked the rifle away from the fallen guard.

Amidst the chaos, Lange grappled with the remaining guard, wrenching the rifle from his grasp.

"Fuck you!" he screamed, his finger tight on the trigger. A hail of bullets tore into the guard's chest, propelling him and Lange backwards. "That's for Martin!" he roared, as the guard's body crumpled to the ground.

Adler glanced over at Day, who was ushering the Dixons

to relative safety on the far side of the tent, using his body as a shield between them and the unfolding horror.

One guard lay dead on the ground. The other, dazed but still conscious, was struggling to regain his footing and come to terms with the sudden turn of events.

"Come on, let's run for it!" Lange cried out, rifle in hand. He grabbed at Price, attempting to pull him from his stupor, but the timid Englishman remained rooted. "Come on!"

Price's eyes darted between Day and Adler. "But... What if...? Do we...?"

"Ah, screw this!" Lange spat, abandoning Price and bolting from the tent. In the ensuing disarray, Adler noticed the remaining guard scrambling on all fours for his rifle.

*Shit.*

She was too far away to stop him, but Day had also spotted the danger. Without hesitation he sprang into action, closing the distance between him and the guard in a few strides and delivering a heavy boot to the face, knocking him out cold. He picked up the rifle and as he straightened he locked eyes with Adler, a silent communication passing between them.

Her mind raced with possibilities. Should they seize this moment and run – follow Lange's desperate lead?

But before a decision could be made, the tent flap burst open. Two more guards with weapons at the ready stormed in, shouting frantically.

"Put the gun down now! Or we shoot you all!"

Day held his ground for a moment, before raising one hand and carefully placing the rifle on the ground. "Okay, don't shoot. We're cooperating."

He offered Adler a crooked half-smile as the guards

ordered them to raise their hands, and the group, now in a fresh grip of fear, complied.

*Damn it.*

They were back to square one. Their brief moment of hope snuffed out before it had started.

Or maybe it was worse than that.

A lot worse.

Chaos reigned in the tent as the young guards struggled to assert control, their rifles swinging wildly from one hostage to another, their commands sounding more like panicked shouts. The Dixons were huddled together, their faces white with terror, whilst Price stood frozen, his earlier bravado replaced by fear paralysis as he stared after Lange.

One of the guards followed his gaze, glancing over his shoulder and jerking his head at the fleeing figure of Lange, just visible through the flap of the tent. "One of them has escaped," he yelled in Spanish. "He's getting away. Go after him. I'll hold them."

His comrade hesitated for a moment before turning and dashing out in pursuit of the runaway. Adler gritted her teeth. The remaining guard, now alone, was still visibly shaken, waving his aim around the tent in an attempt to keep the hostages at bay.

She tensed.

*Was there still a chance?*

That question was answered a second later as Lieutenant Peroza burst into the tent followed by two more armed guards. His commanding presence made the group shrink back as he barked questions in Spanish, his swarthy skin turning a shade of purple. The remaining guard, stuttering and wide-eyed, swiftly reported what had happened.

"Who was on duty? Him?" Peroza demanded, pointing

at the guard Day had knocked out. "He allowed one of them to escape. Idiot!" He headed for the fallen guard who was now conscious but still groggy.

"Lieutenant Peroza," Day said, stepping forward, his hands still raised. "None of us wanted this, especially not the Dixons here. It wasn't—"

He shut up as Peroza punched him in the face. It was a heavy, well-aimed blow that sent Day's head snapping to one side in response. Yet Adler could tell he'd seen the punch coming and had turned his head to lessen the impact. It was a deft move. Not what you'd expect from a former financial advisor who'd spent most of his adult life in an office.

*Who was this man?*

Peroza, now muttering furious incantations under his breath, turned to the fallen guard who was now getting to his feet. In one movement he drew his pistol from its holster and executed him with a single shot to the head, turning away before the guard's lifeless body hit the ground.

The hostages watched on in stunned silence as Peroza glared at them, panting.

"Where is the one that escaped?" he asked, narrowing his eyes at the group, trying to work out who was missing.

"L-Lopez gave chase, Lieutenant," the remaining guard stammered. "The man was heading towards the wall."

Peroza spun around to peer through the tent flap. Adler, from her vantage point, had a good view of the prison grounds beyond. Her heart skipped a beat at the sight of Lange scaling the wall with a desperate determination, his fingers clawing for purchase on the rough surface, his feet finding footholds in the crumbling concrete. The walls were high, she'd have guessed around ten feet, but for a fleeting moment it seemed he might get away, his frantic movements propelling him onward as the guard approached.

"Come on, Lange," she whispered under her breath. "You can do this."

A shot rang out, the bullet pinging off the wall above Lange's head. He stopped. He reassessed his trajectory. More shots followed, each one closer than the last, sending fragments of concrete raining down on him.

It was over. Adler's heart sank as she saw Lopez reach the wall. Jumping up he grabbed hold of the hem of Lange's cargo pants, halting his climb. Lange yelled out, his expression taut with effort and indignation as he fought against the inevitable. But it was no use. Lopez clambered up after him and grabbed onto his pants with both hands, using his body weight to pull him down from the wall. A collective gasp rippled through the tent as Lange fell to the dusty ground and Lopez stepped over him, smashing the butt of his assault rifle into the German's face.

Adler held her hand to her mouth as two more guards ran over and dragged Lange to his feet. He was conscious but only just. Blood was streaming from his nose.

"Oh dear," Peroza said, with a mocking smile as he addressed them. "It seems your friend's plan didn't quite work out." He glanced around the tent, the grim satisfaction evident in his cold, hard stare. When he spoke again his voice was ice. "You are foolish to disrespect me and my operation."

"Wha-What do you mean?" Price stammered. "We were no part of this."

"It was all him, *señor*," Castillo added. "We would never—"

"Silence!" Peroza screamed. He turned to his guards.

"Bring them to the exercise yard," he commanded, his eyes locked onto each of the hostages in turn, like a predator assessing his prey. "I will show you what happens to those who defy me. Those who dare to attempt escape."

## Chapter Twenty-Three

Richard Foster – Dick, to those close to him – strode purposefully down the wide echoing corridors of the CIA headquarters in Langley, the heels of his Bruno Magli Oxfords clacking off the polished floor like gunfire. As he passed a couple of female analysts walking the other way, he noted how they glanced at him reverently before averting their eyes. This was a reaction Foster was accustomed to and appreciated. It affirmed the respect and authority he had cultivated over the years.

Having turned fifty on his last birthday, Foster now fit the mould of a seasoned CIA deputy director of operations. Tall and tanned, his hair was impeccably trimmed and just starting to show hints of silver, which complemented the sharp, analytical gleam in his ice-blue eyes. Always dressed in tailored suits, he presented an image of controlled power, a man who knew the weight of the decisions he made on a daily, if not hourly, basis.

In keeping with this fact, he was currently en route to a round table sit-down with his chief of staff, Mark Gold-

## A World of Sun and Violence

smith, and Lou Simmons, the deputy director of National Clandestine Services. These bi-monthly meetings were vital touchpoints for staying abreast of international operations and a forum to discuss ways they could better shape the nation's covert foreign policy.

Lou Simmons, tall to the point of gangly, rose from his seat and gave Foster a curt nod as he entered the room. "Afternoon, Dick."

Simmons was an experienced operative turned administrator and Foster trusted him with his life, but he'd never seen him smile, not once. His hangdog expression implied he understood the weighty responsibilities they shouldered and was enduring them with quiet resilience.

"Lou, Mark." Foster waved a hand at his colleagues, prompting them to relax the stiffened postures they'd employed when he walked in. "Good to see you both."

He closed the door behind him, listening for the click as he cast his attention around the meeting room, one of the executive spaces they had here at Langley. Designed for function over form, with no windows and a low ceiling, these rooms always felt a little oppressive but they were secure and that was what mattered. The walls were lined with screens displaying maps and data from hotspots around the world, while in the centre of the room, and taking up most of the space, was a large oval table surrounded by ergonomic chairs designed to be sat in for extended periods.

"Who wants to start?" Foster asked as he took a seat, eager to dive into matters rather than waste time on pleasantries.

Simmons cleared his throat. "It seems Iran is heating up," he began. "We've got several assets in Tehran reporting unusual military movements and our satellite imagery is showing increased activity at their missile sites."

"How recent is this?" Goldsmith enquired, his tone deeper and more serious than in other meetings he and Foster attended together. Goldsmith was the youngest of the three men, but Foster held a great deal of respect for him. His dark eyes sparkled with the eagerness of youth but he carried himself with a hardened grit that belied his years, making him an indispensable ally in these high-stakes meetings.

"Our signal intelligence suggests they might be preparing for a demonstration of capability, possibly a new missile test, imminently," Simmons said. "We're monitoring communications closely."

Foster settled back in his chair. "Good. Continue to do so and keep me in the loop. And make sure to inform the president as well. Today. He needs to be aware of everything you've just mentioned."

Simmons nodded in acknowledgement. The notepads and pens laid out on the table were never used in these sorts of meetings. Each of them had a sharp, analytical mind. They didn't need to make notes even if protocol allowed it.

Goldsmith's brow furrowed as he approached his next question. "And what about Ukraine?"

Simmons leaned back slightly, interlocking his fingers. "As we know, Ukraine remains a complex situation. We're running several operations aimed at undermining Russian communication networks. But with them on the backfoot currently, it's a delicate balance to ensure we disrupt their capabilities without escalating tensions unnecessarily."

"The cyber division is stretched but doing well," Foster added. "We've infiltrated key command and control systems on the front lines, though maintaining access is proving difficult. Our efforts took a hit when our allies, the Russian Freedom Legion militia group, were wiped out recently outside of Kharkiv, but we're persevering." He rolled his shoulders back, mentally crossing that point off the agenda. "Let's move on. What's the current situation in Colombia?"

Simmons shared a grave look with Goldsmith, his usually composed face displaying a flicker of concern. "It appears the situation could be heating up. There's been increased chatter about the unrest. We're intercepting communications that hint at a possible military coup. However, the details are still murky."

Foster leaned forward. "But we still have people on the ground there? Infiltrating the key players?"

His colleague made a low growling noise. "One of our operatives is currently near the Colombian border in North Venezuela, gathering intelligence on the Ejército Liberación de Colombia – the ELC... amongst other things."

"Other things?"

Simmons sniffed. "We should discuss it later, sir," he said, eyeing Goldsmith. "It's highly classified."

"I see. And who's the operative?"

"Well, that's the thing," Simmons replied. "It's Vanessa Adler."

Foster took the information onboard without flinching, but it wasn't what he wanted to hear. "*The* Vanessa Adler?"

"Yes. And given the rapid escalation in the region, we're evaluating our next steps. She's a good operative, of course, one of our best. But with her ties—"

"Yes, I'm aware of her background. When was her last report?"

"It's been over a month since her last check-in. But given the nature of her assignment and the depth of her cover as a freelance journalist, this isn't unusual."

Foster frowned. "Why was Adler assigned to this particular mission?" he asked. "It's a volatile situation for a lone operative, regardless of who she is."

"She requested the assignment," Simmons explained. "It was always going to be a solo mission and we were confident in her abilities. But with recent developments and talks of a coup, the situation has become much more precarious."

Foster steepled his fingers underneath his chin as he contemplated the implications. "Fine. Keep me updated on any developments. We might need to consider an extraction plan if things deteriorate further."

"We'll keep a close eye on it."

Goldsmith cleared his throat and waited a moment before interjecting. "All right, what's next on the agenda?"

However, as the meeting continued, Foster found himself preoccupied with thoughts of Vanessa Adler. The challenges of operating in such a turbulent environment were enormous. A potential coup in Colombia would destabilise the region further and the implications for the US were significant.

Throughout his tenure at the CIA, Foster had overseen countless operations, each with its own set of dangers and complexities. But the stakes involved in this particular situation resonated more deeply. Adler was a damn good operative; one of the best. Despite her personal disdain for the baggage attached to her name, she was special. More than just another operative. And her safety was paramount.

## Chapter Twenty-Four

The high prison walls cast long shadows over the arid ground as the hostages were marched over to the exercise yard on the far side of the compound. The thick, humid heat only added to the sense of nervousness hanging over the group. Both Price and Kathleen whimpered softly to themselves, but no one spoke out loud.

As before, Beckett kept a watchful eye over things. His background might have honed his ability to remain calm under pressure, but the precariousness of their situation exacerbated by Lange's botched escape weighed heavily on him. He glanced around, assessing his surroundings and the armed guards who flanked them, their once-eager expressions now a mix of annoyance and grim determination.

He understood their mindset. They'd been made to look like amateurs, and after witnessing Peroza's cold-blooded execution of their fellow guard, it was clear they were all on their last strike. Beckett sensed their keenness to assert dominance, to show the lieutenant they wouldn't tolerate any further disruptions from the hostages.

To his right, Gray looked pensive but was still maintaining her level-headedness. They held each other's gaze momentarily, but neither offered the other anything as trite as a reassuring smile. It had gone way beyond that.

Beckett respected Gray. She was resilient, methodical, and not easily scared. He knew journalists could be that way, but he'd started to wonder if there was more beneath the surface. Her systematic approach, the way she observed and assessed, the questions she asked, the things she said – it stirred a suspicion in Beckett's mind.

"Stop! This is far enough!"

His train of thought was interrupted as Peroza's voice boomed across the yard. The group halted, huddling together in the middle of the exercise yard and exchanging worried glances.

"Why are we here?" Castillo asked. "What are you going to do with us?"

Peroza grinned. "You will see."

"W-We didn't do any-anything wrong," Bruce stammered. "Kathleen and I are old people. We don't want to rock the boat. We're happy to wait and see—"

"Silence!" Peroza barked, holding his hand in the air. "This is on you. On all of you. You will see what we do to those who disrespect us, who disrupt what we are doing here. Now, all of you – on your knees!"

A distraught murmur ran around the group for a few moments until Price pierced the air with a loud cry. "No! Please! We didn't mean to upset you. It was him not us," he cried, pointing at Lange. "It was all him!"

Peroza glared at Price. "On your knees!"

The guards hustled over to the group, shoving and prodding with their rifles until they were kneeling together in a rough semi-circle.

"They're going to kill us!" Price wailed. "I don't want to die!"

"Oh Lord above us, no!" Kathleen joined in. "Please spare us this day. I'm not ready."

Beckett shot Price a look. This was not what they needed right now. He attempted to dial out the group's panicked mumblings as Peroza produced a Taser gun and a metal whistle from his belt. The sun glinted off the whistle as he brought it to his lips and blew a sharp, piercing note.

The group glanced around them, confused and fearful as to what this alert signified. Beckett's instincts, however, directed his gaze towards the wooden hut on the far side of the grounds. As he watched, a large hand emerged and slowly drew the curtain to one side.

"My prize fighter," Peroza announced. "Bracho! Otherwise known as El Demonio Roto. Otherwise known as The Canaima!"

A collective hush fell over the hostages and the guards shifted awkwardly as a large figure stepped out into the daylight.

Beckett couldn't believe what he was looking at. Bracho had to be almost seven feet tall and nearly as wide. Large sinewy muscles bulged under his skin, but it was the deformities that caught his and everyone else's attention, his physicality an unsettling blend of human and monster. He was completely bald, his scalp gleaming under the hot sun, accentuating bumps and welts that covered his skin as he lumbered towards them. His face bore the signs of past conflicts. What was once a nose was now a mess of cartilage and bone, seemingly broken and reset so many times it had lost any semblance of normality. His left eye socket and cheekbone had also been shattered at some point and it looked as if the nerves in his eye had been damaged, which gave him a sinister lopsided gaze.

"Who the hell is that?" Bruce whispered. "*What* the hell is that?"

But no one had a good answer for the American.

Beckett couldn't take his eyes off the huge beast-man as he approached. He was barefoot and limping slightly due to one foot being bent inward and swollen, but that was the least of his horrors. His body, toughened by the sun and years of abuse, seemed more weapon than flesh. He was dressed in a pair of tie-dyed muscle pants, the sort of attire weightlifters wore, and his naked torso was a hideous map of bulbous scars, puckered burns and angular calluses. But the most unnerving aspect of his appearance were the lumps and bumps stretching his flesh, topped off by a sharp bone that protruded grotesquely out of his shoulder, a visible sign of a past injury healed in the most unnatural way. It gave him both a primal, animalistic aura and the sense that he was not of this world. A creature born of darkness and brutality.

It was the brute's right hand – if it could still be called a hand – that concerned Beckett. Like his nose, it must have been broken and reset many times over, and had formed into a large ugly callus. Like a medieval club.

"Whoa... I've heard of this man," Castillo whispered. "He is a legend in the fight clubs of Caracas and El Tigrito. I always thought people were making up stories about him. But now I see it with my own eyes."

"Come, my friend," Peroza called, beckoning Bracho closer. "I have some fun for you today."

Bracho eyed the Taser in Peroza's hand before striding over to stand a few feet away. He glared at the hostages with

## A World of Sun and Violence

a strange expression, his wide mouth contorted into a shape that was almost a smile.

"Do you want to have fun?" Peroza asked, speaking to him in Spanish.

Bracho nodded, repeating the word 'fun' in a gravelly voice. "*Diversión… diversión…*"

Observing him up close, Beckett sensed the big man had limited intellectual capacity, but as Bracho raised himself to his full height and let out a strange high-pitched laugh, even the armed guards appeared unnerved.

Peroza pointed at Price and Lange. "You and you, stand up."

"No! It wasn't me!" Price cried, shaking his head violently. He held his hands out. "I want to help you. I believe in what you're doing here."

The guards forced the two men to their feet. Lange was already bruised and bleeding after his beating, but stood defiant. Price, on the other hand, was now hysterical, promising Peroza the world in an attempt to save himself. Whilst Beckett appreciated that not everyone had the same experience in handling tense situations – and that people dealt with fear in different ways – it angered him to see his fellow countryman acting so cowardly.

"Now you must choose," Peroza said. "Decide which of you will fight Bracho. You will be allowed a weapon, and if you win you will both go free."

Price immediately stepped back and pointed at Lange. "You should do it," he said. "You're a strong guy. You're tough."

"Fuck you!" Lange snarled. "He will kill me."

"You *will* be allowed one weapon," Peroza repeated, although the smirk on his face told them he knew it would do little to level the playing field. "Decide quickly. Or I will decide for you."

"Fine!" Lange said, flicking Price a mean glance before turning to Peroza. "You decide."

Peroza's amusement grew. He moved between the two hostages, waving his finger from one to the other as he launched into a Spanish selection song.

"*Pito, pito, gorgorito. Dónde vas tú tan bonito?*"

The childish rhyme sounded chilling as they waited to see where his finger would land.

"*A la era verdadera. Pim, pam, pum, fuera!*"

He stopped on Lange. Price gasped in relief as Peroza leaned closer to the German. "It's you!" he said. "You will fight El Demonio Roto."

Lange, his features drawn and paling, glanced from Peroza to Bracho, to Beckett. He was terrified. "Nein!" He clasped his hands together, begging. "*Bitte! Es tut mir leid!* I am sorry!"

"Too late for that." Peroza gestured at one of the guards, who spun on his heels and headed away towards the main building. "It is time to fight."

"I will not fight him," Lange spat. "I cannot."

Peroza raised his head as Bracho growled impatiently beside him. "Oh, you will fight him," he said, narrowing his eyes. "Or you and your friend will both be shot where you stand. It is your choice."

## Chapter Twenty-Five

Beckett and the others watched on in silence as the guard returned with a wicker basket full of close combat weapons. He placed it down in front of Lange. Beckett, still kneeling, strained his neck to assess the contents. Inside was an assortment of combat knives, a pair of t-batons, a baseball bat and a heavy steel mace. On any other day, against any other opponent, these weapons would be effective. But against the monstrous Bracho, they seemed like mere toys.

"Pick your weapon," Peroza hissed at Lange, who was now visibly trembling, tears streaking his face. "You have ten seconds to choose or you will face my man unarmed."

Lange peered at each of the weapons in turn before hesitantly reaching for the mace. It was the right choice. Beckett would have selected the same. The mace had weight and reach, potentially useful against a larger opponent.

As Lange held the mace in his grip, Price was dragged to the opposite side of the yard by one of the guards and made to kneel facing the rest of them. Beckett could hear his sobs from where he was kneeling. Beside him, Kathleen, overwhelmed by the threat of death, broke down also. Bruce shuffled closer to comfort her, but the man standing guard behind them steered him away with the muzzle of his rifle.

"You stay still! You watch!"

"Yes, yes… don't hurt us," Bruce whimpered. "We are old. She needs me."

Kathleen continued to sob quietly as Beckett ran his attention around the yard. The guard who had brought the weapons was stood to his right, rifle at the ready. On the other side of the semi-circle, to his left, the man who had dragged Price away had also resumed his position. With the third man standing behind them, he had no room to breathe and any offensive manoeuvre would be suicide. He was powerless to intervene.

All he could do was watch as Peroza approached the hulking Bracho and whispered to him in Spanish. Bracho's response was an eager nod and he peered over his master's head to stare at Lange. Then Peroza stepped back, pointing to Bracho and then to the German.

"*Hasta la muerte.*"

Bracho responded with a high-pitched screech, an unsettling display of excitement. He stomped his feet and pounded his clubbed hand against his chest, echoing Peroza's words. "*Hasta la muerte! Hasta la muerte!*"

"Okay," Peroza called out, holding up his hand. "The fight begins when I blow this whistle. It ends with only one man standing." He nodded at his guards, who adjusted their stance, tightening their grip on their assault rifles.

Lange, standing a few feet from Beckett, was trembling with a mixture of fear and adrenaline. He hefted the mace over his shoulder, holding it like a baseball bat, his arms trembling. Beckett caught his eye, offering a silent nod of encouragement. It was a small, almost insignificant gesture in the face of impending violence, but it was all he could do.

Peroza moved over to stand next to Price on the far side of the makeshift ring and raised the whistle to his lips. He held it there for a moment, revelling in the power. Then blew, releasing a piercing sound that cut through the air like a razor.

This was it.

Beckett knew the only way Lange stood any chance of survival was if he started on the offensive. So he was glad when, with a yell, the German lunged forward, swinging the mace with all his might. The first blow, aimed at Bracho's head, was deflected effortlessly, sending the adrenaline-fuelled Lange off balance. The crowd gasped, but he regained his footing and swung again, this time aiming lower, going for the beast's ribs. Now the mace found its target, but it may as well have struck a wall of stone. Bracho barely flinched, absorbing the blow with an unsettling grin, as if pain were a foreign concept to him.

"*Dios mío!*" Castillo cried.

"Come on, son," Bruce added. "You can do this!"

Lange, his face red, the tendons in his neck bulging, swung the mace again. This time he caught Bracho's good arm, but once again he didn't flinch. Lange swung again, aiming for the ribs. This time his attack was blocked by the clubbed hand.

"*Fick dich!*" Lange screamed, gnashing his teeth as he swung the mace desperately. Beckett sensed his attacks becoming more erratic by the second, his movements driven by panic rather than strategy. He was also tiring himself out.

In contrast, Bracho moved slow and steady. He was still grinning and nodding as if this were all a game. And maybe to him it was. He lashed out with his clubbed hand, an organic mace of splintered bone and scar tissue, which struck Lange in the face with a sickening crunch. The German's already bust-up nose exploded in a cloud of red mist as his head snapped back from the force of the blow.

"Leave him alone!" cried Bruce, as Kathleen lowered her head, no longer able to watch.

Peroza answered his call with a cruel cackling laugh that tightened the muscles across Beckett's shoulders. In front of him, Lange was fighting valiantly to remain standing as Bracho circled him, his expression one of childlike glee. It was as if he were disconnected from the violence he was inflicting, just roughhousing with an old friend rather than inflicting torturous pain on another human being.

Beckett and the others could only watch in muted horror as the fight unfolded and became more and more one-sided. Lange's face was swelling up and he was finding it hard to breathe through his broken nose, but Bracho didn't give him a moment's respite. Advancing on him, he delivered a series of punishing blows to the German's chest and body. Lange, dazed and bloodied, tried to ward off the attacks but his defences were failing and his movements sluggish from shock and pain. He staggered away, but Bracho seized him by the collar, lifting him off his feet with one hand like a rag doll.

Except for Gray, the rest of the hostages were now looking away, but Beckett made himself watch as Lange kicked at the air, his hands clawing at Bracho's iron grip. With a grunt, the beast flung him to the ground, a heavy thud reverberating through the yard. Lange, gasping for air, attempted to crawl away, but Bracho loomed over him like a malevolent giant.

Beckett's jaw tightened.

*Get up.*

Bruce and Castillo offered up their own words of encouragement, urging Lange to move, to get out of the way. It was no use. Bracho reached down and grabbed the German by the hair. Lange struggled in vain against the brute's unyielding grip – he was no match for Bracho's overwhelming strength.

The big man dragged Lange to his feet, spinning him around so he was behind him and clamping his arm around the German's neck. Beckett glanced over at Gray. He knew what was coming, and from the grim expression darkening her features, so did she.

Bracho let out a low growl, peering across at Peroza who was nodding enthusiastically.

"Do it!" he ordered. "Finish him!"

Bracho tightened his grip, his thick forearm like a metal vice around Lange's neck. The German's attempts to break free were growing weaker, his energy gone, along with his hope. The hostages fell silent as they waited, the only sound now Lange's desperate gasps for air, each breath more laboured than the last.

With a sudden jerk Bracho twisted Lange's head violently to one side. There was a sickening snap, and the German's struggles ceased.

Beckett puffed out his cheeks as those around him cried out, recoiling in horror at what they'd seen. Only Gray was silent, her expression one of dismal contemplation at what she'd just observed, as if she were perhaps considering her next move, assessing her options. She was a tough woman, and he was almost certain now there was more to her than she was letting on. In contrast, across the yard, Andrew Price was inconsolable, his wails highlighting the despair that hung heavy over the group.

Peroza regarded them with that same self-satisfied smirk, revelling in the pain he had caused. "Take them back to the holding cell," he ordered the guards. "And one of you escort Bracho back to his hut. Make sure he gets a treat. He has earned it today."

As the group were hauled to their feet and led away, Beckett's gaze lingered on Peroza. The lieutenant moved over to get a better look at Lange's lifeless body before shaking his head and strolling back to his office. But he had made his point. He was the man in charge here. Ruthless, cruel, and willing to do whatever was needed for his cause. And the hostages now knew – any further escape attempts would be met with the same merciless retribution.

## Chapter Twenty-Six

Lange's neck had been completely snapped, his battered head lolling at a right angle to his body. It looked obscene, unnatural, sickening. Adler couldn't take her eyes off it as she was led away. He was almost unrecognisable from the man she'd met just that morning. His face wasn't even recognisable as a face.

"Hey, that's not going to help."

Adler looked around to see Day had fallen in step beside her. "I know," she told him. "It's just…"

"Oh, I get it. Believe me, I get it."

They walked in silence until they reached the large holding tent where the armed guards lined them up outside. Price was still shaking with shock, Kathleen and Bruce were in tears, Castillo looked like he'd seen a ghost. They were all perfectly valid reactions to what they'd just viewed.

"You stay in this tent," one of the guards barked. "You stay quiet, you don't try anything. We all stay happy."

The group nodded and mumbled in agreement before being herded inside where they took up their usual positions

– the Dixons huddled together on one of the church pews, Castillo on another, Michael Day standing tall and composed. But Price, who was normally so animated and full of nervous energy, was a shell of who he once was. He sank down to sitting on the ground. It seemed all ego and sense of self-importance had crumbled away after what he'd just witnessed.

"I have heard of that man," Castillo muttered after a long silence. "They say he is immortal. That he cannot feel pain. I thought it was just stories, but now I've seen him with my own eyes."

"Don't be ridiculous," Price scoffed. "No one is immortal. People feel pain."

"Not everyone," Day replied. "There's a condition. It's called CIPA, I think. Congenital Insensitivity to Pain. It's a rare disorder."

"Yeah, I've heard of it too," Adler added. "But it's not that those who have it are immortal, they're just not born with the nerve cells responsible for transmitting the right signals to the brain. So they can be hurt, they just don't feel it."

"Oh my Lord saviour," Bruce said and sighed, holding his wife tight. "Poor Lange didn't stand a chance against that brute. What are we going to do?"

"We're going to do nothing," Day said, giving Price a hard stare in case he was getting any other bright ideas. "For now we wait. We stay quiet. We do as they say."

"Of course... yes," Bruce said. "It's just..." He shifted uncomfortably as the group focused their attention on him.

"What is it, Bruce?" Day asked.

"Well, the thing is... I've got a bit of an issue with the old prostate and I could do with using the John. Only I don't want to rock the boat."

"Just tell them!" Castillo called out. "They will take you. We've all done it while we've been here. They understand you need to take a leak."

"I know," Bruce whispered, locking eyes with Adler as he gestured to Kathleen still shivering in his arms. "But I don't want to leave her alone after that."

"It's fine," Adler said, going over to the bench. "I'll sit with her. We'll be fine, won't we, Kathleen?"

The older woman lifted her head and nodded weakly. Her cheeks were wet with tears. "Thank you."

Adler positioned herself on the bench beside Kathleen as Bruce rose and shuffled to the door, calling out he needed to use the bathroom. A second later, a young guard entered the tent and grabbed him by the arm. Bruce just had time to give his wife an encouraging smile before he was yanked outside.

"Don't worry," Adler whispered, leaning into Kathleen. "He'll be back soon. And I'm here. We're all here."

"I just don't know what's going to happen to us," Kathleen said. "I know I'm sick, but I've enough of myself left to know I don't want to end up like that poor young man."

"You won't. I promise."

Kathleen looked at her with pale, watery eyes. "How can you say that? How can you be so sure?"

Adler swallowed. "Listen, the US government won't just leave us here," she said, lowering her voice. "There are protocols in place for situations like this."

Kathleen leaned back. "But... they don't negotiate with terrorists," she stammered.

Adler leaned in closer, whispering. "Officially yes, that's the stance. Presidential Policy Directive 30 reaffirms the US's longstanding commitment to make no concessions to individuals or groups holding US nationals hostage. But I know for a fact that isn't always the case. PPD-30 also commits the government to utilise all instruments of national power to safely recover hostages."

She sat back and observed Kathleen, who wiped at her eyes and pulled in a long stuttering breath. "In a nutshell," she added, "what that means is – sometimes they do negotiate."

"I really hope so, dear."

"I know so. Last year the current administration transferred six billion dollars in Iranian oil revenue that was being held in restricted accounts in South Korea – that was in return for the release of six hostages. They also granted clemency to five Iranians imprisoned in the US. So it does happen. Often. You're going to get out of here, Kathleen. I promise."

She was going against all protocols, sharing such information, but the old woman was distraught and seemed to find comfort in her explanation.

Bruce returned to the tent and she gave Kathleen's hand a final squeeze before rising to allow him to take her place on the bench. Walking over to the side of the tent, she stretched her arms above her head, sensing Day watching her. She didn't look directly at him, but she wasn't surprised when out of the corner of her eye she noticed him coming over.

"You know an awful lot about US foreign policy and decision-making," he said. "For a journalist, I mean."

She turned to him. His eyes were sharp and alert but his expression neutral. She felt a twinge of apprehension. "All the best journalists are well-informed."

"I'm sure they are."

"You think you know otherwise?" she asked, folding her arms.

# A World of Sun and Violence

Day's expression didn't change, but his eyes held a knowing glint. "Right now I'm almost certain I know otherwise." He paused and glanced around the room before lowering his voice. "My guess is CIA. NCS, more specifically. The journalist thing is a cover, as is the name Julia Gray."

Adler narrowed her eyes a touch, not wanting to give anything away. "Interesting. Go on."

"Okay. You're possibly working the Venezuelans, but my guess is your target has been the ELC all along. Clearly, there's something new afoot but I'm not sure what it is yet. These people seem chaotic and rudderless – and for a militia group with far-reaching contacts who have been operating for a good few years, that's odd."

"I see." Adler met his gaze squarely, a silent challenge passing between them. "And what's your story, Michael Day?"

"I'm a backpacker, like I told you."

"Come on. I told you my story."

"No, you didn't. I guessed. You haven't confirmed anything."

She didn't take her eyes off the Englishman, wondering how much she could divulge. There were aspects of her mission he didn't know and she could never tell anyone. But if she shared a little more, he might do the same. Chances were he'd see through this tactic, yet in her experience it was a method that worked regardless. An unspoken understanding.

"Are you ex-military?" she asked him. "I need to know."

Day considered that for a second, then gave her the briefest of nods. "Ex-British Secret Service actually," he whispered.

She nodded, having suspected as much. "Quite the coincidence, isn't it? That we're both here."

"I call it bad luck, that's all. I'm ex-everything these days and I really was backpacking. I was supposed to be at Angel Falls."

"Okay," she said, casting her attention around the room. "Let's say you're mostly correct. I've been in Venezuela for the last few months, information gathering on the ELC and trying to get close to Jalen Murcia. The agency is worried about the possibility of a coup in Colombia. Murcia has links to our enemies all over the world and if he seizes power it could destabilise the region and take us back twenty years."

Day raised his head. He looked deep in thought.

"Now it's your turn," Adler told him.

He sighed. "All I'm prepared to say is that I was once part of an off-the-books section of MI6."

"Once?" Adler repeated. "But not anymore?"

"No. I can't – and won't – say too much. Events transpired against me around this time last year and I had to make myself scarce. You need to know I'm not a traitor. But I've annoyed a lot of people, on both sides of the Atlantic. Your people and mine."

"So... what? You're a defector?"

"No. I'm a backpacker. That's the truth. I'm out. Forced out perhaps, but out all the same. My hands were tied. I did what I had to do to save people I cared about." He stared into her eyes, not blinking. "I'm one of the good guys, I assure you. But as you're aware, there are a lot of grey areas in our line of work."

Adler didn't respond straight away, but her gut feeling was that she believed him, and she was glad of that fact. She needed an ally; someone she could talk to. Because right now she was worried. With the coup imminent she wondered how long the ELC would require hostages. And then what?

"I take it Gray is an alias?" Day said.

"Yes."

He carried on looking at her and grinned. "You don't have to tell me... but I won't tell. I can't."

Adler looked away and shook her head. It was potentially dangerous to share her identity with this man, but in her line of work she had to be a good judge of character and she trusted him. Besides, the more she shared, the more she might get in return.

"Fine," she whispered. "It's Adler. Vanessa Adler. But that's between us. In here I'm Julia Gray."

"Of course. Adler. Right." He frowned and tilted his head to one side. "No relation, though...?"

She felt sick suddenly. "No! Hell, no!" She looked away. "Don't make me regret telling you all this. I trust you."

"You won't regret it,' he said, but as she glanced back she didn't like the way he was looking at her.

"And what about you?" she asked. "Is Michael Day your real name?"

He grinned. "Sorry, I can't do it. If – when – we get out of here, I can't risk my name coming up in a debrief."

"Hey!" she snapped. "I just told you everything. My name. The fact that I work for the agency. I think I deserve a name, at least."

Day nodded, about to say more when a scuffling noise behind her alerted them both. Adler spun around to see Price standing a few feet away with a look of intense hatred on his face.

"You're fucking CIA?" he hissed. "I knew it! I knew you weren't a journalist."

"What the...?" Adler raised her hands in an effort to shush him down. "I am a journalist. I don't know what you heard, but—"

"Bullshit! I knew it! I was already suspicious after I mentioned Robert Marple. He hasn't worked at the New York Times for over a year. You'd have known that. And now this! You're bloody CIA!"

Adler felt a surge of panic. "Keep your voice down," she hissed, her heart racing. "We're in a very delicate situation."

But Price, now visibly agitated, turned to the group. "She's not who she says she is. She's a spy. She works for the CIA."

Adler locked eyes with Day, a silent plea for understanding passing between them. He stepped forward, confronting Price. "Shut your damn mouth," he snarled. "That's not helpful."

But everyone had heard.

"Are you here to help us?" Kathleen asked her. "I don't understand."

"I knew it, too," Castillo announced. "There was something off about you, Julia Gray."

"Okay, listen," Adler said, moving in front of the group. "Yes, I work for the US government. I've been working undercover in Venezuela for the past six weeks. But we can't let the rebels find out. Once my people realise I'm missing, they'll do what they can to secure our release – all of us. We're going to get out of this mess, but we have to work together." She shot Price a look, which he acknowledged with a nod. "As far as anyone is concerned, my name is Julia Gray and I'm a freelance journalist at The Times."

"But you can help us?" Bruce asked.

"I'll do everything I can," she told him.

## A World of Sun and Violence

She glanced around the tent, meeting each person's gaze. No one looked particularly convinced or reassured by her admission but at least they'd calmed down. For now.

Returning to sit on the ground at the opposite end of the tent, she was glad when Day came to join her. His voice when he spoke was low but firm. "Keeping this from them is crucial," he said, nodding towards the entrance. He then shifted his attention to Price. "He won't be a problem. I'll keep an eye on him."

"Thank you." She looked down at her hands. She was shaking. "If they find out…"

"I know. Same goes for me."

She shuffled closer to him. For a mad moment she wished he could put his arms around her. He was both an ally and a comfort, and it had been a tough couple of days. "I'm sorry."

"Why?" he asked. "This isn't your fault. None of us are at fault. Let's remember who the enemy is here."

She sucked in a deep breath. "You're right." He was watching her carefully, maybe checking she was holding it together. Which she was. Or she would be if his eyes weren't so piercingly blue, and if she hadn't sat so close to him. They stared at each other for a few seconds, the heightened energy and proximity between them fizzing with a mixture of shared understanding and awkwardness. "I think you were about to tell me your name," she managed to say at last.

"Was I?"

"I'm pretty sure you were."

He rubbed his chin. "Maybe later. But once we're out of here, you'll need to forget everything you know about me. I mean it."

She glanced around at their fellow hostages. "Do you really believe we'll get out of here?"

"I have to." He grinned. Adler attempted one in return but it felt forced. In the shadow of Lange's brutal death, everything was now hanging in the balance, and with the added stress of her identity being revealed she felt unstable and scared. She closed her eyes, allowing herself a moment to gather her thoughts. She hoped her people would come through, that they'd all be rescued like she'd told the others.

But right now, it could go either way.

## Chapter Twenty-Seven

The sun was setting over the prison yard as General Jalen Murcia showered and changed his clothes, opting for a pair of cream trousers and a white linen shirt. Now ready for the evening, he sauntered into the front room of his living quarters. It had been a long day, fraught with moments of disappointment and frustration, but it had also provided clarity.

Murcia had long suspected Peroza's management of the prison was deteriorating into disorder and today's events had confirmed this. Now he was faced with a decision: restructure the operation here and bring it back in line; or shift his focus entirely to the new site, and transfer his old friend into a less volatile role. It would be a lateral move, perhaps to a backroom position in Colombia, or even a less hands-on administrative role. The alternative, of course, was a more permanent solution to the Peroza problem.

It wasn't that Murcia didn't trust his old comrade, but Peroza was the same loose cannon he'd always been, with a belly full of chaos and an insatiable appetite for rebellion. His exuberant and wicked personality had been invaluable during their rise, but as the ELC transitioned towards being a political entity and prepared for a military coup, the old firebrand's skillset was fast becoming at best obsolete and at worst a liability.

Murcia knew he had much to consider, and he always did that best with a little lubrication. He approached the drinks cabinet in the corner of the room and opened the leaf doors to reveal an array of high-quality spirits. The cabinet was well-stocked, as it should be, something that Murcia still insisted on despite his now infrequent visits to the prison. He had always been a man of refined taste, but as his star continued to rise, his desire for the finer things in life only grew stronger. This duality – a revolutionary with a penchant for luxury – was not lost on him. Yet, for Murcia, the revolution had always been a means to an end. He loved his country and knew he could elevate it to prodigious heights, but he had no desire to remain lowly and in the shadows once he ascended to power.

He leaned into the cabinet, his fingers tracing the labels as he surveyed his collection. He paused on a 22-year-old Aston Martin Bowmore, a fine whisky, yet somehow not fitting for this moment. Moving on, he selected a bottle of Suntory's Yamazaki 18-Year-Old Single Malt. Now this was a whisky. It retailed for well over a thousand dollars online, but this particular bottle was part of a gift from the head of Los Cachiros – the Honduran criminal organisation that had recently donated a significant sum to the ELC under the condition their exports to Colombia would continue uninterrupted once Murcia came to power.

He picked up a cut-crystal glass from the lower shelf and was about to return to the couch when he heard a commotion outside. A moment later the door swung open and Peroza strode in.

"I'm sorry, sir, he wouldn't stop," his security guard told him.

"It's fine," Murcia said, dismissing him with a wave before turning to Peroza. "What, you don't knock anymore?"

Peroza spread his arms wide in a shrug. "It's been so long since you were last here, I forgot myself."

The two men held each other's gaze for a moment, neither wanting to look away first.

"Drink?" Murcia asked him, holding up the bottle, choosing to take the higher ground.

"Why not?"

Murcia picked up a second glass and walked over to the couch. Sitting, he placed the glasses on the coffee table in front of him and filled them with the amber liquid, the rich aroma filling the air.

"Come. Sit." He gestured to the second leather couch beside his, masking his displeasure at the disturbance with practised ease. "Let us talk. It has been so long."

Peroza sat and accepted the drink. They clinked glasses. "*Viva la revolución!*"

They drank, Murcia's initial irritation fading as he savoured the whisky's subtle and complex flavours. Yet there was plenty that needed saying and now was as good a time as any.

"You know, Victor, I am a little concerned with how things are being managed here in my absence." He settled back into the couch, which creaked under his weight. "I know you have your ways of doing things and they have worked well in the past, but now I feel there is a disconnect between our actions and the image we need to present. Very soon the whole world will be looking at us and we must be ready to meet that scrutiny in every conceivable way."

Peroza nodded and snorted derisively as if he'd known this was coming. "You worry too much what the world thinks of you, brother," he replied. "We are fighters. We wear the clothing of war even now. Come the revolution maybe this will change, but let's not get ahead of ourselves. Our victory isn't secured yet."

Murcia sipped at his drink. "I'm aware, but with our recent discovery and the potential of the new site we have the opportunity to move things forward quicker than we had planned." He hesitated, wondering if it was a bad idea to say what was on his mind. But it was important. "I am not pleased with the current state of affairs here, Victor. Your approach is too chaotic, too savage. This is not the way a legitimate party should be operating. I mentioned when we spoke last month that with the new site operational, we need to phase out all illicit activities – drugs, guns, hostage-taking."

"Yes, phase out, not stop entirely. Not yet at least!" Peroza sat forward as if to drive his point across. "We're not financially stable enough to forgo the revenue from these *activities*. Lugo has already uploaded two of the hostage videos and forwarded links to the British and American embassies. You agreed that we would continue with this batch of hostages."

Murcia raised an eyebrow. "And if we don't?"

Peroza opened his mouth to reply but hesitated, struggling for the right words.

"I know what I said," Murcia pressed on. "But I've reconsidered my stance. Our priority is legitimacy above all else. No more hostages."

"But the ones we are holding will fetch a good price. As you requested, we left out any mention of the ELC in the recordings. As far as the British and Americans are concerned, their people are being held by some unknown militia group in North Venezuela. Now that we request all ransoms be paid in crypto coin, it is untraceable. We get the money with no blowback on the ELC. It is perfect. You shall see, we will—"

"I do not like it!" Murcia snapped. "This is not how we should be operating. We are not thugs, we are not a rogue militia group – not anymore. We're on the brink of taking back our country, brother. The goal we have been working towards for over ten years is in our sights. If your efforts were as focused on the new site as they are on kidnappings and betting on illegal fights, we could be operational in a month. There is no reason why we can't be at full capacity within six months. This time next year we will have more money coming to us than we ever dreamed of. We can buy an entire army. We can reclaim Colombia. It will all be mine... and yours, brother. We will have our country back."

Peroza finished his drink and placed his glass down on the table. Though he appeared contemplative, Murcia knew his old friend's temperament too well. He could sense the anger simmering beneath the surface. Peroza was a man of action, lacking the patience and subtlety required for their new direction. It troubled Murcia a great deal, but it was something he would confront in due course. He finished his drink and refilled his glass.

"These current hostages will be our last," he said. "Soon we won't need ransom money. We'll have more than enough."

Peroza sneered. "Well, perhaps we should just kill them then."

"Perhaps you should." Murcia raised his glass. "A clean slate. I heard you had trouble with one of them."

"Nothing I couldn't handle." Slapping his thighs, Peroza got to his feet. "If we're done here, I have work to do."

Murcia leaned back. "I'm serious, Victor. The times are changing. You have to change with them or be left behind."

Peroza didn't respond as he headed for the door. But Murcia wasn't finished yet. "If the hostages cause any more trouble," he called after him, "I want you to kill them."

Peroza paused, turning back with a look of surprise. "You *want* me to kill them? You're serious?"

"I am," he replied, the finality in his voice unmistakable. "We don't need them. Any more problems – do it. I don't care how. You, Bracho, it doesn't matter. Just get rid of them. Like I say, we need a clean slate. And soon."

## Chapter Twenty-Eight

Bracho didn't like sunshine. He hated it, in fact. Not being able to sense temperature meant it wasn't the heat that bothered him, but that he was unable to sweat like other people, which meant his body couldn't cool itself properly. A few hours in the sunshine often left him weary and feverish. On a few occasions he'd suffered seizures.

Despite not being able to properly articulate it, Bracho knew he was different from other people, and not just in his appearance. He'd had doctors prodding and poking at him on more than one occasion, especially after Victor took him under his wing. They used long, complicated words like 'hyperpyrexia' and 'osteomyelitis', and phrases he just about understood, like 'thick, leathery skin' and 'inability to feel pain'. But whilst Bracho didn't know the concepts of pain or heat, and would never experience them the way other people did, he knew the sun gave him a hard time and so he avoided it as much as possible. This was why during daylight hours he stayed inside his hut, sleeping or watching the television Victor had given him. Most nights were spent walking around the prison grounds or doing his exercises in the yard.

But after being made to fight in front of the new people, he'd been exhausted and had drifted off to sleep as soon as the sun went down. He'd been dreaming about swimming in the ocean, something he'd never done. In his dreams it felt strange but wonderful. He felt light and airy and unencumbered by his mangled, callused body.

He felt free.

That was until a sound woke him.

Opening his eyes, he sat up and glanced around the dim interior of his hut. The television was still on, showing some grainy soccer game. He rarely had the volume up very high and over the static buzz from the set he heard footsteps outside, then voices.

For a moment he felt a surge of excitement, thinking it might be one of the men who brought him food. But his anticipation turned to dismay and even a little dread as the curtain was drawn aside and the one they called General Murcia stepped into the hut. He was followed by another man, who Bracho didn't recognise.

"Good evening, Bracho." General Murcia greeted him with a big smile on his face, but it didn't look like a happy smile.

Bracho hated General Murcia, the one with the loud voice and neat hair, who always looked at him with hate in his eyes and forced him to do things he didn't like doing. He used to come to the prison often to meet with Victor, but he hadn't visited for a long time. Bracho had hoped he was dead and that he'd never have to see him again.

"Here he is," General Murcia told his friend, his words slurring as he spoke. "Bracho. The prized fighter. The attack dog. The Beast."

## A World of Sun and Violence

The other man stared at Bracho with an open mouth. He had short hair and smooth skin but the same cruel glint in his eyes as General Murcia. "Whoa. And the rumours are true?"

"Oh yes." General Murcia swayed slightly as he moved into the centre of Bracho's hut, his friend following close behind. A strange smell hung around him, mixing with the musty air in the already cramped space.

Bracho straightened up, eyeing the two men warily. He wanted them to leave, to not bother him tonight, to leave him be, but his heart sank as he noticed the Taser in General Murcia's hand.

"It's true, he feels no pain," General Murcia said, speaking out the corner of his mouth. "You can do anything to him and he doesn't care. It makes him a good fighter." He stepped closer and tilted his head to one side, grinning at Bracho in the way people did when they were trying to make you feel uncomfortable. "But he is also retarded, like a child, and he consumes a lot of resources. I don't want Peroza to keep him around much longer. He is not what we want to be associated with. But for now... hmm... he has his uses."

General Murcia flicked the Taser towards Bracho as if he were going to zap him, then abruptly stopped and chuckled to himself.

Bracho knew not to go near the Taser. While it couldn't hurt him, it made his body shake uncontrollably and stopped his legs and arms working properly. Victor had used one until Bracho learnt not to get so angry and do what he was told. He liked Victor. He didn't like General Murcia. He'd always been mean and horrible to him, just like the boys in the orphanage. He shifted uncomfortably, the memories of his harsh past creeping into his mind. The taunts, the beatings, the feeling of helplessness — all these emotions resurfacing as he stared into General Murcia's eyes.

"Just look at the pathetic creature," Murcia slurred, waving his hand in Bracho's face. "He might be strong, but he sure is an ugly bastard."

Bracho's eyes narrowed, but he remained silent as General Murcia pulled a small knife from his pocket and tossed it on the ground in front of him. "Show my guard here your little party trick," he sneered. "Go on. Stab yourself in the leg."

Bracho stared at the knife, his muddled mind trying to deal with the indignity of the command. He hesitated, his gaze drifting from the knife to the Taser, before reaching out with his good hand and picking up the blade. With a resigned grunt, he plunged the knife into his thick, scarred thigh, just above his knee. He didn't flinch. He didn't cry out. He didn't feel anything but a slight sensation of pressure.

General Murcia burst into laughter and a second later his guard joined in, both of them echoing the cruel jibes of his childhood bullies. "Incredible, isn't it?" General Murcia said, slapping the other man on the back. "He's a real-life freak of nature."

Bracho pulled the knife out of his thigh. The place where he'd stabbed it was already covered in callused skin so there wasn't much blood to deal with. He felt the sting of humiliation. That was all.

General Murcia, still chuckling, took a step closer. "You know, Bracho," he said, waving the Taser in front of him, "you're quite the asset. But remember, you're just a tool. Don't ever think you're more than that."

"Leave me," Bracho growled, not looking away. Despite

# A World of Sun and Violence

his limited understanding, he could sense the belittling nature of General Murcia's words. This cruelty wasn't new to Bracho, but each time they met, he left the encounter feeling confused and wretched.

"He talks!" the younger guard said. "I didn't know that!"

"Sometimes he does. Not so much though," Murcia replied. "He has nothing useful to say. You're lucky we found you, aren't you, Bracho? Without us you'd be nothing but a street rat, forgotten and alone."

Bracho remained silent, his thoughts clouded. But thankfully it seemed General Murcia was growing bored. He usually did after a few minutes. Sighing heavily, he grabbed his friend by the shoulder and gestured for the door.

"Get some sleep," he told Bracho. "We might have some use for your... talents soon enough." With a final dismissive glance he turned and stumbled out of the hut, his guard trailing behind him.

Left alone once more, Bracho stared at the television set for a few moments, watching as one of the soccer players kicked the ball into the baying crowd. Then he settled down on his tattered old blanket, and closed his eyes.

## Chapter Twenty-Nine

Dick Foster sat in his office at Langley, his gaze fixed on the door. The room about him, lined with neutral-coloured walls and sparse furnishings, echoed the no-nonsense approach of Foster himself. A dark mahogany desk took up almost a quarter of the room, with Dick's chair in front of the window and two more facing him on the other side. On his right was a bookcase made from the same wood as the desk, and on his left a row of black metal filing cabinets. A secure laptop sat open on the desk, its blue light illuminating his tense features.

Leaning back in his chair, he briefly closed his eyes, exhaling slowly. Dick Foster was a man who always had a lot on his mind, but the escalating situation in Central America, compounded by the lack of contact from Adler, gnawed at his resolve. Add to that mix Xander Templeton – who was still breathing down his neck regarding a security breach in London, and the looming threat from The Consortium – and it felt as if the scales could tip at any moment. It wasn't a good sign.

The click of the door handle broke his concentration and he opened his eyes to see Goldsmith entering the room. His chief of staff's usual stoic expression had been replaced with one of concern.

That wasn't a good sign either.

Foster sat upright, his hands clasped together in front of him on the desk. "What is it?" he asked, his eyes searching the younger man's face for clues.

Goldsmith looked around, ensuring the door was shut before speaking. "It's about Adler, sir."

"I see." Following their meeting with Lou Simmons, he'd asked Goldsmith to put out some feelers and get an update on Adler's status. That they'd had no contact with her for six weeks wasn't unusual given she was deep undercover, but with growing unrest in the area he wanted reassurances. Though as Goldsmith hesitated before answering, his gut told him he wasn't going to get them.

"This morning a recording of her surfaced on an encrypted site on the dark web," Goldsmith said in a low voice.

"What sort of recording?"

"A ransom plea," Goldsmith replied quickly, raising his hand to indicate there was no immediate cause for alarm. "She's alive, appears healthy and unharmed."

Foster's gaze remained fixed on Goldsmith, urging him to continue. "Who has her? The ELC? The ELN?"

"That's the thing. There's no mention of any organisation and the metadata on the upload doesn't give us much to go on. They sent the link to our embassy in Bogotá via a masked email address."

"Shit."

Four years earlier the US had rejected Maduro's proposal to elect Turkey as a 'protecting power' for the

Venezuelan embassy in Washington. In retaliation, he'd forced them to close the US embassy in Caracas. A 'Venezuela Affairs Unit' had been established at the US embassy in Colombia to serve as an interim diplomatic office to Venezuela, but this fact only made things more volatile, and acted as a stark reminder to Foster that whatever they did next had to be done with a light touch.

"Can I see the recording?" Foster asked, pushing his chair back and gesturing at his laptop. Goldsmith moved around the desk and swiftly brought up the site in question.

"It's a close shot with few pointers to go off," he warned, stepping back as the video began to play.

Foster leaned forward, eyes narrowing as he focused on the grainy image onscreen. It was Adler all right, her face recognisable even in the low-resolution footage. The room she was in had concrete walls and a single light source that cast deep shadows on her face. She was sitting in a metal chair, her posture upright and controlled, but Foster noticed a tautness in the muscles around her eyes and mouth that hinted at the stress she was under.

*"My name is Julia Gray. I am thirty-one years old. I am a citizen of the United States of America…"*

Foster sat back as the recording continued. Adler's tone was steady, betraying no hint of fear despite the dire circumstances. She'd been trained well. She was a good officer. Her skin was darker than usual, from a mixture of dirt and sun, and her hair was frizzy and unwashed, but she appeared to be unhurt as Goldsmith had said. Importantly, there was no discernible sign of duress or coercion in her manner.

Adler went on to state that she was being treated well and that her captors demanded a ransom of a hundred thousand

US dollars, to be paid into a Petro wallet. Petro was the cryptocurrency du jour for criminal organisations in Latin America, having been specifically designed to circumvent US and EU sanctions, and with a value transfer only usable between Venezuela and Russia through Russian banks.

The recording ended with Adler informing the viewer they had a month to transfer the ransom – after which, the screen went black. The entire message had lasted a mere ninety seconds and once it ended Foster reached over and closed the laptop.

"Thoughts?"

Goldsmith cleared his throat. "She's maintaining her alias, sir, but the situation is precarious. Even if we had her location pinpointed, any extraction mission must be approached with caution. We can't afford to upset the Venezuelans."

"Have we received any other form of contact from her captors?" Foster asked, his mind flicking through possible scenarios. "Why don't we know who they are?"

"I'm not sure, sir. As you saw, it's similar to recordings we've received in the past from the likes of the ELN and ELC, as well as other militia groups operating in the area. But this one pledges no allegiance to any cause or provides any information on who her captors are. It's an anomaly in that regard."

"And potential locations?"

Goldsmith grimaced. "Nothing certain yet. We're presuming she's still in Venezuela and we have a list of possibilities. I'll keep you updated. Should I prep a team in the meantime?"

"Yes, but hold them back for now. I need to think through our options."

Goldsmith hesitated. "There's the other issue, sir. The senator…"

Foster sighed, feeling exhausted all of a sudden. "Yes, Mark, I'm aware. That's why this particular situation is so precarious."

"Adler knew what the mission entailed. We all did." Goldsmith glanced at the floor. "Do you want me to contact him?"

"No. I'll speak to him personally. It's the least I can do."

"Very good, sir." Goldsmith backed away, ready to leave, but paused at the door. "Sir, if we don't act soon—"

"I'm aware of the stakes," Foster snapped, cutting him off. "Let me handle the senator first. This is delicate, and we need to play it just right."

Goldsmith left the room. As the door closed behind him Foster closed his eyes, his head swirling, fogged with the countless decisions he had to make.

First, before anything else, he had to speak to the senator. It was the last thing he wanted to do this morning but he'd written Adler's risk assessment himself, it was protocol. It was also the right thing to do. He just hoped the old man took it well. But he wouldn't blame him if he didn't.

## Chapter Thirty

Beckett's muscles ached from lack of use as he trudged along the perimeter of the exercise yard. He and the other hostages had only been awake a short time. Despite the discomfort of the airless tent, they'd all been exhausted into sleep, then woken by the arrival of two guards, who took the Dixons away for another round of hostage videos, leaving the rest of them to walk the yard.

He glanced over his shoulder, taking in the weary, already reddened faces of his fellow captives. Castillo was directly behind him, with Price next and Adler keeping pace at the end of their small procession. He caught her eye briefly, giving her a knowing nod which she returned. It was hard for her too. There were a lot of variables up in the air and both of them had a lot to lose if their identities were revealed.

They'd already walked one and a half times around the prison yard – a large rectangular plot of around two hundred by one hundred metres – and were turning the corner when Beckett saw the man who'd stood behind

Peroza on the first day. He had just emerged from the building on this side of the grounds. The man was tall with dark hair and tanned skin, and he stood on the steps, watching them with his head raised and a sneer curling his lips. As the group passed by him, the guards flanking them stiffened and gave the man a sharp salute.

"General Jalen Murcia," Castillo whispered, hurrying to catch up to Beckett. "The leader of the ELC."

Beckett's eyes remained fixed on Murcia. His presence was undeniable, and it was apparent he took great care in his appearance. The crisp, khaki uniform he wore was immaculate – clean, well pressed, the polished metal buttons catching the sun. He certainly looked the part. Like the leader of a country.

"Man, if he's still here," Castillo continued, "I'd say that works well for us."

"Why do you say that?" Beckett asked.

"He's trying to be a politician," Castillo whispered. "I hear he wants to do things legally now. Well, as legal as it gets as the head of a military coup. But if he's here overseeing things, maybe he's considering releasing us. I shall pray for that, anyway."

Murcia, seemingly unaffected by the heat, watched the hostages with an intense gaze. Even from a distance, Beckett could sense his scrutiny, as if he was assessing them. But for what, and why, he didn't know. He'd heard of General Murcia, but had no direct knowledge of him. He had no idea if he was a real general, for instance.

Beckett wished he shared Castillo's optimism, but he'd been in enough perilous situations to know something was amiss. From day one he'd sensed a tension and unease in the camp, not just from the hostages but something more. Then there were those weird noises coming from the jungle, which were still audible even over Castillo's laboured breaths.

They made their way down the far side of the compound, toward Bracho's hut. Price began muttering to himself as they neared the entrance, but the curtain remained drawn and there was no sign of the beast-man.

One of the guards looked nervous as they passed the hut, and his colleague laughed. "Don't worry," he said, speaking in Spanish. "He sleeps all day. The sun bothers him."

"Ah... makes sense," Beckett muttered, almost to himself.

"How so?" Castillo asked.

Beckett shot him a look. "I remember reading how people like Bracho, those who don't feel pain, also have trouble regulating body temperature."

"That's interesting... I guess. I would say poor bastard, but... you know... he broke Lange's neck." He let out a gruff chuckle. It was gallows humour but Beckett didn't join in. "How come you read about it?" Castillo asked. "You read about weird diseases a lot?"

"I read everything. As much as I get a chance. Don't you?"

Castillo sniffed. "Nah, man. I have Netflix."

The group pressed on, the sweat dripping from them and their pace slowing under the relentless sun. Beckett was hungry and tired, and feeling more despondent than he had in a long while, but giving in to despair was not an option. As they started their third lap of the grounds he remained alert, casting his attention around them. A group of four soldiers were running exercise drills on the opposite side of the yard and two more stood guard outside both of the main buildings. Beckett had been counting heads since he arrived at the prison, observing and remembering faces, and estimated there were twelve hostiles; fifteen if he included Peroza, Lugo and Murcia. It wasn't an unreasonable number to deal with. But most of them carried assault rifles and he didn't even have a stick.

He continued to scope out the compound as they walked past the outbuildings, searching for any security weaknesses. His attention kept returning to the two gates on either side of the prison yard. They were tall, each comprising double swing-hinge doors constructed out of steel bars and aged wood. They appeared sturdy, but they were old and didn't look to have been serviced in a long time. With the right explosives, he speculated, they could be breached. But he also had no explosives.

His gaze shifted to the largest of the three outbuildings. Today was his first opportunity to closely inspect this side of the compound, and as he had thought, the building appeared to be the camp's primary storage facility. The doors were securely locked but there were tracks in the sand outside, as if crates had been dragged in and out. Big, heavy crates, from the size and depth of the tracks. The indents also seemed relatively fresh, suggesting it was in frequent use.

The building likely contained food and medical supplies, but potentially more valuable items too. Like guns. Like gasoline. His mind buzzed with the possibilities, a collection of scenarios playing out in his head. While they were all long shots and would require a great amount of luck and good timing, they were starting points. If he could get into that outbuilding and have a look around, they might have a fighting chance.

"We have to stop. I think I'm going to faint."

Beckett looked around as Price's high-pitched whine

broke his concentration. Regardless of their shared kinship, he found himself increasingly irritated by Price, but he did have a point. The group were exhausted and dehydrated. "I need rest and some water!" Price insisted.

The guards gave him a hard stare before mumbling to each other in Spanish. Finally, one of them jerked his head over to the large awning where they'd gathered the day before. "Follow me," he said.

The group, sapped of energy and drenched in sweat, trudged towards the canvas shade. Once there, they were relieved to find a simple meal of cornbread, fruit and some cured meat laid out for them, along with four one-litre bottles of fresh water.

"Thank God!" Price rushed for a bottle and glugged half of it down in one go. Beckett and the others followed his lead. The water was lukewarm but refreshing all the same.

"I saw you checking out the outbuilding over there," Adler whispered, sidling up to him. "Be careful. If I noticed, so could they. If they think you're planning something…"

"No one else saw," he replied. "I made sure of it." He picked up a piece of cornbread and bit off a large chunk, chewing it as he continued scoping the area. The guards, disinterested and bored, lounged at their posts, their rifles hanging loosely in their hands, but they were young and eager and Beckett had to assume they'd be fast to draw their weapons if one of them tried anything.

"So… are you?" Adler asked. "Planning something, I mean."

"I wish I were." He turned to look at her. "What about you? Any ideas strike you on our walk?"

She shrugged and picked up a banana from the table. "I'd like to get inside that outbuilding too."

Beckett observed Adler closely. She was undeniably attractive, with large expressive eyes and a cute nose that turned up a little at the end. But looking at her now, lost in her thoughts with her mouth twisted to one side, it hit him like a slap to the face.

*Of course…*

He'd suspected it yesterday when he'd asked her about her name. She'd turned away, physically deflecting the question. But now he knew for certain.

*Shit.*

*No wonder she was tense. If they found that out…*

"They're back!"

Looking up, Beckett saw Kathleen and Bruce coming their way, with Peroza and Lugo flanking them. He and Adler instinctively moved apart as they came closer. The Dixons had been gone a long time, longer than it had taken for Adler and Price to record their videos. Kathleen's face was streaked with tear tracks and Bruce looked green.

"What is it?" Price asked, as they got under the shade. "What's happened?" His wide-eyed gaze flicked back and forth from Kathleen to Bruce, then to Peroza, searching for answers.

"Hey, calm it down," Beckett whispered, placing a hand on Price's shoulder.

"Go to hell," he spat, twisting around to glare at him. "What is it, Bruce? Tell us what happened, what did they make you do?"

Peroza chuckled to himself as Bruce shook his head. "We had to do a video," he said quietly. "To the folks back home. The both of us together…" His last few words were drowned out as Kathleen began to sob. Beckett tightened his grip on Price as Bruce continued. "We had to say… they

## A World of Sun and Violence

made us say... that they'll execute us if they don't get what they want."

"I knew it!" Price shrugged Beckett off and stepped towards Peroza. "You didn't make me say that. Why these two?"

Peroza grinned. "They are American. And also, our priorities have changed."

"How much?" Price asked him; then to Bruce: "How much do they want?"

Bruce swallowed. "A hundred thousand per head. In crypto."

Price's reaction was immediate and frantic. He cried out, turned to the group with his eyes filled with tears, then back to Peroza. "You're going to kill us if you don't get the ransom money in time?"

"Of course," Peroza replied with cold indifference. "What did you think would happen?"

Price's panic reached a fever pitch. "No. You can't do that. I'm a journalist. It's not right. It's not fair." But his desperate pleas only made Peroza chuckle. Price shuffled closer to him. "Listen to me, I can help you. I swear. I have important information if you let me go."

Beckett's hands curled into fists. He shot a glance at Adler.

*Don't do it, Price.*
*It's not worth it.*

But it was too late. "You have a mole," Price announced. "There's a spy in your midst!"

Beckett's heart sank. He wanted to grab Price, to silence him in any way possible, but he was too far away. He and Adler exchanged a grave look.

"Price, think about what you're doing," she said. "This isn't going to end well for any of us."

But Peroza's interest was piqued. "There is a spy? Here? One of you?"

Price nodded vigorously. "Yes. Now agree to let me go. My information for my freedom."

Beckett growled. "Enough, Price! Don't be reckless!"

But Price ignored him. He was beyond reason, his desire for self-preservation overriding any sense of camaraderie or logic.

"I can't die here," he whined, staring into Peroza's confused face. "There is a spy in this camp, and I'm prepared to tell you who it is. Just please, let me go!"

## Chapter Thirty-One

The atmosphere in the tent was suffocating, the air charged with static electricity.

Time seemed to grind to a stop.

Beckett stared at Adler. Her jaw was tense, the tendons in her neck bulging. She looked more scared than he'd seen her since they'd arrived. But now he understood why and it wasn't just because this idiot, Price, was ready to unmask her. That would be bad, of course, but not as bad as these people knowing who she really was.

It had come to him in a flash just now, recalling their conversation yesterday evening and the way she'd reacted when he probed about her name. He'd felt, briefly, that something was odd, but then the talk had moved on and he'd let it go. Except his instincts had known, even if his fatigued brain had taken a while to catch up.

Price, suspecting he was teetering on the edge of freedom, moved closer to Peroza as if picking a side, his weasel face a rictus of desperation.

"I want to help you," he pleaded, his voice quivering. "You need to know who you're dealing with."

Beckett's focus remained on Adler. He could almost see the wheels turning in her head, calculating the risks and consequences that might be about to unravel. If the rebels discovered her true identity they could panic and make an example of her.

"All right, enough of this bullshit," Peroza barked, as his guards moved beside him, alert and glaring at the hostages, their fingers tight on the triggers of their weapons. "Tell me who this spy is. Now!"

"You'll release me if I do?" Price asked.

Beckett was silently urging Adler to hold it together. But the heat and the tension were getting to her and she seemed to be crumbling before his eyes. Her lips parted as if ready to speak, but no sound emerged. She looked like a deer caught in the headlights.

"I will think about it," Peroza told Price.

Beckett's fists tightened. He was furious at his fellow Englishman, but with two assault rifles aimed at him, he was helpless to do anything.

Or was he?

Because at that moment Beckett realised he had another play. It was a gamble and would put him in danger, but the more he considered it, the more he knew it could work. And perhaps on many levels.

He stepped forward, drawing the attention of Peroza and the others. "It's me," he declared. "I'm the spy."

Price turned to Beckett as Castillo and the Dixons gasped in shock. "What?"

Peroza's eyes narrowed as he regarded Beckett. "You? A spy?"

Beckett could feel the eyes of the entire group, Adler

included, burning into him, but he held Peroza's gaze without flinching. He was aware of the jeopardy he was facing, but he also knew, having worked in the field, that calculated risks could be the difference between success and failure, between death and glory.

"Yes. I'm the spy."

"I don't believe you," Peroza replied, with a sneer. "You think I am stupid? We would know."

"No one thinks you're stupid," Beckett said firmly. "But what I say is true." He stepped closer, giving Price a hard stare as he did, silently warning him not to interfere. It was imperative that Peroza believed him – trusted him, even – and he couldn't have that duplicitous oaf ruining things. "Let the others go. I'll help you."

"*You* will help *me*?" Peroza scoffed. "How will you do that?"

"I used to work for the British Secret Service," he started, keeping his tone steady and his voice low. "I was a member of an elite team called Sigma Unit, a covert section of MI6. I was involved in secret operations all over the world. But no more. I am a defector. A traitor to my country. I'm on the run and I have information I can share with you, relative to many different countries. Information that could help your cause a great deal."

"Is that so?" Peroza drew a pistol from his belt and stepped up to Beckett, shoving the muzzle in his belly. Someone gasped; possibly Price, possibly Kathleen. Beckett stared forward, not moving. For a moment he thought he'd blown it. But then a grin slowly spread across Peroza's face. "Okay, let's see. You come with me. Now."

He waved his gun, gesturing at the building across from them. One of the guards appeared and shoved Beckett forward with the butt of his rifle. Keeping his pistol drawn and jammed in Beckett's side, Peroza escorted him across the dusty compound, their shadows stretching out in front of them under the burning hot sun. Beckett's heart pounded, not from fear but from the adrenaline surge of his high-stakes gambit. He knew it was a long shot, but this was no impulsive act for Beckett; it was a calculated risk, a product of his extensive training in covert operations.

As they traversed the compound's central area, their progress was interrupted by a shrill whistle and then a voice calling out to them. "Hey, Victor! Wait!"

Beckett looked over to see General Murcia, accompanied by an armed guard, striding towards them.

Peroza turned away, cursing under his breath. *"Mierda!"*

The translation was not lost on Beckett.

"What is going on here?" Murcia enquired, as he got closer. "Who is this man?"

"He is no one," Peroza replied, with a nonchalant wave of his hand. "Just another of the hostages. English. I am taking him to record a video." He offered Murcia a sly grin. "You don't care for these matters. Let me handle it."

But Beckett, seizing his chance, straightened up to engage Murcia directly. "General Murcia, I am far more than just a hostage. I'm a former operative for the British Secret Service. I have information that will be invaluable to you and your party."

Murcia's expression shifted from confusion to intrigue. Beckett observed him closely, noting the subtle arch of his eyebrow, the slight tilt of his head, both indicators of a man reviewing the scenario.

"Is this true?" he asked, turning on Peroza.

"He says so," Peroza muttered, unable to hide the irritation in his voice. "I planned to interrogate him, use some of

## A World of Sun and Violence

my trusted… methods to extract more information and verify his story."

Beckett remained silent, though he'd anticipated as much. 'Trusted methods' – meaning torture. He'd met countless men like Peroza throughout his career. Cruel, thuggish men, so conceited and paranoid they thought everyone was as twisted and deceitful as themselves.

Yet Beckett sensed Murcia was different. At least, that was what he was counting on. He was no doubt as equally cruel and egotistical as Peroza, but from what Beckett had heard and seen, he was a man with a grand vision, a forward-thinker. If he aspired to legitimise the ELC, as Castillo had suggested, then Beckett could work that.

"I possess top-secret intelligence relating to numerous administrations and ongoing operations all over the globe," he continued, focusing solely on Murcia. "My knowledge as well as my expertise would be a significant asset to you and your cause."

"Why would you do this?" Murcia asked.

"Because my country deserted me when I needed them most. The Americans want me dead and the British cast me aside. I'm a wanted man. If I go home I'm a dead man. I want the British government, as well as the Americans, to pay for what they did to me. And you can help me do that. We can help each other. If you use what I know, what I'm willing to share with you, you could fast become a significant player on the world stage."

Murcia considered this for a moment, closing his eyes in contemplation. Then he opened them, and with a decisive nod gestured for Beckett to follow.

"Come," he said. "I believe we have much to discuss."

## Chapter Thirty-Two

John Beckett was a man well-versed in thinking on his feet and adapting and surviving against all odds. He was often several steps ahead of the game, plotting, planning, ready to exploit any weakness or opportunity that might present itself. But as he followed Murcia across the prison grounds, leaving Peroza muttering indignantly in their wake, he knew he was playing with fire.

Yet there was no room now for doubt or second-guessing himself. Trained for such high-stakes scenarios, he knew this was his only viable play. By drawing attention to himself, he protected Adler's true identity, and at the same time he hoped to gain Murcia's trust and sow discord between him and Peroza, potentially destabilising their operation from within. In exchange for information, he might even be able to negotiate the release of some of the hostages.

Not that Beckett would ever disclose anything vital – in his heart he was still a soldier and would die before he did that – but he had to buy himself some time and convince

Murcia he was a valuable asset, whilst he came up with phase two of his plan.

As they reached Murcia's quarters, Beckett prepared himself for the conversation ahead. He was aware the general was sceptical of his claims and every word, every gesture, would be scrutinised.

"Would you care for a drink?" Murcia asked, leading him into the building and pointing at the cabinet opposite the door, stacked with liquor bottles.

"Thank you, I'll pass," Beckett replied, casting his attention around the room. To his left, two huge tan-leather sofas formed an 'L' shape around a low coffee table. A bookcase dominated one wall, while the others were adorned with large modern art canvases. Everything looked expensive, even down to the whisky in the drinks cabinet, a stark contrast to the austere prison camp outside.

Murcia lingered momentarily by the cabinet but decided against a drink. "Let us move into my office," he said, leading the way through an open doorway into a short corridor. Beckett followed, maintaining his focus on the general as they entered another room and Murcia took a seat behind a leather-topped desk. His office was what you'd expect: the desk, some chairs, filing cabinets, a bureau, a world map on the wall, a laptop on the desk – but they all looked to be top-of-the-range items.

"So, here we are," Murcia purred, gesturing for Beckett to take a seat opposite him at the desk.

"Indeed." Beckett settled into the chair, crossing his legs. "I appreciate you listening to what I have to say. I believe we could be of mutual benefit to each other."

"You haven't even told me your name," Murcia said.

"It's Beckett. John Beckett," he replied. There was no merit in lying about it.

"John Beckett… John Beckett," Murcia repeated, rolling the name around. "And you claim to be with the British Secret Service."

"I was. Not anymore." He allowed his lip to curl in disgust just subtly, enough that Murcia would pick up on it. "They betrayed me."

"And what makes you think I won't?"

Beckett held his gaze. "I know collaborating with you is my only chance of survival. I can't risk my government or the Americans knowing where I am. I already don't exist – officially. If you decide to execute me and the other hostages, that's one thing. If you release us, and the CIA gets its hands on me, the best I can hope for is to spend the rest of my life locked up in some black site. I don't like either of those options. I want a third one." He paused, ensuring his next words carried weight. "But I don't want anyone else to die. If I do share my knowledge with you, I need your word that the others will be released, ransom or no ransom."

Murcia laughed, his eyebrows arching in surprise. "You're in no position to make demands, John Beckett."

"I know. But I also know the value of the intelligence I possess. It's worth a lot. A hell of a lot. You want to be seen as more than just the leader of a militant group. You want diplomatic muscle, to be an influential player in the geopolitical landscape. I can help you achieve that."

Murcia reclined, a sly smile twitching at his lips. "You know, I started as nothing more than a foot soldier," he said, his eyes glassing over. "It was Peroza and I together, fighting among the ranks of the ELN. Back then it was about the struggle, the fight against what we saw as an oppressive regime. But over the years I have seen too many of my brothers die and too many mistakes made." He slammed his fist on the desk. "You see, Mr Beckett, the ELN, despite its ideals, became entangled in the same cycle of corruption it sought to eradicate. That organisation was my entire world, but then they agreed to a ceasefire and I lost all faith in them. They got too comfortable here in Venezuela. They forgot their true mission, to overthrow the corrupt regime back home. So I started my own organisation – The Colombian Liberation Party – intending to overthrow Petro's regime."

Murcia's face hardened. "We have fought hard over the years, both in Colombia and here in Venezuela where we raise finances for our insurrection back home. But as time passes, I see that we have been going about this all wrong. If we are not careful we will become no better than the ELN – just another group ready to lie down and have their bellies scratched once their snouts are in the money trough."

"And you don't want that," Beckett added.

"Exactly! I envision a new Colombia!" Murcia's voice rose with passion. "I realise now that the path to change doesn't come through bullets and bloodshed alone. It's through seizing real power. The kind that sits in government halls, not in the jungles of Venezuela."

"I agree," Beckett said. "Yet I sense some of your people are resistant to this change…"

"You mean Lieutenant Peroza?" Murcia sighed. "Victor and I were like brothers once. We fought side by side for years. We shared the same goals. But he is a revolutionary and a soldier. He might say differently, but he'd rather remain as the opposition and have something to fight against than achieve actual success. He has no flair for politics and no vision for the future."

Beckett nodded, taking in Murcia's words. It was what he had assumed – what he was hoping – might be the case.

"Now it's your turn, Mr Beckett. Tell me who you are. And explain to me what makes you so valuable."

Beckett smiled. What he said in the next few minutes would be critical. He had to convince Murcia of his worth without revealing too much.

He began by outlining his military background, including his time with the SAS, followed by Sigma Unit. He explained that S-Unit was an elite task force, whose members were handpicked from the United Kingdom's Special Forces and Defence Intelligence, and who worked covertly alongside MI6, the CIA, and Mossad.

"I've been involved in some of the biggest clandestine operations across the globe," he continued, maintaining eye contact the entire time. "I know, for instance, that there's been a lot of chatter over the last five years regarding the ELN's close relationship with Russia."

He paused, gauging Murcia's reaction. Though the man's expression remained guarded, there was a flicker of curiosity in his eyes. Beckett pressed on.

"If you plan to take Colombia by military force, then you'll need the ELN onside in some way, even if you eventually quash them completely. Having Russia in your debt will be a big help in that regard. I can give you information that you can trade in return for their assistance. The same applies to other regimes. The North Koreans, for instance. I have intelligence they would happily pay for or exchange for favours. You need these people in your corner if you're going to stand your ground on the world stage. And in terms of the UK and the US – I have firsthand knowledge of most of their current strategies, their internal conflicts, the key players. I have insights into all these aspects. Insights that could be leveraged to your advantage."

Murcia rubbed at his face, thinking. "And why should I

believe a word you say? By your own admission, you're a spy. You could be feeding me misinformation."

Beckett nodded. "Agreed. You don't have to take my word at face value, General. But consider the potential benefits. I'm offering you a unique opportunity to gain an upper hand."

"And all I have to do in return is… free the hostages."

"Yes. But I sense that kidnapping, as a tactic, is rather… below you these days anyway."

Murcia stuck out his bottom lip and gave a slow nod. "Once it was a necessary evil for financial gain, but we're fast approaching a time when such methods will be redundant. We'll soon have all the resources we need."

Beckett was about to probe further when it hit him.

*Of course.*

It all made sense now. Murcia's confidence about the future and his shift in strategy – along with the distant noise Beckett had been hearing since his arrival – could only mean one thing. He had enough experience with military coups to know that success often hinged as much on financial backing and powerful allies than the strength of your army. If he was right about Murcia's source of confidence, then soon the general would have all the finances he needed for a successful coup, more than he'd ever get from ransom money.

"But you must appreciate, I am not prepared to let them go so easily," Murcia added. "This is still Lieutenant Peroza's base of operations, and despite his questionable methods he is still part of the ELC."

"I get that it's a complex situation. But think of the bigger picture. With my intel, you'll have the ears of the world and their balls in your hands. All I ask in return is for you to let those people go free. You don't need them. You won't need me once I tell you everything I know."

"Is that so?" Murcia rubbed again at his chin, a calculated gesture as if trying to make Beckett squirm. But Beckett didn't flinch. "Your offer is tempting, Mr. Beckett. But I must first verify your identity and the veracity of your claims." He motioned to his guard standing by the door. "If you prove to be a valuable asset, I shall then consider the fate of your fellow captives. Not before."

"I understand your point but that might be a challenge," Beckett replied. "Like I said, I never officially worked for the SIS. As far as any records are concerned, my military career ended abruptly in 2008."

"Don't worry. I have the best tech team in Colombia working for me. If you are who you say you are, they'll be able to find out, and we'll talk again. If you're not… well, we won't."

He spoke to his guard in Spanish, who then placed a hand on Beckett's shoulder and instructed him to stand.

"Peroza is a loose cannon," Beckett added, as he got to his feet. "And what got you to this stage won't get you to the next one. You need a different approach. I think you know that."

Murcia smirked but said no more, dismissing him with a flick of his hand. As Beckett was escorted from the building, he ran a quick assessment of the situation. He knew that playing to Murcia's ambitions was key, but there were numerous other variables he couldn't control. If Peroza realised his plan to undermine him, the situation could go wrong very quickly. He had to shift the needle, move into a proactive position. But it wouldn't be easy.

Striding across the compound back to the holding tent,

## A World of Sun and Violence

he could hear the clinking noise in the distance. But he knew what it was now. And he knew what it meant.

Soon Murcia would have all the financial power required and would no longer have use for the hostages. He could free them; it would be the simplest option. But whilst Murcia may have illusions of legitimacy, Beckett had noted the latent cruelty in his eyes. He could just as easily execute the hostages and remove the problem that way. Likewise, Beckett might have his ear for now, but he wasn't prepared to give him any useful intelligence; and if his plan to stir up a mutiny within the prison failed, then Murcia wouldn't hesitate to execute him as well.

Right now it was all still to play for. But the more he knew of the situation, the more he realised that his life and the lives of his fellow hostages were balancing on a knife edge.

## Chapter Thirty-Three

Adler was angry. She was also worried and nauseous and filled with just a trace of dread. But mainly she was angry. Now back in the holding tent, she kept glaring over at Price.

*That dumb bastard.*

He'd endangered them all and possibly signed their death warrants. And for what? Did he really think someone like Peroza was going to show leniency and let him go free?

Murcia was the thinker of the organisation, the tactician, the trailblazer. It made him more dangerous in some ways than his brutish counterpart, but at least he understood the game of war, he could be reasoned with. The more she saw of Peroza, the more she knew he was the sort of man who just wanted to blow things up. There was that old saying – one man's freedom fighter is another's terrorist. Peroza was a terrorist through and through.

The stifling heat in the tent seemed to be amplifying everyone's anxieties, transforming the canvas shelter into an unbearable pressure cooker. Rather than wind herself up focusing on Price, Adler walked over and sat beside the

Dixons, who offered her some semblance of comfort with their worried, empathetic eyes.

"I'm sure Mike will be okay," Bruce said. "He's a good guy. He's tough. Clever."

"I know." She forced a smile.

"What's going on, dear?" Kathleen whispered, leaning over her husband. "Do you know?"

Adler hesitated, taking in the older woman's harried expression. Maybe it was time to come clean. Either way, she couldn't carry on like this any longer.

Steeling herself with a deep breath, she got to her feet. "Okay, listen, everyone." She raised her voice enough to be heard by those in the tent but not the guards outside. "It's me. I'm the spy. I work for the CIA as a deep-cover operative. I was in Venezuela gathering intel when I was captured. Now I need your trust and cooperation. We still have a chance to get out of this alive, but we need to start working together."

Her gaze darted between Price and Castillo as she said this. They were both staring open-mouthed at her. Price looked away.

"You can help us get out of here?" Castillo asked.

"Oh, thank God!" Kathleen added.

Adler turned to the older couple. "I'll try, but we have to all be on the same page in this. Price, do you understand? What happened today can't happen again. When Mike gets back, we need to be a solid team. No more division or trying to save your skin at the expense of others. I mean it."

"You really think Day is coming back?" Price asked, his nasal tone dripping with sarcasm.

"Yes. I do!" Adler said, but she wasn't sure which one of them she was trying to convince the most.

The truth was she was concerned about the enigmatic

Englishman. She kept going over his recent admission, the shock of it, and the implication. She'd suspected he was more than he claimed, perhaps Special Forces, but him being part of an elite MI6 unit had taken her by surprise. It seemed he was the real deal.

*Or was he?*

He was certainly savvy enough that he could be playing her at her own game, sharing a secret to gain a secret. Yet the connection she felt with him was undeniable and the unspoken understanding they'd shared from day one hinted he was for real.

"Well thank the lord you're here!" Bruce exclaimed, pulling her from her thoughts. "Once the CIA know you've been captured, they'll come get us all out of here, right?"

Adler glanced briefly at Price and Castillo, then back to the Dixons.

*I wish that were true, Bruce.*

*Unfortunately, it's not as easy as that.*

Her thoughts were interrupted once more as the tent flap rustled open. A collective sigh of relief drifted around the space as Day stepped inside.

Adler rushed over to him. "Thank God you're alive!" She wanted to hug him but stopped herself, already a little embarrassed by her outburst. She stepped away, composing herself as she looked him up and down. "Did they hurt you? What happened?"

Day remained unruffled, his presence instantly calming the tent's charged atmosphere. He spotted Price at the back of the tent and strode over to him.

"No. Please!" Price gasped, covering his face with his hands. "I was scared. I wasn't thinking straight... I'm sorry..."

Day's fists clenched, the muscles in his forearms rippling.

"You idiot," he snarled. "You think throwing one of us to the wolves is going to save your neck with these people?"

"I didn't... I wasn't..." Stumbling over his words, Price backed away further until the back of his knee hit the edge of the wooden bench, causing him to tumble awkwardly to the ground. Day stood over him and shook his head.

"You're not worth it," he said, pointing a finger at him. "So we're good. But don't you dare pull another stunt like that."

Price nodded frantically as Day turned and walked back towards Adler.

"We need to talk," he whispered.

Adler followed him to a quiet corner of the tent. "What is it?" she asked, once they were out of earshot.

"Peroza was planning to torture me for information, but Murcia showed up and I managed to leverage the situation to my advantage. Murcia is clever and ambitious and the talk about him is true. He sees himself as a politician, the rightful leader of Colombia. But he and Peroza are clashing regarding the direction of the ELC. I picked up on it before, but now I'm certain of it. We can use that to our advantage."

Adler liked the sound of that. "So... what? We play them off against each other?"

"Yes. If we create enough chaos and confusion in the camp, we might have a chance to escape."

"And you think waiting it out isn't an option?"

Day exhaled deeply. "Both the US foreign affairs unit and UK foreign office will be up to their eyeballs right now with the conflicts in the Middle East and Ukraine. Likewise, they won't send troops in to deal with a hostage situation that could ruin their diplomatic relations with Maduro's regime."

"And we're running out of time."

"Precisely. Murcia no longer needs the financial rewards hostages provide and now I know why. But we have another issue. Your cover as a journalist… it's fragile. If they find out why you're here, and who you are…"

Adler stared into his eyes and her stomach turned over.

*Shit. He knows.*

*This guy is good.*

"I know," she whispered. "I'm a ticking time bomb in this place."

Day's expression softened. "I'm not going to let anything happen to you. But we need to put a plan together."

"What do you have in mind?"

Day lowered his voice even more, so she had to lean in to hear. "I'll make Murcia believe I'm of real value to him. That means I'll have to give him something concrete, but nothing too extreme. Meanwhile, I'll look for ways to widen the rift between him and Peroza if you do the same with the lieutenant. Any way you can think of that doesn't put you in danger. If we can stir up enough unrest, we might find our chance."

"That could work. But it'll be risky."

"Everything here is risky," Day replied, a wry grin on his face. "But we don't have a choice. The longer we stay here, the greater the danger. Murcia wants to be rid of the hostages; he doesn't need the hassle any longer. I'll try to convince him it's better he releases us via the front gates rather than in body bags, but I don't know how successful I'll be."

Adler frowned. "What did you mean before about him not needing the financial rewards?"

Day leaned in, his voice low but intense. "Oil."

"Oil? How do you mean?"

He glanced around, ensuring no one was listening. "On the flight over here I was reading an article about Venezuela's oil industry. It's fascinating and troubling at the same time. The Orinoco Belt region was once a thriving hub that turned the country into a global energy giant. Back in the day, when oil prices were high, Chávez used billions of dollars to fund the country's social programs. But he also failed to reinvest in the industry. Despite having enormous oil reserves, he and his cronies ran Venezuela's oil trade into the ground. But over the past few years there's been a resurgence. It's moving slowly, but it's going to happen. Venezuela has the world's largest crude oil reserves and there are thousands of abandoned fields all over the country."

He paused, gauging Adler's reaction. "You think Murcia is getting into the oil business."

"I'd bet my life on it. Have you heard that weird clinking sound coming from the east of the compound? I couldn't place what it was at first. But then I realised, it's a refinery. Murcia must have found an old oil field close by and is restoring it. My guess is it's only a matter of time before the pumps are fully operational again. Good for him, not so good for us."

"I get it." Adler's mind was working fast to connect the dots. "Once upon a time, hostages, guns and drugs were the main source of funding for their rebellion. But with oil money behind him, even if he sells the completed refinery to the Venezuelans or an established company, Murcia is going to be mega-rich. Rich enough to buy his way into power. Plus, our group is becoming a liability. So there's a very real possibility they kill us all and blame it on some rogue militia, rather than messing around with ransoms and diplomacy."

"My thoughts exactly," Day said.

"Shit!"

"Yeah, that was my next thought."

She rubbed at her face. "Okay, it's a gamble, but I agree, we have to do something and fast. The longer we stay here, we're all dead."

"Our first step is getting into that storage unit. I'm hoping there are some spare rifles in there. Explosives would be even better."

Adler chewed on her lip as she considered this. "Next time we're out for exercise, I'll slip away from the group and check it out. If it's locked, there has to be a key. If it's guarded, there has to be a way around the guard."

"Okay, great," Day said, with a hint of a smile. "But don't take unnecessary risks."

She returned his smile as a shiver of nervous energy ran down her back. "Well, like you said… everything here is risky."

## Chapter Thirty-Four

In the current climate, Victor Peroza liked the fact that his deputy was more street thug than soldier, but even he was a little shocked as he strode into Lugo's office to be met with a scene of unbridled excess. Lugo, sprawled in his worn leather chair and wearing just a pair of cargo pants and a grubby undershirt, didn't lift his eyes from the pornographic video playing on his computer screen. In his hand was a half-empty beer bottle, which he rested on his sizeable gut.

"Turn that off!" Peroza shouted, over the sex noises coming from the laptop speakers. "We have business to discuss."

Lugo flashed him a roguish grin, seemingly unbothered by the interruption, but sat up and paused the video. "What's going on?"

"Bring up the secure message forum," Peroza ordered. "I want to see if the Americans or British have responded."

"No problem."

Lugo's expression shifted to one of mild interest as he

pulled the laptop towards him and tapped away at the keyboard. Peroza took a seat, surveying the room as he waited. Lugo's office was a third of the size of his own and comprised just a small, laminated desk and two plastic chairs. Yet his deputy had certainly made it his own. Empty beer bottles and scrunched cigarette packets fought for floor space amongst piles of torn paper and girly mags. On the wall behind Lugo was a calendar featuring a blonde woman in bra and panties holding a Kalashnikov. The office was a reflection of Lugo himself, Peroza mused – messy, lewd, and with a strange odour he could never quite place.

"There is nothing as yet," Lugo said, turning the laptop around to show the lieutenant. "But these things usually take time."

Peroza narrowed his eyes at the encrypted communication channel. "Yes, you're right. All part of the game." He glanced at Lugo's beer. "Give me one of those."

"Sure."

As Lugo reached under his desk, Peroza pressed on. "We've got a bigger issue, my friend. A suspected spy here on the base. The tall Englishman with the blond hair."

"Whoa, fuck!" Lugo handed Peroza a bottle of beer. "Is that bad?"

"I'm not sure yet," Peroza replied, opening the bottle on the edge of the desk and swigging half of it down. "I planned to interrogate him, see what he knew, but Murcia got to him first and took him away. As they were walking together, they were acting kind of chummy, then were in his quarters for over an hour. I don't like it."

"No. Me neither." Lugo drained his beer. "You know, the general and one of his men were in with Bracho last night. They were messing with him."

## A World of Sun and Violence

Peroza sneered. "He hates Bracho. He wants us to get rid of him."

"Him and the hostages," Lugo added. "What the hell is he doing? It's as if he's turned his back on everything we built."

Lugo's agreement pleased Peroza. He'd hoped his deputy would be on his side but he couldn't assume. "Murcia's playing with fire, if you ask me."

Footsteps sounded behind them. "But no one is asking you, Victor."

*Mierda!*

Peroza tensed as Murcia strode into the room. Lugo made to get up but the general waved him down. "Are we celebrating something, gentlemen?" he asked, gesturing at the beer bottles.

"I don't know. Are we?" Peroza sneered, not ready to back down. So what if Murcia had heard him just now? He needed to hear it.

"I've just got off a call with our tech unit in Colombia," Murcia told them. "The Englishman, Beckett, was indeed British Secret Service."

Lugo let out a cackling laugh. "MI-fucking-6. So we're going to kill him?"

"Don't be foolish," Murcia snapped. "He's of use to us."

"Okay, torture him, find out what he knows, then kill him," Peroza added, grinning at Lugo.

Murcia shot him a vicious look. "Not so fast, Victor. Beckett could be instrumental to our next phase. He says he is a defector. He says he hates his country. From what I have ascertained, I believe him."

Peroza and Lugo exchanged a wary glance. "You're sure of this, Jalen?" Peroza asked. "I say he's playing you. Either way, it's too big a risk. He's MI6, not some random turncoat. We can't have someone like that loose in the compound."

Murcia placed a hand on his shoulder. "I know what I'm doing. He stays alive. For now at least."

"And the hostages?" Lugo asked.

Murcia hesitated. "I have not yet decided."

"Well, let us know when you do," Peroza muttered, and chugged down the rest of his beer. He knew Murcia didn't like them drinking on duty, but he didn't care. If anything, he wanted to piss him off. "I say we give their countries five days to make contact, then we start chopping off heads. How about that?"

Peroza's glare intensified as he turned to face Murcia, but the general met his gaze squarely, pointing a finger at him. "Don't do anything without my say-so, understand?"

"Sure," he muttered.

Murcia left the room and Peroza motioned for Lugo to fetch more beers. They popped the caps and drank in silence for a few minutes. He had a lot on his mind but didn't know how to even start articulating his ideas.

"General Murcia has gone soft," Lugo mumbled, his voice echoing down the neck of the beer bottle as he held it to his lips. "Sounds like he's forgetting where he came from."

Peroza stared, trancelike, at the wall. "I agree. He's changed. I wish it was different but I have to accept it. He's become a pussy, only interested in chasing power, forgetting the roots of our struggle. He's turned into everything we once despised."

"What are we going to do about it?" Lugo asked.

Peroza gripped his beer bottle, overcome with an intense sense of loss. He missed his old friend and the ideals they'd once shared, but Murcia had made it crystal clear – the two of them were no longer on the same path. The general was playing a very dangerous game, taking matters into his own hands.

Perhaps it was time he did the same.

## Chapter Thirty-Five

Beckett's eyes snapped open as the cold muzzle of an assault rifle was pressed against his cheek. Disoriented, he tried to focus on the figure looming over him.

"Get up. Come with me," the man commanded in a harsh whisper. It was dark in the tent, but as Beckett's eyes adjusted, he recognised him as one of Murcia's security detail.

He got up and pulled on his trousers and shirt. Through the tent flaps he saw that dawn was still some time away, and none of the others stirred as he was escorted outside. The air was cool but refreshing on his skin as the guard led him across the exercise yard and down the side of the compound towards Murcia's building.

Two trucks were parked near the main gate and a patrol of young soldiers were unloading crates of fruit, bread and water and carrying them to the storage unit on this side of the yard. The doors were open and Beckett bristled with alertness as their path brought them within thirty metres of the front of the unit. Under the solitary halo of a halogen bulb at the entrance, he could just make out the interior, noting three large freestanding shelving units loaded with crates, and more importantly, a rack of assault rifles on the back wall.

*Bullseye!*

Continuing towards Murcia's quarters, Beckett glanced back over his shoulder. Two guards were walking towards the holding tent to relieve the two on duty. It appeared that many procedures in the camp took place before the hostages were typically awake.

Another guard approached, carrying a tray with a whole roast chicken and cornbread. It smelled amazing and for a moment Beckett hoped the food was for him, but the guard carried on past, heading towards the hut belonging to Bracho.

El Demonio Roto. The broken demon. The huge beast-man had lingered in Beckett's thoughts since his brutal handling of Lange. Despite his imposing size and ferocity, Bracho was clearly a vulnerable individual, exploited and possibly mistreated by Peroza and his crew. Beckett wondered if he could use that fact to his advantage.

But how?

He shook the thought away as they arrived at Murcia's building and the general emerged, holding his arms out. "Mr John Beckett. Apologies for waking you so early, but I was eager to continue our discussion."

Beckett stopped and squared his shoulders as his escort continued towards an old US military jeep parked nearby. "I take it your team have verified my story?"

"Indeed they have," Murcia replied. "It was difficult for them, as you said it would be. But we were able to gain classified documents seized by the Iranians, relative to a mission you were involved with in Syria four years ago."

Beckett remembered it well. But that only confirmed he was once SIS. "And you trust me regarding my intentions?"

"Let's just say, we've done our homework. It's amazing what you can find out if you speak to the right people. You are quite the contentious figure, Mr Beckett. It seems you have managed to ruffle feathers in both the CIA and British intelligence."

"Exactly why I want to work with you," he said, seizing his cue to press his point. "I want to screw them over just as much as you do, and anyone who stands in your way. Release the hostages and we'll work together."

"Why this insistence on saving these nobodies?" Murcia asked, jutting out his chin. "If what you say is true, why do you care?"

Beckett kept his expression neutral. "I believe you're a man of great vision, General, and those people are extraneous to your needs and a pointless drain on your time and resources. I know you don't need the ransom money, but you also don't need to kill them. Think about it. We could twist the narrative to make it appear as if you facilitated their release from a local militia. You want to be seen as a valid and reasonable leader; this is the way to go. With the right spin, we can paint you as a hero. The great President Murcia." He paused. He'd been thinking on his feet just now and was worried he might have gone too far with that last comment. But Murcia's eyes lit up.

"You know, I like you, Beckett. You've got real balls. Okay, come with me," he said, waving his hand in the direction of the jeep. "I want to show you something."

Murcia walked down the steps and over to the parked jeep. His security detail, now sitting in the driver's seat, started the engine as Beckett jumped into the back of the vehicle alongside Murcia. As the gates were hauled open and they drove away, he braced himself for action. They could be taking him anywhere.

"The man Bracho is certainly a… unique asset," Beckett said, seeking to build on the rapport he'd initiated. "Where the hell did you find him?"

Murcia's expression soured. "He is Lieutenant Peroza's pet, not mine. I find him repulsive. He's a brute, a gimmick, nothing more. He won't be kept around for much longer."

Beckett nodded, playing along. "A means to an end. I get it."

The jeep veered onto a dirt path flanked by dense jungle, and Beckett released a long breath, purposely settling his tone into one that was casual yet respectful. "You have an impressive setup here, General. But I know you have higher ambitions. And rightly so for a man of your prestige."

Murcia, glancing sideways at Beckett, allowed himself a small, satisfied smile. "Yes, it's taken a lot of work. My efforts are finally bearing fruit."

"I was involved in a similar situation in Africa, back in 2012. We were supporting the United Front of the Niger Delta in toppling Kabir Chukwu's Democratic Progress Alliance." He paused, allowing the point to land. His years of experience in covert operations meant he could become whatever his subject needed him to be, and whilst time was of the essence, he didn't want to come across as too eager. "It was an interesting time, but as you're no doubt aware, regime change was needed."

The reference was designed to resonate with Murcia's ambitions, and also demonstrate his insider knowledge and depth of experience. Murcia's broadening smile indicated the tactic was effective.

"I can help you achieve the same," Beckett continued.

"I know what you have here. They had the same – a field, just like yours, better than any goldmine. It turned the whole power dynamic in Nigeria on its head."

Murcia raised an eyebrow. "And what do I have, Mr Beckett?"

"Oil, General. You have oil. And if my instincts are correct, I'd say you have a lot of it."

As the jeep rumbled onwards, the landscape transformed dramatically. Emerging from the dense jungle, they drove across a sprawling wasteland, the barren ground and lack of trees almost alien after the lush greenery they'd left behind. The clinking noise was growing louder. They were almost there.

"The UFND harnessed their oil fields to sway political power, much like you're planning," Beckett carried on. "It's an excellent strategy. Masterful, even." He shot the general an admiring glance. His time spent undercover, as Rufus Delaney's right-hand man, had not been wasted. Delaney had been just as ambitious and egotistical as Murcia, and Beckett knew how to play to these traits. "After all, oil is money, money is power."

Murcia chuckled. "I agree, but this is about more than mere financial gain. It's about reshaping the political landscape. I love my country and I have grand plans for it. Colombia will be great once more. I know this."

Beckett shut up and leaned back, giving Murcia room to elaborate whilst absorbing every detail and nuance of their interaction. Each fragment of information provided helpful insight into Murcia's psyche.

"This is how I achieve my vision," the general said, gesturing in front of him. "This, here, is key."

As the jeep drove around a bank of trees, the oil field sprawled out before them. In the early light of dawn, the scene had a surreal, ethereal quality. The elaborate network of pipes, towers and machinery stretched over a considerable area, and the new day's sun painted the industrial landscape in hues of orange and red.

They came to a stop about fifty metres from the first of six rusty drilling rigs. Up close the noise was relentless and all-consuming, an endless hum of mechanical groans and clinks that set Beckett's teeth on edge. The air was thick with the smell of crude oil, a pungent odour that overpowered all other senses and seemed to push nature itself away. There wasn't a single bird or critter in sight. The grass here was brown and brittle.

"Very impressive," Beckett shouted over the din. This was no lie. The sight of the noisy complex, sitting on the edge of the jungle, spoke volumes about the scale of Murcia's grand ambition. It also confirmed to him that the hostages, and any potential ransom, were low on the list of the general's priorities.

"This is the future," Murcia announced, waving his hand over the scene. "Black gold. Better than any green, right? This field, it's more than just oil. It's power, it's influence, it's the key to everything I've been planning."

Beckett nodded as he took in the scene. "Will you funnel the crude oil back to Colombia?"

"Possibly," Murcia mused. "But whatever I decide, it will bring about our victory."

"So you're poised for a full-blown coup d'état?" Beckett asked. "To overthrow the current regime?"

Murcia's eyes glimmered with determination. "Oh yes. Petro has overseen too many scandals and my people are more disillusioned than ever. The ELN had a chance to change things, but over time they lost their edge. They're weak and unwilling to take the necessary action. But not me. I see the bigger picture. First Colombia, then South America. Then…"

"Interesting," Beckett said. "Once you take Colombia, your options are boundless. But you'll need strong allies, powerful backers." He paused, allowing Murcia the space to respond.

"And you can help with this?" he asked.

"I can. Along with this oil field, the information in my head, my training and experience, it could be a real game changer for you." He leaned in closer, holding his voice steady. "I have intel worth millions to certain parties and catastrophe to their enemies. I can help you forge powerful alliances with Russia, North Korea, the Saudis, even ISIS and Hamas if that's the way you want to play it."

Murcia stared at Beckett, clearly trying to discern if what he was saying was true. "You are prepared to do this, turn your back on your country, on everything you've fought for your whole career? Why?"

Beckett, well-versed in such situations, held the general's gaze. "Self-preservation, pure and simple. MI6 and the CIA want me dead. I'm an exile, a pariah. I want them to pay for their betrayal. I have nothing to lose. I can never return home. Plus, I'll be honest with you, General Murcia, the prospect of being a kingmaker appeals to me. I know I have what it takes. You're the man. I could be the man behind the man."

Murcia twisted his mouth to one side, considering the statement. Then he smiled. "You're a man after my own heart, Mr Beckett. Come, let us return to the compound. I have something I would like you to do for me."

Murcia's words echoed around Beckett's head as they returned to the prison. He kept quiet, subtly scoping out the surrounding area as they drove. There were two dirt roads leading away from the prison; the one they were on that connected them to the oil field, and another that curved around the side of the compound and cut through a section of the jungle. This second road, Beckett hoped, would lead back to civilisation eventually.

Ten minutes later the jeep pulled up outside the prison's high walls. Beckett turned to Murcia as the gate creaked open for them. "What is it you want me to do?" he asked.

Murcia made a tutting sound as if displeased by his impatience. "I believe you have potential, my friend," he said. "But I need more than just words. I need to see proof of your loyalty."

Peroza was standing in the middle of the exercise yard as they pulled up, flanked by two guards. Murcia climbed down from the jeep and walked over to him. Beckett waited for the driver to climb out, noting he switched off the engine and left the keys in the ignition, then followed suit. Standing on the dusty ground, Beckett observed from a distance as Peroza and Murcia spoke in hushed, hurried whispers.

Something felt off suddenly. He didn't like it.

"What's going on?" he asked, walking over to Murcia as Peroza turned and headed for the holding tent, signalling at his men to follow.

"Don't worry," Murcia replied. "You will soon find out."

Beckett was about to say more when he was interrupted by a woman's screams.

*Adler!*

He couldn't make out what she was saying, but as he turned, he saw her being dragged from the tent by Peroza's men. The other hostages shuffled along behind her, watching the scene play out with a mix of horror and disbelief.

Beckett's heart pounded as the realisation hit him. He knew what Murcia was going to ask him to do. As she got closer, he suspected Adler knew also.

"Get off of me!" she cried, trying to free herself from the guards' grip. "I'm an American journalist. I have immunity. I have rights."

Peroza, striding behind the hostages, wore a self-satisfied smirk, clearly relishing Adler's distress. The guards shoved her to her knees in front of Murcia and Beckett. Her complexion was pale, her eyes wide with terror. She stared up at them, searching the general's face for a hint of what was to come.

"Here you go." Murcia drew a pistol from his belt and held it out to Beckett. "Take it."

Beckett stared at the gun as Adler's desperate pleas filled his ears. It was a Córdova 9mm, a typical service pistol made by the Colombian Indumil company. Murcia was certainly on-brand.

"If you hate your country and America as you say, it is time to prove it," Murcia hissed, his voice low and threatening. "Show me where your allegiance lies, Mr Beckett. Lift the gun, shoot this journalist bitch in the head."

"You don't need to do this!" Adler whispered. "Please…"

She stared, frozen, as Beckett took the gun, feeling its weight. The reinforced polymer grip was cold against his skin despite the air around him suddenly feeling a lot hotter. In his peripheral vision, he noted Peroza's guards had their assault rifles trained on him.

"Do it!" Murcia urged. "Show me you have what it takes."

"No!" Adler begged. "You can't do this. I don't want to die."

## A World of Sun and Violence

Beckett sensed the eyes of the other hostages burning into him, their anticipation and dread almost palpable.

Adler continued to stare up at him. She had tears in her eyes. Her breath was shallow. Beckett held the gun, his hand steady despite the turmoil raging inside him. He'd been put in this position before. The last time it happened, he'd pulled the trigger to protect his cover. The man he'd killed had been a vicious arms dealer and human trafficker who deserved everything he'd got, but morally it blurred the lines.

But then, what was new about that in his world?

"Kill her!" Murcia demanded, gritting his teeth. "Do it!"

The moment stretched on, each millisecond an eternity. Beckett rested his finger on the trigger. He knew whatever he did next would change everything.

He took a deep breath.

## Chapter Thirty-Six

Adler tensed as Day — or rather, Beckett, as Murcia had called him — raised the gun to her head. Her eyes searched his, desperate to know his intentions. Getting closer to Murcia was part of his plan, but he couldn't have primed himself for this eventuality. Would he sacrifice her to save himself and the other hostages? Should he? Would that serve a greater purpose?

Her mind raced with too many questions and not enough answers.

She thought of her mother and father, picturing their faces, a mixture of pride and concern, on the day she'd told them she was joining the agency. They had known not to discourage her, that it would only make her more determined, but she was still their little girl. They worried about her even now.

Would they ever learn what happened to her?

It was another unhelpful question that faded from her mind as Beckett's finger lingered on the trigger. Her breath caught in her throat. It wasn't the first time she'd faced death, but it never got any easier.

Beckett towered over her, his expression fixed and cold. Was he hesitating, perhaps playing for time whilst he plotted his next move? Or was he readying himself to take the shot? Adler had been trained in how to read people and understand their intentions, but Beckett was an enigma.

An insidious fear swelled inside her. She wasn't ready to die, not like this, not now. She thought again of her loved ones, of the life she had yet to live. Tears formed in her eyes, but she held them there without blinking, refusing to show weakness in her final moments. Off to her right, she heard Kathleen sobbing and Bruce trying to comfort her. She closed her eyes. She waited.

"What the hell are you doing?" Murcia hissed.

Adler opened her eyes to see Beckett lowering the pistol. He looked at the general. "You don't want this," he told him. "She's more valuable to us alive."

Murcia scoffed. "How do you mean? Explain!"

Beckett held his composure as he turned back to meet Adler's gaze. "She's the daughter of Senator Adler," he said. "He's an influential figure in the US government. There's talk of him being a presidential candidate in the next election."

Murcia's eyes narrowed as he stepped forward. "Is this true?"

"Yes," Adler said. "Senator Simon Adler is my father."

She'd suspected Beckett had worked out who she was but this confirmed it, and whilst his intervention had saved her life, the uncertainty of his motives left her with a sense of unease despite the immediate relief. Now her captors knew the truth about her. It still felt like she had a gun held to her head.

"All right, get her up," Murcia said.

Peroza walked over and grabbed the pistol out of Beckett's hand before signalling his men to follow Murcia's order.

"What are we going to do with her?" Peroza asked, walking over to confront Murcia whilst Adler was hauled to her feet. "And why didn't he tell us this sooner?"

The general took the pistol handed to him, eyeing Beckett with suspicion as he holstered it. "I have no idea. I need to consider these new developments. For now, take her and the others back to the holding tent." He pointed at Beckett. "You, come with me."

Adler hoped Beckett might glance back at her as he followed on behind Murcia. Right now she needed reassurance, a silent reaffirming of their alliance, but it didn't happen. The other hostages stood motionless in a tableau of fear and uncertainty. Kathleen's face was damp, her hands clasping at Bruce's for comfort. Price's face was pale and drawn.

"Move!"

Peroza's command jolted them into action. As they trudged across the prison yard, Adler couldn't help but notice his predatory gaze fixed on her. After the events of the last few minutes it made her feel uncomfortable and like she might throw up, but she also saw an opportunity. Despite feeling a little shaky, she steeled her nerves and approached the lieutenant.

"You wanted him to kill me?" she asked.

"I want what's best for my people and my cause," he replied. "It is never personal."

Adler doubted that. "I just think it's odd, that's all…"

"What is odd?" Peroza looked her up and down, eyes settling on her chest. "What do you mean?"

## A World of Sun and Violence

"Well... I thought this prison was under your leadership," she replied, resisting the urge to cross her arms. "Yet you follow a lot of orders for someone in charge."

Peroza stopped and spun around to face her. His eyes were like slits. "I am in charge," he hissed. "These are my men."

Adler suppressed the knot of fear tightening inside her. "You might want to let General Murcia know. From what I see, he's the one pulling the strings."

She was playing with fire, she knew that, but it seemed to be having the desired effect. Peroza had turned a deep shade of crimson and a vein pulsed angrily at his temple. He stepped closer, invading her personal space.

"You know nothing," he spat. "Now get moving."

He shoved Adler on in front of him and they set off again, her heavy pulse resounding in her ears as they headed for the holding tent.

Once back in the confines of the canvas prison, the atmosphere was more charged than ever. Price, who had been uncharacteristically quiet on the walk back, now became animated as Adler entered followed by Peroza.

"What does this mean for us now?" he asked, making a beeline for the lieutenant. "Does this change things?"

"Sit down," Peroza told him. "Be quiet."

"You have to tell us what you plan to do with us," Price went on. "This isn't fair. It's against the Geneva Convention, against the UN's Declaration of Human Rights. If you want legitimacy, free us. Let me contact my people, I can move things along, get your ransom money paid."

He was speaking fast, without taking a breath, a man grasping at the vanishing threads of hope. But Adler sensed his pleas were only aggravating the already enraged Peroza.

"Price," she warned. "Let it go."

But he wasn't listening. He stepped closer. "I've got money saved, plenty of it. I can wire you whatever you need right this second." Adler winced as the frantic Englishman grabbed at Peroza's lapels. "Release me, please. I just want to go home."

Peroza recoiled as if struck. "Don't touch me!" he cried, shoving him away.

Adler's body instinctively went into fight mode as Peroza lunged forward and punched Price in the head. Beside her, the two guards stiffened to attention, quickly training their rifles on the remaining hostages as the smaller man stumbled backwards. The Englishman was no match for Peroza's brute force as another right hook knocked him to the ground. He tried to scramble away, his arms flailing in a futile attempt to shield himself, but Peroza stalked after him, setting about him with a series of punishing kicks and punches.

Adler watched on, helpless, as Peroza kicked the poor bastard in the stomach. Instinctively Price doubled over, which is exactly what the lieutenant wanted. He followed up with a boot to the face, snapping Price's head back as his nose and lip exploded.

Blood poured from his face. He was done. On the edge of unconsciousness. But Peroza, still red in the face and with saliva foaming at the corners of his mouth, appeared far from satisfied. He towered over Price's prone form before stomping down on his face.

Across the other side of the tent, Kathleen screamed and buried her face into her husband's neck. Bruce wrapped his arms around her, but like Castillo, like the two guards, like Adler herself, he was unable to tear his gaze from the horror unfolding before them.

"*Estúpido y patético bastardo!*" Peroza spat, his boot

colliding once more with the swollen, bloody mess that was once Price's nose.

The Englishman was no longer moving or making a noise. He was knocked out, possibly worse. Adler grimaced as Peroza rolled him onto his front and then raised his boot, bringing his full weight down on the nape of Price's neck with a brutal crunch, a sound reminiscent of a turkey's leg being pulled from its carcass. She wanted to look away. She couldn't. Price's body twitched once, then was still.

"Oh Lord, save us!" Bruce's voice was muffled as he burrowed his face in his wife's hair.

Peroza stood back, chest heaving, fixing the rest of them with a fierce glare. "This is what happens," he gasped, pointing at Price's body. "You will all meet the same fate if you don't fall in line."

With measured, deliberate movements, Castillo moved forward, holding his hands up to Peroza as he gestured at Price. "Can I...?"

Peroza raised his chin and sniffed. "Go."

Kneeling, Castillo placed his fingers on the side of the Englishman's broken neck. Adler felt this was a rather pointless exercise. A moment later, a dour nod from the old cop confirmed what she knew. Price was dead.

Peroza gave a flick of his hand and his men moved in, lifting Price's body and dragging it from the tent. Adler remained still, her poise betraying the turmoil bubbling inside her as she grappled with all that had transpired.

"Watch your mouth from now on." Peroza pointed at her as he marched out. "Or your father will receive your head in a box."

He left and a heavy silence fell over the tent, broken only by the soft sobs of the Dixons' and Castillo's ragged breaths.

Adler slumped onto the nearest bench, overcome with trepidation and guilt. She'd pushed Peroza too far and Price's blood was on her hands. She imagined herself ripping the tent down and going after Peroza, making him pay, but reality anchored her firmly in place. Yet this settled it once and for all. They had to escape this rotten place. Peroza was unhinged and they couldn't afford to wait around in the hope their government would intervene.

Doubts about Beckett gnawed at her soul. She had trusted him, but she now had to make peace with the possibility he might have played her – gathering information that he was now using to save his own neck.

She shuddered; the image of Price's bloody form imprinted on her mind.

For now, she would still cling to the hope Beckett was the ally she believed him to be. He'd acted out of necessity, she told herself. He'd done what he had to. But the fact Murcia now knew who her father was only added layers of complexity to an already fraught situation. Would he increase his ransom demands now he knew the truth? Use her as leverage in other ways?

An image of her father, sitting in his Washington office, flashed in her mind. He was a good man and a damn good senator. Beckett had been speaking the truth earlier. There was a real possibility he could become the Democrats' pick in the next ten years, VP at the very least. She wondered if he knew of her peril, if he was in talks with the CIA right now demanding action. She knew her father would pay the ransom himself in a shot, but her covert role within the agency complicated matters significantly. Would the CIA intervene, or would they deem her expendable for the sake of national security? If they sent a Special Forces team in to extract her, it would place the other hostages in even greater danger. She didn't want that.

In the field, decisions were usually clear-cut, guided by protocol and strategy. But here, in this lawless jungle prison, there were no rules. Almost every choice carried the weight of life-or-death consequences, not just for her but for the Dixons, Castillo, even Beckett.

She glanced around the tent. Kathleen and Bruce were huddled together, shrouded in grief. Castillo sat on a bench at the back of the tent, staring at the ground in stunned silence. The air smelled of death.

"What the fuck do I do?" she whispered to herself, and maybe to some higher power. Not that Adler believed in God anymore. She'd seen too much horrible shit over the years for that.

Murcia was both cunning and shrewd and would be assessing his options right now, working out how he might utilise these fresh developments. That bought her a little time, but not much. Peroza, however, was a different story altogether. The cruel brutality he'd displayed against Price was a glaring reminder that no one was safe under his watch.

Glancing through the tent flap, she caught sight of one of the young guards positioned near the entrance. She sized him up, noting his stance, the way he held his weapon. She was confident she could overpower him, but another guard was standing on the other side of the doorway. Two at once was risky. Doable but dangerous.

For the moment she stayed where she was. She focused on her breathing, trying to stay focused and not give in to despair. The urgency of their situation was clear. Time was slipping away, and they needed to find a way to escape before it was too late.

But the big question was how, and at what cost?

## Chapter Thirty-Seven

Over in Washington, Dick Foster was sitting in Senator Adler's hideaway office on the top floor of the Capitol Building. He'd spent the last fifteen minutes briefing the senator – in as much depth as protocol would allow – on what he currently knew of his daughter's situation. It was a tense conversation, not made any easier by the grandeur of the setting. The room, like the echoing corridors that had led him to it, was spacious and elegant. High ceilings and large, panelled windows allowed natural light to enter, throwing a warm glow over the polished mahogany furniture. A bookcase lined one wall, filled with volumes of legal texts, historical works, and a plethora of awards and mementoes. The walls were adorned with framed black-and-white photographs of the senator with various dignitaries – Jimmy Carter, Clinton, Obama – each image a testimony of his distinguished career.

"You have to bring her back, Dick," Senator Adler implored. His thick hair was now white, but he still had the tall, athletic build of his younger self in the photographs.

He glared at Foster with pale blue eyes filled with fatherly concern. "Margaret and I... we never envisioned this path for Vanessa. But she's always been fiercely independent and headstrong."

Foster, a father himself, empathised but maintained a professional demeanour, having prepped himself for this moment on the flight over here. "Senator, your daughter is one of our best operatives. I assure you, we're doing everything we can."

Senator Adler's gaze lingered on a silver-framed photograph of a much younger Vanessa on his desk, her face beaming with youthful promise. "She's achieved so much already," he said. "Top of her class at Langley, a key player in dismantling that arms ring in Eastern Europe, not to mention her covert operations in the Middle East. She's already made significant sacrifices, Dick."

"I'm aware of her record, Senator. It's impressive, to say the least. We value her greatly."

The senator picked up the photo and held it in front of him. "She was meant for great things... not this. Not to be held captive by a bunch of lousy guerrillas in the middle of nowhere. Do we have any idea about her captors?"

"As of now, we have no concrete identification, Senator." Foster's expression remained stoic, but his mind raced with the urgency of the situation. "But rest assured, we're mobilising all our resources. I give you my personal commitment; we're doing all we can to ensure Vanessa's safe return."

The senator held Foster's gaze, the fatherly twinkle in his eyes dropping away. "You'd better. You know as well as I do, she's not just my daughter, she's a vital asset to our nation. Her safety is paramount."

Foster stood, extending a hand. "Senator, you have my word. I'll do everything in my power…"

Senator Adler stood and took his hand, giving it a firm shake that seemed ripe with subtext. "I know you will, Dick. Keep me updated, regardless of the hour."

Exiting the senator's office, Foster was already planning his next move in this high-stakes chess game they called international espionage. As he made his way towards the elevator, he powered on his phone, seeing three missed calls from Goldsmith. He hit redial and his chief of staff answered on the first ring.

"Sir, I've been trying to reach you."

"I know. I've just finished with Senator Adler. You could say it went as well as could be expected." He glanced around, mindful of prying ears. "How's the situation in Venezuela shaping up?"

"We've made some headway," Goldsmith informed him. "Drone surveillance identified four potential sites in Northern Venezuela, and a facial recognition scan conducted just twenty minutes ago confirms Vanessa Adler is alive. She's being held with five others in a remote prison compound south of El Tigrito."

Foster reached the elevators but found the landing area bustling with suits. Opting for discretion, he looked for the fire escape. "What do we know about this place?" he asked.

"It's an old site, built in the mid-eighties by the Democratic Action party. It was thought to be decommissioned."

"Okay, good work." Foster pushed through the fire door and hurried down the stairwell. "Continue monitoring the situation for the time being, and once I'm back at Langley we'll assemble a full task force. I'm catching the next flight."

"Understood, sir," Goldsmith said. "But there's more. The drone footage also revealed an oil field approximately ten kilometres east of the compound. This too was thought to have been decommissioned but it looks to be operational. We're currently analysing its significance."

"That's a good lead," Foster gasped. "If these people are drilling for oil, they might be more ready to negotiate. They have to sell it somewhere, right? We need more intel on that."

Goldsmith cleared his throat. "There is one final matter, sir."

"What is it?" Foster reached the ground floor but remained in the stairwell rather than exit into the lobby. Something about Goldsmith's tone told him this was a conversation to be had away from the bustle of congressmen and lawmakers.

"We've identified the other hostages. Two are US citizens. But there's one individual who… Well, it's best if you see the file. I'm sending it over to you now."

Foster's heart sank. "Is it bad?"

There was a loaded pause before Goldsmith answered. "It potentially could be, sir."

## Chapter Thirty-Eight

The sun was dipping low over the Venezuelan jungle, casting long shadows across the compound where Peroza and Lugo lounged under a canvas awning. The afternoon heat still lingered, overbearing and sticky, barely alleviated by the cheap, battery-powered fans they both held.

The fire in Peroza's belly was still raging, the muscles in his jaw yet to fully relax following the day's events. This despite him being four beers down and now starting on his fifth.

He leaned back, the plastic garden chair beneath him groaning under his weight. To say the chair had seen better days would be an understatement. Along with a rickety plastic table currently holding a bucket of ice filled with beer bottles, the once-white garden furniture was now mottled with green mould and warped from the sun. The chair Lugo was sitting in had a crack in the seat and one of the arms had broken off, leaving a sharp point. The chairs were comfortable enough, they served a purpose, but it had been a long day and this was no way for a leader to be spending his downtime. For Peroza, this only highlighted a much bigger issue. Murcia was so obsessed with his power struggles in Colombia that he no longer cared about the prison's upkeep. An oversight Peroza found both unfair and insulting.

Lugo lifted a beer from the ice bucket and gave Peroza a sly look as he shook off the drips. "You really did a number on that whiney English journalist. How did Murcia take it?"

"He doesn't know about it yet," Peroza replied, wiping sweat from his forehead with the back of his hand. "But you know what? I don't give a shit how he takes it. This is my prison. He's too wrapped up with that Beckett guy. Thinks he's got a new best friend, a new ally."

"Do you reckon he's genuine?" Lugo twisted the cap off his beer. "This Beckett guy, I mean. You think he's going to help our cause?"

Peroza shrugged. He was a little annoyed at himself for letting the American bitch get to him earlier. He shouldn't have lost his temper and killed that guy. His battered body was now in a shallow grave outside the compound with all the other dead hostages. Yet, the fact remained, what the American said had angered him because it was true. He should be the one in charge here.

His attention shifted as one of his men walked past carrying a tray of food and water towards the hostages' tent. Lugo leaned over and raised an eyebrow, gesturing with his bottle towards the guard.

"Look at that, man. Those vermin in that tent eat better than some of us. Sitting around all day, draining our damn supplies."

Peroza's gaze lingered on the guard. He didn't like the situation any more than Lugo, but Murcia's line had always been that captives were well-fed and looked after. Well, right until they were released or executed, at least. But that was back when the general actually cared about the hostage game. Nowadays, their old practices seemed to be a source of embarrassment to him. Peroza understood his rationale but it didn't mean he liked it. Although he would never admit it to anyone, lately he'd been feeling increasingly powerless and redundant. Yet he and Murcia had once stood shoulder to shoulder.

"It's ridiculous," Lugo went on. "We're supposed to be fighting a revolution, not running a hotel for foreigners. I say put them all in one of the outbuildings, feed them gruel once a day until the ransom money is paid. If it isn't soon, we kill them. And, man, what I wouldn't give to have a go with that American chick..."

Peroza started to laugh but it died somewhere between his chest and mouth. He sighed. There was a lot to think about, but his mind was hazy with alcohol and fatigue. He took a hefty swig of beer and set the bottle down on the arm of his chair.

"It's Murcia," he growled. "He's lost his way, lost his focus. All he cares about is that damn oil field and how he looks to the world. I don't like the way this is going."

Lugo leaned in, his expression serious. "You think he's gone soft on us?"

"Soft or not, he's distracted and I don't like this Beckett guy. I don't trust him."

He stopped as they caught sight of Murcia and Beckett on the far side of the compound, engrossed in conversation. Peroza scowled as he watched them, his grip tightening on his beer bottle.

"I see what you mean." Lugo shook his head. "Who exactly is this guy?"

Peroza's eyes narrowed. "He claims to be ex-MI6. A

defector. Says he's going to aid our cause. But if you ask me, he's a snake and Murcia's playing right into his hands."

Lugo sneered. "Seems like the general has forgotten who calls the shots around here. This isn't right, Murcia taking his cues from a British spy. We should do something. This is our prison, our revolution. He's making us look like fools."

Peroza took a long swig of his beer, the alcohol fuelling his growing indignation. Lugo was right. He was invisible to his old comrade now. All the blood, sweat and effort he'd put into this fight, and for what? To be sidelined when victory was in sight. To be treated like an embarrassing relative that Murcia wanted to brush under the carpet.

*No.*

*It wasn't going to happen.*

His gaze drifted towards Bracho's hut as a risky yet compelling idea sparked in his mind.

It was approaching dusk, and the air was cooling with every minute that ticked by. Bracho would be awake soon. He'd be eager to play.

So maybe he'd let him.

Peroza drained his beer and grabbed himself a fresh bottle as his plan took shape. He smiled to himself, feeling a surge of energy in his chest and belly. This was it. He was done sitting back and watching the ELC transform into something weak and unrecognisable. They were rebels, for Christ's sake, warriors. It was time for a change, time for him to take control.

It was time the world knew who Victor Peroza really was.

## Chapter Thirty-Nine

Beckett maintained a relaxed demeanour as he strolled the length of the compound alongside General Murcia, but his senses were on high alert, sharply attuned to his surroundings. They'd been talking for some time, mainly regarding the general's vision for Colombia once he took power, but they'd also touched a little on how he planned to get there, and Beckett's role in these plans.

It was now dusk, the heat and humidity on the wane and a slight breeze offering some respite to the intensity of the daytime. Yet as they walked, Beckett was acutely aware of a storm brewing within the camp. He'd seen the way Peroza and Lugo had been staring at them just now. If he kept stoking the flames, he was confident the conflict between Peroza and Murcia would reach boiling point. It was just a matter of when.

Beckett was now certain the general trusted him. He'd carefully divulged bits of information, nothing too damaging to UK interests, but sufficient to cement his story as a defector and a vital source of intelligence. His main objectives remained the same – to secure the hostages' release, whilst at the same time staying alert for opportunities to further his plan within the prison. Gaining Murcia's trust was crucial, as it would allow him the freedom to move around the camp and access essential areas, namely the storage unit.

However, he was also conscious of the need to speak with Adler. He imagined she might be questioning his loyalties right now, and he needed to reassure her he was still onside.

"You've gone quiet," Murcia said, as they passed alongside the exercise yard. "You are thinking deeply about something?"

"I suppose I am," Beckett replied, sensing the opportunity to steer the conversation. "You see, we know you want power, real power, not just as a rebel leader but as a legitimate political force. But do you have a strategy for achieving that in the long term?"

Murcia slowed his pace as he considered the question. "Don't tell me – that's where you come in."

The statement didn't faze Beckett. He already knew Murcia was a savvy individual. "Exactly. I know you're still a little wary of me and that's understandable – I'd be concerned if you weren't – but I can help you. It's clear you are a great military general, and with the right backing and finances I'm confident you'll pull off a successful coup. But what then?"

Murcia chuckled. "I am under no illusion, Mr Beckett, that after the revolution is when the real work begins. I need to be seen as more than just another militant leader. My vision for Colombia goes way beyond mere rebellion."

"That's where the challenge lies," Beckett continued, carefully observing Murcia's reaction, keeping his tone

## A World of Sun and Violence

steady and nonchalant. "Transitioning from military force to political strategy requires a delicate balance, and I've noticed unrest among your men. Particularly Peroza. He could be a problem for you."

A flash of concern crossed Murcia's face. "Peroza has always been impulsive and rowdy. But he's under control."

"Okay. I'm sure you know him best," Beckett replied. He knew he had to tread carefully, offering advice without revealing his true intentions. "But if both those things are true, I'd suggest you also know Peroza isn't going to be an integral part of your vision going forward. Which is fine, I agree. But if he feels sidelined, that could lead to betrayal. You need to strengthen your authority and make your intentions clear. A true leader can't tolerate dissent. I'd also suggest that distancing yourself from some of the controversial aspects of your past might be prudent. Abducting civilians, for example."

Murcia nodded as he considered Beckett's words. "I know this. With the refinery nearing completion, I instructed Victor to cease taking hostages but he didn't listen. He had his men abduct you and the others without my knowledge. Since arriving here I've ensured the situation isn't linked to the ELC in any way. Any ransom money will be routed through an untraceable crypto wallet that can't be linked to me or the party."

"Maybe this time," Beckett said. "But it's a worry... and I was thinking, you could twist the narrative in your favour."

Murcia looked intrigued. "How?"

"Start by acting more like a politician, less like a revolutionary. Own up to your past mistakes, control the narrative. It's a risk, but people respect transparency."

"And the hostages?"

"Release them. Let Peroza take the fall for their capture.

Inform the Americans he acted independently, against your orders. It shows respect and strong leadership."

Murcia stopped. "You want me to show respect for America? After everything they've done?"

"It's not about respect for America but for international law, for human decency. You want legitimacy, General Murcia – *President Murcia* – this is how you get it."

They set off walking once more. By the look on Murcia's face, he was uncomfortable with the idea, but Beckett stood his ground, aware of the risks he was taking with these suggestions.

"I don't mean to speak out of turn," he continued, holding his hands up. "But Peroza strikes me as problematic. He's too attached to the old ways, chaotic and reckless. What happens the next time he doesn't agree with an order? You need people around you who share your vision, and who embrace change. By putting the hostage situation purely on Peroza, you kill two birds with one stone."

"Maybe you're right," Murcia replied, as they neared the cluster of outbuildings. "I shall think hard about what you say. We will talk again." Halting, he faced Beckett, his stare cold and intense. "However, I expect more from you soon. I need information I can actually use. What you have told me so far has aroused my interest in your country's clandestine affairs, but it's not the depth of information you promised."

"I get that," Beckett replied. "But you have to appreciate my position, General. I have a lot to lose."

"You have a lot to gain, also."

"Which is why I'm doing this. Like I told you."

Murcia sniffed. "Fine. You can stay here from now on." He led him over to the closest of the three outbuildings and opened the door. "We used these rooms when there were more of us onsite. They are rarely used these days, but are comfortable enough."

Beckett stepped inside, finding himself in a room about ten by fifteen feet, with a desk and chair adjacent to the door and a double bed facing it. On the wall next to the bed was a basin, and in the corner a shower pod. As he moved further into the room, there was a musty smell.

"It'll do," he said. "Thank you."

"I'll have my security guard bring you some food and supplies," Murcia told him, backing out of the room and easing the door closed. "Get some sleep. We'll speak again in the morning."

Beckett waited as the door clicked shut and then for the sound of a key turning in the lock, but it never came. He pulled his shirt off over his head and hung it across the back of the chair, then took his trousers off and draped them over the desk. Once done, he tried the door handle to make sure. It opened. A faint smile played across his lips.

Stripping out of his underwear, he walked over to the shower pod. Up to now he'd had to make do with brief sink washes in the toilet blocks, and the prospect of a real shower was inviting. Afterwards, he would try to get some rest. The seeds of doubt had now been planted in Murcia's mind, but the general was an unknown quantity and Beckett needed to be alert for what came next. He opened the pod door and twisted on the water. It was ice cold. Perfect.

## Chapter Forty

Peroza had left Lugo and was now alone in his quarters, sprawled on his dirty, sagging couch with a bottle of rum in his lap. The room, with its peeling paint and shabby furnishings, felt more like a prison cell than a living space. A solitary bulb dangled from the ceiling, casting distorted shadows on the walls that in his drunken state Peroza equated to the dark thoughts swirling around in his mind.

He lifted the bottle of rum, already a third empty, and glugged down another mouthful. It was rotten, cheap liquor from some moonshine place in Caracas, but his taste buds had been shot to pieces long ago. He drank and he stewed, the anger boiling in his belly. He hated the situation unfolding in his camp, hated Murcia's overbearing presence, and most of all, he hated the way his old comrade had made him feel pathetic and ineffective. He got up off the couch and paced. Kicked the wall. Drank some more. Sat down. His thoughts were a whirlwind of fury and determination.

## A World of Sun and Violence

*Enough!*

He had to do... something.

He got up and walked over to the window. Outside, the prison lay bathed in moonlight. Across the other side of the compound the lights were on in Murcia's suite and he saw movement in the window. Peroza imagined him there, sipping fine wine while plotting his rise to power. A glance at his watch showed it was almost 2.30 a.m.

"Screw it," he muttered to himself, snatching his gun and Taser from the table and holstering them as he headed for the door.

It was time.

He was ready.

As he paced across the yard, his rage felt like a physical force, propelling him onwards. He stormed into the soldiers' tent, where he found six of his men sitting around playing dominos and drinking beer. They looked up, startled by his abrupt entrance, their expressions shifting from surprise to apprehension.

"Get up! Get your weapons!" Peroza barked. "Come with me!"

The men, accustomed to his volatile nature, hastily scrambled to their feet. They scurried about, grabbing their discarded rifles and berets as fast as they could. Only one of them, a young recruit whom Peroza had found begging for his supper up in Anaco, dared to speak.

"What's going on, Lieutenant?" he asked, his words a little slurred. "It's getting late. Why the rush?"

In a flash, Peroza lunged at the young soldier, his hand clasping tightly around the kid's throat. He shoved him back, pinning him against the tent wall, his grip tightening. The fury coursing through him was intense.

How dare this pathetic prick question him and his authority?

Did he not know who he was?

The young man choked and gasped, clawing desperately at the lieutenant's vice-like grasp. Peroza was going to kill him. He was going to choke the life out of the rotten bastard. But in a moment of clarity he realised – he needed all the soldiers he had. With a grunt, he shoved the kid to the ground and stepped away from him.

"Because these are your orders!" he growled. "Now get up! All of you, follow me."

The young soldiers, now fully aware of the seriousness of their situation, scrambled into formation, following Peroza as he marched out of the tent and across the compound. As they went, he briefed them on their mission. They were to apprehend the general but take him alive. Peroza lowered his head, eyes fixed on Murcia's building as his resolve tightened along with his fists.

He could do this. He had to. It was his rebellion inside of a rebellion, and he would make his move or die trying.

The atmosphere was charged with the electric anticipation of impending violence as they approached Bracho's hut. Peroza stopped and turned to his men. "Wait here," he hissed. "But stay alert."

Pulling aside the velvet curtain, he entered the dim hut. The sight of Bracho, his deformed colossus, looming in the shadows at the back of the room, reminded him of a tiger he'd once seen at the zoo, caged and pensive, eager to be unleashed, ready to kill. A smile spread across Peroza's lips. This was exactly what he needed. Yet he approached with caution, his hand resting on the Taser in his belt, fully aware of the raw and unpredictable nature of his prized fighter.

"Bracho, my dear friend," he greeted him, keeping his

tone jovial and light. "I have a special task for you tonight. Are you ready to fight?"

Bracho looked up, an expression of confusion playing across his mangled features. "Fight? Kill?"

"Yes. That's right." Peroza held out his hand. "You know General Murcia? The man who torments you, who treats you so cruelly? I need your help to deal with him. Can you do that?"

Bracho nodded. Then he laughed. A high-pitched noise full of delight and eagerness. "Mur... cia!" he growled, the word garbled in his clumsy mouth. "Yes! Yes! Yes!" His eyes, usually dull and lifeless, sparked with a glint of excitement.

"That man has wronged you, my friend. But tonight you will get your revenge. The man who hurt you... it's time for him to pay." Bracho stood up, all six feet nine inches of him. He and the lieutenant stared at each other for a moment. "There are soldiers outside with guns," Peroza told him. "But they are our friends. Don't be concerned, just do as I say."

Bracho nodded eagerly and Peroza led him out into the moonlight. Without a word, he and his men walked together towards Murcia's building. No one spoke. Except for Bracho's heavy panting, no one seemed to even dare breathe.

As they reached the main entrance to Murcia's building, one of his security detail emerged and blocked their path.

"What do you want at this hour?" he asked, eyeing the angry posse before him with suspicion.

Peroza stepped forward. "I want to speak with General Murcia."

"He is otherwise engaged this evening. He does not want to be disturbed."

Peroza turned around. This was it, the moment of

truth. Do or die. Slowly, he walked over to Bracho and whispered, "Kill him."

The beast's response was both swift and ferocious. He lurched forward, his massive hand swiping the guard's rifle away, sending it clattering against the concrete steps. Before the guard could react, Bracho grabbed him in a vicious bear hug, hoisting him off the ground as he crushed the air out of him. Unable to get enough breath to even cry out, the guard struggled as best he could but his efforts were futile against Bracho's overwhelming strength. Bracho glanced at Peroza, seeking reassurance for his actions, and after receiving a curt nod, he slammed the guard to the ground and stamped on his head, crushing his skull beneath his bare foot with a sickening crunch.

"That's the way to do it!" Peroza hissed, gesturing at his men to enter the building, with Bracho and himself following closely behind.

The interior of Murcia's suite was peaceful. But as they advanced down the hallway, two more of Murcia's guards emerged from a side room. Their eyes widened in alarm at the sight of Peroza's men and the towering figure of Bracho. One of them raised his rifle and fired into Bracho's shoulder as he lumbered forward, but the beast-man absorbed the bullet with little reaction and seized the guard by the throat. With a single brutal swipe of his clubbed hand he knocked the second guard against the wall, before returning his attention to the man in his grip. His good eye grew wide with delight and he released a high-pitched squeal as the guard's face turned red, then purple, and then blue, before there was a loud snap and his head went limp. Flinging the spent body to the ground, Bracho strode over to the remaining, downed guard. With a final brutal movement he stomped his foot, crushing the man's face into the back of his skull like it was a piece of fruit. Finished, he looked over at Peroza, his deformed grin indicating his readiness for more.

"Very good, my friend," Peroza said, relishing the scene as he took in the stunned faces of his men. "Now let's find Murcia."

Peroza signalled for his men to continue into the building, the alcohol in his system, coupled with vast amounts of adrenaline, making him almost giddy as he followed them.

"Sir. He's here."

Peroza walked into Murcia's office to find his old friend cowering behind his desk, pistol in hand.

"Victor, what the hell is going on?! Call your men off." He stared on in grim realisation as Bracho lumbered into the room. "No, Victor! This is wrong! Stop this!"

Peroza hesitated for a moment, savouring Murcia's distress before calling out. "Halt, Bracho! Not yet."

The giant paused in front of the general, his hulking form vibrating with pent-up aggression as he turned around and noticed the Taser in Peroza's hand, a clear reminder of who was in control. Even Bracho couldn't win out against neuromuscular incapacitation.

Reluctantly he stepped back, leaving Murcia cowering on the floor.

"You pig! You fucking pig!" Murcia glared up at Peroza, his face twisted in rage. "You have no idea what you're doing."

"Oh, I know exactly what I'm doing, *brother*."

Peroza was enjoying this. Jalen Murcia, the polished politician, the strategic rebel leader, now reduced to a vulnerable, cringing wretch.

"Don't do this, Victor. Let's talk about it. I know I've

excluded you of late and I apologise. But we are so close now. Things can change…"

Peroza stood over him. "Things have already changed," he said, the venomous pleasure in his voice not doing justice to the excitement he felt. He drew his pistol. "You took things too far, my friend. Your time is up. Now we do things my way. *Viva la revolución!*"

## Chapter Forty-One

Beckett was lying on his bed with the lights out, going over a mental map of the compound, when he heard a single gunshot. Senses heightened, he opened his eyes and sat upright, waiting for more.

When none came, he rose from the bed and switched on the light. Without a watch he had no idea of the exact time but guessed it was around 3 a.m. – the perfect time to ambush someone in their bed. Or their suite.

He walked to the desk and pulled on his trousers and shirt before heading for the door. Gripping the handle, he eased it open a crack. There was no one in the vicinity, but over to his right he could hear shouting coming from inside Murcia's building. Peroza. It had to be. And from the sounds of it, the situation was at breaking point.

Beckett hadn't planned on things happening so fast, but whilst disorder and panic reigned, he had to capitalise on the situation. Most of the guards lacked combat experience. They'd be confused and unsettled right now.

He opened the door wide and stepped outside. The air

was cool on his skin, a welcome change from the daytime humidity. He moved down the side of the outbuilding, slowing to lean around the corner. The storage unit was a hundred metres in front of him, but an armed guard was standing outside it. The youngster looked pensive, glancing around him with his rifle drawn and ready.

Beckett waited. The kid looked to be in two minds whether to stay at his post or join his buddies over at Murcia's place. If he moved on, Beckett's path would be clearer. If not, he could still approach the unit in a wide arc and neutralise the guard using stealth. But it had to happen soon, whilst the camp was still in disarray.

Footsteps to his right caught his attention. Looking over, he saw two more guards running towards him, heading for Murcia's building.

"Hey!" Beckett called out, counting on them having seen him with Murcia earlier. "I am here as the general's guest. What's going on?"

The guards stopped and stared at him, their youthful faces creased with fear and uncertainty.

"We do not know!" one of them said. "We are going to check."

"I heard gunfire and I need you to stay with me," Beckett told them, adopting a tone of urgency. He pointed to the largest of the two men. "You. Come here. You have to protect me."

The guards exchanged nervous glances. They looked terrified. Like they'd found themselves in a war they never wanted to be part of. Beckett had seen it happen often in Africa and the Middle East, as well as in South America. Young kids get recruited into these guerrilla or terrorist outfits with the promise of status and success. Their recruiters tell them they'll be fighting for an important

## A World of Sun and Violence

cause, that they'll be heroes – and these kids who grew up playing Call of Duty and watching action movies, like the idea of being a soldier, so why not? Yet they soon find the reality of war is a lot different to the movies. And when they get shot, they can't start the game over again.

"These are the general's orders!" Beckett continued, pointing at the two men. "You – stay here. And you – go see what is happening. They need you." The men nodded in unison. The one Beckett had selected stepped closer while his partner turned and hurried towards Murcia's building.

"Now, follow me," Beckett commanded, leading the young guard back to his room. "Come inside. I need your help with something."

The guard, his confounded expression now fixed in place, shuffled into the building behind Beckett and looked around.

"What help do you need?" he asked.

Beckett let the door swing shut. "I need your uniform," he said, slamming his fist down on the barrel of the man's gun and following up with a sharp elbow to the jaw, rattling his brain against his skull. The guard's eyes rolled back and he dropped to the floor, unconscious.

Beckett wasted no time. He stripped the guard and then himself, before changing into the guard's uniform. Although not a perfect disguise – the fatigues fit a little too snugly over his broad frame – it would suffice, from a distance. He hauled the still unconscious guard onto the chair and secured him with torn strips of bedsheet, binding his ankles and wrists, then securing him to the seat to ensure he was immobile. A gag made of a sock and more strips of bedsheet muffled any potential alert he'd try to make when he came around.

Picking up the fallen assault rifle, Beckett slung the strap over his shoulder and moved to the door. His mind was laser-focused and his objective clear. Get the hostages to safety.

Outside, the night air buzzed with the sounds of conflict. But for Beckett, it was a call to action.

And he was more than ready for it.

## Chapter Forty-Two

Adler had heard the gunshot, too. She was now sitting on the tent floor, trying to piece together some kind of plan. Further cracks echoed in the distance, each one amplifying her worry, but also igniting a spark of hope. This could be their chance.

Propelled into action, she got to her feet and peered around. Through the tent flaps she saw it was dark outside, darker still in the tent. It was also chilly. She'd fallen asleep dressed in her jeans and an undershirt and she felt around for her shirt, slipping it on as her eyes grew accustomed to the gloom.

The tent was silent. She crept to the doorway, straining her ears. The lack of voices, the absence of movement or rustles of uniform, it was unsettling.

"Hello? Guard?"

It was normal for one of the soldiers to poke their head through if one of the hostages needed to use the bathroom. But there was no response.

"Hello, can you hear me? Is anyone there?"

Still no reply. She waited for a count of ten, but sensed no presence outside the tent. With a cautious hand she lifted the canvas and stepped out.

Her heart raced. The armed men were gone, possibly having left their post to deal with whatever was going on across the other side of the prison.

*This could be it!*

Her gaze swept the compound, registering the noticeable absence of guards. In the distance, near the main building, she saw silhouettes of people running, illuminated suddenly by the flash of gunfire. She also clocked two military jeeps parked in the corner near the gate on the far side. Glancing back to the main building on this side of the compound, she counted two more jeeps – more than enough transport for them all to escape. If only they could get those damned gates open.

She shivered, the night air acting as a catalyst for the mix of excitement and trepidation coursing through her veins.

Slipping back inside the tent, she moved over to where Bruce and Kathleen were both snoring softly. "Hey, Bruce, wake up," she hissed, placing her hand on his shoulder and giving him a firm shake.

"Huh, what's going on?" he mumbled. "What is it?"

"You need to wake up," she replied. "We have to move. Now!"

On the other side of him, Kathleen stirred. "Bruce? Is everything all right?"

"Everything's good," Adler said. "But I need you to get up and get ready to leave here in the next two minutes."

Castillo was already awake and sitting up as Adler approached. "We're making a break for it," she whispered. "We've got a good window. But I need your help."

He rubbed at his eyes. "Okay, I got you. What's the plan?"

She glanced back towards the entrance. "The camp's in disarray," she told him. "There are two jeeps parked by the main building. If we can get them started and get the gate open we can escape."

"That's a big if," Castillo replied, staggering to stand. "What if they catch us?"

"It sounds as though there's some kind of skirmish over on the other side of the yard. With the confusion they won't have time to notice us. But we have to go now or we might not get another chance."

The Dixons, now fully awake, looked at each other. "Are you sure?" Kathleen asked, her voice quivering. "Shouldn't we wait?"

"Someone will come for us," Bruce added. "They have appeals for these sorts of things. We've all seen it. People are good. They'll help get us home. We should wait. It's safer."

"Bruce, I don't think it's that easy," Adler told him. "We have no idea what will happen here tonight and I don't want to wait around to find out. The situation is too volatile. Please, you have to come. It's now or never."

"She's right," Castillo said. "Listen to the noise out there. We can't miss this chance. We could all be killed if we stay here, either on purpose or in the crossfire."

Bruce puffed out his cheeks as Kathleen gave him a nod. "Fine. Let's do it."

"Good man." Adler helped him and Kathleen to their feet. As they prepared to leave the tent, her focus was singular – get everyone out alive. The chaos outside provided the perfect cover, but it was also an unknown danger.

She was gathering the group together when the tent flap opened and a guard entered.

*Shit.*

Adler froze, thinking on her feet to explain why they were awake and standing by the entrance. But then she saw his face.

"Beckett?" she exclaimed, a mix of surprise and relief washing over her.

"Oh Lord! He's one of them!" Kathleen spluttered.

"No. I'm not," Beckett said, walking over to them. "I overpowered one of the guards and took his uniform."

As he was saying this, Adler strode up to him. Her relief had quickly been replaced by an intense rage that bubbled up inside her. At least, she thought it was rage. She got up to him and slapped him hard across the face. "Bastard!"

Beckett took the hit and didn't flinch. "I probably deserved that," he said, holding her glare. "I know divulging that information put you in a bad position, Adler, but it was all I had except for shooting you in the head. I had to keep Murcia onside."

"Why should I trust you?" she hissed.

"Because this is our chance. I've been scoping out the place and I think we can do this if we work together."

She listened intently as Beckett outlined his plan, explaining to the group how he'd identified the storage building as a potential source of weapons and that he could get inside. More crucially, he knew how to get through the gates.

"The wood is old and rotten in places," he said. "If we can get our hands on some explosives, we can blast them open – at least do enough damage to get through."

Adler watched him carefully as he spoke. Beckett's plan was risky but straightforward. He would get the gates open and then create a diversion, giving Adler and the others a chance to escape in one of the jeeps.

"I'll be right behind you," he assured them, before he hesitated. Looking around the group he asked, "Where's Price?"

Adler glanced at Castillo. "He…didn't make it," she said, quietly.

Beckett groaned. But seemingly, this was enough of an explanation for him, which came as some relief. The last thing any of them needed was to be reminded of Price's fate.

"How will you do it?" she asked him.

"Do what?"

"Create a diversion, distract an entire camp of armed rebels?"

His eyes flashed. "I haven't worked out all the details yet. But I will. When the moment comes I'll figure it out."

"Easy as that?" she said, shaking her head.

"It's our only way." His face was serious. "You know it as well as I do. But this has to happen now. So…"

Adler considered that and agreed, this was their only shot. Despite her doubts about Beckett's allegiance, the urgency of the situation left no room for indecision.

"Fine," she said, her voice low but firm. "Let's do this."

## Chapter Forty-Three

It was a few minutes after 8 a.m. in the UK, and despite having been on garden leave for over a month, Robert Locke was up early. Indeed, he'd been awake since 5 a.m. when his alarm had sounded, and had showered and eaten a hearty breakfast, followed by a drive in his new gunmetal-grey Range Rover to Upchurch River Valley Golf Course, ready to play a glorious eighteen holes in the fresh air.

Now, standing on the green of the first hole, putter in hand, he felt fitter and more alive than he had done in months. Retirement had gently rounded his once-lean frame, and streaks of grey now dashed through his jet-black hair, but his doctor had informed him last week that his stress levels and blood pressure were now almost normal again.

Locke was the sort of person who was constantly wired for danger, full of adrenaline and nerves, even in these seemingly peaceful surroundings. But day by day he was learning to become a civilian again. He had no regrets.

"Come on, Rob, get a bloody wriggle on."

He glanced up at Terry, his oldest friend, waiting patiently at the edge of the green, and winked. "Now, now. You can't rush these things, old boy."

He returned his focus to the ball, adjusting his stance and then his grip on the putter. His eyes, sharp and perceptive, flicked from ball to hole and back again. He pulled in a deep breath, held it and released, slowing down his heart rate as he lined up the shot. He was ready to take it when his phone vibrated in the pocket of his chinos.

*Bugger.*

Why hadn't he turned the damned thing off?

Pulling the phone from his pocket, he saw a US number on the screen. "Bloody hell," he muttered. "Who the hell is calling at this hour?" He motioned to Terry, signalling for a brief interruption. "Sorry about this. Give me a minute, would you?"

Walking away from the green, he answered the call, lowering his voice and turning his back on Terry as he did. It was more out of habit than reason, yet something in his gut told him this call was important.

"Hello, Robert Locke here."

"Bobby, I'm glad I caught you. It's Dick Foster."

"Dick. Heavens, it's been a while."

Foster chuckled. "That it has, my friend. How's retirement working out for you?"

"Oh, you know. Keeping myself out of trouble."

Locke had known Foster for over ten years, from back when he was the head of the CIA's NCS division and Locke was gearing up to take over at Sigma Unit. They'd run many joint operations together and liked and trusted each other. But Foster was now deputy director of the agency and Locke was retired. As such, it was strange and rather worrying that Foster was calling him out of the blue like this.

"Listen, can you talk freely?" Foster asked, his voice now serious.

"Erm… yes, I suppose. I'm out in the open. No one around." He glanced over at Terry and mouthed 'sorry'. "And there was me thinking you were just calling to see how I was."

"Maybe some other time. I'm afraid I've got a favour to ask."

Locke looked at his watch, quickly working out that it would be 3 a.m. in Washington. That didn't make him feel any better about the call. If Foster was in his office at this time, then it was serious.

"How can I help?" he asked.

Foster's reply was straightforward and devoid of pleasantries. "I need information on one of your operatives. I know it's a big ask. But it's important."

"Dick, you're barking up the wrong tree," Locke told him. "I'm retired. And regardless, you should be talking to Calder at MI6 if you need that kind of intel."

Foster cleared his throat. "This is… deeper than that, Robert."

"I see." Despite not mentioning Sigma Unit directly, the implication was clear in Foster's tone. Locke sighed and looked around, turning a full three-sixty. Terry was leaning on his putter, scrolling through his phone, and there was no one else in sight. He lowered his phone to see the number. He still didn't recognise it, but he could be confident Foster was calling on a secure line. "I wish I could help you, but it's the same answer, Dick. I'm retired. I have no clearance. Contact Victoria Harwood, my successor. She's good. Very thorough."

## A World of Sun and Violence

"I need this today, Bobby. Now. I can't say too much, but between you and me it's an incredibly delicate and potentially disastrous situation. We have US hostages being held by a group of Colombian rebels down in Venezuela. We've reached out to the Venezuelans but they're not playing ball and the situation is escalating fast." He paused as if considering his next words. "One of the hostages is a woman called Vanessa Adler. She's CIA, over there on a black ops mission. We can't let the Venezuelans get wind of that. But the thing is... she's also the daughter of Senator Simon Adler." He paused again, allowing that information to sink in.

And what a lot of information it was. Locke blew out a long breath as he considered it. "That's quite a mess."

"Damn right. But we think – well, we know – that you have intel on one of her fellow hostages. He worked for you. Closely."

"Do you have a name?" Locke closed his eyes. He knew the answer before he asked. But he had to ask.

"Beckett," Foster said. "John Beckett."

Locke's silence stretched for a few seconds as he processed Foster's revelation, his thoughts racing at a thousand miles an hour. "Have you spoken to Xander Templeton about this?" he asked.

"Not yet. I wanted to get your take on it first."

"Good. Well, don't. If you want my help, that's my only request. Leave Templeton out of this."

Foster snorted in amusement, the sound distorting down the line. "I know you're not a fan of the guy, but Templeton's regarded as one of our finest section chiefs."

"I think we'll have to agree to disagree on that one. John Beckett is a good man and an even better operative. But he and Templeton... clashed. Which is putting it mildly. It's one of the reasons why Beckett is no longer…"—he paused, searching for the right phrase, the one that would best paper over the reality of what happened—"…part of Sigma Unit." It was the best he could do. There was little point in going over what had happened. Besides, it was highly classified and he wasn't prepared to divulge that information, not even to Dick Foster.

"But you vouch for this man Beckett?"

Locke raised his head. "Oh yes, let me be clear – John Beckett is one of the bravest and most loyal men I've ever met. He's tough, highly trained, incredibly resourceful, the best of the best. If he's with your people, they have a chance. No matter what."

"I can trust you on this?"

"You know you can. That's why you called me at silly o'clock on a Tuesday morning."

"Okay, thanks. And…" Foster's voice turned grave. "I can count on your discretion with this, Bobby?"

"You have my word," Locke replied. "Who am I going to tell? I'm just an old retiree trying to better his handicap."

"Good man. I appreciate it."

Foster hung up and Locke stood motionless for a moment, his gaze fixed on the horizon, a thousand memories flickering in his mind's eye.

Beckett was alive. He was still in the game.

"But of course he bloody is," he murmured to himself. "He's John Beckett."

Returning to his golf ball, Locke realigned his putt. For a brief moment just then, he'd almost missed being part of the cut and thrust of international intelligence. But this was where he was meant to be now.

Beckett was still alive. He hoped he'd stay that way.

"Best of luck, John," he whispered into the morning air.

## Chapter Forty-Four

Beckett crept along the perimeter of the compound, blending into the shadows cast by the early dawn. Despite wearing the guard's uniform, the disguise wouldn't hold up under close scrutiny and so staying out of sight was crucial.

As he edged closer to Murcia's building, he noticed a sentry stationed outside and pressed himself against the prison wall. From this vantage point he could see through into the front room of the building. Inside was Murcia, battered and bloodied, slumped on a couch with Peroza standing over him, gun in hand. The lieutenant was swaying as he shoved the Magnum into Murcia's face, laughing boisterously, mocking the general. Beckett tensed. Peroza was wild and thuggish at best, but with a mixture of booze, bravado and power, he was a bomb ready to go off.

As the sentry turned away, Beckett seized the opportunity, darting across the open ground and concealing himself against the nearest outbuilding. He assessed the layout.

Another of the smaller buildings stood in front of him, and beyond that, the main storage unit. The same young man stood guard outside, rifle in hand. Beckett braced himself. He knew this was a long shot, but time was slipping away. He had to get the hostages out before sunrise.

Breaking cover, he lowered his head and fell into a steady walk as he traversed the side of the outbuilding and approached the storage unit.

"Hey, I'm here to take over," he muttered in Spanish as he got close.

"That's not right. I'm here until morning," the young guard replied.

Beckett held his nerve. He tried again, keeping his tone firm. "I don't know, man. These are Lieutenant Peroza's orders."

"That doesn't make sense. Where is he?" The guard's confusion turned quickly to aggression. "What's your name?"

Beckett couldn't let this escalate. In one stride he closed the distance between them. His left hand shot out, slamming down hard on the barrel of the guard's rifle, pinning it against his body. In the same movement, he stepped around the smaller man and snaked his arm around his neck. The guard gasped and struggled, but it was no use; the more he struggled, the tighter Beckett squeezed. Five seconds ticked by, then ten. At the twenty-second mark the guard's body went limp, his arms falling to his sides.

Beckett gently lowered him to the ground and pressed two fingers to his throat. He was only a young man, unprepared for this conflict, and for a split-second Beckett felt a twinge of something approaching remorse. But he swiftly pushed it down deep inside himself and retrieved the man's rifle, slinging it over his shoulder before getting to his feet.

Glancing around, he was relieved to see the compound remained oblivious, but the noise coming from Murcia's suite sounded even more celebratory and debauched. That was a bad sign.

He tried the door to the storage unit door. Locked. He searched the guard's pockets and belt. No key.

*Shit.*

He tried forcing the door open, but it was too robust and any further attempts would attract unwanted attention. He looked over to the holding tent, noticing Adler peering out. She saw him and gave a nod, confirming the hostages were ready to move. He nodded back and dashed back towards the first outbuilding, then made his way along the prison wall using the shadows as cover, heading towards Peroza's quarters.

As he approached Peroza's building, two guards were leaving through the main entrance carrying beer crates. Beckett ducked down, watching as they crossed the yard towards Murcia's suite, the beer bottles clinking as they went.

It was another bad sign. Peroza and his men were already full of booze and insurgence. More alcohol would only make the situation more dangerous. Both Peroza and his man Lugo were old-school thugs, capricious and cruel. In their heads they'd ousted Murcia; but then what? Would they come for the hostages, decide to make an example of them? The lieutenant was a vain and vindictive man. Beckett could imagine him forcing the remaining hostages to face Bracho. Just to prove to everyone he was in charge. Just because he could. Beckett was armed but out in the open, he could engage some of the guards but not all of them. There was also a chance the hostages would get caught in the crossfire. He couldn't risk it. The plan remained the same. But it was now or never.

He emerged from his cover and sprinted the rest of the

way to Peroza's building. After leaping up the steps in a single bound he slipped inside, entering a wide corridor with a stairwell at the far end and doors leading off on either side. He moved diligently through the building, searching each room for the keys to the storage unit.

In a room near the stairwell he found a large desk with two computer screens and a server tower, its green and red lights flickering silently in the gloom. But no keys. He was turning to leave when footsteps echoed on the stairs. As he listened, they stepped down into the corridor, too close for him to make a run for it. Swinging the assault rifle off his shoulder, he aimed at the door before reconsidering and flipping it around the other way. It would be reckless to shoot if he didn't have to. The noise would attract more guards, and besides, these heavy Colombian rifles doubled up perfectly as blunt instruments.

He shifted into a fighting stance as a large man appeared in the doorway. Beckett had clocked this guy when they first arrived at the prison. He was the biggest of the guards, tall and broad and with a feral demeanour that suggested he could be trouble.

A look of surprise creased his big features as he saw Beckett. "*Qué carajo?*" he growled, reaching for a large knife hanging from his belt.

In these situations, landing the first blow was vital. Knowing this, Beckett immediately became the aggressor, swinging the rifle butt at the soldier's head. But he was surprisingly agile for his size and shifted out of the way before contact was made. Beckett stumbled forward and the big man grabbed him around the back of the head, slamming him with force against the wall. Recovering quickly, Beckett spun around in time to evade a deadly knife swing, the blade missing his face by mere inches. He gripped the man's wrist, attempting to gain control, but the man was also stronger than he looked and delivered a forceful punch to Beckett's jaw, sending a wave of pain shooting through his skull.

Exploiting the situation, the guard pushed forward, knife in hand, aiming directly at Beckett's heart. Beckett was dazed and unsteady on his feet, but with years of experience in close combat his muscle memory and instincts took over. With a burst of energy he sidestepped the man and grabbed the knife-wielding arm once more. This time he made it count, stepping past him and twisting violently, forcing the elbow joint against itself. There was a crack and a pop and the man let out a roar of pain as his arm lost all power and the knife clattered to the hard floor.

Beckett shoved him away and scooped up the knife. The man, overcome by excruciating pain, was momentarily defenceless and Beckett didn't hesitate. Stepping forward he plunged the blade up through the big man's ribcage, driving it into his heart. The man stared at Beckett for a second, his eyes widening in disbelief, before he collapsed to the ground.

Not wasting any time, Beckett recovered his rifle and searched the room, yanking open the desk drawers and turning out every box file. He found an old map of the area, which he glanced over before stuffing in his pocket, but no key. Time was running out. He was about to try upstairs when he glanced again at the guard's lifeless body. Crouching, Beckett searched the man's pockets. He found only chewing gum wrappers and cigarettes, but the movement alerted him to something else and he hauled the big lump over onto his front. A bunch of keys hung from his belt at the back. The one for the storage unit had to be on there. Breathing heavily, Beckett unhooked the keys and sprinted out of the building. His body ached and his lip was bleeding, but he pushed himself onwards. The sun would soon be visible over the horizon and he didn't have much time.

With gritted teeth he ran along the side of the barracks, making for the first outbuilding. But as he crossed the exercise yard he saw a hulking silhouette coming towards him. Bracho, unmistakable even in the dim light of dawn, was returning to his hut.

Beckett tried to alter his course, to run for cover, but it was too late. Bracho had seen him. Their eyes met and Beckett slowed to a stop. His instincts screamed at him to run, but he was paralysed, staring into the eyes of the giant man.

Then, with a sinister growl, Bracho began to move towards him.

## Chapter Forty-Five

Beckett remained rooted in place, his breathing shallow, as Bracho trudged ever closer to him. The giant's deformed eye was weeping, and as his lips parted into a manic grin, he revealed two rows of black and yellow teeth. The growl emanating from him was primal. More like a wild animal than a man.

"Hey there," Beckett whispered, raising his hands in a non-threatening gesture and reverting to Spanish. "It's okay."

Bracho stopped a few metres away. Up close he was immense. Beckett could sense the raw, untamed power radiating from him. It was like being cornered by a wolf or a grizzly bear. One wrong move, one hint of aggression, and he'd be torn apart.

With one hand still raised, Beckett tapped his chest with the other. "Friend," he said softly. *Amigo.* "I want to help you."

Bracho tilted his head to one side, perhaps contemplating Beckett's words. His good eye, which still held a flicker of humanity, widened. "Friend?"

"That's right." Beckett smiled. "Friend." He risked a step forward, keeping his movements slow and steady, observing Bracho's reaction. The big man didn't move, but his hands remained clenched into fists.

As Beckett took another step forward, the rifle slipped off his shoulder and swung outwards. Bracho recoiled as if in pain, his growls intensifying as he gnashed his teeth.

"No, no, it's fine," Beckett assured him, lifting the rifle to show him.

Bracho's eyes fixated on the weapon and he grinned. "Gun."

"Yes. That's right. Would you… like it?"

Bracho stared at him, his mouth hanging open. He nodded. "Yes! Yes, yes!"

"Okay, fine. I'm going to give it to you." Holding Bracho's gaze, he swiftly ejected the magazine and pocketed it before offering the rifle over.

Bracho snatched it from him and stepped back, holding the weapon like a child might hold a toy gun, his delight evident in his wide grin. "Friend. Gun!"

"That's right," Beckett said, taking the opportunity to edge away. He pointed to the sky. "But the sun is up soon. Very hot."

Bracho glanced up at the brightening sky and scowled. Clutching the rifle to his chest, he wandered back to his hut and disappeared behind the heavy curtain without looking back.

*Bloody hell…*

That was close. Too close.

Beckett paused, ensuring Bracho was now settled in his hut before pulling himself together and setting off again.

## A World of Sun and Violence

Navigating his way past the building where he had spent the night, he wound his way between the two smaller outbuildings. His heart was racing with a mixture of adrenaline and urgency as he reached the storage unit and pulled the keys from his pocket. The first two keys failed, but on the third attempt the lock clicked open. He slipped inside and closed the door behind him, immediately greeted by the musty scent of diesel, paint, and metal. He flicked the switch next to the door and an LED bulb dangling from the ceiling burst into life.

He made a beeline for the back wall where he'd spotted the rifles a day earlier. Hanging on a rack were four Galil Córdovas – more than enough firepower for their escape. Spying an old military holdall on a shelf, he spread it open on the concrete floor and carefully placed the rifles inside. Underneath the rack, a squat chest of drawers contained enough boxes of ammunition to arm the entire compound three times over. He grabbed up six boxes as well as four spare magazines and stuffed them into the bag under the rifles.

But what he needed were explosives.

He moved around the unit, lifting tarpaulins and opening boxes, but found nothing of note except for one lousy hand grenade. It was an M67, which could potentially take out one of the gates, but only if it went off at a strategic point. That could be tricky and he didn't want to put all his eggs in that basket. He needed more.

Turning, he cast his attention around the room. The storage unit offered limited options but he was determined to find a solution. In the far corner he found a stack of old fuel cannisters and a jerry can. He lifted a couple of the cannisters, shaking them to gauge their fullness and feeling the liquid sloshing inside. He also found a pile of old uniforms and a sheet covered in paint. A plan began to form.

He spread the sheet on the floor and piled the fuel canisters in the centre, enough to make it count but not so many he'd have trouble carrying it. Yet fuel on its own was flammable but not explosive. He needed to increase the potential for combustion. He scoured the shelves, desperately searching for inspiration. At the bottom of the middle shelving unit, near the wall, he found what he was looking for – a box of spray paints and some white spirits, likely used for maintenance around the prison. He carried the box over to the sheet and dumped the contents on top of the fuel canisters. To amplify the impact, he laid the old uniforms on top and doused the whole thing with the contents of the jerry can. Lastly he returned to the chest of drawers and grabbed the remaining boxes of ammo, stacking them on top of the uniforms. Rather than force the bullets down a barrel, in this setting the gunpowder would cause the casings to act like shrapnel, enhancing the explosive impact.

Gathering up the corners of the sheet, he used a roll of electrical tape to bind the whole thing together. His eyes were streaming and his throat raw from the fumes, but he was satisfied it would work.

After hauling the makeshift bomb onto his back, he collected the holdall containing the rifles and ammunition. The load was heavy and cumbersome but he only needed to carry it a short distance.

Leaving the storage unit, he made his way towards the main gate near Peroza's building, keeping close to the shadows of the outbuildings and tents. Away from the revelry in Murcia's suite, this side of the compound was quiet, almost eerily so. Dropping the holdall down, he moved over to the main gate and positioned the bundle of explosives strategically in the centre of the two panels.

Once done, he turned his attention to the twin jeeps parked nearby. He checked each of them, finding the keys had been left in the ignitions as he'd hoped. Retrieving the bag of weapons, he carried it swiftly across the exercise yard to the holding tent.

Adler was outside as he approached. "Did you manage it?" she asked.

"Affirmative. Everything is in place." He lay the rifles down at her feet. "Get everyone to make their way to the steps in front of the main building. You'll be safe from the blast there. Once the gate blows, get everyone in the jeep as quickly as possible and get the hell out of here."

"What are you using?" she asked. "Did you find explosives?"

Beckett coughed. "I had to improvise, but it should work."

"*Should?*" Adler glared at him. "How will we detonate it?"

"With this." Beckett reached into his pocket and pulled out the grenade. "It'll also provide part of the blast. Once we're all in position I'll toss it."

"O… kay. Are you a good shot?"

He grinned. "Let's hope so."

"Don't kid around," she snapped, but there was a twinkle in her eyes as she said it. "What happens then?"

"Once the gate blows, you drive out of here as fast as you can. I'll get in the second jeep and wait for Peroza and his men to appear. Once they've seen me, I'll set off and lead them away from you." He pulled the map from his back pocket and showed it to her, pointing at key areas as he explained. "You'll head down this road here. It'll take you around the side of the jungle and eventually crosses the river before reaching the town of San Luzardo de Aragua. At the same time, I'll draw them away down this road here. But we'll be leaving them with two jeeps. If they split up and come after you, you've got these rifles. Use them – you and Castillo. We'll meet at the rendezvous point here." He stabbed his finger at the map.

"Got it." Adler nodded slowly to herself as she scanned the details in front of her. She looked up and frowned. "Wait, can't we blow up their other jeeps? Incapacitate them at least?"

Beckett glanced over her head at the far building. "I thought about that, but there's an armed sentry standing guard nearby. It's too risky. Plus, we need all the explosive material available to blow the gate. I know this isn't the most elegant of strategies, but it's all we've got." He picked up one of the rifles and checked the magazine. "Now gather the others. It's time to move."

He turned to leave but Adler grabbed his arm. "Beckett!"

"What is it?"

"Good luck. I think we'll need it."

He smiled. "Thanks. You too. Now go."

## Chapter Forty-Six

Peroza was enjoying his newfound power so much more than he'd ever imagined he would. And he'd imagined it a lot. He was currently standing at one end of Murcia's once-immaculate suite – now a scene of raucous celebration – with the stub of a Cuban cigar smouldering between his lips and a glass of expensive brandy sloshing from a glass in his hand. Salsa beats boomed from out of the speaker system in the corner, mixing with the laughter, cigar smoke, and heavy stench of alcohol.

His gaze landed on his old comrade, slumped in the corner of the couch. The great General Murcia, the man who'd once been like a brother to him, was now a defeated figure. Bloody and broken. Reduced to whimpering beneath his gag like a little bitch.

Peroza caught his eye and shook his head. "You should have listened to me, Jalen," he called over. "You underestimated me, like you always did. But it's the last time you ever will." He laughed. More to taunt Murcia than from genuine amusement, but what was the difference?

Lugo and the rest of his men, drunk on liquor and victory, danced around in the middle of the room, spilling beer and whisky on the furniture, their laughter coarse and loud. Some of them would be cleaning this mess up later, but for now Peroza would let them have their fun. Why not? They were revelling in their new leader's success, after all. He smirked as one of the youngsters sidled over to Murcia and tousled his hair with mock affection.

Yet despite their merriment, and Peroza's sense of pride in what he'd achieved, he couldn't shake the niggling voice in the back of his mind. It was the same one he heard sometimes when he was lying awake at night. It told him he was completely out of his depth. That he'd made a terrible mistake.

And maybe it was right.

He'd not thought far enough ahead. He had no plan for what happened tomorrow or the day after. All he'd cared about was getting the better of Murcia, making him pay for leaving him in the dirt.

He pulled on his cigar. It had gone out, so he flicked at his lighter. The flame burned his fatigued eyes as he touched it to the end of the Cuban and drew in a mouthful of smoke. He exhaled, before complementing the taste of bitter tobacco smoke with another gulp of brandy.

*Stop this worrying.*

It was all fine. It was all good. Because he deserved this. He watched his men, a smirk playing on his lips. He reached for the bottle of brandy. As he poured himself another glass, one of his men stumbled over to him.

"*General* Peroza," he slurred. "Thank you for such a great party. And for being such a wonderful general. Viva la revolution!" He gave a sloppy salute and staggered away, leaving Peroza with a bemused smile on his face.

Still, as he sipped his brandy, Peroza's gaze involuntarily drifted back to the defeated Murcia and darker thoughts clouded his mind. Despite having no real plan of action, one thing was certain, he would eventually have to execute his old friend. The realisation pained him, but he saw no alternative. Murcia had become a threat, his ambitions too aligned with the very forces they'd once fought to overthrow. They were supposed to be revolutionaries, for Christ's sake, but the idiot was already imagining himself in the presidential suite.

What was it they said?

The day after the revolution, the rebel becomes everything he hates.

Peroza drained his glass. Yes. Murcia had to die and it had to be soon. Tonight. Or rather, today. A glance out the window told him the sun was now peeking over the horizon. Either way he had to kill his old friend, and before he could talk himself out of it.

He grabbed the bottle of brandy. More deaths would follow, but they would be less of an issue. In fact, he was going to enjoy them. Beckett, that meddling Englishman, would be next, and then each of the hostages. He'd let Lugo deal with the American woman. His new lieutenant seemed to have a thing for her.

A grim resolve settled over him. It was time to show the world who the ELC really was. But a moment later his thoughts were shattered by a loud explosion from outside.

"What the fuck…?"

He looked around as confusion and panic erupted amongst his men. Some dropped to the ground in fear, others sought shelter behind the couch.

"Get up!" he screamed at them. "Find out what's going on?"

No one moved except Lugo, whose drunken stupor had been replaced by a heightened alertness. He stepped forward and grabbed Peroza's arm and they rushed to the front door. Outside, the new day's sun was yet to fully show itself, but the prison was alight from the flames licking up the front gates, now blown off their hinges. Thick black smoke spiralled up into the sky.

"No!"

Peroza stormed back into the front room, barking orders over the din. "Turn that damn music off!" he yelled, gesturing wildly at the speaker system. "Grab your rifles and get out there. Move!"

The men scrambled to comply as Peroza marched over to Murcia, still cowering on the couch.

"I didn't know!" he spluttered, as Peroza yanked the gag from his mouth. "I swear it! I thought he was—"

"I knew it!" Peroza cut him off, spittle flying from his mouth. "This is your friend's doing. That MI6 prick. I told you he was trouble. Idiot." He slapped his old friend around the face with all the force he had left. "This is on you, Jalen. I'll make you pay for this."

Turning, he saw his men huddled together by the door, their faces pale, their demeanours a mixture of fear and bewilderment.

"Go on then!" he screamed at them, pulling his pistol from his pocket and racing for the door. "*Vamos! Ahora!* Get that fucking Englishman!"

## Chapter Forty-Seven

The acrid stench of chemicals and burning wood followed Beckett as he raced back to the jeep and jumped in the driver's seat. Through the clearing smoke he surveyed the aftermath at the main gate. His makeshift bomb had done its job, albeit not as extensively as he'd hoped. Only one panel was hanging off, but there was enough of a gap down the middle that a single jeep could pass through.

"All right, drive!" he yelled to the others. "And don't stop!"

Castillo was behind the wheel of the other jeep. He waved his hand in a vague salute as the vehicle lurched forward. Adler was seated beside him, clutching a rifle. Her eyes were sharp and focused, her face rigid with concentration. The hostages had a good chance with her onboard, Beckett thought, as he watched them go.

Now it was his turn.

He counted five, then manoeuvred the jeep around and stopped in front of the gate, keeping the engine running. A glance in the rearview mirror revealed the chaos unfolding across the other side of the compound. Peroza and his men, unsettled and impaired by alcohol, were bustling out of the far building, yelling and pointing. Beckett counted eight hostiles in total, his eyes finally resting on Peroza, whose face he imagined twisted with rage as it dawned on him what was happening.

Gunfire rang out, but it was only more proof that these young soldiers were nothing more than unsophisticated amateurs. Even if they weren't drunk, no one was going to hit him from that distance.

As the rebels hastily piled into their remaining jeeps, Beckett waited a few more critical seconds, then sat back and gripped the wheel once they were on the move. It was now or never. Slamming the accelerator to the floor, he propelled the jeep through the billowing smoke and out of the compound.

The early morning sun, just beginning to assert itself, cast a mosaic of light and shadow on the dirt road leading from the prison. Up ahead, the road forked and Adler's jeep was visible driving away down the right-hand track. Beckett veered left as planned. This road snaked around the side of the prison, ending up at the oil field. He'd told Adler he hoped to take Peroza and his men on a wild goose chase, before doubling back and meeting her at the rendezvous point. However, he suspected Adler knew that was a lie.

Beckett couldn't risk leaving Peroza in play. The current instability in Venezuela was one thing, but Peroza's influence spread to most of the towns in the region. Even if the hostages got to freedom, it didn't guarantee their safety.

He had to finish this. Today.

The surrounding jungle was a blur of greens and browns as Beckett pushed the jeep to its limits, navigating the winding, uneven road. His attention alternated between the path ahead and the rearview mirror, vigilant for any sign of pursuit. Despite the ruggedness of the terrain and the vehicle's protesting suspension, his hands remained steady on the wheel, holding his nerve with military focus. At the same time his mind was racing with tactical considerations, calculating distances, potential routes, anticipating his pursuers' movements.

Glancing back over his shoulder, he saw the first jeep tailing him by fifty metres. Good. They'd taken the bait. As the road straightened, gunfire erupted, bullets zipping past and hammering into the surrounding trees, dangerously close. Beckett jerked the wheel, zigzagging the jeep across the road to dodge the incoming fire. With one hand gripping the wheel, he reached for his rifle, firing off shots more as a distraction than an attempt to take out his pursuers. No one hit a moving target one-handedly using an assault rifle whilst driving on this rugged terrain, but Peroza's men were young and inexperienced and if he could give them cause to back down, all the better.

Down in the valley to his left he saw the flicker of lights from the town, a beacon in the murky dawn. Adler and Castillo would be there in thirty minutes. With any luck he'd join them in the next hour or so. But he had to deal with these bastards first. He gritted his teeth and stamped on the accelerator, the jeep's engine responding with a strained growl. The road here was treacherous, bordered by an impenetrable wall of dark green, but up ahead he saw it curved and then disappeared around a blind bend.

Beckett smiled to himself. This was what he'd been waiting for.

As he got around the bend, he eased off the gas and brought the jeep to a stop in the middle of the road. The thick foliage on either side provided perfect cover. He killed the engine and, rifle in hand, leapt from the cab and moved swiftly into the trees. Once concealed, he ran a quick status assessment. He'd been counting his rounds. He always did. It was something he'd learnt in basic training and after a while it was in his blood. He had twenty-nine rounds left. More than enough.

Crouched low, his senses sharp, he waited. Each second felt like an hour. His breath grew shallow and controlled. Ten seconds ticked by, then twenty. Finally, the first jeep appeared around the bend, the men inside yelling as they were met with the abandoned vehicle blocking the road in front of them. Beckett had entertained the idea of a collision taking out the first jeep, but the driver's quick reflexes prevented it and the tyres skidded to a halt as the others raised their rifles. There were four of them, all armed, all alert.

Undeterred, Beckett moved like a ghost, his hands steady, his focus unwavering. He rose from his hiding spot, shouldering the rifle and firing with deadly precision. Four shots took out four men in rapid succession, their heads snapping back violently as the bullets ripped through their pre-frontal cortex. It was over in less than a second, the soldiers' lifeless bodies slumped over the side of the jeep.

But it was far from done.

Shifting his position closer to the road, Beckett dropped to his knees to wait for jeep number two. The first team had been an easier takedown than he could have hoped for, but Peroza and Lugo were in the next vehicle, men much more experienced and vicious than their young disciples.

He waited. Five seconds... Ten... No jeep. He moved closer. All he could hear was the sound of the jungle waking up. No engines.

Keeping his aim high, he stepped onto the dirt road.

Had they already pulled up? Were they hidden amongst the trees, waiting to ambush him? Moving steadily and keeping to the side of the road, he advanced around the bend.

But the road was empty. No jeep. No soldiers. Just the wild, untamed jungle.

*Shit.*

Peroza had gone after Adler and the others. Not what he wanted to happen.

Beckett sprinted back to his jeep, his thoughts racing faster than his feet. He'd been driving for five minutes and they'd set off half a minute before him. That meant it would take him about eleven minutes to reach where the others were now – if they were stationary. Catching up with a moving vehicle was nearly impossible. Yet he couldn't go to the rendezvous site knowing they were in trouble.

He fired up the engine and swung the jeep around, the tyres tearing through the dirt and gravel.

He had to help them. He had to try.

## Chapter Forty-Eight

Even over the roar of the jeep's engine, Adler was acutely aware of the terrified cries coming from the back seat. Poor Kathleen. She shouldn't be here; she shouldn't have to be dealing with any of this.

"Hey, it's going to be okay," Adler told her, twisting around. "We're almost there."

Kathleen forced a thin smile and nodded. Beside her, Bruce appeared to be handling the situation a little better. His face was fixed in grim concentration, his eyes on the road ahead.

"We're almost there," Adler repeated, mainly to herself as she turned back to the road.

She mentally traced their route on the map Beckett had shown her. Her guess was they were about twenty minutes out from San Luzardo de Aragua. Once there, they'd head straight for the police station and get a message to the US embassy. They'd be safe. They'd be free.

But they weren't there yet.

She adjusted her grip on the rifle, bracing herself

against the jeep's jarring movements as Castillo manoeuvred them along the dirt road.

"How are you doing?" she asked him.

"You know me, *chica*," he replied, gritting his teeth as he steered around a rough bend. "I'm good. I got this."

"That's what I want to hear."

He nodded, keeping his eyes on the road. "Listen, I'm sorry about what happened in Guayana City. I shouldn't have dropped you in it the way I did. But they threatened my family. I was… scared." He glanced over.

"You did what you had to do," she replied. "I don't blame you. Let's just get to safety and make sure these people return home in one piece."

"You got it!"

Adler leaned back. She hadn't taken a full breath since the gate blew, but she couldn't relax just yet. As the jungle on either side of them thinned out and turned to grassland, gunshots echoed through the trees.

"Shit, we got company!" Castillo yelled.

Kathleen screamed as a hail of bullets peppered the dirt road to their right, sending clouds of dust into the air. Adler spun around in her seat, rifle at the ready. A jeep, containing Peroza and two of his men, was thundering down the road behind them, closing the gap rapidly.

"Get down!" she yelled to the Dixons, raising her rifle to return fire.

Bruce grabbed his wife and they ducked low in their seats as Adler clambered into the back seat between them.

"Put your foot down," she told Castillo. "We can do this."

The old cop was a veteran behind the wheel, weaving the jeep from side to side, swerving and accelerating as he drove them out of the jungle and alongside the river.

Behind them Peroza was standing up in his seat firing his handgun at them, but it was clear he was driven by anger rather than precision, as the distance between the two jeeps was growing larger every second.

Adler squeezed off a few more shots, aiming at Peroza, aiming at the jeep's wheels. They were too far away and moving too erratically for her to take a decent shot, but that went for both parties and it gave her hope. Up until now she'd been telling the others what they needed to hear, but now she found herself believing it too.

They could do this.

"*No! Mierda!*" Castillo's shouts pierced the air and the jeep swerved violently, throwing Adler into Bruce.

"What is it?" she yelled back, a jolt of adrenaline surging through her veins as she fought to regain her balance against the bounce of the jeep. Her eyes widened in shock as she saw a motorbike had emerged from a side path in front of them, blocking the road. "Shit. It's Lugo."

She pushed against the seat, trying to get herself upright whilst realigning her aim. But her elbow was trapped against the front seat and centre console.

"I can't get a shot at him," she shouted frantically.

"I can handle it." Castillo floored the accelerator and steered straight for Lugo. As they got closer though, the Colombian drew a pistol from his belt and fired. Adler cried out, trying to warn Castillo, but it was too late. The shot resounded over the roar of the engine and the old cop jerked back in his seat, his shirt blooming red from a shot to the heart. Adler tried to grab for him but he was already gone, and the jeep, now driverless, decelerated and then lurched forward as the clutch disengaged.

Adler's heart was pounding in her ears as they rolled to a stop in front of Lugo. Peroza's jeep pulled up alongside them, the lieutenant's face formed into a cruel sneer, his triumph evident.

"Oh dear," he sneered. "It looks like your little plan has failed."

Adler eyed the guard in the back seat behind Peroza. He was standing with his rifle aimed at them, but he wouldn't shoot without Peroza's command. At least, that was what she was counting on. With a cry of pain, she yanked her arm free from the console, her bicep muscle searing as she straightened up and aimed her rifle squarely at Peroza.

"Drop your weapon!" she yelled at the young soldier. "Or he dies."

Peroza chuckled. "You think you're in any position to make demands on my men?"

Adler ran a quick assessment of the situation. Peroza's gun was drawn, but from what she could see, all six chambers had been emptied. The driver and the armed guard in the rear had both been up all night and appeared frazzled, but the rifle remained raised and its owner stared at her, the standoff teetering on a knife edge. Over to her left, Lugo had climbed off his bike and was walking over, gun in hand.

Keeping her rifle on Peroza, she carefully stepped out of the jeep. "Get over here," she called to Lugo.

"Fuck you, bitch," he snarled. "You aren't walking away from this."

"Put the guns down," she repeated, shoving her rifle at Peroza. "I swear I'll kill him."

But Lugo kept coming. She had to do something. Kathleen and Bruce were both sobbing, their voices hysterical as they whispered to each other. But fair enough, this was a dire situation. They were outnumbered and outgunned and Lugo was closing in. This was it. They were all going to die.

"Wait!" she said. "Let these people go."

"What?!" Peroza screwed up his face. "Why would I do that?"

Adler swallowed. "Because... it's me you want." She gripped the rifle for dear life, her stomach churning. "Beckett was telling the truth. My father is Senator Simon Adler. If you've not heard of him, you will soon enough. He's tipped for the presidency in a few years."

Peroza's expression shifted as he considered her words. He glanced at Lugo and gestured for him to hold back.

"You can use me," Adler continued. "Now you're assuming power, show the world who you are. I could be your ticket to getting what you want."

Peroza scowled. "How do I do this?"

"You make demands," she said, her head spinning as she fought to arrange her thoughts into some kind of order. "Your rebellion has been going on for years. You must have allies imprisoned, both in the US and Central America. You start by demanding their release. Then you ask for guns, money, whatever it is you need. The US government's line is they don't negotiate with terrorists or respond to blackmail. But they do when it counts. They do if the life of the future president's daughter is at stake. But to get that leverage you need me alive."

A tense silence descended on the scene as Peroza weighed his options. Then a sly grin crept across his face. "Fine," he said. "You come with me. We let the old people go."

"What are you saying?" Lugo barked. "We can't just free them..."

Peroza silenced him with a glare. "Do not forget yourself, my friend. I am your leader. This is my decision."

Adler's heart was beating so loud she feared Peroza

would hear it. She glanced at the Dixons still cowering in the back of the jeep.

"Bruce, get behind the wheel," she said, her voice as firm as she could manage. "Now. Do it."

Bruce, his face ashen, nodded and quickly moved Castillo's body to one side as he clambered into the driver's seat. Kathleen watched on, tears streaming down her face.

Adler kept the rifle trained on Peroza, her eyes never leaving his. "Let them drive away," she said. "And I'll return to the compound with you. I'll talk to those in charge. Get you what you need."

Peroza bared his teeth in a sinister grin. "Maybe I have other uses for you too, huh?"

"Don't push it."

He laughed. "Fine, we have a deal." He gestured at the kid with the rifle. "Let them go."

"*Esto es una broma,*" Lugo muttered to himself, as the young soldier lowered his weapon.

"Bruce, you can do this, you hear me?" Adler called out. "Drive fast, stay low, and don't stop for anything."

Bruce exhaled deeply as he started the engine. The jeep jerked into motion, quickly gaining speed as it sped away. Adler watched them go. Then she lowered her gun, a sense of defeat washing over her as Peroza's man jumped down and grabbed her.

As she was led to the other side of the jeep, gunfire erupted behind her. She turned to see Lugo firing at the fleeing vehicle.

"No! This is not what we agreed!" she yelled, turning away, not wanting to see the outcome as Peroza's mocking laughter echoed in her ears.

"Oh, I am so sorry," he sneered. "I think he may have killed the woman. Oops."

The laughter continued as she was hustled into the rear of their jeep. She suspected he was lying. She hoped he was. Because if not, what the hell had she achieved by offering herself to these bastards? She knew Beckett was still out there, but would he realise what had happened and come to her aid? She shuddered. Hope was an unhelpful emotion. In volatile situations such as this, action and strategy were what mattered. But right now, as the jeep turned back towards the prison, what Adler really needed was nothing short of a miracle.

## Chapter Forty-Nine

Beckett sped along the rugged dirt road, taking the curves and bends without slowing for a moment. Up ahead he could make out the silhouette of another jeep making its way down the side of the river. He leaned forward, pressing the accelerator pedal to the floor, the old engine roaring in response as he closed the distance between them. When he got closer, he saw Kathleen and Bruce. But no Castillo. No Adler.

"Hey, Bruce!" he called out. "It's Beckett. Slow down."

Kathleen glanced back at him, but her face was a picture of distress. He held his hand up, gesturing for them to stop. Kathleen tapped Bruce on the shoulder and said something, then the jeep came to a juddering stop.

Pulling up alongside them, Beckett saw the blood spatter on the windscreen and the body of Castillo slumped on the passenger seat. "What happened?"

Bruce was white-knuckling the steering wheel. His pale blue shirt was soaked in blood from a shoulder wound.

"W-We were almost cl-clear," he stammered. "But they ambushed us. Peroza and his men. They took Adler. She sacrificed herself for us."

"She's a damn hero!" Kathleen whimpered.

But Beckett didn't like that word, *sacrificed*.

"She's dead?" he asked.

"No," Bruce replied quickly. "She was talking about her father, telling Peroza he could use her to get what he wanted. They took her back to the prison."

"I see." Beckett peered around as he considered his options. There was only one. Adler needed him. Despite the risks, he had to go back.

He was a soldier. It was what he did. It was who he was.

Never leave a comrade behind.

"Are you okay to drive?" Beckett asked Bruce, nodding at his injury. The bullet had passed through cleanly. Painful but not fatal.

"I think so," Bruce replied. "If it's not too far."

"Keep driving the way you're going, as fast as you can," Beckett told him. "In about fifteen minutes you'll arrive at a town called San Luzardo de Aragua. It's a small place, but it looks big enough to have a police station. Head straight there. Tell them everything and ask them to contact the US embassy. They'll patch you up while you wait."

"Got it." Bruce nodded weakly, his face sagging with the weight of responsibility. "And what will you do?" he asked.

"I'm going back for Adler." Beckett shifted the stick into reverse. He gave Bruce a nod, a silent gesture of solidarity, before turning the jeep around and heading back to the prison.

As he drove, he tried to empty his mind of anything but the mission in front of him He mentally rehearsed his path into the prison as well as assessing the schematics of the compound and the number of surviving rebels. He knew he was heading into a viper's nest and he needed to stay focused. Adler's life depended on it.

As did his own.

It took less than five minutes for the high walls to loom into view. From his angle of approach, Beckett could see the gates were still hanging open, and there was no one in sight.

Was this an ambush?

Were they expecting him?

Yet the lack of guards didn't necessarily mean it was a trap. Peroza's crew had been depleted considerably in the last hour and could be closing ranks.

Either way, he should approach with caution.

Parking up behind a row of trees, Beckett grabbed his rifle and made a dash for the compound, slipping silently in through the damaged gate. Staying close to the walls for cover, he approached the back of the main building. Peroza's jeep and a motorbike were parked in front of a long structure comprising three units. He moved past the first one, catching sight of what could only be the kill room. The faded blood spattered up the walls and the stench of death did nothing for the tension nipping at his shoulders.

He pulled in a deep breath, slowing his heart rate in the process as he continued along the rear of the building and traversed the side elevation, rifle at the ready. As he neared the entrance, muffled voices and laughter drifted out from within. With light steps he hurried inside the building and moved down the shadowy corridor, leading with the rifle and snapping his aim into each room as he passed. The body of the man he'd killed earlier still lay in the same place, but someone had rolled him up against the wall.

Stepping over the body he ascended the stairwell, which was made of stone and thankfully made no sound as he went. He paused at the top, faced with another corridor, the same footprint as downstairs but in reverse. The voices were more distinct now, coming from a room at the far end. The door was hanging open a few inches, but from his position he couldn't see inside the room.

He advanced closer, moving with practised restraint, every muscle and nerve honed for moments like this. Raising his rifle, he peered through the gap in the door. Adler was bound and gagged, strapped to a chair in the centre of the room, flanked by two guards. The young men were chatting, their conversation vulgar and threatening, seemingly trying to outdo each other in terms of what violent and obscene acts they'd like to do to the American woman. She looked enraged, like she was ready to castrate them, or failing that, just slit their throats. The men were speaking Spanish, but Beckett understood them and so would she.

Without hesitation he pushed the door open and stepped into the room. The guards barely had time to register his presence before he dropped them both with fatal headshots, as efficient, precise and deadly as he'd ever been. The room fell silent except for the soft thuds of the guard's bodies hitting the floor.

Adler's bloodshot eyes met his, a flicker of relief behind her tears as he moved into the room. But as he got closer her eyes grew wide and she tried to yell, her words muffled by the gag. Beckett only had a split second to register the creak of floorboards behind him before he felt the cold muzzle of a gun against the nape of his neck.

"Back so soon, Mr MI6?" a voice said, as a hand

reached around and relieved him of his rifle. "Now, put your hands up and turn around. Slowly."

He complied, turning to face Peroza who stepped back and aimed the gun at Beckett's forehead.

"You thought I'd let you just walk into my prison and take her?"

Beckett remained silent, his training keeping him outwardly calm as he searched for a solution. He made no sudden movements. Peroza had backed further away, and he wouldn't be able to reach him before he fired. It would be suicide to try.

But while he couldn't fight his way out, maybe he could negotiate. "Well done," he said. "We're completely at your mercy."

"You killed my men," Peroza spat. "Good men. Proud men. I'll need to recruit once more."

"But you've taken control. You're the leader now and you'll be a damn good one. We both know Murcia messed up, but he got some things right. I can help you. We can—"

"Enough!" Peroza snapped, cutting him off. "Talking is over."

Beckett lowered his chin. "Is Murcia dead?"

"Forget about Murcia. I'm the new general around here." Peroza eyed the two guards who appeared in the doorway. "Untie her. Bring them both out to the yard and keep a close watch on them. If they try anything, shoot them."

Peroza exited the room and Beckett felt a rifle muzzle poke the small of his back. Behind him he heard the second guard releasing Adler and getting her to her feet.

"Did you see the Dixons?" she whispered, as she appeared beside him.

Beckett nodded. "They're okay. Whatever you would have told them to do… that's what I told them."

"Good."

They held each other's gaze for a moment but their silent exchange was cut short. "Move!" the guards ordered. "Now!"

They were led downstairs and escorted out into the early morning sun. The yard was already heating up. It was going to be another hot one. Beckett wondered how much of the day they would see.

With rifles prodding at their backs to ensure compliance, he and Adler were marched across the prison grounds to the exercise yard where Peroza and Lugo were waiting. Lugo watched the captives approach, his weapon drawn, his expression one of amusement and anticipation. Peroza stood a few feet away, his eyes burning with a fury that promised retribution. Beckett could almost feel the intensity of his glare as they reached the yard.

"Bring them here," Peroza ordered, waving his pistol at the ground a few metres in front of him. "Line them up."

The guards did as instructed, and once Beckett and Adler were in position, Lugo sauntered over, his predatory gaze shifting between the two of them and his gun wavering as if choosing his first target. Beckett braced himself. There was no way he was going to give this creep the satisfaction of seeing his fear.

"I think… we'll start with… you!" Lugo sneered, aiming his gun at Beckett's head.

Adler tensed beside him. This was it. Beckett raised his face to the blue sky above and thought of his father. He waited.

"Stop!"

Beckett exhaled, turning to see Peroza with his hand up.

"Not like this." Peroza's eyes glinted with malice. "It's too… clean."

Lugo threw up an eyebrow, confused. But Beckett knew what was coming. Unfortunately, he knew.

"I want to make this more interesting," Peroza said, turning to his men. "Go fetch Bracho!"

## Chapter Fifty

Beckett and Adler watched as the guards hurried across the prison grounds towards Bracho's hut. In front of them, Peroza pulled a whistle from his pocket and blew it sharply, signalling his deadly charge, the shrill sound cutting through the tense atmosphere. The guards paused, cautious, as Bracho's huge, calloused hand yanked the velvet curtain to one side and emerged, blinking, from his lair.

"Bring him here," Peroza called out. "Come, Bracho. I have work for you, my friend."

The giant looked over, a hint of confusion on his face. But years of conditioning to obey Peroza's orders overrode any momentary doubt. He lumbered forward, his steps heavy and deliberate, and his grotesque features just as unsettling as the first time they'd encountered him.

Reaching the yard, Bracho paused and stared at Beckett, a strange expression on his face. There was a hint of what might have been compassion, but it was fleeting, not enough to change anything. With a growl, Bracho straightened to his full height, his fists tight and ready, his gaze fixing on Peroza. It was a display of both his formidable presence and tragic lack of free will.

"You are going to fight for us, my champion," Peroza told him, gesturing at Beckett and Adler. "Tell me, which of these treacherous fools would you like first?"

Bracho made a low growling noise as he considered Peroza's words, his one good eye examining Beckett and Adler in turn.

"I'll go first," Beckett announced, before the decision was made for them. "Let me fight him."

Peroza turned to Lugo and shrugged. Lugo grinned. "Very well. Mr MI6 will go first."

"And if I win?" Beckett asked. "Will you free us?"

His question was met with scornful laughter from Peroza, a sentiment echoed by Lugo and his men. "No need to think about that," he said. "You won't win."

"Bastard!" Adler hissed. "If we die—"

Beckett cut her off with a firm look. "Vanessa! It's okay," he said, lowering his voice. "This has to happen."

She looked up at him, her face creased with fear and concern. "He's a monster," she whispered. "You can't win against... that."

"We don't have any other choice. If I don't fight, they'll kill the both of us."

"He'll kill you!"

"Maybe. But this is our only chance." He pulled his shirt off over his head, feeling the heat on his bare skin. A few feet away, Peroza was giving Bracho a strict talking to, instructing him to show no mercy. Beckett moved closer to Adler and whispered, "Stay alert and watch Peroza and his men. If you see an opening, take it. If you get an opportunity to escape, go. Don't worry about me."

Adler opened her mouth to reply but shut it again. She nodded.

Beckett shifted his focus to Bracho. There was a momentary flicker of recognition in the giant's eyes, perhaps recalling their previous encounter. Yet any semblance of connection was clouded by Bracho's blind obedience to his master.

"Take your positions!" Peroza called out, signalling for Beckett and Bracho to move closer, as Lugo and the remaining guards spread out to watch. Slowly, Beckett made his way into the centre of the makeshift ring, subtly nudging Adler as he passed, guiding her closer to Lugo.

He could feel his heartbeat in his neck and chest. The adrenaline surging through him made his teeth ache. He took a moment to mentally prepare, breathing deep and slow as he rolled his shoulders back and stretched his arms. Beckett rarely felt fear, he was too well-trained, too focused on the task in front of him to allow his imagination to knock him off course, but as he took in Bracho's monstrous appearance – the deformed club that was once a hand; the bone protruding like a spike from his shoulder – he couldn't deny it. He was scared.

"All right, get ready!" Peroza boomed. "One round. One fight. No stoppages. The winner is the last... man... standing."

Bracho nodded, panting and eager to get started. Beckett raised his fists.

"Begin!"

Peroza leapt back as Bracho lunged at Beckett, his deformed hand swinging wildly. Beckett dodged out of the way, feeling the rush of air against his skin. Correcting himself, Bracho swung again, this time catching Beckett with a blow to the ribcage that knocked him off his feet.

Scrambling up, Beckett immediately put distance between them. It felt like he'd been hit by a car. He retreated further as Bracho glanced over at Peroza, perhaps seeking approval or instruction.

"Kill him!" Peroza yelled.

With a roar Bracho charged forward, the ground seeming to tremble as he advanced. Beckett sidestepped him and delivered a solid punch to the kidneys, but it was like hitting a new leather sparring bag, firm and unyielding, and the big man didn't flinch. As he turned, Beckett leapt out of the way, but he underestimated Bracho's impressive reach and his clubbed hand slammed into the side of his head.

For a moment he didn't know his name or where he was. It felt like his sinuses had exploded. As the world spun around him, he fought to stay upright and conscious. From somewhere in the swirl of colour he heard Adler shouting his name. From deep inside himself he heard his father.

*Come on, John. Keep it together.*

*You can do this.*

He regained his bearings in time to dodge out of the way as Bracho charged. Crying out in frustration Bracho grabbed for him, but Beckett, already slippery with sweat, managed to twist away before he could get purchase.

That was too close. If Bracho got his arms around him and started to squeeze, it would be over.

Beckett danced around the perimeter of the makeshift ring, tuning out the taunts and jeers coming from Peroza and his men and focusing only on Bracho. He felt blood trickling down the side of his face, and his left eye was swelling shut, but he was too full of adrenaline to care. Yet with the man in front of him feeling no pain at all, and almost twice his size, he knew the odds were dire.

A direct confrontation with Bracho's raw power wasn't

just daunting, it was futile. But Beckett also knew a purely defensive stance wouldn't win him this fight. He needed another way. Whilst he couldn't match Bracho's brute strength, he had speed and stamina on his side.

And also, something else.

As he stared at Bracho panting and readying his next attack, he recalled a crucial aspect of the big man's condition. He couldn't sweat, or regulate his body temperature. With the sweltering heat intensifying, this could be the edge Beckett desperately needed.

"Bracho, what are you waiting for?" Peroza yelled. "End it! Crush his fucking head!"

The giant charged forward, his clubbed hand cutting through the air with lethal intent. But Beckett was already up on the balls of his feet and evaded the blow, dancing away with the agility and precision of a seasoned boxer. His mind was now clear, focused only on prolonging the fight as long as possible and turning the oppressive heat into his ally.

He darted around the ring, a nimble middleweight against Bracho's hulking street fighter. Each time the heavy club came crashing down, Beckett was already somewhere else, striking back with calculated jabs to Bracho's kidneys, then retreating before he could react. Though the pain wouldn't wear him down, his body still received trauma, and the repetitive strikes and unabating sun were visibly sapping his energy.

Peroza and Lugo continued their jeers, egging on their prized fighter. But Beckett was persistent, ducking and weaving away from every attack, drawing Bracho into a tiring chase. The giant's frustration grew with each near miss, his movements becoming slower and more laboured as his massive frame struggled to keep up with Beckett's pace.

With every minute that passed, Bracho's steps grew

heavier, his attempts on Beckett more desperate. Though wet through with sweat and panting, Beckett maintained his rhythm – dodge, strike, run, repeat. He couldn't let up for a second. The moment he faltered he was dead.

As Bracho lunged forward with renewed fury, Beckett saw his opening. Dodging aside, he leapt up onto Bracho's back, locking his arm around the giant's thick neck. Bracho roared, a guttural noise of animalistic rage, as he tried to shake off his attacker. Beckett held on tight, his hand locking onto his other wrist to strengthen the chokehold.

Around them the prison yard erupted into chaos.

"Get him off you! Destroy that son of a whore!" Peroza's voice rose above the din, hoarse with anger and disbelief. "Fight, Bracho! Kill!"

Lugo and the other guards were also bellowing encouragement, but Beckett remained singularly focused, his muscles straining as he squeezed his forearm against Bracho's carotid artery. Pain might not break Peroza's champion, but all brains needed blood, and all bodies needed brains.

Seconds stretched on like days as Beckett maintained the chokehold. He could sense Bracho growing desperate. The giant flailed wildly, grappling to remove him, but his strength was fading and each attempt was weaker than the last.

"No, Bracho!" Peroza screamed. "Do something!"

But it was too late. Letting out a deep groan, Bracho dropped to his knees. His enormous frame trembled, and with a final, shuddering breath, he pitched forward. Beckett rode him down, his arm still wrapped like an iron bar around Bracho's neck until the giant's movements ceased. Only then did he cautiously release his hold and slide off Bracho's lifeless body.

The crowd was silent now, the uproar replaced by a stunned hush. Peroza stood, frozen, his expression one of disbelief and fury as Beckett, breathing heavily, rose to his feet.

"You bastard," Peroza snarled, marching over to Beckett and pointing his gun in his face. "You killed him."

"Wait!" Adler yelled. "That was a fair fight. He won. You can't do this."

"Can't I?" Peroza replied. "Watch me."

Beckett locked eyes with Peroza, finding no hint of mercy, only hatred. He knew he was about to die. Every muscle screamed from the exertion of the fight and Peroza had stopped too far away for him to do anything. He glanced at Adler. She shook her head.

He waited once again for death to take him, before a new voice shattered the heavy atmosphere, bouncing off the prison walls.

"*Cerdo traicionero!*"

It was Murcia, battered and bleeding, and waving a pistol in front of him. His eyes were wild with determination as he staggered forward.

"*Cerdo traicionero!*" he repeated. *Treacherous pig.*

Peroza sneered, about to reply. But before he could utter a word, a sharp crack split the air and a bullet tore through his arm, sending him reeling backwards. Capitalising on the chaos, Beckett charged at Peroza, wresting the Magnum from his grip. In the same fluid movement he smashed his elbow into Peroza's throat and stepped back, finishing him with a single shot between the eyes.

As Peroza's body crumpled to the ground, Beckett turned, ready to confront Lugo and the remaining guards. But Adler had already sprung into action. She struck Lugo in the face with the heel of her hand, snatching his gun and forcing the barrel under his chin as he fought through the pain. There was a crack, as skull and brain matter burst out the top of Lugo's head and he dropped lifelessly to the ground.

"Enough!" Murcia yelled, firing a warning shot into the air. "Put your weapons down."

Beckett and Adler hesitated. The two remaining guards had now regained focus and had their rifles aimed at the two of them.

"Drop your weapons," Murcia yelled, his face contorted with rage, pointing his pistol at Beckett and then Adler. "Now! I mean it!"

Beckett glanced at Adler, then at the armed guards. They looked terrified, as if they'd just realised whatever reward they were due to receive was not worth all this bloodshed. Yet despite their appearance, they were still young and excitable. He couldn't risk them opening fire.

"Do what he says," he told Adler, calmly placing Peroza's gun on the ground. "It's going to be okay."

Adler scowled at him. "But we... We've got to..." The guards adjusted their grips on their assault rifles and she complied before leaning into Beckett and lowering her voice. "What now?"

Beckett raised his head, looking each of the young soldiers in the eye. "These men betrayed you," he told Murcia. "Are you sure they'll follow your orders now?"

"*You* betrayed me!" Murcia yelled at him. "You ruined everything."

"This is on Peroza," Beckett replied. "He did this, not me. I still want to help you. Together we can do great things. You know it. Just let—"

"Silence!" Murcia thrust his pistol towards Beckett. "You talk too much, you know that? You're full of shit."

Beckett swallowed. Murcia was beyond reasoning now, his judgement clouded by betrayal and fury. He glared at the young men, speaking through gritted teeth. "Get. Them."

But the two guards hesitated.

"These men don't want to fight anymore," Beckett said, speaking in Spanish as he maintained eye contact with the young soldiers. "This isn't their fight. They want to go home."

"They want what I tell them they want!" Murcia snarled, turning to the guards. "Seize them now!"

Beckett clenched and unclenched his fists as the young men lowered their rifles to the ground.

"*No, Generales,*" one of them muttered. "*Ya no más.*"

"Pathetic idiots!" Murcia snarled, as the men backed away. "I am surrounded by imbeciles. But no matter. I shall deal with the two of you myself." Adler inched closer to Beckett, her fingers finding his and clasping his hand tightly as Murcia stepped in front of them.

"I've been betrayed by everyone!" he raged, gesturing wildly with his weapon. "But I'm not finished. Far from it. I *will* be president. I will make my country great again. And I will do that by destroying my enemies. Every single one of them."

"This isn't the way," Beckett said. "Kill me and no one cares. Kill Adler and you make powerful enemies for yourself. There's a better way. A more diplomatic way."

"Screw diplomacy. And screw you, Beckett. I'm done listening to you." His eyes narrowed as he aimed the pistol at Beckett's head.

Beckett swallowed. Despite the threat of death being a familiar sensation for him, it never got any easier. But as Murcia continued his tirade, Beckett noticed movement behind him. Bracho was stirring. His neck muscles were so thick he'd only been rendered unconscious by the punishing chokehold.

With a surge of strength, the big man pushed himself to his feet. Murcia, so caught up in his furious diatribe, didn't notice until it was far too late. He spun around, only for Bracho to grab him around the throat. A gunshot rang out and Bracho's torso contorted but his grip remained firm. With a grunt he swung his heavy clubbed hand at Murcia's head, the sheer force of the blow snapping the man's neck with an audible crunch. Bracho dropped the general's broken body and staggered back, a fatal bullet wound evident in his chest. He looked at Beckett, a look of bewilderment in his eyes, before letting out a high-pitched sigh and stumbling to the ground.

All at once the prison yard was silent.

Beckett, his body aching and with adrenaline still coursing through his veins, staggered over to where Bracho lay. The formidable giant now looked almost peaceful in his stillness.

Beckett knelt beside him, wondering what it must be like for this man to bleed out whilst devoid of pain. Bracho's eyes, one clouded and the other showing a glimmer of awareness, met Beckett's. It was hard not to feel sorry for him. There was a tragic innocence there, a soul that had been twisted and used for others' vile purposes.

"I'm sorry," Beckett told him. "You deserved better." He reached out and touched Bracho's shoulder, feeling the weight of their shared humanity, of the circumstances that had led them both to this point. Enough pain and suffering had been inflicted, not just on Bracho, but on all those who had been caught up in conflict and power struggles.

Getting to his feet, Beckett felt Adler's presence beside him as he watched Bracho's eyes flicker shut. Her hand rested gently on his arm. "Come on, soldier," she said. "Time to get the hell out of here. I'm sick of this damn place."

Beckett looked at her and smiled. He couldn't have put it better himself.

## Chapter Fifty-One

Beckett sat at a café in El Tigrito's main square, the atmosphere around him buzzing with the energy of a typical Venezuelan evening. A bottle of Solera beer stood, untouched, on the table in front of him.

It was almost thirty hours since he and Adler had left the compound in the remaining jeep, driving north to San Luzardo de Aragua. Once there, they had spoken with the local police, who transported them over to El Tigrito where the US government had already booked hotel suites for the Dixons and any remaining hostages. Beckett had swerved the offer of luxury accommodation, for obvious reasons, but he was glad to hear Kathleen and Bruce were safe and being looked after until arrangements were made to get them home.

The rustic wooden chair beneath him creaked as he reached for the beer. The condensation on the bottle was cold against his hand, a soothing contrast to the humid air. He drank, savouring the taste as the ice-cold liquid ran down his throat. The beer, along with the hearty meal of steak and potatoes he'd just devoured, would be viewed by many as scant reward for surviving the events of the last week, but these days John Beckett was a man of simple needs. It was more than sufficient.

He leaned back, cautious not to move too fast and disturb his bandages. A local medic in San Luzardo de Aragua had patched him up, getting carried away and wrapping almost an entire roll of gauze around his midriff. He assumed they didn't see a lot of action in the small town, because the truth was he'd walked away with just a few cuts, a couple of bruised ribs and a dislocated cheekbone. He would heal in time.

His gaze wandered across the bustling marketplace as the sun began to dip below the horizon. Venezuela, despite everything, remained undeniably beautiful. The vibrant hues of the setting sun painted the sky in strokes of orange and pink, reflecting a warm, serene glow onto the streets. Around him the market was still a hotbed of activity. Families and friends gathered, laughing and chatting as they browsed the stalls and drifted towards the bars and restaurants.

In the distance, the silhouette of the mountains stood out against the pastel sky. Angel Falls, hidden somewhere beyond those peaks, remained an unchecked item on his list. Now, as he looked at the peaceful scene before him, he felt a twinge of regret. Another day, perhaps.

But for now, it was time to move on.

He closed his eyes, and was pondering where he might end up next when he sensed a presence in front of him. He immediately knew who it was.

"I thought I might find you here," Adler said.

He opened his eyes, squinting as he gazed up at her. Her hair was down around her shoulders, and the light perfectly

## A World of Sun and Violence

highlighted her strawberry-blonde locks. She was also wearing a little mascara, which accentuated her pale blue eyes, still bright and alert but now with a hint of mischief.

"Mind if I join you?"

She was wearing a sleeveless cream shirt, tucked neatly into a pair of black jeans. In her hand she had a tumbler of whisky on the rocks. It looked like a double.

"Please, be my guest." Beckett sat up and gestured at the chair opposite. "I'd offer to get you a drink, but I see you've already got one."

She sat. "I like to pay my own way."

"Yes, I thought that would be the case."

She lowered her chin. "What does that mean?"

"Only that you're someone who gets what you want and on your own terms. I imagine you had to be that way for your superiors to put you on that mission, given who you are."

She chuckled to herself as she swirled her glass gently, the amber liquid reflecting the last rays of the sun. "You have no idea."

He narrowed his eyes and lowered his voice as he spoke. "You weren't here on a 'fact-finding' mission, were you?"

Her smile faded and expression turned serious. "How did you know?"

"This is my world too," he replied. "Or at least it was. Murcia was readying himself for a military takeover of Colombia. The CIA wouldn't have wanted that, not with the way things are in the region. It's ticking along right now and there's too much happening on the other side of the world for them to want unrest on their doorstep. I thought it was odd they'd send someone like you on such a simple assignment, especially alone. And then it hit me. You were here to assassinate him."

Adler sipped her drink. "I can't confirm or deny that theory, Mr Beckett."

"Quite right."

"But if it were true, then you did me – and the agency – a big favour. So, thank you. For everything."

Beckett grinned, his eyes lingering on hers. "I should be the one thanking you. Just so long as you keep my real name out of any reports."

"I'll try."

He hoped she'd do more than that. But there was no telling what might be said when she was back home and behind closed doors in debrief. He took a long swig of his beer then asked her how the Dixons were doing.

"Both good. They've been offered counselling but turned it down. They're holed up in the hotel, making use of the spa instead."

"Is Bruce's shoulder okay?"

"Yeah, he'll be fine. It was just a flesh wound. There's a team on the way to deal with the fallout from the ELC and get everyone safely back to the States."

"That's good to hear," Beckett told her.

There was a pause. Adler studied him. "You could come with us, you know," she said.

Beckett shook his head. "I really can't."

"You sure? I've got some sway. I can talk to the right people. Once they know what you did over here…"

Beckett chuckled. "Thank you. But I really don't think that's going to help. And I meant what I said before – I know it's a big ask, but I'd appreciate it if my name wasn't mentioned."

Adler chewed on her lip as she thought about it. "What shall I tell them? Who helped me?"

"Tell them there was an English hostage with you called

Michael Day, a backpacker. He used to work in finance but that's all you know. Tell them he slipped away before you could get his contact details or a forwarding address. Say he was a quiet guy and didn't want any of the limelight."

"You'll think they'll buy that?" she asked, with a sly smirk.

"You're a resourceful person, Vanessa. You'll think of something."

She sighed and sat back, glancing across the square. "I'll see what I can do."

"That's all I ask." Beckett finished his beer and stood up, feeling the pull of the open road once more.

"Leaving so soon?" Adler asked, looking him up and down. "You won't stay for another drink... maybe dinner?"

"It's tempting. But I should go."

She nodded and sipped her drink. "Where to next?"

"Best you don't know," he said, with a knowing smile.

He turned to leave, pausing for a moment but not looking back, before setting off across the marketplace. He'd already stayed here too long. The jungle prison had been an unexpected detour in his life – a detour that had brought both pain and a strange sense of connection. But Beckett knew he had to keep moving; his life was a transient one these days, always staying one step ahead of his troubled past. As the sun dipped below the horizon, he took one last look at the mountains and headed for the bus station.

Like the woman had said, it was time to get the hell out of here.

# Epilogue

Adler rubbed at her face.

How long had she been sitting in this damn interview room?

It felt like hours; it was probably less than fifty minutes. She picked up the paper cup in front of her and drained the last drops of water from it. She thought about asking for more, but her hope was the debrief was nearly over.

She'd been in the States for almost a week now and this was her first day back at Langley. It was Thursday. Tomorrow she was due to take two weeks' leave until the end of the month to rest and recuperate, to get her head together after the trauma of her kidnapping. Yet protocol required she come in for this debrief first.

"Are we almost done?" she asked. "I've told you everything I can remember. And I'll be producing a report on my return. Like I've already told you, Deputy Director Foster has agreed to this personally."

The man sitting across from her, who she knew only as

# A World of Sun and Violence

Lewis, didn't look up from his notes. "We're almost done, Special Officer Adler."

"Good to hear."

She leaned back, glancing around the room for something of interest to focus on. There was nothing. The interview rooms here at Langley were all like this, especially those on the top floor. The walls were grey and featureless, there were no windows, just a single door with no glass in it. A metal-topped table sat in the centre of the room with two basic metal chairs on either side. You'd call the look 'functional minimalism' if you were being kind. A harsh fluorescent bulb hummed softly overhead, spilling a cold, clinical light over the table. The air was still, with a faint smell of antiseptic.

"Is there anything else you want to tell me at this stage?" Lewis asked.

"Like what?" Adler hit back. "The mission was disrupted somewhat, as you're aware, but ultimately we got what we wanted. The ELC are in tatters. They're no longer a threat. And I'm lucky to have made it out of there alive."

Adler glared at Lewis. He seemed as unremarkable as their surroundings. His suit was dark grey, the same colour as his tie, and he had a slow, robotic way of speaking that set her teeth on edge. He didn't look as if he needed to shave, but was one of those people who could be any age from early twenties to late forties. His hair was neatly combed, his expression inscrutable behind a pair of round glasses.

He looked up and gave her a thin-lipped smile. "This man – Michael Day – is there anything else you can tell me about him?" he asked, pen poised over his notepad.

Adler could sense herself growing pricklier the longer

she sat here. She was sick of talking about what had happened. She might be safe, but she was still processing the events that had transpired in Venezuela. She needed some downtime.

"No, that's all," she said. "Everything will be in my report. Including a detailed analysis of the ELC power structure and Jalen Murcia's network."

She was already mentally detaching from the briefing, and from Washington itself, picturing herself in the tranquillity of her parents' home in Connecticut. She was due to spend the entire two weeks with them, and the prospect of seeing her father again brought a smile to her face. She'd missed the old man.

"Fine." Lewis placed his pen down and closed the ringbound notepad. Smiling, he rose from his chair. "That concludes our debriefing," he said. "I'm aware you are now on leave, but we will need that report in the next three weeks."

"Understood." Adler nodded and smiled, relieved it was over. She was more than ready to put physical and mental distance between herself and work, eager to be surrounded by the warmth and familiarity of her childhood home.

"Oh," Lewis added, seeing Adler was making to get up. "If you can stay here for now."

"Is there something wrong?"

He glanced at his watch. "Wait here, please. It won't take long." With those words he turned and left the room, closing the door behind him.

"What the…?" Adler muttered, sitting back and folding her arms.

What was Lewis doing?

Why was she still here?

Confused, she waited, her mind spinning with questions. Moments later the door opened and a man entered. He was tall and broad, with thick white hair and a chiselled jaw. He was wearing a pair of beige trousers and a navy shirt that accentuated his solid build. Closing the door, he looked at her and smiled. His piercing blue-grey eyes seemed to bore into her very soul.

"Vanessa Adler," he said.

"That's right." She felt a shiver of apprehension. "And you are…?"

He pulled the chair out and sat, making himself comfortable before he answered. "My name is Xander Templeton," he said. "I'm currently the CIA section chief based in London."

Adler swallowed and nodded, playing it cool as her heart skipped a beat. She didn't recall the name, but she knew there were people at the agency gunning for Beckett.

"I was listening to your interview just now," Templeton said, pointing to the microphone in the corner. "Your insights on the ELC and General Murcia's network will be invaluable, no doubt. However, there's a particular detail that I'm interested in. This man, Michael Day."

"Okay." Adler maintained her composure. "He was another of the hostages. He was captured with the Dixons. I didn't speak to him much."

"But he helped you out – he was instrumental in your escape?"

Adler cleared her throat. "We all helped each other out. It was a group effort."

"How lovely." Templeton grinned, revealing two rows of perfect white teeth. "But you don't know what happened to him?"

"No. Like I told Lewis, he must have slipped away once we arrived in El Tigrito."

"I see." He reached over and picked up her empty cup, glancing inside it with a smirk. Then his eyes were back on her. "And you didn't discuss anything with this man. About who you were, what you were doing over there?"

Adler paused before answering, uneasy about where this was going. "I did not."

"Are you sure about that?"

"I am."

Templeton's lips curled into a half-smile, as if privy to a secret joke. "Did he tell you who he was?"

"A financial advisor. An *ex*-financial advisor. I think he's backpacking around the world using inheritance money."

"Is that so?" Templeton leaned back, not taking his eyes off her. It was damned unnerving. He sighed. "Let's stop beating around the bush, shall we, Ms Adler? I've recently viewed satellite recon as well as drone surveillance of the prison where you were held. Would it surprise you to learn that this Michael Day is, in fact, an ex-officer of the British Secret Service?"

Adler held Templeton's gaze, unsure how to respond. "Oh?" was all she could find to say.

"Oh, indeed!" Templeton replied. "His real name is John Beckett. Do you know that?" He smirked. "Don't worry, I can see from your face you do. Did he ask you to lie for him, to cover his tracks?"

Adler stared at him for a second then looked away.

Templeton snorted. "Of course he did."

"You have to understand, sir," she said, meeting his gaze directly. "He's not what you think. He saved us. We wouldn't have made it out without him."

Templeton's fist came down hard on the table. "That

man is a liability that we can't afford, Ms Adler. He needs to be brought in and questioned, at the very least."

She tried to interject, to defend Beckett further, but Templeton raised a hand, silencing her.

"I appreciate the circumstances you've been through, and given who you are – and who your father is – we'll let this slide. But tread carefully in future, Ms Adler. Be wary of who you confide in. Allies like John Beckett can become burdens very quickly."

Adler nodded, feeling like a scolded child. She hated men like Templeton, full of gruff machismo and their own sense of importance. At least Foster wasn't like that. But no doubt Templeton had spoken to him about this matter and she'd get her hands slapped on her return. Except the truth was she hadn't done anything wrong. She hadn't personally divulged anything she shouldn't have done.

"What happens now?" she asked.

Templeton sniffed. "To you? Nothing. I may have more questions for you as they come to me, but for now you're free to go."

"Thank you." The relief she felt was palpable as she gathered herself together.

"Yes... you have a pleasant vacation," Templeton said, getting to his feet. "Connecticut is so beautiful this time of year, isn't it?" He shot her another wide grin – his way of telling her he knew everything about her life.

"Yes... Yes, it is."

She pushed against the table, about to stand, when Templeton raised his finger. "Just one more thing, Ms Adler. I don't suppose our friend Beckett mentioned where he was heading next?"

Adler's mind raced, but she knew better than to lie. "No. I don't know."

Templeton nodded, more to himself than to her. "No matter. We have our methods and now we have a starting point, too." He moved over to the door and paused with his hand on the doorknob before looking back. "You know, Ms Adler, John Beckett is very good at what he does. But so am I. I'll find him. If it's the last thing I do – I'll find him."

## Next in The John Beckett Series

vinci-books.com/beckett4

**A rogue agent with deadly secrets and a race against time to stop a global catastrophe.**

John Beckett thought he'd left the world of espionage behind. But when a mysterious woman seeks his help, Beckett is ambushed, blackmailed, and thrust back into a dangerous game with a ruthless CIA adversary. Beckett's pursuit takes him to a high-stakes gathering of powerful elites. With millions of lives at stake, Beckett faces an impossible choice that will test his loyalties and could alter the course of his life forever.

Turn the page for a free preview…

## A Bullet for the Past: Chapter One

When you had nothing to do but wait by a window, Stuttgart was the same as any other European city – cold, impersonal, soulless; a sprawling panorama of concrete and neon stretching out to the horizon.

It was late afternoon here in the Swabian metropolis, and the air creeping in through the gap in the window was cold against the man's skin. He adjusted his position, just enough to stave off the creeping muscle cramp in his right shoulder and keep his blood moving.

Wearing short sleeves in the fall, especially in Germany, had been an oversight on his part, but he appreciated the ease of movement the simple t-shirt provided. He preferred that over comfort. Tonight's shirt was black, though he sometimes wore dark navy. He had three of each colour in the holdall by his feet, along with a change of underwear and a leather bag containing essential toiletries.

He waited.

The room behind him was silent, devoid of the usual signs of habitation. No ticking clock, no hum of appliances, just the faint rustle of the curtains in the evening breeze. The only furniture was a wooden table and two mismatched chairs, one of which he'd been sitting on for the last two hours. The walls were bare except for a single faded print of a landscape that could have been anywhere. The carpet was threadbare, the walls a dull beige. The view, however, couldn't have been better, providing him with a clear sightline of Wolframstrasse and the modern Hampton by Hilton hotel.

Like always, he'd spent days meticulously researching the location, down to the smallest detail. He knew the Hampton's layout, its entrances and exits, and the timing of the employees' shifts. He knew the delivery schedules and the patterns of pedestrian traffic. Knew too that this specific apartment he'd chosen was ideal for its position and privacy. He'd found it on the rental market and, after a couple of phone calls, discovered the broker was on holiday and the owner lived in Berlin. It was perfect – no one would disturb him, no one would come knocking. And he would be gone in an hour, maybe less.

He glanced at his watch before returning his gaze to the street, resuming his statue-like stillness.

He observed the flow of people and cars with unwavering patience.

He watched the driver of a white van unloading crates of alcohol into the back room of a local bar before driving away.

He waited.

His was a solitary existence, but he preferred it that way. Even if he wasn't doing this, there would be no close relationships in his life. He enjoyed his own company and the silence that came with it. Years in the US military and then as a specialised skills officer for the CIA's Special Activities

Center had honed his ability to wait for hours, even days if necessary. It was all part of the job.

Waiting. Watching.

Staying ready.

He adjusted his grip on the cold metal of the high-powered sniper rifle in front of him. The Mk 13 was a masterpiece of lethal engineering, but tonight it was an extension of himself. The scope, a Schmidt & Bender PM II, offered unparalleled clarity, allowing him to observe his target with precision detail. He leaned closer and adjusted the focus until the crosshairs were sharp. Up here he was a silent force, a godlike presence in the sky, ready to cast down his judgement on the depraved and avaricious mortals below. He rested his finger on the trigger, his focus narrowing as he slowly swept the area.

He knew his mark was inside the hotel, involved in a clandestine meeting with a high-ranking member of the Hessen Bruderschaft – one of the most powerful organised crime groups in the world. But he also knew the meeting wouldn't last long. Because what the mark had for sale was too expensive, even for the Hessen Bruderschaft.

He exhaled slowly, consciously, keeping his heartbeat steady. Down below, a flicker of movement caught his eye. He leaned into the sight as the front door of the hotel opened and three large men emerged, scanning the area with stern expressions. Bodyguards, professional and alert, but not his concern. His focus shifted to the smaller man following them.

Dressed in a sharp charcoal suit with a pale blue shirt open at the collar, the man had neatly styled short black hair, and aviator glasses with photochromatic lenses reflecting the streetlights. He looked important. He didn't look like a scientist, but they never did in his experience.

Especially not the ones sitting on an invention worth millions of dollars to the right people – or the wrong ones.

Through the scope he tracked the man as the bodyguards herded him towards a waiting car, a sleek black sedan with the engine already running. He had seconds. Maybe less. He tightened his grip on the trigger, releasing his breath in a measured flow.

*One... two...*

He paused as a man in a light grey suit stepped forward, placing a hand on the mark's chest to stop his movement. The man in grey glanced across the busy road towards the apartment block, his gaze sweeping directly past the open window where he was holding his position.

But there was no way he could see him from that distance.

He couldn't know.

His finger hovered over the trigger as he watched through the scope, realigning the crosshairs with the mark's head. Except now his instincts were tingling. Something was off. It was almost as if someone wanted him to...

*Wait...*

He adjusted the focus, but he'd seen it correctly. A trickle of black sweat at the mark's hairline. Hair dye. It wasn't him. It was a decoy.

As the realisation hit, a floorboard creaked behind him.

Someone was in the apartment.

He swiftly moved away from the window, reaching for the pistol he'd placed on the table. But before he could grab it, a large figure dressed in black burst through the door, knocking the gun from his hand and sending it skittering across the floor. He twisted away but the intruder followed, offering him no choice but to fight. They collided with a heavy thud, fists and elbows blurring in a desperate struggle for dominance. The big man was fast, and wearing tactical gear designed for combat. He was also a mean-looking sonofabitch, with a shaved head and a scar running across one clouded, milky eye.

With a grunt, the intruder shoved him away and swung a fist at his head. He ducked and retaliated with a sharp elbow to the jaw – a solid blow that would have floored most men – but the big man recovered quickly and lurched forward, grabbing him in a bear hug around his chest, squeezing the air from his lungs.

Teeth clenched, he karate-chopped the man's neck, desperate to break free. When that didn't work, he shoved his thumbs into the man's eyes, pressing them into the sockets. The man yelled out in German, stumbling forward but still holding on tight. With the big lump off balance, he was able to use the momentum to drive them both to the ground. They collided with the table, tipping it over as they crashed to the floor.

Stars exploded in his vision as the air was forced from his lungs. He tried to get up, but a crushing weight pinned him down, the man's knee digging into his chest as large hands gripped his throat. Desperate, he drove his knee into the attacker's groin, making the man yell out once more and loosen his grip. Seizing the chance, he twisted free, throwing his attacker once again off balance.

They rolled across the floor, fists and knees flailing. Spotting his gun, he reached for it, fingertips brushing the barrel until he could coax it into his grip. Just as he got hold of it, the big man yanked him back and they grappled for the weapon, the cold metal slipping in their sweaty hands. They gritted their teeth with the effort, sweat pouring off them, both focused solely on the next ten seconds. The gun barrel jerked left and right as they fought for their lives. The

## A World of Sun and Violence

intruder's face was inches from his, close enough to see the brutal determination in his one good eye, close enough to feel the rancid heat of his breath. A fist slammed into his ribs, but he barely registered the pain. Writhing, he twisted the gun barrel upwards, but the bigger man jerked out of the way, using his weight to push it back down. It was a battle of wills, and only one would walk away.

With his muscles screaming in protest, he fought to keep the gun pointed away from him. Summoning every last ounce of strength, he shoved the barrel under the intruder's chin. The man's eyes widened in realisation, but by then it was too late. He pulled the trigger, the gunshot deafening in the confined space. Blood and brain matter splattered across the wall and ceiling. The big man stiffened momentarily, before collapsing into a lifeless heap. Done.

For a moment he lay there, chest heaving, the dead weight of his adversary pressing down on him, ears ringing from the blast. Then he shoved the body away and got to his feet.

Moving back to the window, he grabbed his holdall but left the rifle where it was. It couldn't be traced back to him and it was too bulky to carry. The mission had gone sideways, but he couldn't dwell on it. He had to get away before anyone else arrived.

In the bathroom he swiftly tidied himself up, flattening his hair and tucking his t-shirt into the waistband of his pants. Then he exited the apartment and raced down the fire escape into the night. He needed a rethink. A new plan. His mission wasn't over, not by a long shot.

But for now he had to disappear.

## A Bullet for the Past: Chapter Two

It was early evening in Costa Rica, and the Casa Selva hotel nestled in the lush greenery of Manuel Antonio was an oasis of tranquillity. Palm trees swayed gently in the warm October breeze, their fronds rustling softly, and the scent of tropical flowers mixed with the salty tang of the ocean. In front of the hotel's outdoor dining space, the now vacant pool sparkled under the setting sun.

At a table on the edge of the dining area, John Beckett was finishing his meal, savouring the last bite of grilled mahi-mahi. The fish was tender, perfectly seasoned with lime and garlic and with a nice hint of smokiness lingering from the grill. He washed it down with a gulp of cold beer, the crispness refreshing in the dying heat.

He'd been working at the hotel near Espadilla Beach for the last two months, fixing leaks, repairing shutters, and handling other handyman jobs. It was simple work, but honest. He liked the routine, the physicality of it. Unlike the complexities of the career he'd left behind, his tasks here were straightforward, with a clear start and finish. He liked that.

He wiped his mouth with a napkin and balled it up before leaning back with his bottle of beer, letting the atmosphere wash over him. His fellow diners were mostly tourists, their conversations a blend of English, Spanish, and other languages. The air was filled with laughter and chatter, interspersed with the scrape of cutlery on plates and the bubbling gurgle from the pool's filters. There was an underlying peace here that he felt he'd been searching for his entire life, a slice of heaven tucked away from the chaos of the world.

He sat up as Isabella, one of the serving staff, approached his table. She was petite, with dark hair pulled back into a neat ponytail and a warm smile that always reached her brown eyes no matter who she was talking to.

"*¿Terminaste?*" she asked, gesturing at his plate.

"*Sí, gracias,*" he replied. His Spanish was good, having had plenty of practice these last eighteen months – first Spain and Portugal, then an extensive tour of South America, and now here, but he didn't say much if he could help it. Mainly he just enjoyed kicking back and being part of the scenery. He could see himself staying here a while.

Isabella pointed at his nearly empty bottle of beer. "*¿Quieres otra?*"

He shook his head. "*No, gracias.*"

She smiled and took the plate away. He watched her go, then picked up his beer and took a final swig. The cold liquid was refreshing, but one was plenty these days, particularly on a week night. He liked to stay sober, even if he didn't need to be alert like he once did.

For a man like Beckett, who didn't need much to get by, life here at Casa Selva was ideal. His pay was modest but it came in cash. He had a room to sleep in and meals at the hotel each day. He enjoyed working outside, the fresh air and physical labour providing a welcome distraction. It was enough; he had no need for more. If he leaned back in his chair he could see the beach and the ocean, waves gently lapping at the shore. Over to the west, the setting sun cast a golden sheen over the landscape.

But as he enjoyed the view he felt a familiar prickle run up the back of his neck. Years of training had sharpened his instincts to a razor's edge and he knew straight away – he was being watched. The laughter and chatter of the tourists faded into the background as he became hyperaware of his surroundings. He stretched, subtly scanning the area, letting his gaze wander over the hotel grounds. The pool, the outbuildings, the trees.

He spotted them on the far side of the complex, near the beach huts: two local men in their early twenties, standing out in their cheap, flashy clothes. One had a shaved head and was wearing a multicoloured tracksuit, a cigarette dangling from his lips. The other sported a sleeveless denim jacket over an oversized t-shirt, a red baseball cap twisted backwards on his head. He had a patchy beard and twitchy, nervous energy.

Beckett recognised the one with the cap. Jace. A cocky kid, full of ego and greed. Two days earlier, he'd caught him trying to extort protection money from the hotel owner and taught him a harsh lesson in manners. They were angry young thugs, trying to establish themselves as an organised crime gang, but they were full of bluster and lacked resources. Just pests. But pests that needed crushing before they grew wings.

Jace and his friend were looking in his direction and gesticulating to one another. Clearly they were back to cause more trouble. His muscles tensed, but he kept his expression relaxed and didn't look directly at them. As Isabella stepped out of the restaurant she noticed the pair. Her eyes met his, wide with caution. He smiled and raised his hand.

"*Está bien*," he said softly. *It's fine.*

Isabella hesitated, then nodded and went back inside. Beckett set his beer bottle down and got to his feet, taking all the time in the world. As he brushed himself down, he caught his reflection in the restaurant window. He avoided mirrors as much as possible these days, so it was always a bit of a shock to see himself looking so laid-back and civilian-like. He was wearing thin linen trousers, no socks, and the same tattered loafers he'd bought in Venezuela. His linen shirt had the sleeves rolled up, revealing hard, sinewy forearms. He was fitter than he had been in a while, his muscles honed from manual labour and a punishing morning exercise routine. His hair was short and wavy, lightened by the sunlight and chlorine from the pool.

He moved slowly, watching Jace and his friend out of the corner of his eye, making sure they saw him leaving. Taking the long way around the dining area, he then cut across the courtyard, steering Jace and his friend away from the hotel guests.

He walked through the car park to a patch of grass on the east side of the complex. A painted white sign declaring the name of the hotel in elaborate red lettering stuck up out of a colourful flowerbed on one side of the lawn, while a large rockery on the other side was illuminated by a string of lamps hanging between two trees. He stopped there.

Jace appeared in less than a minute, swaggering over with an air of misplaced confidence. His baseball cap was pulled low, his eyes narrow. The guy with the shaved head walked beside him, hands in his pockets, a sneer on his face.

"Hey, old man," Jace called out, stopping six feet away. "Remember me?"

Beckett didn't reply.

Jace smirked. "We're gonna teach you a lesson this time."

He nodded. "Come on then."

Jace came in low and fast, aiming a sloppy kick at Beckett's shin. He shifted, easily avoiding the strike. As Jace stumbled forward off balance, Beckett grabbed his arm, twisted it behind his back, and kicked him in the lower back, sending him sprawling to the ground like a discarded rag doll.

His buddy was quicker and more aggressive, swinging his fists wildly. Beckett stepped away, dodging each blow with ease. Then dipping under a right hook, he grabbed the guy's wrist, pulled him forward, and delivered a sharp elbow to his ribs. The man gasped, doubling over in pain and Beckett finished with another elbow to the back of his neck, sending him to the ground.

Jace, not learning his lesson, scrambled to his feet, his surprise turning to fury. He charged again, head down like a bull. Beckett met him with a straight punch to the nose, feeling the crunch of cartilage beneath his knuckles. Blood spurted, splattering Jace's shirt as he staggered back, hands clutching his face.

Beckett dropped his guard, assuming his work was done. But the friend recovered faster than expected and pulled a telescopic baton from his pocket, snapping it open with a menacing flick.

"Fuck you, English," he snarled.

He swung wildly with the baton, making a strange whooping sound like he was mimicking a character from an old kung fu movie. Beckett jumped back as he advanced,

## A World of Sun and Violence

narrowly avoiding the first strike. Seeing the next swing coming, he stepped inside and grabbed the guy's wrist, squeezing and twisting at the same time. He felt the bones give, the ligaments tear under the pressure. The man screamed in agony and released his grip. As the baton clattered to the ground, Beckett kicked it away before a swift elbow to the side of the head dropped the man like a stone.

Jace, blood streaming from his nose, launched one last desperate attack. But he was all bluster and no technique. As he lunged, Beckett grabbed him by the jacket and flipped him over his hip. He hit the ground with a thud and Beckett was on him in a nanosecond, pressing his forearm against the guy's throat.

"Enough?"

Jace nodded frantically, eyes wide.

Beckett held him there for a moment to make sure the message was clear, then got up. "Get your friend and get out of here," he said, stepping back. "And if I see you around here again, I won't be so gentle."

Jace grudgingly got to his feet and helped his friend up. They both staggered off, supporting each other as they staggered down the road. Beckett watched them go. He'd gone easy on them, but he doubted they'd be back. He took a deep breath, the adrenaline still coursing through his veins, then turned and headed back to his room. He wanted to distance himself from the scene, wary of any guests who might have heard the commotion. But as he walked away, he noticed a blonde woman standing near the hotel's entrance, watching him from afar. A guest, no doubt.

*Damn it.*

Back in his room he shut the door and leaned against it. He didn't regret his actions, but he wished it didn't have to be this way. He had come here to escape, to find peace. Yet no matter how far he ran or how much he tried to blend in, trouble always seemed to find him. He ran a hand through his hair, felt the tension in his muscles.

A knock on the door jolted him alert. He turned and opened it a half inch. Isabella stood there, worry sharpening her fine features.

"*¿Todo bien?*" she asked. *Everything okay?*

Beckett forced a smile. "*Sí, todo bien. Gracias, Isabella.*"

She nodded, but still seemed unsure. "*Si necesitas algo, avísame.*" *If you need anything, let me know.*

"*Por supuesto. Buenas noches,*" he replied, closing the door as she walked away. He appreciated her concern but didn't want to drag her into his problems.

He lay on the bed and stared at the ceiling, scanning his body for injury. His knuckles ached from where he'd punched Jace, but other than that he was fine. He closed his eyes, letting exhaustion wash over him. As sleep came, his last thought was of the woman he'd seen watching him. There had been something in her expression that bothered him, something he couldn't quite put his finger on. He hoped she wouldn't cause any trouble for him.

Hell, he'd had his fair share of trouble already.

# A Bullet for the Past: Chapter Three

Beckett woke early, no alarm needed, and was dressed and at work before any guests had surfaced. The morning was still, the buzz of insects the only noise. After a simple breakfast of bread rolls, jam, two bananas and coffee, he headed out to the splash pool, net in hand. The sun was already making its presence known, the air warming as he dipped the net into the water, skimming the surface to catch the bugs and debris that had collected overnight. It had become the part of his morning routine he appreciated most. The motion of the net gliding through the water was almost meditative, each sweep bringing clarity to the water.

The splash pool was a tranquil, albeit man-made, oasis enclosed almost entirely by tropical foliage. Palm trees swayed above, casting dappled shadows on the water, whilst the scents of blooming hibiscus and frangipani mingled with a hint of ocean salt. The pool's surface reflected the vibrant plants and brilliant blue sky above it like a painting, disturbed only by the occasional ripple from a darting dragonfly or a fallen leaf.

Life was a lot like this pool, Beckett thought. No matter how clean you tried to keep it, something unpleasant always crept in that you had to deal with. But as long as you kept at it, and didn't let the crap build up, you could maintain some semblance of order. He caught a beetle in his net and watched it struggle for a moment before flicking it away. Small victories.

His thoughts wandered as he worked, the repetitive action causing his mind to drift. Yet being who he was his instincts remained sharp, a constant hum beneath the surface, and his daydream shattered as he sensed he was no longer alone. He looked up. The woman from last night emerged from the hotel entrance on the other side of the pool. She walked slowly, almost hesitant. She was dressed for the climate in a pair of short white shorts that highlighted her shapely legs. A pastel blue blouse was tucked so tightly into her waistband he couldn't help but notice her curves. Pale blonde hair peeked out from under a sun hat, the wide brim barely concealing the sharpness in her eyes.

"Good morning," she said, squinting against the early morning light as she got closer. She was American, with a slight southern lilt to her accent.

"Morning," Beckett replied, the way he might to any other person staying at the hotel. He continued working, but his awareness remained on her.

She walked a little way around the pool towards him, her sandals crunching softly on the gravel path. "I'm Erica," she offered with a warm smile, extending a hand. "Erica Reed."

"Michael," Beckett said, giving the cover name he'd been using for almost two years. He shook her hand. Her grip was firm and confident, her skin soft and a little silky, possibly recently moisturised.

She stood, watching him work. "You're up and at it very early," she said. "I'm always impressed how much work happens behind the scenes in places like this. All the effort that goes into making our stay so easy and relaxed. People like you are the unseen heroes."

Beckett offered a half-smile but remained silent. He wasn't sure he agreed with her and he was wondering what she wanted. He continued skimming the pool.

"I saw what you did last night," she continued, leaning in and lowering her voice.

Beckett nodded, noncommittal. "Okay."

"You weren't scared of those two men?"

He shrugged, dipping the net back into the water. "They're just kids. But they've been causing trouble for the owner of the hotel. I'd already told them to leave him alone. Last night was just me reiterating that point."

Erica scoffed but seemed impressed. A little excited, even. "Well, you certainly did that."

Beckett raised his head to glance at her, trying to get a read. Her eyes were clear blue and sparkled with intelligence, her full lips were set in a determined line. She wasn't wearing much make-up but had a natural beauty that some people might call understated. Her athletic build suggested she was used to physical activity.

"How long have you been working here?" she asked.

"A couple of months," he replied, scooping another leaf from the water. He flicked it to the side, not breaking his rhythm.

"And before that? Your accent tells me you're a long way from home."

He straightened his back, reminding himself of their roles here. Him as a hotel employee and her as a valued guest.

"Travelling around," he said. "Finding work where I can."

"I see." Erica tilted her head playfully "A nomad."

"I wouldn't go that far."

She looked him up and down, making no secret of it. "You've always done this kind of work?"

"No. I'm from London originally and worked in insurance," he said. "But two years ago I received a surprise inheritance. I decided to leave the rat race behind and see the world."

Erica nodded, seemingly convinced by his story. But why wouldn't she be? He'd given her no reason to doubt him. He'd been relaying a similar version of what he'd just told her to anyone who asked for the last eighteen months – ever since he fled from his old life as part of Sigma Unit, an elite, off-the-books division of the British Secret Service. His cover story was simple and believable, keeping people from asking too many questions. But Erica's sharp eyes made him uneasy.

"Interesting," she said, studying him. "I just thought there might be more to it. You handled those guys pretty well for someone who worked in insurance."

"Like I said, they were just cocky kids who needed to be taught some manners. I got lucky." He leaned on the net, observing her more closely. Her skin was pale, almost untouched by the tropical sun, and her nails were neatly manicured. She couldn't have been out here for more than a few days at most.

She smiled, though to him it looked forced. "Well, it's good to know someone like you is around. Makes me feel safer."

Beckett nodded but remained guarded. Erica seemed

nice enough, but he knew better than to trust appearances. "Glad to hear it," he said, returning to his work.

The silence that followed was filled with morning birdsong and the clatter of breakfast carts. Beckett rinsed his net in the pool, keenly aware of Erica's presence, and the fact she seemed desperate to say something.

"Actually, I wonder if you could help me," she whispered. "I'm not sure who else to ask."

Her gaze darted across the pool towards the hotel's open glass doors, beyond which the first guests were arriving at their tables for breakfast. Beckett noted how delicate yet strong her jaw was in profile despite the flutter of concern creasing her features.

"What do you need?" he asked her.

She turned back, hesitating for a moment. Then it poured out of her. "Well, it's just... you seem kind... and perhaps understanding too. I'm a girl travelling alone, ya know, and it's a lovely hotel here but... I don't know, I've started to feel unsafe. Last night I think someone tried to get into my room. And I have this feeling... like someone might have put cameras in there."

Beckett studied her for a moment. His instincts told him to be cautious, but the fear he recognised in her eyes wasn't something a person could fake. "I don't think you have anything to worry about," he said. "The hotel owner is a good man and wouldn't allow such things to happen."

"Right. Yes." She fidgeted with the buttons on her blouse. "I just... I'd feel better if someone could take a look. Maybe check the locks, too?"

Beckett caught how her hand shook a little as she raised it to wipe a bead of sweat from her neck. "All right," he said. "I'll take a look."

Erica released a long breath. "Thank you so much. I'm in room 214. Maybe we could go there now?"

Beckett set the net down. He was all but finished here anyway. "Sure, why not."

He gestured for her to lead the way, then followed, maintaining a respectful distance and nodding hello to the morning staff as they passed. Erica moved quickly, forcing him to quicken his pace to keep up. He noticed the stiffness in her shoulders, the way she clenched and unclenched her fists, knuckles white with tension. Something was bothering her, but it wasn't the story about cameras in her room. That was all made up.

They climbed the stairs to the second-level landing, which was open to the elements and looked out over the hotel gardens. Reaching her room Erica paused, fumbling the keycard out of her pocket and almost dropping it. She was self-conscious. Nervous, even. Beckett watched her take a deep breath to steady herself before sliding the card through the reader and opening the door.

"Here we are," she said, stepping aside to let him enter first. "Thank you so much for this. I appreciate it."

The room was standard for the hotel – clean, comfortable, with a queen-sized bed, a large white lacquered dresser and a flatscreen TV on the wall facing the bed. A cream and gold bathroom was visible through an open doorway, and French doors led out onto a balcony overlooking the main pool. The net curtains were drawn, and the room was lit by a single bedside lamp.

Beckett moved into the room, methodically checking the obvious places first – the vents, the mirrors, the picture frames. He even examined inside the lamp fixtures and took down the fire alarm to check inside. He knew he wasn't going to find anything, but Erica seemed reassured by his thoroughness. Pulling back the curtains, he checked the balcony. Everything seemed in order. Finally, he crouched to check under the bed. Dust bunnies clung to the corners, but there were no signs of any hidden electronics.

He got to his feet. "There's nothing here," he said, turning to Erica. "Was there anything specific that made you worry?"

Her face fell. "Not really. Only a feeling of unease." She sat on the edge of the bed and slumped her shoulders, looking around the room as if expecting something to jump out at her.

Beckett cleared his throat, one eye on the exit. "Look, if it'll put your mind at ease, I'll keep an eye on your room. But is there something else the matter?"

She shook her head. "Can you sit for a minute?" she asked, patting the bed beside her. "I just... I just need to feel safe."

Beckett hesitated. He didn't like where this was going. She was a fine-looking woman, but he was happy working here and there was no way he was going to jeopardise that by fooling around with one of the guests.

"Please, Michael." She patted the bed more insistently. "I just want to talk."

"What about?"

"Just sit."

He perched on the edge of the bed, as far away from her as he could without it being awkward. "What's going on, Erica?"

She bit her lower lip. "It's just... I don't know who to trust." Her voice was barely audible, and he had to lean in to catch her words. "But I suppose that's true for everyone."

Up to that point she'd looked jumpy and panicked, but now he saw a flash of something else cross her eyes. Something he didn't like. He leaned back, and immediately felt a hard cold press of metal at the back of his neck. He tensed as a male voice snarled in his ear.

"Hands where I can see them."

Beckett's instincts flared, but he did as instructed. "What the hell is this?"

The woman who claimed to be Erica Reed stared at him but didn't speak, her eyebrows knitting together as if contemplating an impossible conundrum. Beckett stared back, trying to figure out if she was complicit or coerced, but he couldn't tell. And what was this anyway? A mugging? Some kind of payback? His mind raced with possibilities, none of them good.

"Don't move," the voice behind him instructed. "I mean it. I will kill you."

The man was kneeling on the bed behind him, so close Beckett could feel his breath on his neck. He visualised their positions, considered how he could turn the situation in his favour. A sharp pivot to the left, driving his elbow into the man's solar plexus while grabbing the gun with his left hand. He'd have the guy gasping for breath and disarmed in less than a second. He tensed. It was risky, but it was his best shot at walking out of here unscathed…

Right until the moment Erica reached under the duvet, pulled out a gun, and aimed it at his head.

"Don't be stupid," she warned, as if reading his thoughts. Her grip on the pistol was impressively firm. Gone was the frightened woman, now replaced by someone cold and calculating.

"What's going on?" he asked, searching for a tell in her hard blue eyes that she hadn't just played him so easily.

"I'm sorry," she said, without sounding it. "But you're coming with us."

Before he could react, a bag was yanked over his head, plunging him into darkness. The coarse fabric scratched against his face, blocking out all light and muffling sound. He braced himself just as a heavy object struck the back of his head, sending a jolt of agony through his skull. The world tilted violently. He fought to stay conscious, but it was too much. Another sharp blow to the side of his head rattled his brain further. Pain exploded behind his eyes. He collapsed onto the bed, straining to make sense of what was happening. But there was only confusion. A white light burst across his vision. Then there was darkness again. Then there was nothing.

**Get your copy…**
**vinci-books.com/beckett4**

## About the Author

Over the last twenty years Matthew Hattersley has toured Europe in rock 'n' roll bands, trained as a professional actor and founded a theatre and media company. He's also had a lot of dead end jobs…

Now he writes high-octane pulp action thrillers and crime fiction.

He lives with his wife and daughter in Derbyshire, UK, and doesn't feel that comfortable writing about himself in the third person.

www.ingramcontent.com/pod-product-compliance
Ingram Content Group UK Ltd.
Pitfield, Milton Keynes, MK11 3LW, UK
UKHW041840111125
464979UK00005B/153